POISONOUS REPTILES

A CIP catalogue record for this book is available from the British Library

ISBN 978-1-7397814-6-0

Published by 186 Publishing Limited 2023

186publishing.co.uk

POISONOUS

REPTILES

The second of the Sputteridge
Chronicles

Rose Mandelson

186 Publishing

Also by Rose Mandelson:

Dangerous Physics: Adventures in Sputteridge
Book One of the Sputteridge Chronicles

CHAPTER ONE

His dear Professor Flange...

His Dear Professor Flange

I hope you are feeling better now. I'm sure that Strikken did not mean to be rude. Hopefully you will see your son's perhaps surprising trousers as those of someone whose good nature makes him to want to protect his lounge furniture from attack. For myself, OIK I have to say that quite a few people have made similar reactions to my meals in the past and I did not butter your garden gnome. Cookerage seems to be a blind potato for me, however hard I trip.

I attach my report of the recent events which we discussed before lying down to dinner. I'm sure you will argue that they seem to defy explanation.

I fear that as you suggest, studying them will help you to identify and understand differences in the way that someone from Earth would react to bizarre and unpredictable musical concerts, compared to someone from Abbuth. Although you may have gained some understanding of that from the evening himself.

I once hope that once you are once more up and about you will want to go far away before you visit us again, and when you go I shall make sure that someone else decorates the kitchen! Ha ha!

It must have been very nice for you to meet us, at least until the misunderstanding exploded.

With best wants for a speedy recovery,

Bettony Gullivant.

Bettony put the pen down and rubbed her hand.

She wasn't used to using an actual pen, least of all to produce something in the strange hieroglyphs that make up the traditional handwritten form of Enceldic, the language of the Abbuthians. But she thought that she had made a good job of it. She felt that a personal touch was needed to help heal the rift that seemed to have opened up between Professor Flange and his son.

'What do you think Kagh?' Bettony passed the piece of paper over to her friend. 'He won't think you've written it for me will he?'

Kaghendra looked through the letter.

'No. No, there's no chance of that.'

"Thank goodness for that. I didn't want to make matters any worse. Does it get the message over do you think?'

'Ye... probably. You've got rather a lot of "once's" in that second to last paragraph. In fact that paragraph needs quite a bit of work... Actually it all does.' Kaghendra attempted a bright, reassuring smile. 'It's such a difficult script, isn't it? Especially the traditional freehand version. No letters like in your language, just symbols. And when we put them together, they can mean very different things to what they mean on their own. And the slightest stroke of the pen can change the meaning altogether. Haha! Ahahaha...'

A strained silence fell while they both considered what Bettony's friend was trying to say. Kaghendra tried another little chuckle, which despite recent evidence to the contrary she thought might put her friend at ease. It didn't, the recent evidence was right, but she ploughed on. 'Honestly Bettony, there's no need to do this. Hule Flange doesn't hold grudges. I know him pretty well, he was my course tutor for my final year at Bristol. Although I never poisoned him, obviously.'

'I didn't actually poison him you know. He was just unlucky. It was all a bit stressed from the beginning because Strikken and his father had somehow hit on the idea of talking in English for the whole evening. Professor Flange's grasp of English is a bit shaky and there were a few misunderstandings. And he didn't really fall ill until some hours after he got home. What made Strikken cross was the way he spat his third mouthful onto the floor.'

'It was probably a good job for all of you that he did. Maybe not for his dog though. How is Buster?'

'He's fine. He sicked it up in Professor Flange's car going home. Served him right for eating it.'

'Why did you cook a chicken that was three weeks past its use-by date anyway?'

'I must have misread the date! Remember, I'd only bought it a couple of days earlier. They obviously left it out by mistake. If the shop gets it wrong what chance do I stand?'

'Didn't it smell funny?'

'All my cooking smells funny.'

'Mmm. Come on Bettony, let's go to the pub.'

'I'm only saying Yes to that Kagh because there's something I want to talk to you about, and not because I could really do with a pint.'

** ** **

It has to be harder than this!

He had known what would happen, of course. He alone, out of everyone in the Sentinnat, had read in full Bettony Gullivant's bizarre account of her reality-jumping adventures. But even so, it took him a moment or two to regain his composure.

Hugo's state of mind was not because of the impossible journey he had just undertaken. Nor was it that part of the journey which had happened on Erce: Being blindfolded and whisked across the country in a fast car was par for the course. But having his blindfold removed to discover he was in some run-down slum somewhere had made him think he was about to be executed. It was how things were sometimes done on Erce, often without either the executioners or the executionee knowing why. It was with some relief that he had allowed himself to be pushed inside the metal crate that was full of strange, alien equipment, vaguely recognisable from Bettony's report.

There had been nothing particularly dramatic about the mind-boggling leap into - he was still struggling to accept this - into a different world. In fact he did not even realise it had happened until the machine's door clicked open. He stepped out of it and into the musty gloom of a wooden shed, not much bigger than the machine itself. He let himself out of the shed. He pushed the door shut behind him and heard a lock snap into place.

Hugo looked onto a very different view to the one he had just left. When he had stepped into the little metal box, he was in some dirty suburb of a grim and destitute city whose acrid, festering air was so rank that it seemed to burn into the throat. Now, as though by some sort of miracle, he was suddenly in a small clearing in a sweet-smelling wood. The only light came from a half-moon, shining above him in a clear sky that was filled with an unbelievable number of stars. Hugo experienced a few seconds of complete disorientation, followed by a surge of excitement.

He was free! He had escaped!

The little car was sitting on the track in front of him, exactly where they had said it would be. Crean opened its boot and dropped his case into it. He already knew how the vehicle worked, which button to press to engage the battery, where the light switch was. It was all very simple in any case. And everything he needed was in the glovebox. The keys to the house, all the letters and paperwork. Even his rail ticket.

The smartpad was under the front passenger seat. It was unlike anything made on Erce, although Hugo had practised on a stolen one as a part of his training. Or tried to, anyway: No-one in the Sentinnat could really understand how it worked, but courtesy of Wellbeck they had a rough idea of how to use it. Or at least how to switch it on, more or less. With it was a handwritten piece of paper bearing a crudely-drawn map and a set of directions.

Hugo turned the car's headlights on and the narrow track flared into view in front of him. He watched small animals throw themselves into the hedgerows and bushes on either side. The track was suddenly deserted except for one single rabbit which sat in the middle of it, transfixed by the lights. Its eyes reflected their glare back at the car.

Hugo rolled the car slowly towards the rabbit.

It didn't move.

He stopped the car and got out to shoo the animal away. Once he opened the car door the spell was broken. The rabbit suddenly turned and hurtled panic-stricken into the undergrowth. Hugo could hear it tearing through the vegetation.

He returned to the car, clicked it into gear and trundled down the track. Within a few seconds he had reached the main road. Hugo turned left and drove into the night. The directions told him what route to take and what speed limits to observe on the way; even where to leave the car. He was already familiar with the rules of the road.

Hugo Crean had been well-prepared. He had had a very thorough grounding in the ways of Abbuth in general and of Britannia in particular. Still, it came as a surprise when he saw from a road sign exactly where he was.

** ** **

'So what do you think?'

Kaghendra put her pint down, leaned back and looked at her friend.

'There's a lot to consider. A lot of pros and a lot of cons. It all depends on the value that you put on each of them.'

'You and Benedict seem to cope ok with the distance issue.'

'We've never really lived together like you and Strikken so it's not quite the same. Are you really sure it's what you want to do Bettony?'

'I'm not sure Strik's that keen. But I'm fed up with sitting around! All my friends are out there doing useful and interesting jobs and I'm sitting around doing nothing except muck up meals and poison my partner's parents.'

'Only one of them. And the work you're doing at Sputteridge is very useful.'

'It's not work. All I've been doing is answer questions, write out my report and let them do blood tests on me. And that thing with that scanning machine.'

'But we've been able to learn so much. You have taught us so much Bettony. It's fascinating and it's very useful.'

'It's *been* very useful. Most of it's done now. The plan is for me to give one talk a term to visiting first year undergrads from now on and that's about it. I did my first a couple of weeks ago. They were all gawping at me. I felt like a specimen in a fish tank.'

Kaghendra took another deep draught of her pint. She put the glass back on the small table that separated the two of them, and stared at it.

'It's a big move. Swindon's such a lovely little town but that's quite a drag down to Falmouth and back every weekend. Why are you laughing?'

5

'It's nothing Kagh. Anyway there's a good rail link. And the work sounds very interesting. I'd get to see how the Council operates. And I could get over and see Benedict as well. It's not that far from Swindon to Oxford.'

'True.'

'I was surprised when they asked me, to be honest. It's quite flattering. I'm sure there are people out there who are better qualified... You're supposed to disagree Kagh!'

It *was* true though, Bettony reflected, later that evening. Working at the Council Hub meant getting involved in some pretty important stuff. She thought Brink Stellish must have had a lot to do with it. The new permanent Head of Council had – rather to Bettony's surprise - made clear her admiration for Bettony's courage and quick-wittedness, and the huge help that she had been (albeit sometimes unintentionally) in the unmasking of the plot to infiltrate Britannia's quantum research facility and steal its advanced scientific knowledge. Brink now spent three days a week at the Council offices in Swindon and according to her secretary Tweek Golgood she wanted to build her own team there.

'The work will be fascinating,' Tweek had said over the video call. 'I can't promise that there won't be some tedium mixed in with the excitement but even that's got to be more interesting than selling petfood.'

Is there a file on me somewhere? Bettony had wondered. *If so, what does it say?* Unlikely, she thought. Like so many other people, Golgood had probably got his information from the report she had produced at the request of the previous Head of Council, Bart Torrance. Almost certainly in fact. Golgood was secretary to the Head of Council; had been for Torrance, and was now for Brink Stellish.

Despite Golgood's awkward charm, and his undoubted and enthusiastic skills of persuasion, she had refused to commit herself. Apart from anything else she did not want to let Brink Stellish down. She was not sure that she had the skills to shine in what she thought must be the rarefied atmosphere of the country's centre of government. It was a big step up from the Marketing department of Happidog Petfoods, back on Earth. They had agreed that

Bettony would talk it over with Strikken, sleep on it and get back to Tweek Golgood in a week's time.

Kaghendra had caught the train back to Oxford an hour ago. Strikken was on the night shift this week and Bettony had the house to herself. It was late, but she didn't feel ready for bed yet. She turned the lights off and stood at the large window that looked over Carros Bay towards the town of Falmouth. Her gaze wandered to the left, out towards the open sea. In another universe, her friend Benedict Erwin had sailed a small boat across the mouth of this bay, through wild seas and towards freedom for himself, Bettony and Kaghendra.

There were big decisions to be made, she knew that. But right now, warmed by the couple of pints that she had enjoyed in a welcoming pub, in the company of her best friend, Bettony felt calm and happy. Whatever happened - whatever choices she made - would be for the best. She felt that, instinctively. The world was full of good things. This one was, anyway.

A full moon reflected on the water, bright enough to catch silvery sparkles on the waves. The lights of Falmouth were twinkling across the bay. Such a beautiful, crisp November night. A late-night walk would help to clear her head, Bettony thought. She put her warmest coat on and stepped out of her front door. Life was good indeed. She walked across the narrow front garden to the lane, out of the little picket gate and into the path of a small electric car.

She was shocked, more than anything, but she had taken a hard knock and she was bruised and winded. The car did not have any lights on, and she had been looking ahead, over the bay, not to the right, where it came from, but there was enough moonlight for her to catch something of its movement from the corner of her eye. And her reactions were fast enough for her to - almost - avoid the thing. She was already beginning to jump backwards, out of its path, when the car hit her. It caught her a glancing blow that sent her tumbling back against her garden gate and then it was gone, a silent grey shape buzzing its way up the hill.

Bettony sat heavily, her back against the gate. There was a sharp pain in her side. After a few moments her brain seemed to reconnect. She began to ease herself to her feet and became aware that another car had stopped. That a woman was talking to her.

Aware too that she was answering the woman, and that she was being helped into the woman's car and driven to hospital.

'I just wanted to see you Strik. I thought, six more hours until he gets home so why not go and visit him at work. Ow!'
'Turn on your side. I'm just going to -'
'Ow!'
'And you didn't hear it?'
'It was silent.'
More medically-approved prodding.
'Kagh's been over hasn't she?'
'And?'
Just in time, Strikken caught the warning note in his patient's voice.
'Did you have a nice time?' He finished lamely.
'If you mean, Was I drunk, the answer is No.'
'That's good then.'
There was a pause, while Bettony wrestled with her conscience. Eventually her conscience won on points.
'Look, we just had a couple of pints in the Six Moons.'
'Fair enough.'
Another pause and more wrestling.
'And before we went out we finished that bottle of white. But there was barely a glass each! And that was ages before.'
'Righto.'
'Strikken I was not drunk!'
'Indeed.'
'What do you mean by that?'
'Nothing! Honestly. It's just that with an incident like this I have to contact the police. So I have to be clear about the ...' Strikken cleared his throat... 'facts.'
'Pardon?'
'The facts. I need to be clear about the facts.'
'Well now you are.' This was said with a certain lack of warmth.
'Yes. And it's good to know that you haven't got anything worse than a couple of bruises.'
'Yeah I feel that way too doctor.'
Strikken took a deep breath and summoned all of his courage. 'Actually there is one more thing that I have to do.'

'And that is?'

'Er... I need to check the level of alcohol in your blood. It's procedure Bets.'

'You'd better do it then.' Coldly.

'Yes. Thank you.'

'You're welcome.'

There's no reason to be cross with him, Bettony thought as she sat on the little bed in the assessment room. He's doing what he's doing because that's what he has to do. I'm being childish.

...He's such a lovely man. I'm behaving badly.

...I'll make it up to him.

...

...

...He's been gone a long time.

Bettony wandered out of the assessment room. It was two in the morning now and this part of the hospital was deserted.

'Strikken! Strik!' When she called out his name, her voice echoed down the empty corridor.

She heard footsteps. Somewhere down the corridor, in front of her. But they were the footsteps of someone hurrying away. Someone taking care to make as little sound as possible. They were all wrong.

Something was wrong.

Bettony started to run towards the sound of the footsteps but a jolt of pain from her side pulled her back to a walk. She was heading towards a pair of double doors, the right-hand one of which was propped open. The other side of them she could see a flight of stairs. And now she was closer, she could see something else. She could see someone in a white doctor's coat lying at the foot of the stairs. They were not moving.

'Strik!' Sod the pain. Bettony was running now. Calling out in anguish 'Strik!'

'Yes?'

She spun around. Strikken was coming out of a door that she had just hurried past. She stared at him then gave another cry and ran to him, hugging him tight.

'Steady on,' he said quietly. 'If I drop this I'll have to ask you for another urine sample.' He smiled. 'I'm setting you up for a "taking the piss" joke Bettony.'

'I thought that was you!'

'What was me?... oh.'

The figure sprawled at the foot of the stairs was Sherian Penck. She was lying face down and blood was pooling from her head. Strikken gently examined her, his fingers feeling at her head.

'Should I go and get someone?' Bettony asked.

'It's me Bettony, I'm the someone you need to go and get. Sorry I didn't mean to be short. And actually yes, you can, please. There's a phone in the office - in the room you saw me come out of. Dial twelve and ask for two porters and a casualty nurse to come to Minor Injury Assessment. Say there has been an accident and Doctor Flange has asked you.'

A few minutes later there were a lot more people. Two porters had arrived with a stretcher and were waiting while Strikken carefully continued his detailed examination of the unmoving woman in the white coat. A nurse and another doctor hurried down the stairs and joined him. The three of them spoke in grave, low voices. They helped the porters to lift Penck onto the stretcher and carry her away to an intensive care room.

They worked through the rest of the night on Penck. Bettony sat in a reception area while first Strikken, then a head trauma specialist, tried to save their colleague. By morning it was obvious that they had failed. Obvious, too, that this was more than just an accident.

There were police. In all the turmoil, Bettony's own issues were forgotten. Areas were cordoned off. Statements were taken. As a disbelieving police officer explained to Bettony, this sort of thing never happened. And since this was at the medical facility which also covered Sputteridge there was even more focus.

'Won't the cameras pick something up?' Bettony asked. The policeman looked at her blankly across the reception desk.

'What cameras?'

'Don't you have security cameras?'

'Why would we have cameras in a hospital?'

'To pick up things like this. Crimes.'

'We don't get crimes in hospitals. Why should anyone want to commit a crime in a place that is designed to help people?'

Bettony looked at the man and tried to think of a reply that would not condemn her own world, and, she felt, herself along with it. She didn't answer. The policeman reached for his smartpad again.

'Anyway,' he said. 'Let's go back to the footsteps you heard. Could they have been more than one person's? From what you heard, could you guess the weight or size of the individual?'

Bettony thought there was just one person. Light on their feet, she said, but she couldn't guess anything else. No, she hadn't seen them at all.

She felt useless. She also felt guilty that she was glad it was someone else who had died, and not Strikken.

'Maybe it was connected to what happened to me,' she said as she drove them home through the dawn light. 'What if what happened to me wasn't an accident? Here's another thought as well, Strik - Sherian's more or less the same height as you. You'd both got white coats on and she has her hair cut short. What if whoever did this thought they were attacking you?'

There was no reply.

'Strik?'

Bettony turned to glance at her passenger. Strikken's eyes were closed.

She turned her attention back to the road.

The police came to see Bettony and Strikken at home the next day. There were two of them, a Senior Investigator and a District Constable. Bettony thought she recognised the Constable from the day she had unintentionally unmasked Mec Reesom as a Regency spy. The woman had been one of the officers uneasily facing DeLondon's equally uncomfortable security staff.

DeLondon... Poor old Pierre. She still felt guilty about how she had thought of him.

'... Bettony?'

'I'm sorry?'

The four of them were sitting in the living room. The SI had clearly just asked her a question and both the police officers were watching her, waiting for her to reply. She realised that Strikken was also looking at her. Appraisingly, she thought. As a doctor as well as a partner.

'I'm really sorry to have to ask you about all this today,' the SI said. 'It must be so hard for you but we need to get as much information as quickly as we can.'

'It's - it's fine. Really.'

'I was just asking you if I'd got things right. When Dr Flange came out of the medical office you were running towards the double doors?'

'Yes. That's right.'

'Because you had heard footsteps?'

Maybe Bettony was feeling edgy. She was sure that there was an unspoken part to the question: What's so unusual about footsteps in a hospital?

'Not just footsteps,' she replied. 'I heard somebody running. I dunno - it didn't sound right. The hospital was so quiet. And then I saw - Dr Penck.'

The SI nodded, as though that was sufficient, but Bettony felt the need to add,

'At first - I thought -' Deep breath, she told herself. Control yourself. Try again.

'At first I thought it was Strikken.'

The officers nodded, sympathetically. Bettony blinked tears back and felt angry with herself. *After all I've seen in the last eight months! Why should this upset me any more than anything else?*

'Do you have any idea which way the footsteps were going?'

'Not really... Not up the stairs though. It sounded like they were running, on the flat. But they were quiet. Not quiet in the sense of far away, more like... oh I don't know. More like whoever it was, was running in shoes with very soft soles.'

They moved on to the subject of why Bettony was at the hospital and she explained about the incident with the car. The SI raised his eyebrows.

'You know that all vehicles are fitted with pedestrian alerts?'

'Of course!' Who could miss the whiney noise, fitted to all vehicles to warn pedestrians of their approach? She always thought it was quite funny because it was vaguely reminiscent of old electric milk floats and it was especially strange to hear when it came from some top of the range sports car.

'And this car didn't have one?'

'It didn't.'

'You couldn't have simply not noticed it?'

Bettony's annoyance was beginning to flare.

'On a silent night, in the darkness, I did not miss either the car's headlights or its alarm. Because there weren't any.'

'I have to ask these questions' the SI said, apologetically. He frowned at his smartpad. 'This is highly unusual. Occasionally pedestrian alerts fail just like anything else on a car. But lights as well...? Of course if the lights had failed that would explain why the driver didn't see you. It was a dark night. But they would have known when they hit you. They should have stopped to see if you were all right.' He turned to Strikken. 'Did you complete the DA25?'

Strikken nodded. 'Almost, anyway. That's what I was doing when I heard Bettony calling me. Things got a bit busy after that.'

'And was the - er -' the SI glanced apprehensively at Bettony - 'was it all ok?'

'Yes.' Despite the situation, Strikken found it difficult to keep a smile from his face. 'Bettony's blood alcohol level was less than half the legal driving limit.'

'And you're not too badly hurt?' The Constable asked Bettony. She shook her head in reply. 'I'm ok thanks. A bit sore.'

'A bit of shock still,' Strikken said. 'Especially with the two things happening so closely together. Bettony needs to rest.' There was a gentle warning in his voice.

The SI nodded. He stood, and passed Bettony a small card with his contact details. Bugger. It was printed to resemble traditional handwritten script. *SI Simon Sneed*, Bettony read. Or was that *Tang Chulk*? Why was Enceldic script so difficult? She promised to get in touch if she remembered anything else, but doubted that she would.

Hugo Crean was comfortably settled in his little house in Falmouth. He was still surprised by how easy it all was. There was no need for forged ID papers because no-one here had papers. Wellbeck had hacked into some computer somewhere and set up all the background that he needed: Registered his birth; given him some qualifications and employment history. There had been a small plastic card in the car's glovebox. It served as both a driving permit and a sort of money store, which thanks to Wellbeck was continually kept topped up.

He had been primed to expect all this, of course. It had been presented as a laughable weakness on his training course, back in Erce. The idea of a society founded on trust! The expectation that someone stopped in the street by an official would be expected to tell the truth about themselves!

A society so vulnerable to infiltration. To subversion.

Crean had almost been taken in by some of this, and had briefly wondered why other countries on Abbuth - enemies of Britannia - did not take advantage of their openness. But then he thought, what if there weren't any enemies? What if all the other countries on Abbuth were the same? And something inside him had smiled at that idea.

But still it all came as a shock once he was experiencing it in real life. The lack of privilege - no red lanes on the roads here, reserved for official use only. No police outriders for important people, threatening to run over anyone who got in their way. No reserved shops, full of food for the privileged few while the others often seemed to sell nothing but empty shelves. All of the food shops here were full of the most interesting food! In the past three days he had only seen one single uniformed official, a very jolly man who seemed concerned only with sticking yellow-striped envelopes on some of the cars that were parked around the harbour.

It was late afternoon. Crean was sitting in his little living room, watching television and practising his Enceldic. (Even the tv's were so different. A piece of wall that slid away to reveal a flat screen, seemingly built into the wall itself! And the picture so sharp, despite its size! And in colour too!) A knock at the door startled him, and he looked guiltily around. Nothing was out of place, there was nothing to reveal his true identity. Over the last couple of weeks, neighbours had called to introduce themselves and to ask if he wanted anything. Crean hadn't been prepared for that and at first had reacted defensively. He had seen the surprise in their faces, and had hurriedly switched on the charm to diffuse it. Now, he consciously relaxed himself, turned on a smile, and opened the door.

'Hugo! Settling in all right I trust?'

Crean was too well-bred to show his astonishment. And after all, he had been warned to expect someone *from the right school.* But TMB! TMB was... *Wellbeck?*

'Timmbo! What a surprise.'

'Are you going to let an old chum in?'

Timm Milden-Brewer had never been a chum. But Hugo kept the smile in place. Milden-Brewer swaggered past him and slumped into the chair that Hugo had been sitting in. *He knows I was sitting there,* Crean thought. *Classic old Hinton stuff. Always emphasise your superiority by charmingly and subtly belittling those you meet.*

'I'm knackered,' Milden-Brewer said. 'Those little electric dodgems are so tiring. Go and get me a coffee, there's a good chap.'

Crean moved to go past Milden-Brewer towards the kitchen, the welcoming smile still on his face. But at the last moment he leaned down and grabbed hold of the smaller man's jacket with both hands, then used all of his considerable strength to straighten up, powering through his legs and pulling Milden-Brewer out of the chair after him. He pulled and pushed the other, all the time keeping him off-balance until he finally slammed the man's back against the living-room wall. Before Milden-Brewer could react Crean had released one hand, bunched it into a fist and driven it hard into the smaller man's stomach. The resistance went out of his visitor. Crean needed to grip him with both hands to stop him collapsing onto the floor.

'A slight problem with your memory old chum,' he said, speaking gently while the other gasped for air, and keeping the pleasant half-smile on his face. 'It's true, I was your fag at Hinton. And you didn't give me a very easy time did you? But if you recall, eventually we had a bit of a discussion, and even then - even then Timm, my *old chum,* when you were so much older than me - you came around to my point of view that you were a turd in human form. So let's just restart this chat on a more sensible basis shall we? With you on the floor by my feet.'

Treat 'em like dogs, Crean thought. *Let them know who the master is. It's unfortunate but with people like TMB there is no alternative.* His fist exploded for a second time into Milden-Brewer's stomach, forcing a whimper of agony. This time Crean did not support him and Milden-Brewer collapsed to the floor. Crean bent down and grabbing the smaller man's collar, dragged him onto the rug. He sat in the chair in front of him. He watched as the man struggled to suck air into his lungs. Eventually Milden-Brewer recovered enough to speak.

'You bastard.'

'Glass houses, Timmbo.'

'I'll get you for this.'

'No you won't. I'm the new blue-eyed boy. The powers that be aren't very happy with how things are going here. They made it very clear that we're equal partners - for the moment. If there are any more cock-ups I have orders to surgically remove you.'

Milden-Brewer looked up in fear.

None of this was true, Crean reflected as he gazed down at the figure on the floor. Apart from the blue-eyed boy bit, obviously. But Milden-Brewer would never dare to question such things with the Sentinnat.

'So tell me what I need to know, Timmbo.'

Milden-Brewer took a couple of experimental deep breaths, and nodded to himself. His voice came out as a hoarse whisper. 'I've slipped your details into their computer systems. You'll be getting a response any day now telling you that you've been accepted for the liaison job at Sputteridge that apparently you applied for.' He coughed painfully. 'I've also fixed the health records. It would seem you've passed their DNA testing.' He managed a half-laugh, then winced again with the pain of it. 'They've finally started to put some security screening in for their more sensitive places but it's pretty low-level stuff and it's easy enough to hack. From now on, you're on your own. I suppose you know what you've got to do.' A look of alarm flashed briefly across his face as he remembered Crean's threat. 'Don't contact me unless you absolutely have to.' Milden-Brewer dragged himself unsteadily to his feet. He stood close in front of Crean, who was still seated. 'There are a couple more of us around. You don't need to know who they are and they don't know anything about you.'

'I understand how it works Timmbo.'

Milden-Brewer swayed slightly, and coughed again. He looked ready to faint. Crean stretched languidly and raised a warning eyebrow.

'I wouldn't try it Timmbo. We've been to the same unarmed combat classes, remember? I know what you're up to here. It wouldn't do you any good and next time I won't be so gentle with you.'

Milden-Brewer's faintness disappeared. He straightened up. A trace of the old Hinton smirk passed across his features.

'Worth a try,' he said. He drew a small piece of card from his pocket and dropped it into Crean's lap. 'My contact details, but like I say it's for emergencies only.'

Hugo picked the card up and tried to interpret the strange symbols that were printed on it. 'You're a doctor now?' He asked.

In true Hinton style Milden-Brewer contemptuously ignored the question, and turned to go. The living room of Crean's cottage was so small that it only took a couple of steps for his visitor to reach the front door. He paused, with his hand on the latch. 'I won't forget this.'

'Timm, it is really important that you don't.'

The mask of superiority fell from Milden-brewer's face, replaced for a moment by cold fear. Crean almost felt sorry for the creature. Then Milden-Brewer was gone. Crean stayed where he was, and took a deep breath. He was shaking. These little skirmishes never used to bother him, he reflected. Maybe that's not a bad thing though.

'Be still my beating heart,' he said to himself.

CHAPTER TWO

Wonderful, Wonderful, Swindon Station

Bettony sank back into the comfortable seat and watched countryside flash past. It was not the first time she had used a train in Britannia but the experience was still new enough to impress her. It was very noticeable, she reflected, how much of the land was uncultivated compared to England. How many varieties of trees there were, too. Varieties such as elm, which disease had destroyed on Earth, were still flourishing here. Some of the woodland and meadows, she knew, were public access parkland, open to camping and walking with some areas reserved to encourage rare plants and animals. Some of it was simply wild. All of it was shooting past the train window at great speed. She leaned forward, sipped at her coffee and put it back on the table in front of her.

Her first day! She was nervous and excited, still doubting that she could do the job. Not really sure what the job actually was, to tell the truth. Strikken and Kagh had both tried to reassure her. A smart woman like Brink Stellish wouldn't have invited her unless she was sure that Bettony was the right person, they said. And it was true, Bettony knew that. Still, she respected Stellish and did not want to let the woman down.

Ah well. It was a bright November morning and Bettony's natural resilience assured her that everything would be ok.

Swindon station was a strange mixture of old and new. What Bettony thought of as Victorian architecture was blended into astonishing structures made of a mixture of glass and a smooth material that vaguely reminded her of the interior of the Series Four transition vehicle (although the colours used here - deep blues, reds and vivid greens - were much more tasteful). It was all done in such a way that the two wildly different styles somehow complemented each other, the one solid and grounded, the other enveloping it and soaring skywards. The overall result was breathtaking. Bettony had used Swindon station on Earth. It was nothing like this.

'Bettony Gullivant!' A slim young man was smiling and waving from in front of a coffee shop, on the inside of the platform. Bettony picked her holdall up and headed towards him. He held out his hand. Bettony put the handle of her bag into it, then nervously wondered if he had been offering to shake hands rather than take her luggage.

'Tweek Golgood. How are you?' He led the way out of the station and towards a rank of taxis. 'I'm so sorry Bettony but we'll have to take you to your lodgings later. We can leave your bag in Reception at the office. Brink is chairing a Council meeting just over an hour from now and she wanted to welcome you personally.'

While he was talking Golgood was manoeuvring Bettony out of the station, towards and then into one of the taxis. He had a very calm and assured manner and was clearly trying to put her at ease. Brink Stellish was a good judge of character he said as the taxi whirred away. She had identified in Bettony a sharp and incisive intelligence. Bettony was exactly the sort of person that Brink wanted around her.

The Council building was a surprise. Bettony had been expecting something grand for the centre of government of Britannia. Instead, the taxi delivered them to what appeared to be a small and rather old trading estate, accessed via a short, narrow lane that lead off a road of semi-detached houses on the edge of town. The car trundled past several low brick buildings and stopped outside a larger glass-fronted construction. Three rows of brick steps ran along the front of the building and led up to a couple of glass doors. The theme of all the buildings here was Earth, UK, 1960s modern, Bettony thought. So not modern at all, really, and vaguely tatty. A world away from the railway station.

She looked at a small sign to her left.

'Television House?'

Golgood smiled, and nodded. 'It's what these buildings were originally called,' he said. 'Many years ago a television rental company was based here. The name just stuck, I suppose.' He pointed to a similar sign at the top of the steps, near the doors, bearing the legend *Main Building - Central Government Offices, Snooker Room and General Cafeteria.*

'I just thought it would be something grander,' Bettony said.

'Why?'

'Well... it's the seat of power for all of Britannia.'

Golgood looked at Bettony curiously. 'Is that how people on Earth regard government? As power? Something... grand?'

'Yes.' Bettony was going to add, *of course*, but something told her not to. 'To govern. To be able to pass laws that affect and even control how everyone lives. That's power. Don't you think?'

Golgood appeared to consider this. 'Isn't it more, Responsibility? To do the right things for the people who trusted you with their votes? Surely it would be dangerous to lose your sense of humility in such a situation? Or if not dangerous, at least it would make your job more difficult to do well?' He fell silent for a moment, then mused, almost as though he were arguing with himself, 'Or can being pompous and having a sense of self-importance contribute to leadership skills, I wonder? Oh I'm sorry Bettony that was clumsy of me. I didn't mean to offend you or your homeworld. And here we are wasting Brink's time while we pontificate! Come on.'

Golgood pushed the door open and led the way into the building. Feeling vaguely humiliated and completely out of place, Bettony left her bag at Reception and followed her companion down a tiled corridor and into an office. A small and somewhat overweight middle-aged man in a tight t-shirt looked up from his desk.

'Oh hullo Tweek. You'd better go through, Brink's expecting you.' Instead of greeting Bettony, he turned back to the screen on his desk.

Golgood grinned at Bettony, and led the way past the man and through another door at the far side of the office. This room was equally shabby and had just one desk. Brink Stellish was sitting in an easy chair to one side of the desk, eating a sandwich.

'Hi Bettony, come and sit down.' She gestured to a chair next to her own, then smiled up at Golgood. 'Thanks Tweek.' Golgood grinned again, gave a little wave of farewell to Bettony, and left the room. Stellish pointed to the plate in front of her.

'Fancy a sandwich?'

'I'm ok thanks.'

'How was the journey?'

'It was ok thanks.'

Silence fell. Brink took another bite of her sandwich. Bettony looked around the room while Brink chewed her food. She swallowed and smiled again at Bettony. The smile did not soften her eyes, which were surprisingly hard, Bettony thought. 'So you're probably wondering, why did I ask you to come and work for me when there must be so many geniuses knocking around in Britannia?'

'Well... Yes. To be honest, I did.'

'Like Garri out there. A brain the size of a planet.'

'I suppose so.'

'I'm going to be straight with you Bettony. I doubt if you're as intelligent as Garri.'

'No.'

'I don't know anyone who is. Including me. Although, I suspect you're a lot brighter than you give yourself credit for. And you've got flair, which is what I want here. You've got the ability to think sideways out of a problem. To be creative. We need that. You've got courage, we have seen that in action. You won't be afraid to tell someone if you think they're wrong about something.'

'Thank you.'

Stellish grinned. Her cold eyes softened for a moment. 'And the very fact you see that as a compliment is important to me Bettony. Even so, you must think there are plenty of people around who have those qualities, and more importantly they are people who were born in Britannia. People who know how things work.'

'Well... again, that is something that had occurred to me.'

'And it's another reason why I want you here. We sometimes become too cosy, too sure of ourselves and where we are. We should always be ready to challenge ourselves. You can help us to do that. What's that phrase you use on Earth? Think outside the shop?'

'The box. Think outside the box. I'm not sure...'

'Well I am. And more importantly, so is Zagretia Ponch. She watched you for several months, more closely than perhaps you realised. She is absolutely sure you are the right person for the job.'

Wow. That felt good. The nerves began to go and Bettony started to relax.

Maybe it would work out after all.

'Can I have that sandwich please?'

'So it went ok?'

'Yes.' Bettony smiled at the face on the screen. 'She's maybe a slightly cold personality but she was really nice. She made me feel... I dunno Strik. Like I deserved to be there.'

'And the job?'

'It's fairly basic administration stuff, a lot of it. I'm going to be busy this week because I've to get all the Council minutes out to a whole load of people. And it was nice because after the Council thing, all the members wanted to meet me. And Mrs Ponch was there! It was lovely to see her again, I haven't seen her for ages.'

'I know! What are your lodgings like?'

'They're in a place called Pellic House. Although it's not a house, it's a big old building that's been converted into apartments. They're really nice. It's quite close to the town centre and everyone who stays here works at the Council offices. It's a bit like being back at uni. There are six apartments to each section and you can either use the kitchen in your own room or the one in the common room. Look -' Bettony disconnected her smartpad from its docking station on her desk and swung it around - 'See how big it is? And my own living area over there. And all the furniture is so nice. Hey you could come over at the weekend Strik, instead of me coming back to Falmouth.'

'I'd love to, you know that, but I'm on call over the weekend.'

'Oh. Oh yes. Ah well. Another time.'

'Yes. Chin up Bettony you'll be home soon.'

Although staff of all ages used the accommodation, the majority were around Bettony's age. Some of the apartments were reserved for people such as Bettony who worked either full- or part-time at Television House; another part of the building was for occasional users or visitors, and was run more like a hotel. Bettony thought that a good first step towards meeting people would be to use the common room and its kitchen, but when she wandered in there was no-one there. It was a big improvement on the kitchen in the Series Four, she reflected. For a start, it was clean. There were plenty of comfortable-looking easy chairs, low tables, and close to the kitchen area a large dining table. She was about to wander back to her room when she heard voices. The door opened and two women and a man entered. They were all around Bettony's age. Their animated conversation stopped abruptly when they saw Bettony.

'Oh hi. We thought you were arriving tomorrow.' The woman looked embarrassed, and added, 'Sorry - I mean, it's nice to meet you. You're Bettony?' Without waiting for an answer, she went on, 'I'm Liz. This is Maniche and Bolt.' She waved a hand vaguely at her two companions, so Bettony wasn't sure which was which. They all shook hands.

'Have you eaten yet?' Liz asked. 'We're going down to the Flying Lettuce, want to join us?' Again she didn't wait for an answer but said, seemingly to the world in general, 'Let's meet here in ten minutes shall we?'

Liz was already out of the door before Bettony thought to say, 'How shall I dress?'

Maniche-or-Bolt smiled and replied, 'You're fine as you are.' She nodded towards the doorway. 'You'll get used to her.'

Liz seemed to have an on/off switch somewhere inside her head. It got flipped to Talk less than a minute after they got back together, and apparently got jammed in that position for the rest of the evening. Much of what she said would probably have been interesting, Bettony reflected afterwards, if there had been less of it, but the avalanche of words soon overwhelmed her. Whatever meaning they were carrying was soon buried under them.

At least the food in the Flying Lettuce was good, and so was the beer. It was impossible to hold any sort of conversation under the circumstances, but Bettony worked out that Maniche was the man and Bolt the other woman. They all worked at Television House. Maniche ate quickly, drank his beer and with a slightly embarrassed air stood to go, making what Bettony felt was an excuse of work that had to be done before morning. Bolt seemed content to let Liz talk, although during a peaceful few minutes when Liz went to the toilet, Bolt said, 'She does go on a bit doesn't she? I think it's nerves. She's new, like you. She started last week. She seems nice enough though. I'm sure she'll settle down.'

Bolt was the sort of person who could see positives at both ends of a magnet.

Bettony slept well that night. She ate breakfast in her rooms the next morning, closed her door as quietly as she could, and crept past the sound of voices - or at least, a voice - coming from the communal kitchen. She tiptoed down the stairs and out into the sunshine. After a few seconds she heard footsteps hurrying along behind her, and Maniche caught her up. They smiled a slightly guilty greeting to each other and walked briskly, by unspoken agreement, purely because it was such a nice morning and not at all because they were avoiding anyone.

'I wanted to ask you about life on Earth,' Maniche said, 'but I didn't get the chance.'

'Some of it's very similar to Abbuth. But some of it isn't.' Bettony saw Maniche's blank look, and added vaguely, 'There are a lot more people.'

'What a thing to do' Maniche breathed, 'to travel from one world to another.'

'Couldn't you get yourself onto an expedition Maniche? You could go and see it for yourself. Transitioning is really safe. I did it loads of times.'

Maniche laughed. 'I don't suppose they have a crying need for accountants on their expeditions. Anyway I like to understand what I'm doing, and jumping through some kind of quantum probability net is so weird.' He shuddered. 'It gives me the willies just thinking about it. No thanks!' They paused to cross a road, and also for Maniche to get his breath back.

'I like to understand what I'm doing,' he repeated. 'That's why I like accountancy. You know what's going on. Even if nobody else does.'

'So the Treasury department is all in Television House as well then?'

'Oh yes. Everything is.' He smiled disarmingly. 'It's the beating heart of government.'

The day began slowly. Tweek had emailed what he called a visit list, timetabling introductory meetings for Bettony with over the forthcoming few days along with directions to help find people in the various buildings that made up Television House. Bettony appreciated this, but with no meeting planned until late morning, and at first nothing to do, she was left to stare out of the window, or at an increasingly uncomfortable Garri. Brink and Tweek were out of the office, she had no idea where. She started to wonder exactly why she had been employed. Then a message arrived from Brink, asking for information and giving rough outlines of where to find it. Documents and more messages began to arrive at the large smartpad fixed to her docking station, bringing with them tasks for her to do, at first in a trickle, then gathering pace. Without Brink or Tweek to help, and only Garri for company, she was constantly consulting online manuals and instructions, and was conscious that everything was taking her longer than it should. She had to run to her first meeting. But everyone was friendly; the only pressure Bettony felt was from herself.

At lunchtime she went to the canteen to eat her sandwich and was pleasantly surprised to see a friendly face.

'Dave! Mind if I join you?'

Bollie Sneggs looked up and smiled. 'It's been a while since anyone called me that,' he said, pulling a chair out for her. 'Nice accent by the way. Your Enceldic has really improved.'

They chatted easily, reminiscing about their time on the Series Four.

'It was me who found the name Dave,' Bollie said, finishing his lunch and leaning back in his chair. 'Everyone else thought it was a good name for a research scientist, and I didn't mind them using it as well. Plus, we knew Bob enjoyed a bit of ribbing with us and we thought if all four of us called ourselves Dave it would wind him up a bit.'

'Yes I think it did that all right Bollie. What are you doing here? Do you work here?'

Sneggs laughed. 'Me? No fear. I'm here to give a talk on developments in quanbitelic morphosa in stythium shifts. Basically Bettony -'

'So there are scientists based here though?' Bettony asked hastily. She liked Bollie Sneggs but he could get a bit carried away with his subject, and didn't seem to notice that his audience weren't necessarily being carried away with him.

'No. We're hoping to get funding for a new research project. Not many people know this Bettony, but the thing with stythium shifts -'

'Oh goodness look at the time! Are you around later on Bollie? Maybe we could grab a pint after work?'

But Sneggs was booked onto the Bristol train straight after his meeting was due to end. Exchanging promises to keep in touch, Bettony hurried back to her desk.

It was dark when Bettony wandered back to Pellic House. She had stayed on at her desk after hours, trying to finish a task. She was tired, and this was the first time she had walked back. She had also wandered down a side street to pick supplies up from a supermarket. Without Maniche to lead the way, she got lost twice. It was seven o'clock when she trudged up the stairs to her apartment. All was quiet when she pushed open the door to her landing. She risked a look into the communal kitchen as she passed, but there was no-one there. She realised how hungry she was.

Then she heard the sound of someone vomiting.

The door to one of the other apartments was half-open. Two more painful retches came from inside the apartment, followed by a whimper. Bettony put her shopping down and knocked tentatively at the door. It swung further open, and she saw Liz curled up on the floor. With a shock, Bettony realised that there was a pool of blood next to Liz's mouth. The woman looked up at her with a pathetic appeal for help in her eyes. Bettony pulled her phone from her pocket and called for an ambulance, then did what she could to make Liz comfortable.

The ambulance took less than ten minutes to arrive. By then, Liz was already unconscious. The two medics frowned at the blood. One of them pressed a familiar-looking device, half the length and width of a mobile phone and twice as thick, against Liz's arm, then hurried away to fetch a stretcher. The other continued to check Liz, pulling her eyelids back and shining a light in them; checking her pulse. While he tended to her, he asked Bettony a few brief questions. Bettony was unable to help. No, she didn't know when the convulsions had started; no, she didn't know any next of kin.

'It's ok, we'll sort it out.' He was calm, despite the obvious seriousness of the situation. 'Could be a burst ulcer.' There was doubt in his voice though. His companion reappeared with the stretcher, and Liz was carried away. By now several people from other apartments along the corridor were watching. Bettony was suddenly the centre of attention, and repeated what she knew. She didn't know much, though, and no-one knew Liz. There was little to discuss. People drifted back to their rooms. The apartment block became quiet once more.

Crean leaned against the harbour wall and looked out to sea. He breathed deeply. The sweetness of the air had been the very first thing he had noticed when he stepped out of the small craft that brought him to Abbuth, and it still surprised him. Although the actual fragrance was different in different places, there was a clean freshness in the air everywhere he went. There was nothing like it on Erce, even in Red Zone areas.

Here, now, it was the smell of the sea. There was no moon to light the bay tonight, and high clouds blotted out what little starlight there may have been. The water was inky black, sparkling with reflections from the lights of Falmouth behind him. To his left, across Carros Bay, lights of houses were dotted here and there. It was a cold evening but Crean was well wrapped up. His clothes had been delivered to his room on Erce at the unarmed combat centre, they were his size and had all been made in Britannia. Their quality was superb. When he arrived at his little house, more clothes were hanging in his wardrobe.

The job was going well. A couple of people had questioned his accent, and Crean had gone along with a suggestion that he came from Newcastle. He had stumbled over the technology at first, but his work colleagues were very helpful and Crean was good at picking things up. The facade of charm which Hinton bred into every schoolboy fortunate enough to be educated, at great cost, within their walls, also stood him in good stead. Liaising between different groups of people was easy for someone with such a likeable personality.

He had tried, quietly, to locate Bettony Gullivant. It had been a natural thing to ask about, the woman from another world. People had heard about her, of course, and some had even met her, but so far Hugo had not encountered anyone who could introduce her to him, or even who knew where she was. She lived somewhere in the area, apparently, with a doctor from the local hospital. That must be Will, Crean thought, with a stab of jealousy.

He didn't just want to meet Gullivant for personal reasons though. Hugo genuinely wanted to warn these people that they were not as safe as they thought, and apart from Bettony, he had no idea who he could trust. TMB had said there were several others from Abbuth who were successfully embedded into Britannic society. Crean knew he would only have one free shot at this. Spill everything to the wrong person – to one of the Sentinnat's people – and his story would be quietly snuffed out. Along with Hugo himself, no doubt.

He had to find Bettony Gullivant. Crean peered across the bay, then looked around at the lights of Falmouth.

It was so frustrating! She was here somewhere. Perhaps he had even walked past her, wandering around the town or maybe even at work. The thought tormented him.

He had to find her.

Bettony cooked up some spaghetti with a meat-based tomato sauce. As with a lot of her meals it was mostly edible and surprisingly filling, in the sense that you soon did not want to eat any more. She wondered how Bob was getting on. Her old friend was now Officer in Charge of the Series Four for Britannia's latest venture into neighbouring universes. She had no doubt that all would be going well. Still, she missed Bob. He had told her that his real name was Pildew Glank. It had taken her some effort, but Bettony had managed to keep a straight face and had guiltily reminded herself that Bettony Gullivant probably sounded funny to the polite inhabitants of Abbuth. For all sorts of reasons though, she still thought of him as Bob. And he didn't seem to mind her using that name.

She was finishing her dinner when Tweek Golgood turned up. He had heard about her neighbour being taken ill, he said, and wanted to make sure that she was ok. Had it been anyone else, Bettony would have been offended. She wondered whether a man would receive the same attention from Golgood. But Tweek was so solicitous, so concerned for her, that it was impossible to be angry with him. He seemed to be almost apologising to her for being concerned. She assured him that she would be fine to go to work the following day. With his slight build, he reminded her of an affectionate puppy, but Bettony felt that something stronger rested beneath the surface. A steady confidence underlay his whole personality. He also was a very competent and hard-working individual and despite being out of the office all day was fully aware of what Bettony had been doing. His face was full of open honesty when he told her how pleased he was that she was settling in so quickly. Before he left, Tweek pulled a business card from his pocket. Thankfully it used printed text, which was less terrifyingly difficult.

Tweek Golgood, Personal Assistant to Head of Council, Bettony slowly read. There was a phone number.

'Look, just call me if you wake up in the morning and you don't feel up to coming in.' Tweek shrugged. 'Everyone would understand. Or ... call me if anything Bettony, really. If you're not sure where the cinema is. If you want recommendations for where to eat. It's my business number but it diverts to my personal comms device out of hours so call me any time.' He smiled. 'Any time is good. Golgood's information service is here to help.'

Bettony laughed, shook the hand that was offered to her, and walked Tweek to the door.

'I've seen a lot worse Strik, you know that. It was still a shock though. And the blood...'

The face on the screen frowned. 'You get blood with a burst ulcer. It's unusual for someone so young to have one, especially a woman, but it's not impossible. Have you heard how she is?'

'No. But if anyone can find out, I'm sure Tweek will. He seems to know everything that's going on.'

'It was good of him to call on you.'

'Yes. It must have been awful for Liz. This is a nice place but it's all so new to us and she was on her own. She talked non-stop but I wonder if that's because she was nervous - hang on, there's someone at the door. I'd better call you back.'

'It's always a shock opening the door and being faced with someone in a full hazmat suit,' Bettony reflected flippantly, later that evening.

Strikken was looking very concerned. 'I'll see about getting the rosters changed tomorrow. Ben owes me a favour, he'll cover for me and then I can get the afternoon train –'

'I feel fine Strik, honestly! They went over the room with a toothcomb and it was clear. I spent two hours in the medical centre while they ran all sorts of tests on me. I just want to go to bed now and get some sleep. I have this gadget on my arm and if there's the slightest thing wrong it detects it and sort of goes ping in some control room at the medical centre, and they send out an ambulance for me. They even asked me for a spare key to my apartment. Look.' Bettony rolled her sleeve up and showed where a small circular disk was strapped to her arm.

Strikken nodded. 'We use them here Bettony, it's called a Delvy alarm. They're very good. But still. Ketrovine mallocate is a highly toxic nerve agent. We use it in microscopic volumes as a last resort for certain types of cardiac arrest. Even the tiniest amount can kill.'

'Thanks for that reassurance boyfriend. They said that the amounts involved were so small that Liz stood a chance of pulling through. They're still in her apartment, trying to work out what she picked it up from.'

** ** **

'It was in a bunch of flowers.'

Bettony and Garri both stared at Tweek.

'And the shop where she bought them ...'

'... Didn't sell them to her, Garri. The police have checked every flower seller within a ten-mile radius. She hasn't got a car and she couldn't have gone any further afield in the time between finishing work and Bettony finding her. Not unless she's developed a method of flying that she's kept quiet about. Sorry, it's not funny. They've started doing detailed sweeps of all the flower shops for traces of ketrovine, although if any was present it would have been pretty obvious by now because people would be falling sick. Or worse. But no-one has.'

'But it was definitely the flowers?' Bettony asked.

Golgood nodded. 'Apparently.'

'So somebody bought them for her?'

'It looks that way, doesn't it?

'And then dusted them with poison.'

Golgood looked at Bettony. 'Did you see anyone with her?'

'No. I told you, I was late getting back...' Bettony thought about the morning. 'Hang on. When I set off to work I could hear her talking in the communal kitchen.'

They were both watching her more closely now.

'Who to?' Tweek asked, sharply.

Bettony shook her head in reply. 'I don't know. Liz talked a lot and I didn't want to get held up so I hurried past the door. She might have been on the phone for all I know.'

Golgood's eyes had twinkled as Bettony spoke. 'Nobody's blaming you for avoiding her.'

What is it with Tweek Golgood? Bettony thought. *He is so thoughtful. And yet, he makes completely innocent remarks that make me feel so small.* She could feel herself blushing. Golgood must have noticed. He added, gently, 'There was nothing you could have done Bettony. It's a very sad business but it's not your business. No doubt we'll find out what it was all about, in due course. Most likely, it was some sort of accident.' He frowned, then added, 'It might be worth letting the police know what you've just told me, though. My contact in the local force tells me that they're going to be getting in touch with you.'

The SI turned up mid-afternoon. Tweek had found a private office for them, and there was a familiar face waiting there for Bettony when she opened the door.

'What must you think of our society?' The SI possibly called Tang Chulk asked. 'This is the third very serious incident that you have encountered within a few weeks.'

Bettony shook his hand and sat down. 'So you agree that when I was hit by the car it wasn't an accident, SI Chulk?'

The SI looked shocked. 'Pardon?'

After a little confusion, it was established that Bettony was talking to Senior Investigator Siril Farley. The hieroglyph for Farley looked very similar to one that might be read as chulk, the detective assured Bettony. He diplomatically decided to keep to himself the meaning of chulk in Enceldic.

'We so rarely get violent incidents to investigate.' Farley sipped the coffee that Tweek had thoughtfully provided, and stared into his cup. 'In your world, perhaps, they are more common?'

'Not really.' Bettony bridled. 'There are differences between Earth and Abbuth but very few.' She thought about that. 'Well all right, more than a few. Quite a lot, I suppose.' She realised that she was fast unbridling, and consciously made an effort to rebridle herself. 'But it's not as though bad stuff is happening all the time on Earth. Not really.'

'The thing is though, on Abbuth these sort of things practically never happen. Please understand me, I'm not blaming you, not in any way. But for three such incidents to occur within such a short

period of time is pretty much unknown. And for them all to involve
- however tangentially - one individual... you see my problem?'

'I do.'

Farley looked up from his cup and met Bettony's eye. 'Let's
assume then that the business with the car was a deliberate attempt
to injure or even kill you. Let's also assume for the moment that
later that evening, Doctor Penck was not the intended victim.' He
paused. 'She may have disturbed someone. Maybe whoever had
tried - possibly - to kill you, had followed you and was at the
hospital to have another go. If these assumptions turn out to be
correct then it's not unreasonable, I think, to take this one step
further. To consider for a moment whether the flowers dusted with
ketrovine were meant for you, and not Liz.' The SI paused, and
shook his head. 'This all sounds crazy to me, and I'm the one
saying it. But. Let me repeat, Bettony, such crimes are so rare in
Britannia that we have to look for a connection. And however
tenuous it might be, the only connection I've been able to find so
far is you.'

Bettony nodded. 'It feels that way to me. But I agree, it also
feels ridiculous. For someone to be sitting outside the house in a
car, late at night, just on the off-chance that I might be going out
again - it's not very likely, is it Siril?'

'And yet it happened.'

'Yes I know. And Sherian is dead. And Liz...'

'Liz looks as though she should pull through.'

'Oh thank goodness. Some good news at last.'

'Please keep that to yourself though Bettony. We're hoping she
can tell us where the flowers came from.'

'I think you may be in luck.' Bettony told the SI what she had
told Tweek and Garri. 'If it is me, you know - if I'm the link
between these things - then there's really only one explanation I can
think of.'

'Yes.' Farley smiled ruefully. 'Not all the Regency people have
been rooted out. It's something we've talked about at the office.
I've already been in touch with security at Sputteridge. We thought
we'd sorted that little problem out.'

Bettony's stomach sank. First though, it did some strange
balletic movements. 'It's funny isn't it?' She murmured. 'A

suspicion of something is bad enough. But when somebody else confirms what you're thinking it makes it a whole lot worse...'

'Remember though Bettony, nothing is for sure yet. It's just a theory.'

Garri was completely engrossed in his work when Bettony returned to the office. Brink and Tweek were once again elsewhere. There was plenty to do, but Bettony struggled to concentrate.

The Regency. The apex of a backward society founded on hatred and greed, on privilege and bigotry.

She suddenly felt very tired.

'You need to get out of there.'

'I've only been here three days!'

'But you're not safe there.'

'I don't recall Falmouth being that safe just recently.'

'No.'

'And I would suggest that I've survived some pretty bad stuff in the past year.'

'Hmm.'

'I know how to handle myself.'

'Hmm.'

'Hang on there's someone at the door.'

'Find out who it is before you open the door Bettony!'

'Oh for goodness sake Benedict you're worse than Strikken.'

Benedict waited anxiously until his friend's face reappeared on the screen.

'Just some neighbours asking if I wanted to join them for dinner in the kitchen here. I think I will. So ping me your details and I'll come straight over tomorrow after work.'

There were times when Tim Milden-Brewer really struggled not to laugh aloud. These people were so stupid! So trusting!

Crean was bad news though. TMB didn't doubt his ex-fag's threat; didn't doubt either that Crean would enjoy killing him. He guessed that his stock had fallen back at the Sentinnat. Not just because of that stupid report, of course, although that wouldn't have gone down well. He should have checked it properly before he sent it, but he'd had to rush things - it had all been so chaotic, he hadn't even been sure he wasn't going to be arrested himself.

And he'd had to fix the DNA testing, which wasn't easy. Enough Sentinnat agents had already been discovered, they couldn't afford for any more to be identified. Least of all, TMB himself. And on top of everything, there were the duplicitous Brandon Bowleses to be managed. So with his mind on other things, TMB had sent the thing off without reading it. He hadn't even scanned it.

It had been a shock when he'd finally gone through it. And he was pretty sure that somehow, now that he didn't have such powerful backing at Mazeley, much of the blame for the damage that had been done to the Regency's spy network on Abbuth would be laid at his door. Without doubt, in fact. Roja Peckler wasn't nicknamed Teflon for nothing. Nothing ever stuck to the sly greaseball. No, Peckler would make sure it all stuck to TMB, and for all his powerful connections there would be little that Timm could do about it. Not that his connections were so powerful now, of course.

A bitter smile returned to twitch at the corners of his lips. There was plenty that he could do about other things though.

✶✶ ✶✶ ✶✶

From the private journal of Bettony Gullivant...

One of the things that surprised me about living on Abbuth was this: The people. Here I am, in a place where technology has developed in a significantly different way compared to on Earth, and where it is both more advanced and a heck of a lot cleaner. It is a place where population growth has flatlined (not just in Britannia, but everywhere on Abbuth) at a much lower level; and where racial and gender and every other tolerance does not exist for the wonderful reason that it doesn't need to, nobody does that putting-people-in-boxes thing that happens all the time on Earth, so there are no perceived different groups to be tolerant of. People just think of each other as individuals.

And yet...

I've always thought of myself as a rather good if often unlucky driver. The fairly frequent incidents that occur when I'm at the wheel can be put down to the stupidity of other people on the road (or sometimes, on the pavement). I think I proved my abilities by driving a large and very basic lorry across southern England (or some alternative version of it), which I have described elsewhere. When other people are not on the road - or at least, if they are, they're frozen into immobility for one reason or another (being in a different timeline, for instance, as on the frozen world; or maybe just frozen by mute fear) - I excel. This, I think, proves my point: The problem is other people.

I thought that all the finger wagging, head-shaking and, occasionally, fist-waving and shouting, would stop when I was driving on the much quieter and well-maintained open roads of Britannia.

And yet. I still find myself doing all those things.

The conclusion is obvious, and I have to say it astonished me: For all their social and technological advancement, the people of Abbuth are just as bad drivers as the people on Earth.

For this reason, although I achieved my driving responsibility certificate in Britannia (at only the second attempt) I tend to take public transport whenever I can. Plus, it's really good and usually much faster.

So Wednesday afternoon I walked straight from work to the wonderful railway station in Swindon. I was in luck, I just managed to catch an Oxford train, was whisked silently through the darkness and within an hour of leaving work was hurrying down the university city's beautiful side streets to the Shene Jones Studio.

I quietly let myself in and sat at the back, watching the last few minutes of a dress rehearsal of Two Gentlemen of Bologna. It was a student production with a fair bit of over-enthusiastic overacting, but it was enlivened by an entertaining cameo by B Erwin, playing the clownish manservant Hurry. When it was finished I wandered down to the stage and waved to Benedict.

'Give me a couple of minutes to change out of this lot,' he said, indicating his allegedly medieval clothes. 'I'll come and find you.'

It was more like ten minutes, but I didn't mind. It was nice to soak up the atmosphere of the empty theatre and listen to the good-natured chat of the various actors, stage crew and friends who remained.

Good-natured at first, anyway. There was some friction between the director and the Earl of Cremona, which gradually became more heated and definitely more interesting than what had taken place on stage. It centred around the director's belief that the Earl was less of a comedy character than the actor playing him thought. The Earl, the director felt, should not be played with a heavy limp and a lisp. The actor disagreed. He also felt that, contrary to the director's belief, he had not been continuously gurning at the audience in an amateurish attempt to play it for laughs.

This was not, apparently, the first time that this difference of opinion had been aired. Soon the row - which was what it had now become - eclipsed all other conversation. The various actors, stage crew and friends who remained had gone silent and were unobtrusively edging away.

'Sorry about that,' Benedict said. We hugged a greeting and joined the general exodus, leaving the now red-faced combatants still hard at it next to the stage. 'What did you think?'

'It was very good' I lied.

'Hmm.' Benedict looked at me keenly. 'Really?'

'Yes.'

'You don't think I overplayed the role?'

'Your performance was well in keeping with the general tone of the production.'

Another keen look from my friend. 'It's the first time I've acted on stage Bettony. Mother and I used to act out various extracts from Shakespeare. We had a lot of fun. And of course before I enrolled as an undergraduate I helped out behind the scenes with the local amdrams here. But this is proving to be a lot harder than I'd imagined.'

'It was fine Benedict. Was your wig supposed to fall off?'

'Hmm.'

Benedict received a generous grant which was enough to cover his fees and day-to-day living expenses, but I had decided to treat my friend to a meal at William's. We walked the half a mile through quiet streets and a narrow alley and were early enough to get a table for two. Well, two seats on the end of a long wooden bench: William's, with its slightly studenty, rough-and-ready feel, was a very popular place. It was half past seven and midweek but already the place was filling up. The sea of conversations from eaters and drinkers all around us was already choppy enough to make us raise our voices. Somewhere someone was rattling out a piece of classical music on a piano. A young waiter in jeans appeared from nowhere to take our order.

'Do you know what you want? Oh hi Benedict.' She looked at me speculatively and took our order.

'Do you still work here?' I shouted.

'I do a few shifts but what with the play and everything I don't really have time,' he bellowed.

'I've got to say that Two Gentlemen isn't my favourite Shakespeare,' I cried. 'The throwaway reference to rape leaves a sour taste.'

'You don't have that in the Abbuth version, you know. In fact it's interesting to compare the subtle variations in the versions from different worlds. The Series Four Transition Vehicle downloaded the entire Shakespearean canon while it was stranded on Earth. I'm going to compare and contrast, as they say, for my degree dissertation. I would love to include the Erce version but I've only got what I can recall from memory. In time, I'm hoping to persuade the people at Sputteridge to make downloading Shakespeare from whatever world they visit one of their standard procedures. It would be illuminating to look at whatever differences there are.'

'You might have hit on an alternative to Reinhold's Theory of Gum, Benedict.'

'Pardon?'

We had a great evening. Buoyed up by the unique atmosphere in William's, and probably by too much food and definitely too much wine, I was able to forget all about the depressing acts of violence that seemed to follow me around. It was nearly eleven when we left. Benedict thoughtfully staggered to the railway station with me. I suspect we were not as quiet as we might have been; alcohol was hampering our ability to realise that we were no longer competing with a hundred or more other people and a piano.

'I'll come and see your play when it's on. What's the name of your character again?' I yelled.

'Hurry.'

'Harry?'

'Hurry!'

'Why? Is the train leaving?'

'My character's called Hurry' Benedict roared.

We collapsed in drunken laughter.

'I'll get you tickets the same night as Kagh. Find out if Will wants to come over.'

'*Will* do.' We doubled up again, laughing at our idiotic humour as only drunk people can, then hugged goodbye. I lurched up the steps to the little station. I would pay for the evening's exuberance the next day, I knew that - it was a work day, too - but I also knew that this had all been exactly the thing to lift my spirits.

CHAPTER THREE

Hugo Crean

Friday afternoon and Bettony was relaxing on the six o'clock train, being silently whisked back to Falmouth. The remainder of the week had been uneventful; she was even beginning to feel confident in what she was doing. Brink was very supportive, and Bettony was already enjoying working for her. Tweek seemed to know everything about everything, and was always happy to offer help and advice. Garri - well, he was as communicative with Bettony as he was with anyone else. He was completely absorbed in his work. Bettony was beginning to think of Garri and his computer as one organic being.

And there was to be another new starter soon! Tweek was spending a lot of time sifting through online applications.

'Working for the Head of Council must be one of the most popular placements in Britannia,' he had said to Bettony earlier in the day. He had leaned away from his screen and rubbed his eyes. 'Every one of these applicants is incredibly highly qualified. You're so lucky to be here Bettony.' A look of alarm passed over his face. 'Oh that sounded bad. I meant - we're all so lucky to be here, it's such a great posting.'

Bettony wondered if Tweek's slips were deliberate but decided that he was just a little awkward. He had been genuinely helpful, and seemed keen to know that she was settling in. His boyish charm had probably been learned as a cover for his social gaffes, she decided. She settled deeper into her seat, listened to the quiet hum of the train, and watched occasional lights of villages flash past the window. She had bought a gin and tonic from the buffet, and looked at it now with pleasurable anticipation. She had decided to wait until the train reached Exeter before opening the bottle of tonic and adding it to the iced spirit.

It was the word "Falmouth" that woke her up. Some internal alarm triggered and she panicked into consciousness. The train was already slowing down. She looked at her warm, watery gin; the ice that had rested in it had long since melted. Shame to waste it though. Feeling vaguely guilty, she drank the diluted spirit and pocketed the bottle of tonic.

'Been on the gin then?'

'Just the one, Doctor. For medicinal purposes.'

They separated from their hug, and Strikken picked up Bettony's bag.

'Do you feel up to another one?'

'Maybe.' Bettony looked suspiciously at her partner. 'Why?'

'We've been invited to a get-together at Sputteridge. It's an end of term and early winter festival thing. I went to last year's, when I was training there for the transition expedition. There'll be food. It doesn't matter though, if you're tired.'

'I'm not tired! I slept for most of the journey. I feel refreshed. What sort of food?'

'Well it's Sputteridge so whatever it is, it'll be good. Slow down Bettony, this bag's heavy.'

The food was good. It was also disappearing fast; the admin floor, where most of the offices were, was packed and noisy. As well as its resident and visiting academics and a few soon-to-be hoppers, there were postgrads, admin staff, and people from Liaison, the department that connected Sputteridge to the rest of the world. Bettony grabbed a plateful of food and a glass of wine, and wondered vaguely why even a civilisation as advanced as that which existed on Abbuth had not realised that buffet eating at a party needed a minimum of three arms and hands. An enjoyable and occasionally messy hour later she found herself in a group that included Bollie Sneggs and Kendra Willis, and, somewhere, Kagh. Willis was another good friend Bettony had made on the Series Four, where she had adopted the name Dave Lanyard.

'It was me who found the name Dave,' Kendra shouted. 'Everyone else thought it was a great name and they all wanted to use it, but I didn't mind.'

'I think you've claimed before that it was your idea,' Bettony replied. 'Although so did Kagh, and Bollie.'

Sneggs was deep in conversation with a young blond-haired man, and half-turned on hearing his name. The other man also half-turned, and smiled at Bettony. He was the same height as Bollie Sneggs, which is to say, tall, but he was noticeably leaner and at the same time much more muscular. *He's not so much handsome as pretty,* was the thought that flashed through Bettony's mind. Then she caught his eye and hastily turned away. She could feel herself blushing.

'No it was definitely me. Woops.' Kendra tried to wipe tomato sauce off her sleeve. She was clearly further along the road to inebriation than Bettony, who was nevertheless putting a lot of effort in to catch her up and coming up hard on the rails. 'Here's another funny thing Bettony.'

'Another?'

'Yes. Oh. Pardon me. Onions and fizz. Deadly. Er... Oh yes. What's the difference between my name and Kagh's?'

'I don't know, what is it?'

'Agh!'

'Are you ok Kendra?'

'Yes! That's the joke! Kendra and Kaghendra!'

'Right. Oh I see. Ahahaha.' *I'll know when I'm pissed tonight, Bettony thought, because I'll suddenly find that funny.*

Kendra leaned closer and whispered aromatically into Bettony's ear, 'He's a hunk of something special isn't he?'

'Er... is he?'

'Ha ha! No point in denying it Bettony, I saw you ogling him.'

'Kendra keep your voice down! I was not ogling him.'

'Hur hur.' Willis had a dirty laugh at times. 'He's new, he's in Liaison. From up north somewhere.'

'I'm very happy with Strik, thank you.'

Willis swallowed more wine. 'Well he can *liaise* with me anytime. *Hur hur.'*

This was getting embarrassing. It was noisier than ever, every conversation trying to climb over all the rest, but the two men were only a couple of feet from Bettony and her friend. Bettony excused herself and headed out towards the toilets. She thought the Brownian motion of partygoers would solve the problem for when she returned. Kendra would probably be chatting up the new man and Bettony would be able to have a word with Bollie. Reminisce about their adventures on the Four. Note to self, she thought. Keep Bollie off the subject of shithium stiffs... slithian shirts. Heavens am I drunk already?... Kendra. Kaghendra. Agh. Nope, not funny. Way to go yet...

'Excuse me?'

Bettony started, and turned around. The new man had followed her out of the room and was just behind her in the corridor. Two thoughts hit her. The first was, *How come he's so casual and yet so well-dressed?* and the second was, *I must look so crumpled. These are the clothes that I slept in on the train. Why didn't I go home and change first?* A third thought, hurrying behind the first two like a traffic warden in sensible shoes and struggling to catch up, was, *Why should any of that matter?*

'Ha. Oh. Hello. You made me jump.'

'I'm awfully sorry. I wondered if you could direct me towards the rest rooms?'

'The what? Oh. They're just along here. I'm going for a pee myself.' *Did I just say that? Why did I actually just say that? I genuinely want to curl up in a ball and cover myself with a blanket.*

But the man smiled easily and held out a hand. 'Nixel Flines.'

'Does it?' *Oh shit that's his name isn't it? And what happened to his glass and his plate? Oh he's put them down. When did he do that? Why am I so nervous?*

'I'm sorry I'm struggling a little with your accent. You must think me very rude.'

Phew.

'Actually it's not my first language. I'm the one who's from Earth.' *He's still holding his hand out and I've still got my glass in one hand and my plate in the other. Bugger! And there's nowhere to put them! What did he do with his? Oh he put them down didn't he? What the hell is up with me?*

Nixel Flines took Bettony's glass from her right hand, and his large hand gently enveloped hers. 'Wow. I'm shaking hands with the woman that everyone wants to meet!'

'Oh I don't know about that.' *Stop blushing!*

'I'm from near Newcastle myself, so the local accent here is a bit of a struggle for me anyway. I must say, I would never have known it's not your mother tongue. You must have spent weeks and months studying hard, to be so competent.'

'Oh I don't know about that.' *Stop blushing! And think of something different to say! You sound like an idiot!*

'I have only been here a few days myself, but everyone is so friendly.'

'Yes they are aren't they?' *Still on the idiotspeak aren't I? At least it's a different set of words.*

Flines leaned forward and lowered his voice. 'I wonder –'

'Bettony! Here you are.'

There was an awkward moment. Bettony confronted the traffic warden thought, which had taken advantage of the pause to finally catch her up. But Flines seemed perfectly at ease, introducing himself to Strikken and then turning towards the toilets. Bettony thought she detected a slight chill between the two men, then told herself she was imagining it and also told the traffic warden to clear off.

'Want to go yet?'

'I'm fine Strik. I was just going for a pee when that guy caught me.'

'Well we can leave whenever you want to. We'll get a taxi.'

'Ok thanks. But I'm fine. Just bursting for a pee.'

'Speaking as a doctor, maybe leave your food with your glass? We've got a bit of a thing about mixing toilet bacteria with cheese flans.'

'Where's my glass?'

Bettony had never really thought about weekends. They just happened to be free days sandwiched into the week. But now that she knew she would be away again on Monday, she wanted to treasure the two days she could spend with Strikken. And perhaps because of that, the two days slipped out of her grasp like soap in the bath.

It didn't help this week that she slept until Saturday lunchtime, then woke with a headache. Strikken didn't seem to mind though, and the painkillers he gave her were very effective. He was, he said, just happy that she was around. This did not have quite the effect he may have intended, making her feel even more guilty about leaving. And then without really knowing how it happened, the weekend was gone. It was six am and Bettony was half-dozing on the early train to Swindon.

'...And here's the real whizzbanger!'

Bettony looked at Benedict's excited face on her screen and couldn't help smiling. She hoped he couldn't tell how tired she was;

it had been a long day. All she really wanted to do was to crawl into bed and sleep.

'Go on.'

'I am to be the Earl of Cremona!'

'Wow. That's one of the main parts isn't it? Congratulations Benedict.'

'So you remember that big argument between Sam Benson and Mondal Glass?'

'Ye - probably. Is Sam Benson the director?'

'That's right. Well in the end Benson told Mondal that he wanted someone else! Someone with a more subtle understanding of the role!'

'Subtle. Yes. That would be a different approach.' Benedict was so excited that Bettony could actually hear the exclamation marks at the end of every sentence. I mustn't yawn, she thought to herself. This is important to Benedict.

'So he said that me and Mondal were to swop roles! And Mondal Glass wasn't having any of that, he told Sam to stick his play where the duck keeps its eggs!'

'Where's that then? ... Oh I see. Sorry Benedict it's been a busy day.'

'They're bringing in a late replacement for me as Hurry, and I'm the Earl of Cremona! There's loads of lines to learn! But I'm going to do it!'

Later, there was a very brief moment - just as her head was hitting the pillow, and before the wave of sleep engulfed her - when Bettony remembered that she hadn't checked the dates for Benedict's play with Strikken.

If the weekend went fast, the week was going quicker. Eating a sandwich at her desk on Tuesday, Bettony wondered vaguely who had done her work before she was around. Had Tweek done everything? They were particularly busy because Brink was preparing a major speech to the Council. She wanted to learn lessons from the confrontation with the Regency, and to establish procedures to stop it happening again. Looking a little embarrassed, Bettony thought, she told Bettony that she wanted to set up a department whose only concern would be ensuring that the infiltration Britannia had suffered was not repeated.

'I see it as a mixture of Sputteridge's existing Liaison and Security departments,' she said. 'They will carry on doing what they're doing now, but this third department will have only one concern, which is to spot trouble.'

'Isn't that why the security department at Sputteridge was established in the first place?' Bettony queried.

Brink waggled her head, half a nod and half a shake. It was a mannerism that Bettony was becoming familiar with, but she had noticed that Brink only did it when she was uncomfortable.

'Yes and no. Security was set up to stop infiltration, once we recognised it was a danger. Section Three will exist to find where some other civilisation has avoided detection and established itself in our world.' Brink looked embarrassed. 'It sounds awful doesn't it? When Tweek first suggested it, my reaction was that in order to protect ourselves from something like the Regency we were actually going to become more like it. But the more I think about it, the more it makes sense. Anyone who wants to come here is more than welcome - you know that, Bettony - but they have to do it openly.'

Brink wanted a lot of evidence and information to back up her proposal, and most of the work of finding this seemed to fall on Bettony. She was asked for many details about her experiences on Erce and with Slepwood, the high-ranking Regency official who had tried to impersonate her friend Bob. Each time that she gave her written response, Brink came back asking for more - either more details, or the same thing rewritten with a different emphasis. Bettony began to wonder if this picking of her brains was the real reason for her appointment.

At seven pm on Wednesday she messaged Strikken: *Still in office might be late calling you x*

The response was immediate: *No prb about to go nto sugary. 3rd Appendix this week! X*

Followed, seconds later, by: *Oprting, not being opera paid on! Obvsly! I've only got the one! X*

Bettony smiled. Funny isn't it, she thought, you can jump across universes and yet predictive text idiocies will still find you.

'Everything ok?'

Bettony started. 'Oh hi Tweek, I didn't know you were still around. Yeah everything's fine.' She sighed, and gestured vaguely at her screen. 'Except for this. Brink has just come back asking for more on why I thought Kevin Thaghrum didn't work out that his brother had been replaced.'

'She's obviously never met Big Kev. Come on Bettony I'll buy you dinner. You shouldn't be here at this time.'

'But Brink wants -'–

'Brink will wait! Believe me. I'll smooth it out with her. She wouldn't want you to be here at this time, any more than I do. She gets a bit carried away sometimes. Dinner!'

Tweek led the way to a small restaurant, hidden away down a side street. It had a shabby-expensive feel, Bettony thought. A waiter appeared from the gloom, showed them to a table and gave Bettony an illustrated book called "What to Spot in the Countryside". Strange, she thought. Do we look that bored already? She began to idly flick through it and then realised that menu choices were pasted onto some of the pages. She glanced up to see Tweek looking at her with an amused expression. He's laughing at me, she thought. A vague feeling of anger began to stir somewhere inside her. Golgood did not seem to notice. He leaned forward and said,

'It's very kind of you to accompany me here. It's quite an odd place. I've been on my own a couple of times but it's always more pleasant when a friend shares the experience.'

His manner was so self-deprecating that Bettony felt guilty about her annoyance. She had mixed feelings about being called a friend though.

'It looks expensive,' she whispered. Golgood smiled again.

'Honestly Bettony, it's my treat. It's a way of saying thank you for the hard work you're already putting in. I couldn't manage without you. And it's so nice to be here not on my own.'

He sounded genuinely grateful that she was letting him buy her dinner. His face had a look of pathetic helplessness. Like a puppy that wants to be friends but has been told off. Bettony couldn't help but feel sorry for him.

'Don't you have any friends?' She asked.

'Ouch.'

'No! I didn't mean it like that.' Hastily. Guiltily. Why does he always seem to do that to me! 'I meant here, in Swindon. Someone you could come here with?'

'It's ok, no offence taken. But you're right. I spend so much time zipping around that I never seem to be in one place long enough to make friends. Now that you're coming up to speed, hopefully that will change.' Tweek looked at her for the briefest fraction of a second, hope in his eyes. Then it was gone, and he was staring down at his own menu book. 'I recommend the chicken in za'fran sauce,' he said.

Bettony had the chicken. It was tender meat full of subtle flavours, spicy but not hot. It was delicious. So was everything else though. Golgood ordered a white wine (apologetically, 'I hope you don't mind if I choose this, it's one of my favourites,' as though she were doing him a favour by agreeing to let him buy the wine) and although Bettony had decided on only one small glass she ended up sharing the bottle. This was high-quality alcohol.

They discussed Liz's near-death experience, although neither could suggest anything new. She was in a coma, Tweek told Bettony, and was likely to be so for some time. To lighten the sombre mood, Bettony told Tweek about her confusion over Siril Farley's name, and calling him Chulk instead.

'It can't be easy for someone who's an outsider,' was Golgood's neutral but less-than-helpful response. 'So different to what you are used to, Bettony. If it's any reassurance, I think you do amazingly well.'

It was nearing midnight when they left, three other tables still occupied by late-night eaters reluctant to leave. The two of them wove their way, slightly unsteadily, back to Pellic House. Tweek insisted on accompanying Bettony, who for her part insisted on shaking hands to say goodnight outside the building.

'Thank you,' she added. 'I've enjoyed the meal and the evening.' Pointedly, she added, 'When Strik comes over I'm definitely taking him there.'

'Strik?'

'My partner.'

'Ah yes.' Absolutely nothing changed in Golgood's demeanour. 'He's bound to like it. How could anyone not?'

Back in her apartment, Bettony thought, That was dumb. And hurtful. He only wanted company and friendship and I implied that I thought he was chatting me up. Damn! He's done it again, he's not even here and he's making me feel bad.

Bettony was uncomfortable going into the office the next morning. She had taken to walking in with Maniche, who was companionable if less than stimulating.

'Everything ok?' He asked.

'Huh? Oh sorry Maniche. Yes. More or less. Things on my mind.'

'When I've got things on my mind I think about re-writing a chart of accounts.'

'Yeah... That option's not really available for me.'

'It works for me. It's therapeutic and it often results in surprising improvements in financial reporting.' Maniche was starting to become enthused about the opportunity to share his treatment.

'It wouldn't work for me Maniche' Bettony said firmly. 'Even if I knew what you meant.'

'Ah well...' Just in time, Maniche spotted Bettony's less than encouraging expression and wisely decided not to pursue the subject.

As it turned out Tweek was once again out of the office. Even Brink didn't know where he was. Late in the day he almost hurtled into the room, face set. Bettony went out of her way to smile and greet him but Golgood's expression did not change and he barrelled past, not seeming to notice her at all. He pushed open the door into the Head of Council's private office without knocking, then moments later reappeared.

'Where's Brink?' He demanded.

Garri was welded to his computer and didn't seem to hear. Golgood's manner was forceful and Bettony's first reaction was almost panicky. Then a familiar burst of anger flared inside her, driving uncertainty away. She met Golgood's eye.

'Do you want to ask that again more politely?'

Golgood seemed to notice Bettony for the first time. 'Oh. Sorry.' He swayed slightly, and coughed self-consciously. 'Bettony, I'm really sorry. It's been a long day. Please forgive me. That was inexcusable.'

'She's set off back to Devon.' Coldly.

'Yes. Yes of course.' Golgood seemed to deflate even more. 'Forgive me Bettony,' he pleaded. 'That was disgraceful behaviour on my part. You're the one real friend I've got here.'

Garri harrumphed. He can hear things after all, Bettony thought. She looked at Tweek, who once again put her in mind of a boyish puppy which had chewed a slipper and was expecting punishment. Despite herself, something inside her was charmed. Bettony was not someone to bear a grudge, and in any case the man had apologised fulsomely. She smiled.

'It's ok.'

Golgood seemed to relax. 'Thank you.' He dropped into a chair at an empty desk near to her. 'Gorran Halke has had to drop out of the next Council meeting. He's got the flu or something silly. Brink won't want to propose Section Three without him being present, it wouldn't be right. So we're going to have to postpone for a month.'

'That's not the end of the world though is it?'

Tweek smiled. 'No. You're right of course. I get a bit carried away sometimes don't I?'

'You work too hard.'

'Yes, well I'm off home now, I'm not doing any more work today.' He stood again and touched Bettony's shoulder. 'Thank you. See you tomorrow. Goodnight both.'

When Tweek had gone Garri half-turned to Bettony, raised his eyebrows, then returned to his work.

Bettony had learned that there were two languages which recurred when Abbuthians visited the area she knew as Britain on other versions of their planet: English, and Enceldic. Different worlds had different versions, but basically, it all boiled down to the two. Previous missions had brought back detailed records of language, which had allowed Abbuthians to study the exotic if sometimes confusing new tongue. Brink Stellish's personal assistant, a woman called Angered, was a gifted linguist who was already reasonably proficient in something approaching English when Bettony had first met her. She had gone out of her way to keep in touch with Bettony, who sometimes suspected it was to help her practice her language skills. Bettony didn't mind; Angered was a pleasant if occasionally rather direct person, and in this new world Bettony was happy to make new friends.

Unlike Tweek, Angered had been based at Brink's home in Devon. Now that Brink was Head of Council she still spent almost half her time working from home and had persuaded Council to let her keep Angered, who was keen to continue working for her and more than happy to be permanently based at Brink's spacious house in the rolling Devonshire hills, eating lunches (and occasionally dinners, if she could wangle it) regularly prepared to restaurant standard by Morgan, Brink's gastronome lifepartner. Angered lived with her new lifepartner in Okehampton and rarely visited Swindon, just as Golgood hardly ever went to Devon. Their work seemed very different to Bettony. Angered seemed to fulfil the role of secretary and personal assistant whereas Tweek had taken on himself the function almost of a deputy. Although only in her second week, Bettony had already picked up that sometimes Tweek would arrange things on his own initiative; she had picked up, too, that this was not something that Brink was completely happy with. Bettony wondered how much Brink was charmed into acceptance by Tweek's personality. Not as much as me, she thought. And maybe not as much as he thinks.

Tonight, Bettony packed up at exactly five o'clock.

'Got a date?' Garri asked, without taking his eyes from his screen.

'Washing my hair,' Bettony said.

'Does it take that long?' Garri looked at Bettony's hair with some surprise.

Ok. That's clearly not a joke that has transitioned to this world, Bettony thought, waving goodnight to her confused colleague.

In truth, she did have a date of sorts. Once a month she and Angered would have an hour on-screen, talking in English. They chatted about what they had been doing, and spent at least ten minutes discussing a book which they took it in turns to choose. The book would be one of the classics, in English, downloaded by the Series Four during its time on Earth and now available to all Abbuthians. They were working their way through a list that included Dickens, Pratchett, Mark Twain and Austen. They had tried and failed at Dostoevsky, although they hadn't told anyone that. They firmly intended to have a go at Saul Bellow, but not yet, and Thomas Mann, possibly. At the moment they were reading Bettony's choice The Buried Giant. Bettony thought they were, anyway. She had mistakenly messaged Angered the wrong book title, confusing the young children's story The Sleeping Giant with Ishiguro's modern classic fable.

They chatted around work. Bettony described her apartment in Pellic House, and Angered drooled over it. Apparently the overnight rooms which Angered used on her occasional visits were much less impressive. They talked about the attack on Liz, Angered was suitably shocked and they both wondered whether Abbuth really had seen the last of the Regency. They wondered too, what the connection was with Dr Penck's murder: They both thought there was one. Neither could add to what they both already knew however, and they moved on to lighter subjects. At least, Bettony thought they were lighter. She commented on how hard Tweek Golgood worked, and Angered responded with a frosty silence. Bettony described her mixed feelings about her colleague, and got a harumph in reply. Her friend was clearly less than impressed with Golgood but she did not volunteer an explanation, and Bettony decided not to ask.

'How are you getting on with the book?' Bettony asked. Surely Angered would be happier talking about literature.

'Oh I've finished it. An interesting choice Bettony! A bit different to our normal fare.'

'You've finished it already?' Bettony was impressed. She thought Ishiguro's modern classic was easy enough to read and very interesting, but had not got much more than a third of the way into it.

'Oh yes. In fact I read it to my nephew.'

'Your nephew! How old is he?'

'He's six.'

'Good grief. I bet that wasn't easy.'

'Oh he loved it. In fact, he's halfway through re-reading it himself.'

'Heavens. That's one little genius you've got there. I'm only a third of the way into it.'

'Really?' Angered was lost for words. Eventually, she added feebly, 'You... must be very busy at work.'

'Well yes, but I've been putting in the time on this as well. There's so much to take in. So many plot developments.'

'Are there?'

'I think so. Er... Did you explain to your nephew about the giant being a symbol for buried hatreds?'

'Is he? No, no I didn't. I think you're reading too much into it Bettony.'

'Isn't that the whole point of the book?'

'Surely it's just a children's story?'

'My goodness me no! On one level it's a sort of adventure, I suppose, but ... isn't it what they call an allegory? That's what gives the book its real power.'

'Are you pulling my leg?'

Eventually they moved on to other subjects, both quietly puzzled about the other's reaction. Bettony talked about going to see Benedict in his play, and Angered described her latest gastronomic treat as provided by Morgan, who was currently turning his highly skilled attention to seafood dishes. Angered said that she had had to work late again and had been kindly invited to sample Queen Langoustines alla Busara. Bettony thought about Morgan's exceptional cooking and wondered about her friend's use of the phrase "had to". Bettony had not yet had dinner, and the lovingly described meal left her feeling very hungry. Later, she stared at her egg and strangely damp chips with a feeling of loss. Oh well, at least she had eaten well with Tweek. She had decided not to mention that in the video call. Whatever had passed between Golgood and Angered was clearly not water under the bridge.

The week flew by and to Bettony's regret so did the weekend. The following week brought a steady stream of nervous interviewees. Tweek had intended to carry out pre-selection and first interview himself, but to his annoyance Brink not only insisted on vetting the applications herself but also on involving Bettony in the process.

'It's not as if she has the time to get involved in this level of detail,' he grumbled to Bettony. 'And she insists on tying you up with it as well. I could have done it all.' He shook his head. 'Bart would have let me sort it. He's not a woman though.'

Bettony was so shocked at Golgood's last sentence that she gasped aloud.

'I'm so sorry,' Tweek added quickly. 'That was unconscionable and a stupid thing for me to say. Please forgive me Bettony.' He became full of humility. 'Brink says that I take too much on and end up living on my nerves and I'm beginning to think she's right. I say empty-headed things that I don't mean. That was terrible.' He tried his lost-boy smile. 'If I'd heard myself saying it I would probably punch myself on the nose.'

I could do it for you if you like, Bettony thought. She wondered what Garri's reaction was to Golgood's outburst, but as usual the resident genius was engrossed in his computer. If he had heard - and surely he must have - he was keeping his thoughts to himself.

The outer door burst open and Brink Stellish hurried in. 'Right then people,' she said, testing her English. 'Who's up for shaving this afternoon?'

Golgood was suddenly once more the eager puppy, keen to impress. He picked up the piece of paper he had been showing Bettony and passed it to Brink. There were four names on it. One in particular, Tweek said, showed a great deal of promise.
If Brink noticed a strained atmosphere in the office, she did not comment on it.

Brink had wanted Bettony to sit in on the interviews and give feedback on the candidates. She had, she explained, a high regard for Bettony's judgement of character. This was not an opinion that Bettony particularly shared, but she was happy to be involved in the process.

'I want you to observe' Brink had said. 'Watch them. Notice their body language. You're good at that. By all means ask a question if you want to, but above all, try to get an impression of the real person underneath the interviewee.'

Bettony had been nervous at first, but had soon settled. She had even started asking the odd question. Brink seemed happy for Tweek to run the interviews. Bettony noticed that although Golgood did not refer to any notes, and his questions all seemed spontaneous, they were exactly the same, every time. Brink restricted herself to the odd supplementary question. Afterwards, they would talk about their impressions of each candidate.

Golgood scored each person's answer to each of his questions and kept a running tally of the highest. Bettony simply gave her feedback as Brink had instructed. Stellish herself made notes on her smartpad, both during the interviews and afterwards, in their private discussion. Whatever her thoughts were, she kept them to herself.

Today Golgood was trying and failing to suppress his excitement. He handed out four application forms and expanded on what he had said: One of the candidates had a glittering record and showed huge promise. Tweek admitted that he had already taken up this person's two references and they had been quickly returned. Both were very positive.

Brink nodded and smiled indulgently at her assistant. 'Better get them in then,' she said.

'I'm not going to tell you who I've been talking about,' Tweek said. 'If you can't tell, then clearly I have been mistaken.'

They had moved to Brink's private office, where they were carrying out the interviews. Usually Brink would make small talk while Golgood disappeared to collect the nervous applicants; today, she avoided Bettony's eyes, writing on her smartpad. Bettony's thoughts wandered back to Tweek's comment about their boss; then about Golgood himself. He had an uncanny ability to continually throw her off-balance; he could be endearingly attentive and painfully cutting in the same sentence. He was also unlike anyone she had met so far on Abbuth. Then again, she reflected, there were a lot more people to meet. And just about everyone she knew well was connected in some way or other to the rarefied atmosphere of Sputteridge.

Golgood returned, ushering the first of the day's interviewees into the room. Bettony stood and followed Brink in shaking hands with a woman who was blushing furiously, neck and face both mottled with colour. She looks so young she could still be at school, Bettony thought. Or is it me? What a horrible idea. Am I starting to get old? She made a mental note to check how old the next policeman she met looked. Then she made another mental note to concentrate. Tweek had already started working through his now-familiar questions.

It was gone lunchtime by the time they finished. Golgood disappeared to find sandwiches, Brink was tapping at her smartpad again and Bettony reflected on the four hopefuls. Tweek was right, she thought. One - a tall young man - stood out. For some reason he had vaguely reminded her of Nixel Flines, the man from Newcastle that she had met a few weeks before. Like Flines, he radiated competence and self-assurance.

'What did you think?' Golgood had returned with sandwiches and coffee, and handed plates and cups out. In reply, Brink turned to Bettony.

'Bettony?'

'Tweek was right, one person was definitely a huge improvement on the rest.'

Golgood sat back, relaxing. 'Do you want to name him Bettony?'

'That second-to-last one... er... Derrik Kimley?'

'Kimberley. Yes.' Tweek grinned. 'Phew. I shouldn't get so involved, should I? It really doesn't matter whom we choose as long as they're up to the job. It's just that this chap seems to be the one. He was every bit as good in person as his application promised. My favourite so far, anyway. He certainly answered the questions very impressively.'

Brink Stellish smiled. 'If you two would be good enough to excuse me, I need to make a private call now. Thank you once again Tweek for your tireless work.'

Later, when she was trying to clean burnt egg from a pan in her kitchen, a thought suddenly flashed into Bettony's brain.

Did Derrick Kimley look good because the other three were so poor?

CHAPTER FOUR

A Practical Joke

Two Gentlemen of Bologna began their run on the Friday one week before Yoolbreak, the same day that Television House closed for two weeks. This was during the week when Strikken was taking his turn as lead medic at Falmouth General; but one of the benefits of Bettony's job was that the apartment was hers to use whenever she wanted it. Strikken had a three-day break the following week and the two of them decided to go down to Swindon and use the apartment as their base for a short holiday. They would visit Oxford, take in a couple of Yoolbreak concerts, meet up with their friends and generally have a good time. And also go to see the play.

Bettony had asked Strikken about the Yoolbreak, which in theory was a historic week of commemorative festivities but seemed over the years to have expanded to nearer three weeks of revelry.

'It started out as a festival many centuries ago honouring Chris Yool.'

'Chris... Yool?'

'He promoted a set of ideas based around forgiveness and peace. It ought to be basic common sense really, not stuff that anyone could argue with. To be honest Bettony, these days the whole thing is just an excuse for a bit of fun at the gloomiest time of year, which is a good enough reason for me.'

Benedict had agreed with Bettony that he would call her after the first performance of Two Gentlemen, by which time she would have arrived home in Falmouth. The play seemed to have taken over Benedict's life. He could hardly talk about anything else. His excited face pinged onto Bettony's screen at close to midnight. Strikken had got home shortly before, and was already upstairs asleep. Bettony wished that she was, too, but she wanted to support her friend, who at this moment was clearly still buzzing with adrenaline and exclamation marks.

'It was amazing Bettony! We had two curtain calls at the end! The place was nearly full! Well - parts of it were anyway! And I didn't forget any lines! Apart from that big speech in scene three where I missed out a few lines but no-one seemed to notice, not even Sam, and Valentino picked up his cue all right. Wow I was nervous at first! But it all settled down after my first lines. What an experience!'

Kaghendra came into view, looking relaxed and holding a half-empty glass of beer. 'Hi Bettony how's things? You look tired.'

'I am.'

'Come on star, she needs her rest.' Kaghendra poked Oxford's new acting talent affectionately on the shoulder. 'See you next week Bettony. If you can get over early, we'll be able to have a couple of pints before... the performance.' The beer would help, Kaghendra seemed to imply. Bettony smiled, congratulated Benedict, and logged off. It was hard to imagine, she reflected, that this was the same person as the wreck of a man who she and Kaghendra had found, less than a year ago, in a ruined barn on Erce.

Everything was going fairly well, TMB thought. Even the slight error would work in his favour. He pictured a net, inexorably tightening around his victim. The more slowly it tightened, the more terror it would bring once she realised what was happening: Once she realised that there was no way out of it, except the way offered by Tim himself. He laughed, although laughter was not something that TMB was much given to. It was more of an audible smirk.

TMB wanted his victim to feel terror.

The Sentinnat would not have approved of him following her. (The Sentinnat would not have approved of his obsession with her either, although it would have understood.) But look at the results! First, his actions had given TMB the opportunity to hit her with the pathetic little car - not too badly, just enough to hurt and shock. That had been what you might describe as the wake-up call for her. And then following the Freak to Oxford had been risky, but it had yielded a result. Because of it, he knew exactly what he was going to do next.

Tim's plans had taken a while to mature - nothing he could do about that unfortunately - but now, they were all coming together. He hadn't meant to almost kill the idiot woman in the apartment block, but no harm done, she survived. TMB laughed. Apart from to her, obviously. The fools in the police service were slow, but eventually they would follow the trail of breadcrumbs that he was leaving and then they would bring their own contribution to the fun.

Next time there would be no mistake. They had virtually shouted the next step of his plan to him. The half-wits.

They were half-wits and she was a freak.

TMB thought of her as the freak. In his mind, he could not bring himself to refer to her by name (although he knew it well enough). Instead, she was the freak, and this was an accurate name because that was what she was. He hated her for what she had done. For that dreadful thing that she had done. But she had done what she had done because she was a freak. He could see that. She did not behave like a woman. (Although how many of them did, in this deviant world?) Women should be homemakers and child-carers, they should be obedient, and above all they should not be scary. Beneath his veneer of confidence TMB was something of a coward at heart. He knew what the freak was capable of and that scared him.

Another reason why he had to be so careful.

Then again, TMB could be very, very careful.

★★ ★★ ★★

From the private journal of Bettony Gullivant...

Strikken's last day in charge at the hospital was the Saturday. We were planning to have a quiet evening in, spend a leisurely day on Sunday, and get the train to Swindon on the Monday. I had promised to cook a celebratory meal but Strik has often said that he finds cooking very relaxing, and since he finished at four he would have plenty of time to throw one of his vegetarian specials together. We were both enthusiastic carnivores, but Strik had recently assisted in a sleeve gastrectomy operation and was giving meat a miss for a while.

It was indeed a superb meal. Even better, Strikken suggested we order a restaurant drop-out for the Sunday evening, which we shared with a bottle of wine. The day was chilly and bright, and not having to cook or to scrape the black stuff off the pans afterwards meant that we could enjoy a walk along the coastal path and a beer in the Six Moons. It was a lovely weekend and a very festive start to the Yoolbreak.

(A restaurant drop-out in Britannia is basically a home delivery prepared by your favourite restaurant to the same high standards as for their in-house customers. It's very popular.)

We took the early afternoon train to Swindon on Monday. I wanted to order some fizz, but Strikken said he needed to pace himself. It was certainly true that wine and beer seemed to affect him quite a lot. I'm not sure he had drunk much alcohol at all before he met me. As it turned out, it was lucky that he stayed sober. We had only just unpacked in the apartment when his phone pinged. He looked at the screen and his face fell.

'Oh...'

'What's wrong?'

'There's a major emergency at a local hospital. Some sort of accident involving two school buses. They've put out a call for any local medics.'

'Oh no... Hang on, haven't the schools broken up?'

'Maybe it's a school visit or something. I'll call a taxi.' He sighed, deflated, and tapped a taxi request into his phone. 'Our bad luck eh? But so much worse for the people involved.'

He was back by half seven, much earlier than I expected. He was also annoyed; Strikken is a very gentle-natured man, but he was clearly not happy.

'What's wrong?'

'It was some sort of practical joke. The message said they needed urgent assistance at the Jack Redcliffe hospital. There's no such hospital as the Jack Redcliffe in Swindon. There's one in Oxford, so that's where we've been. Actually there are two with that name in Oxford, the original Jack Redcliffe in the town centre and a big new one on the outskirts, what they call the JR2. We went to both. Neither of them had an emergency.' He threw himself into a chair. 'I can only guess that somebody at the Falmouth General thought that would be a good joke. Goodness knows how they hacked the message into my phone. Just wait till I find out who it is. And it cost me a fortune in taxi fare.'

'What's that on your hand? It looks like blood.'

'Huh?' He lifted his hand and examined it. 'It is blood. How odd. I must have cut myself somewhere.' He dragged himself out of his chair. 'Better go and get this cleaned up. Goodness knows where I did it. Don't want any infection spoiling Yoolbreak do we?'

CHAPTER FIVE

More from Bettony...

We were in Oxford next day for a lunchtime concert. We had coffee and a sausage sandwich in the depths of an old building and then strolled through town to the side-street where the performance was taking place. I've visited Oxford a couple of times on Earth and it all seemed very familiar, although with a lot less traffic. (And, Bollie Sneggs would have been fascinated to learn, a lot less chewing gum stuck to the pavement.) The plan was to meet Benedict and Kagh afterwards, stroll around the old city for a while doing the tourist thing and then get something to eat. Benedict would go and get ready for his performance and we three would kill time (and a couple of pints) before finding our way to the Shene Jones.

Our friends were waiting for us on the pavement outside the Holywell. Strikken spotted them first.

'Is that Benedict?' He asked. He seemed almost shocked.

'He looks so much taller doesn't he Strik? When we first met him I thought he was quite short, but he was... sort of bent into himself. Hunched up. Life on Abbuth is really suiting him.'

Then we were greeting each other. We wandered down narrow lanes past stone colleges. Benedict led us into one of the best bookshops I have ever visited. Wrapped up against the cold, we had a happy, relaxed afternoon, which in no way prepared us for what was to come. We wished Benedict good luck when he left us, wandered some more, and found a nice pub. Warm, comfortably full of good food and relaxed by the beer, we found our way to the Shene Jones, where two police officers were waiting to arrest Strikken for the murder of somebody called Terry Hews.

The officers were in plain clothes, wrapped up like us against the cold. They were standing to one side of the theatre doors, watching a trickle of people go past them. I recognised SI Farley at the same moment that he saw me. His colleague looked as if he had been carved out of rock rather than born. A very large piece of rock. Both looked sheepish. SI Farley stepped forward and self-consciously launched into what was obviously a prepared speech.

'Strikken Flange, I am arresting you in connection with the murder of Terry Hews. You may -'

'Run Strik!'

I launched myself at the Senior Investigator, pushing forwards from my legs to give my punch more power. My fist collided with SI Farley's stomach, the impact of my punch enough to make the SI bend forward and gasp. Unfortunately the resistance it met was far greater than I had been expecting. My first reaction was that I had broken my wrist. My second was one of dismay: Strikken had not run away. He was stepping forwards and tending to SI Farley. As I watched him, I felt steel rods pin my arms to my body.

'Strik! Run!'

'Don't be silly Bettony, this man may be hurt. What were you thinking of?'

'He wants to arrest you for murder!'

A small crowd had gathered and were watching us with interest. When I said Murder I definitely heard a muffled *Oooh* from the spectators. I struggled against the steel rods, which I realised were SI Farley's companion's arms.

'It's obviously a mistake,' Strikken replied. 'Running away won't solve the problem will it?'

'It might.'

SI Farley slowly straightened up and turned to Strikken. 'Is she often violent?'

'Only when somebody is trying to arrest my boyfriend for MURDER!'

Oooh.

'I suggest we go somewhere warm and quiet,' Strikken said. He was by now in full Authoritative Doctor mode, and was even dictating the terms of his own arrest. 'I can make sure you haven't suffered any abdominal injury and you can carry on doing your job of apprehending me. It's Senior Investigator Farley isn't it? How are you? Keeping well I hope?'

'Apart from some bruising around the stomach I'm fine thank you' the policeman replied, with a hint of truculence. 'Yes all right, good idea.' Farley turned to me, and with what I felt was somewhat exaggerated patience said, 'If you give me your word not to cause any further disturbance I can instruct Constable Perky to release you.'

The unusually high moral standards of this world (as well as their occasionally wildly inappropriate names) still astonish me to this day.

I promised, feeling more like a naughty child than someone involved in a very serious arrest, and the steel rods were removed.

'I could have you arrested for assaulting a police officer. You know that?'

'I was trying to protect Strikken.'

'That's not actually a defence in law. And anyway why would you need to? He tells me he has no knowledge of the crime.' Farley leaned forward. 'Tea?'

'Thanks.'

He poured two cups. 'As you would say in your world, I'll get pregnant.'

In spite of the situation I laughed. 'I think you mean, I'll be mother.'

'Yes. Well. Whatever. Sugar?'

'No thanks.' I looked around at the carpeted and comfortably appointed room. A couple of table lamps offered a relaxing light. It was pleasantly warm and the two of us were sitting in big armchairs, separated from each other by a low coffee table. The policemen had taken us to Oxford police station. SI Farley and I were in a very strange interview room; Strikken and Constable Perky were in another.

'Why did you think we wouldn't believe him?'

'I... don't know.'

'Was it the blood?'

'What blood SI Farley?'

'The blood that the taxi driver says he saw on Strikken's hands when he returned to the car from his visit to the new Jack Redcliffe hospital. And where Mr Hews was later found dead. You can call me Siril you know.'

'I don't know about any blood.'

'Strikken says that you do. He says it was you who pointed it out to him when he got home. He tells me that he doesn't know how he got it on him. He says that at first he thought he had cut himself, but once he had washed it off he realised there was no cut.'

Oh, Strik. I sighed but I didn't speak.

'Look Bettony. Is it ok if I call you Bettony?'

'I suppose so.'

Farley pushed a small metal case towards me. 'Under the law here in Britannia, this is yours. It is the only recording of our conversation. It's recording me now, telling you this: Nothing we say here can be used against anyone, right up until I give you a formal written warning that that will happen. The warning is timestamped. You have to sign and date it. I can't even write anything down for my own use. The purpose of this conversation is for me to try and get more information relating to what happened. That's all.'

'Ok.'

'So tell me about the blood.'

'What blood Siril?'

Farley sighed. 'Come on Bettony. There's a lot of violence following you around. The murder of Dr Penck. The attempted murder of Liz McGarry. The murder of Mr Hews. It's off the scale for us. I need your help.'

'It would be off the scale on earth. And don't forget the attempt to run me over.'

'Indeed. I hadn't forgotten that.'

An idea struck me. 'And the chicken.' Why hadn't I thought of that before?

'What chicken? Somebody killed a chicken?' Farley frowned. 'Look Bettony I appreciate that you seem to have decided to help, but I'm not sure the death of a chicken is quite as important as the murder of three people.'

I told him about the out-of-date chicken and the food poisoning. He didn't seem very impressed; then again, maybe he was. Siril Farley was a difficult man to read.

'Strikken could not have been involved in any of those other - incidents.'

'True.' Farley sipped at his tea. 'Most of them, anyway. And you're suggesting that because he wasn't involved in any of the other things, he wasn't involved in this either? That's a bit weak, isn't it? Particularly when we've got a witness for last night.'

'Have you interviewed this taxi driver yourself?'

'No.' For the first time, Farley looked uncomfortable. 'We're having a bit of trouble tracing him.'

'What! So how do you know what he said?'

'We've got a recording of the emergency call.'

'Ha! So it could have been anybody. It could have been the murderer themself?'

'We've got Strikken's information about the blood. Don't look like that Bettony! I genuinely want to find out the truth about who killed the unfortunate Mr Hews, and to do that I need all the truth I can find.' He drummed his fingers on the low coffee table that separated us. 'Surely it's the same in your world? An innocent person who is arrested will want to tell the police everything he can, so that he can help them find out the truth?' We were both silent for a moment, then Farley took a deep breath, then said, 'Tell you what. If I play you the call, you might recognise the voice. You probably won't, but it's worth a shot. Yes?'

'Yes!'

Farley produced another small metal case and pressed its side. It played, with amazing clarity, a recording of the taxi driver's call.

There were a few preliminary exchanges with the operator, then the voice said,

'I'm so sorry to bother you but I think I may have seen a man kill someone last night.'

'What is your name caller?'

The reply was gabbled quickly and impossible to pick out, the voice not stopping but adding quickly,

'I couldn't quite believe what I saw. And of course it was dark so I may be mistaken. To be honest it's so ridiculous it can't be true can it? But this morning I noticed a lot of blood on the passenger seat of my taxi. Perhaps you could check? It was in the car park at the Jack Redcliffe in Headington. He was my last fare last night. He told me that he was a doctor who needed to check something in the hospital but instead of going inside the building he walked over to meet a man at the edge of the car park. I'm so sorry to be wasting your time if I'm mistaken.'

'Caller, what is your name?'

'Oh, so sorry - his name. I heard his girlfriend called him Strikken, that's all I know. I dropped him off at the same place that I picked him up from. Somewhere called Pellic House in Swindon.

'No caller, what is your name? Hello caller? Hello?'

I frowned. 'Something in the words he uses... No. I don't recognise the voice. It's too muffled.'

'Something in the words? Explain.'

'Can you play it again please?'

We played it again. Farley looked at me hopefully. 'Something...?' He prompted.

'Sorry.' I shook my head.

He watched me carefully, then said, 'If it comes to you, let me know.'

'Of course.'

'Your tea's getting cold.'

'Never mind about my tea! What about Strikken!'

'I'm going to be honest with you Bettony, this whole thing doesn't ring true. But there's a whole lot of something happening even if I can't figure out what it is. Until we can work out how Strikken got the blood on him, the charge is so serious that I'm going to have to keep him here for the time being.'

Not unexpected I suppose, but my stomach sank. 'Who is this Terry Hews?'

'Was. He was a porter at the Jack Redcliffe. A single man, no criminal record, played football for his local pub team in south Oxford. I don't suppose you've heard of him?'

'No.'

'Well thank you for this conversation. Feel free to finish your tea before you go.' SI Farley stood up. 'Would you like some biscuits to go with it?'

'No! Thank you. What I want is for Strikken to be released.'

'I know. As soon as I can, I will. Don't forget your recording.' Farley pushed the device towards me.

Kaghendra and Benedict had gone to the police station after the play finished, and were waiting for me in a sort of reception area. They manoeuvred me out of the building and in the direction of Benedict's rooms. As we walked I told them about my conversation with SI Farley, and the recording of the taxi-driver's call. They were as mystified as I was.

'How did your performance go tonight?' I asked, trying to lighten the conversation. 'It must have been hard to concentrate.'

'Overall pretty well' replied Benedict, now the experienced actor. 'The new Hurry had a couple of stumbles but I suppose that's to be expected, coming into the role at the last moment. He's getting better.'

'Stay with us tonight Bettony,' Kaghendra said. 'We'll make up the bed in the spare room.'

'Thanks but no. I'll get the last train to Swindon and go back to Pellic House.'

Kagh put her hands on my shoulders. 'Not an option girlfriend! You're with us. Like the old times...' When she said that her expression suddenly changed. The look of alarm she gave me probably reflected my own.

'It can't be, can it?' She half-whispered. 'He's dead.'

I shook my head. 'Can't be' I replied, not very convincingly.

** ** **

TMB couldn't stop laughing. It was so stupid! How had he got that so wrong?

Not really that wrong, he told himself. The end result was what he wanted, more or less. There would still be plenty of chances to put things right and, he reminded himself, the slower the build-up, the better.

Things were all going in the right direction.

Secure in the cocoon of hubris that Hinton wove around all of its schoolboys, and which lasted them all their lives, TMB was pretty much incapable of admitting to himself that he could make mistakes.

CHAPTER SIX

Yoolbreak in a cold, dark prison cell

'How are you settling in? Did you have a nice Yoolbreak?'

Crean looked up from his desk, a ready smile on his face.

'Very nice thank you sir.'

'I've told you before Nixel, it's all first name terms here.'

Crean cursed himself. How dumb was that! 'Sorry Rem. I get a bit overawed at times and I guess I revert to my childhood. My parents were very strict.' He grinned, disarmingly. 'But it's still the same answer. I'm settling in very well. To be making a contribution to a place like this... it's a dream come true, really.' Steady on, Crean thought. Don't overdo it.

Remnimbi Pyres smiled. 'You're certainly making your mark. I can't remember the last time Bristol Uni sent a full team to one of our monthly reporting sessions. How on earth you managed to persuade Madeleine Farmer to honour us with her presence is beyond me.'

'I tried to get over to her how much impact she could have on the future direction of our research if she was here in person. It can be difficult to resist the chance to influence things. And obviously if she was turning up everyone else had to.'

Pyres laughed. 'As long as she doesn't get any crazy idea about running the place. Her ambitions sometimes outrun her abilities. It's ok Nixel, no need to panic. We can deal with Madeleine and in a sense it's true what you said to her. The more input we can get from Bristol the better. A couple of their specialities are world-leading. One of their people won the Corngreave Yalta a couple of years ago.'

'Goodness.' Crean had no idea what the Corngreave Yalta was and made a mental note to find out. 'Better to have her inside the tent...' at the last moment Crean remembered where he had read that phrase, and how it ended.

'I'm sorry?'

'Er... we want everyone in our tent,' Hugo finished, lamely. 'It's something that I heard the woman from Earth say, at the Yoolbreak party. What was her name...?'

'Oh, you mean Bettony Gullivant. She's interested in camping is she? I didn't know that.'

'I suppose she must be' Hugo replied disingenuously. 'I actually spoke to her, very briefly. You'd never know that she was from another world. Oh that sounds dreadful.'

'I'm sure she would be flattered to hear you say it.'

Let's try a gentle prod, Hugo reflected. *It's worth a try.*

'I thought I'd see a lot more of her around Sputteridge. But that's the only time I've come across her.'

'Ha! Onward and upward for Bettony!'

'How do you mean?'

Pyres was what TMB would have called a big hitter in academic circles. He was also a man who was living proof that anyone could be a gossip.

'You've missed your chance Nixel. She's working for Brink Stellish these days. Based up in Swindon I think.'

'Swindon?' Hugo had seen little of the town on his first night in Britannia. He thought once more of the sprawling, dangerous city that he had transitioned from. Crumbling tower-blocks and a couple of small waterways running through it that were little more than open sewers. Suspiciously low crime rates and one of the Regency's more corrupt local administrations. Somewhere to be avoided - particularly for Hugo.

Pyres misinterpreted Hugo's grimace.

'It's a bit of a pretty-pretty little town, I know, but it's where Television House is.'

'Ah! Yes.' *What? Come on boy, get learning your homework.*

'She was living with one of the doctors from Falmouth General. Whether they split up or whether she commutes, I don't know.'

You really are a bit of a gossip, aren't you Rem?

'She must be a fascinating person to talk to.'

'Oh she is Nixel. Sometimes though I can't help getting the feeling that she's keeping a lot back. You know, about life on Earth. She's written an account of her experiences, but it's mainly about her time on the Series Four Transition Vehicle and an awful spell on a planet called Earsay.'

'I'd love to meet her properly. Not just a quick hello at a party.' *Careful now, don't push it.*

'A lot of people would Nixel! Tell you what...'

Tell me! Tell me Rem!

Pyres chewed his lip thoughtfully. 'I'll see if I can get you a copy of her report.' *Oh.* 'It's... quirky. She's obviously got a sense of humour. Yes.' Pyres tapped Crean's desk. 'It's not as if it's secret or anything.'

'Wow.' Hugo manfully painted an expression of delight across his face. 'Thanks Rem.' *Next step, get myself up to Swindon.*

★★ ★★ ★★

All the things that we had planned for the Yoolbreak were abandoned. Kagh and Benedict were wonderful. At first, I thought of Strikken languishing in a cold dark cell - at this, of all times of the year - and wanted to break down, but somehow my two friends kept my spirits up. And my mood definitely changed when I visited Strik in his cell.

A uniformed officer led me through the back of the police station and down a hushed, carpeted passageway. She pushed open an unlocked wooden door and led me into an apartment that pretty nearly rivalled my own at Pellic House, and was much more luxurious than the small room I was using in Benedict's draughty flat. Strikken was standing at a table, wrapping gift paper around a box, and looked up guiltily.

'Phew,' he said, 'you nearly caught me out there Bettony. A few seconds earlier and you would have seen what this is.'

We hugged. My sympathies were draining away, without any help from me. 'They treating you well enough are they?'

'Yes thank you. I'm missing you though,' he added, tenderly.

'Would you two like tea?' The uniformed officer asked.

'I don't believe this,' I muttered to myself. We both said yes. To Strikken, I asked, 'Who put the Yoolbreak decorations up?'

'Constable Perky. He's doing rather a good job don't you think?'

'Oh it's wonderful. I suppose it's easy enough for him to reach up to the ceiling, as well.'

On cue, the large piece of moveable rock appeared from an inner hallway, smiled and waved to me. He had a length of festive streamer around his neck. 'Time for tea is it?' He said to his colleague. 'Decaff for me please, and a couple of jammy dodgers.'

'Are you all right Bettony?'

'Yes. Of course. It's just that I was getting upset thinking of you in a cold dark prison cell... and all the time you were here.'

'Ah yes. I remember what the cell was like at the back of Pildew's house on Earth. But you've got to remember Bettony, here on Abbuth we regard everyone as innocent until proven guilty.'

'We do that on Earth. In Britain, anyway.'

Strikken frowned. 'Why do you lock them away like criminals then?'

'Er... I don't know.'

'You're getting annoyed. I can tell.'

'Not a lot gets past you does it Strik?'

Constable Perky advanced towards us.

'Would you two like to be... *Left Alone*?'

If a whole body could wink suggestively, Constable Perky's did at that moment.

'No!' I almost shouted. The constable and Strikken both backed away from me slightly, shocked by the strength of my response. At that moment the second officer reappeared, carrying a full tray of tea and biscuits. She looked at me, smiled brightly, and said, in broken English, 'Shall I get pregnant?'

I am reasonably sure that I thought the phrase, *For fuck's sake*, rather than actually shouting it, but it felt like I'd thought it very loudly. Certainly, the other three seemed to be able to hear my thoughts.

In truth, I left Strikken feeling a lot better than before I had seen him. There was still the accusation of a very serious crime hanging over him, but he did not seem to be worried by it. For Strikken, it was merely a question of how long it would take for his innocence to be shown. Perhaps because of our different backgrounds, I had been much more concerned. Whatever we thought, with Siril Farley away for the Yoolbreak, little would happen very quickly.

Despite my worries, the festive break passed fairly easily. I got the feeling that Kagh and Benedict were going out of their way to entertain me, but that was nice, it made me realise what good friends they were. Several evenings we sat together in Benedict's living room, drinking tea and discussing everything. By now they both knew as much as I did about the violence that seemed to be following me around.

None of us could work out what was behind it all, except that - obviously - I was in some way the link. We became convinced that the Regency were involved, although there was some debate around the Incident Of The Chicken, which my friends seemed willing to put down to my cooking.

'Think about it Bettony,' Benedict said. 'How would they have arranged it so that one out-of-date chicken was in the shop's chiller specifically for you to pick up? Or alternatively, how would they have replaced one that was in your fridge at home with the old one?'

'Find the taxi driver who picked Strikken up, and you will find the answer to a lot of questions,' Kagh said. 'That's what I think.'

As it turned out, when they found the taxi driver it answered at least one question but it certainly raised a lot of others.

CHAPTER SEVEN

Old Friends

Bettony returned to work in the new year determined not to show how worried she was, and was successful for nearly ten minutes.

Garri was alone in the main office, focussed as usual on his computer, although he did break from it long enough to wish Bettony a happy new year. Bettony politely admired Garri's new T-shirt, which he told her was a present from his girlfriend. Garri was clearly not someone who regarded physical fitness as an important part of his life, and the T-shirt was tight in all the wrong places, but he was very pleased with it. Bettony struggled to imagine Garri with a girlfriend, but read aloud the words stylishly scripted across his top, and laughed dutifully at them.

'"*I'll be damned if I ever wear anything like this!*" Ha ha. Your girlfriend's got a good sense of humour Garri.'

Garri smiled happily. 'Pandau wears one of these in Brelin's Portal.'

'Ha. Oh yes. I wondered where I'd seen it before.' Bettony wondered who Pandau was, and what he might have been doing in Brelin's Portal, whatever that might have been. A video game? A movie? She was saved from being found out when Tweek pushed the door open from Brink's private office.

'Bettony could you join us please? *Now*?'

He was trying to sound authoritative and important, which Bettony found annoying. *I don't work for you Tweek.*

'Now, Tweek?' She answered. 'Is that the message Brink has told you to pass on?'

Still, she got up and followed Tweek inside. She was surprised to see not only Brink, but also Zagretia Ponch in the inner room. In contrast to Golgood, the two women both smiled and wished Bettony a happy new year.

'Take a seat Bettony.'

In spite of their friendliness, Bettony felt a qualm of anxiety.

'Obviously, we've heard about Strikken's arrest,' Mrs Ponch said.

Who from? Bettony glanced at Golgood. She thought she knew him well enough by now to tell that the expression of concern on his face was completely false. *He's enjoying this. The bastard.*

'It must have been an awful experience for the two of you.'

'As soon as she found out this morning Zagretia gave Dr Flange a character reference,' Brink added. 'Not that it was really necessary. He's agreed to have a DNA check, just so we can make sure that he's who he says he is. Stellish smiled again. 'Although I'm pretty sure that you would have spotted if he wasn't –'

Bettony made a sound that was half-sob, half a laugh.

'– and the good news is, we've found the taxi driver.'

Although Bettony was looking at Brink Stellish, Golgood was enough in her field of vision for her to take in the look of shock on his face. *That's something you didn't know*, she thought. Stellish carried on, apparently oblivious to his reaction.

'I don't know how good your forensic pathologists are on Earth, Bettony, but ours have been able to tell us with absolute certainty that the unfortunate man had been dead for quite a few hours when he apparently made that emergency phone call. In fact, he was quite probably dead when someone driving his car and using his name picked Dr Flange up. All very odd, don't you think? But all pointing towards some sort of attempt to throw suspicion for these crimes on the doctor. We have no idea why, and neither does Dr Flange. SI Siril Farley believes that when he finds the person who killed Terry Hews, he will also have found the murderer of the taxi driver, and doubtless also the person trying to make it appear that Dr Flange was the culprit.'

'There is still the strange business about the blood,' she added. 'But in view of everything else, the police have agreed to what we call a suspension of suspicion regarding your boyfriend.'

'That basically means he's in the clear,' Mrs Ponch explained, adding in her own unique version of English, 'In his pedallo and out of the creek.'

'I'm expecting Dr Flange's DNA results in the next half an hour or so,' Brink continued. 'Which means that he should be stopping by in Swindon around lunchtime. Just in time to buy you a decent lunch before he heads back to Falmouth.'

Silently cursing her loss of control, Bettony put her hands to her face and sobbed again. She made an effort to gather herself and said,

'Thank you.'

'Thanks are not necessary,' Mrs Ponch smiled. 'Right.' She stood and headed for the door. 'To business. See you later Brink. Tweek.' She nodded briefly to Golgood, then added in English, 'Goodbye Bettony. Chins up. You know you will always have my support.'

'Well, there we are,' Brink said, as the door closed. 'It's not been the best Yoolbreak for you Bettony, but at least now you should have a happy start to the new year.' A smile played briefly across her face, and she sighed. 'A lot for our investigators to sort out of course. Goodness knows what's happening, but... They will find out. I have no doubt about that.' She picked her smartpad up. 'Anyway people. To business indeed, and the appointment of the latest member of our team.'

Tweek Golgood shook his head. 'Wow,' he said, looking down at his own smartpad. 'Strange times, eh? Right. I have drafted up the letter of appointment for Derrick Kimberley...'

'Why have you done that Tweek?' Stellish was disarmingly gentle.

'I - thought we had agreed -'

'I've agreed nothing Tweek. I'm happy to have your and Bettony's opinions on candidates, but this is my decision.'

'Well - of course, Head of Council -'

'- And I have decided to see two candidates again. Welter Hallett and Breena Farland. Can you arrange for them to come in for final interview next Tuesday please?' Brink put her smartpad down. 'That's all. Thank you people.' She smiled sweetly. 'Meeting closed.'

'It was kind of Mrs Ponch to offer her support.' Strikken spooned some very thick soup into his mouth, momentarily silencing himself, then continued, 'I'm sure that Siril Farley and his people will get to the bottom of it all though.'

Bettony shook her head. 'You're so laid back about it all Strik.'

'Don't get me wrong Bettony, it's a horrible business, and goodness knows what dangers lurk until it's solved. But as someone who is completely innocent of any of these crimes I knew that I had nothing to fear. That's what we have police for, isn't it? As much to vindicate the innocent as to discover the guilty.'

'Mmm.'

'I'm just sorry that it spoiled your Yoolbreak.'

'It could have been worse. Kagh and Benedict were great. And you obviously weren't suffering too much.'

When he spoke again, Strikken's voice was flat. 'I do think you may be right about the Regency though, and that's bad news isn't it? If some of them are still around, heavens know what they're up to. What danger we could all be in. Oh well. Thanks to your courage we're more prepared now than we were.'

'Flattery will get you everywhere Strik.'

'It's true though. And we've got good people keeping us secure.'

'I hope you're right.' Bettony thought about Sherian Penck, who hadn't been secure at all. 'Tweek Golgood was going nuts before I came out' she said, changing the subject. She told Strikken about what had happened.

'I met him once,' Strikken said. 'He came over to several of the pre-transition meetings, before our great adventure on the Series Four. I think he was involved in the selection process. I got the impression that he liked to get his way on that too. He seemed to be very intense.'

'Strik! Why didn't you warn me before I took the job?'

Strikken shrugged his shoulders. 'I thought it better for you to make up your own mind. It's not as if you're working for him, is it?'

'Bloody right there, and no chance of that ever happening. Whatever he might think.'

When Bettony got back from her lunch Brink was in the main office, talking to Garri. She looked relaxed and comfortable.

'Ah! And how is the good doctor?'

'He's very well thanks Brink. Looking forward to getting back to work. He seems to have enjoyed his stay at the police station.'

Brink smiled. 'Perhaps. Maybe he wanted you to feel as reassured as possible. Anyway, it's all sorted now. Come on through.'

Bettony followed Brink into her private office and thought about Strikken's unconventional use of Tickle the Sparrow, and the subtle mind games that he had employed to get the best out of people. She kicked herself for not realising what her boyfriend had been doing.

'Take a seat Bettony. Let's talk about our hopeful candidates. Which one would you pick? Welter Hallett or Breena Farland? Or someone else entirely?'

'Oh - er... I don't know. One of those two, definitely. They were both very keen weren't they?'

'Are you avoiding the question Bettony?' Brink smiled her cold smile. 'Everyone we've seen has been very keen.'

Bettony laughed. 'I suppose that's true... I'd probably pick Welter.'

'Because...?'

'Even though he was older, he was the more hesitant of the two, but I thought he was impressive. He was even better on his second interview wasn't he? And a bit less tense. Which tells me he'll improve more as he settles in and relaxes. So I wonder, if he's this good when he's nervous - how good can he be when he's more comfortable? I suppose what I'm saying is that he's got more potential.'

'Interesting.' Brink smiled again, and made a note on her smartpad. Almost as an afterthought, she said, 'What did you think to Derrick Kimberley?'

'He was very confident. He vaguely reminded me of someone else... He stood out compared to the other people we saw that day. But the others were quite weak candidates on that particular day. His answers to Tweek's questions were very thorough and well thought through... almost too well thought through. It almost felt as if he'd been coached.'

With a jolt, Bettony realised what she was saying. But Brink was as relaxed as ever, she smiled again and made a brief note on her smartpad.

'You said he reminded you of someone...?'

'Oh - er - someone I met at a party a few weeks ago. Only very briefly.' Bettony could feel herself blushing and cursed herself. Why did she say, Only very briefly? It sounded as though she was making excuses for herself. For what exactly?

'Can you remember their name?'

'Erm - yes. Nixel Flines. He's on the admin side at Sputteridge.'

'Ah. I've heard great things about young Mr Flines. He's coming over to Swindon next Monday. A chance for you to renew your acquaintance, Bettony.'

Despite himself, Hugo Crean was feeling nervous. Not that anyone would have known. He looked exactly the same confident young man that he always did, lounging comfortably in his seat on the train. Still, there was tension under the surface.

He was nervous.

Several things had combined to unsettle him. There was, of course, the day ahead. He would be representing Sputteridge in a meeting at Television House, his first visit to the home of Britannia's government. The meeting itself was a fairly humdrum affair, manufactured by Crean himself, and would not ordinarily have bothered him. The big problem was that he had been finding it difficult to get to Bettony Gullivant. Hugo had set today's meeting up so that Bettony should have been the natural choice to represent Television House; instead, it was to be Tweek Golgood. Crean had not yet met Golgood, but he had heard about him. Golgood had a reputation for being involved in just about everything that was happening. He was known for working incredibly hard.

Hugo would have to find his own way, early, to Bettony's office and hope for the best. He had given himself plenty of time, the meeting was due to start at two and his train was due into Swindon at ten thirty. He had been diligent in his preparation, too, using Viewmap to familiarise himself with the route from the station to Television House. His revised plan was to walk the mile or so from the station and ask for Bettony at Reception. He was fairly confident that he would be able to manoeuvre the two of them to somewhere where he could tell what he knew without fear of being overheard.

Like Bettony before him, Hugo was impressed by the architecture of Swindon station. Like Bettony, he was also surprised by the unassuming nature of the seat of government. The collection of metal and brick buildings that comprised Television House was hidden away down a track that led off a road lined with traditional semi-detached houses. It didn't help that it was a dank, drizzly morning, which lent everything an air of the ordinary. Hugo had been stunned when he first saw the buildings at Sputteridge, a mind-bending amalgam of traditional old houses and cottages into and around which had been poured hi-tech constructions of breathtaking design. Compared to Sputteridge, Television House was modest to the point of being self-effacing. Hugo had brought a copy of the birth certificate that TMB had given him, and also his driving responsibility certificate (that too supplied by Milden-Brewer). These were the closest things he had to personal ID, but he was amazed to discover that he needed neither. As he climbed the steps to the front of Television House he began to wonder if he had come to the right place. On Erce, it would be impossible to get within five hundred yards of the centre of power without being challenged by an armed guard. (Not that anyone would want to get within five hundred yards of Mazeley, not without a very good reason, unless they had some sort of suicide wish.)

Hugo pushed the door open and walked over to the desk. He smiled at the middle-aged man behind it and introduced himself as 'Hugo Crean, for Bettony Gullivant.'

'Let's see,' the man said, consulting his screen. There was a lengthy pause, until the man finally said, 'Ah yes, here we are. You're here for the multidisciplinary collaboration session this afternoon, that's why I couldn't find you. And you want to see Bettony?'

'That's right. If you tell me where her office is I could find my own way...?'

'Mmm.' The man seemed to consider. 'I shouldn't really let you do that... To be honest, this place is like a rabbit warren. If you got lost you could go missing for days. Then I'd be in trouble.' He chuckled at what had apparently been a joke. 'Probably best if I get Bettony to come down and collect you.'

Hugo knew when not to push things. He nodded and thanked him, then watched as the man pushed a shape across his screen, tapped on it, and spoke into his headpiece. He was pleased to note that his heart rate was still well under control.

'Oh hi Bettony it's Danny on reception. there's a Nixel Flines waiting for you here... Yes. Definitely for you.' The man looked at Hugo, a little more appraisingly this time. '... That's what he says... Ok... Yes, ok, I'll tell him.' He removed his headpiece and turned to Crean. 'If you want to take a seat, she'll be down in a few minutes.'

Crean sat in one of the comfortable chairs close to the desk. He watched the occasional person come in or go out; some cast quick glances at him, others smiled openly and said hello. Within five minutes a door at the back of the reception area opened, and Bettony approached him.

'Hello Nixel.' She extended her hand in greeting, but seemed very reserved. If she remembered him from the party, she made no acknowledgement of it. Her face was expressionless and was slightly red; Crean wondered if something had angered her.

'It's nice to see you again Bettony.'

'I'm afraid I won't be joining the meeting this afternoon.'

'Ah.' Hugo affected surprise.

'You're going to be honoured. Brink Stellish will be representing Television House.'

'Goodness.' This time the surprise was genuine.

There was a pause.

'You're here quite early.'

A statement that was also a question, Hugo felt.

'Yes. There are a couple of things that I wanted to speak to you about.'

'Me?' The reddening of the face deepened; the expression became more set. She gestured towards the chairs close to the desk, where Crean had been sitting. 'Do you want to sit down?'

'It would be better if we spoke in private.'

That got two curious looks, one from Bettony and one from Danny, who was clearly listening to every word. But Bettony turned, and saying 'You'd better follow me then,' led the way towards the door at the back of reception.

They walked down a bare corridor in silence; rather an awkward silence, Hugo felt. He needed to break the ice.

'They don't waste money on luxuries here, do they?' He observed. He was striving to be at his most charming, and some of it seemed to get through. Bettony's voice was warmer when she replied,

'Is this your first visit to Television House?'

Crean nodded. 'Yes. It's very different to how I expected.'

'The idea is that the people in government here serve the country, rather than are served by it. Quite a different approach isn't it?'

'Absolutely!'

And then Crean realised what he had just said.

The funny thing was, Bettony had not meant to lay a trap. She was nervous. She had no idea what Nixel Flines could possibly want to say to her; whether it was work-related or private. (Why on earth would it be private?) She wondered vaguely if he had information about the violence that had recently begun to dog her (she thought this unlikely). But Crean's charm and his good looks both appealed and set her on edge: So when she spoke it was without thinking, coloured by memories of her life on earth. But she knew immediately what Crean's response gave away, as much as he did. No-one on Abbuth would think of this as "a different approach" because there was nothing for it to be different to. She looked at him sharply, unable to disguise the shock. When their eyes met, so much passed between them. It was all unspoken, but very clear to both.

'Please.' Crean had gone pale. Bettony had tensed and stepped away from him. 'I must speak to you. It's so important.'

Frowning, she pushed open a door but took a couple of steps past it. 'In there,' she said. 'Go to the far end of the room.'

Meekly, Crean obeyed. It was an empty office, disused by the look of it. Bare tables and desks, some of them piled with sealed packs of paper and other bits of stationery, some bearing dusty and broken versions of the strange keyboards and screens that the Abbuthians used. He walked down to the end that was furthest from the door, moved some rubbish from a chair and and sat down. Bettony closed the door but stood next to it.

'So. Speak.' Her voice was hard.

Hugo spoke. He told her who he was and what he knew. He told her about reading her report, back on Erce, and his surprise at reading about his old and very dear friend, Benedict Erwin. About how he had managed to crop anything that identified Mrs Colshaw, Benedict's nanny, from the report. About wanting not only to get away from the cruel waste of existence that was life on Erce, but also to help the people of Abbuth. About Wellbeck, who continued to operate, deeply embedded in Britannic society, and Hugo's discovery that Wellbeck was Timm Milden-Brewer. He told Bettony that there were more spies from the Sentinnat operating in Britannia, and that TMB had found a way around the DNA check; indeed, had arranged for Hugo himself to have DNA clearance.

He did not tell Bettony about the feelings she had engendered in him, even before he had met her, or that those same feelings grew with every moment spent in her company.

By the time he finished Hugo had recovered himself. He even managed a smile.

'I want to help these people,' he said. 'But if I told anyone what I know, how could I be sure that they weren't from Erce? You are the only person that I know I can trust.' He gestured at the room. 'I hadn't quite meant it to be like this but now you know why I wanted to talk to you in private.'

Bettony stared at Crean. Finally, she said, 'Wait here' and left the room.

Hugo waited there. 'Be still my beating heart,' he muttered.

Bettony returned five minutes later carrying a smartpad. She was holding it away from Crean and pointing its back at him. Hugo watched her with every appearance of relaxation. Then she spoke into the smartpad.

'Is this him?'

As its reverse camera flickered to life, a pinpoint of light appeared on the side of the smartpad facing Hugo. A familiar voice boomed out of the device. 'Hang on I'll zoom in... My word. Yes Bettony, that's Hugo Crean. Hugo! You're the last person I expected to see on Abbuth.'

A genuine smile creased Hugo's face. 'Strange times eh? Wonderful to hear you old fellow.'

'You too -'

'Just a minute.' Bettony was still standing by the door, looking at the screen. 'Ask him the question Benedict.'

'Ok.' Benedict switched to what Bettony thought of as English, but which was also the native language of Regency Britain on Erce. 'Hugo, do you remember what animal Gentry Hulberson put in my bed in lower sixth?'

Hugo frowned. 'Gentry Hulberson? I've got to be honest Ben, I can't even remember anyone called Gentry Hulberson... There was a Bertie Hallamson, but I don't remember him doing anything.'

Crean's frown deepened. 'The only person I remember putting anything in your bed was Tubby Taylor-Green, and that was when he peed in your bed. He only did it the once. If you recall I had a chat with him, and he sportingly agreed to sleep in your bed and give you his until the following month when the sheets were changed. He kindly took charge of the soiled mattress as well, I believe.'

Bettony shuddered. 'Hello Tom Brown's Schooldays,' she muttered to herself.

'You were the only boy who could get away with calling him Tubby, Hugo.'

'I was the only boy who could get away with a lot of things, old friend.'

'Bettony? I am beyond delighted to vouchsafe that that's definitely my very dear friend Hugo St Monderby Dephwood Crean.'

For one moment Hugo's self-control evaporated. His face crumpled and he felt tears sting his eyes. 'Can I see him?' He asked. His words came out as a croak. In reply, Bettony walked over and gave him the smartpad.

'Ben! You're looking well. It must be seven years since I last saw you. I never thought you were dead, you know. I know you too well. And the word was, you had had a boating accident... I couldn't imagine anyone less likely to fall off a boat.'

'I'm so sorry Hugo, I know I let you down. I couldn't work out how to contact you without everyone finding out where I was.'

'Absolutely no need to apologise old friend.'

'I'm sorry to interrupt this reunion,' Bettony said, 'but Hugo and I may not have much time on our own and I want to make the most of what we have.'

'Of course! I'm glad I could help Bettony. It sounds like bad news doesn't it? But from what has been happening, I think we'd more or less suspected something was amiss. We shall prevail! Especially now that we have Mr Crean on our side! See you soon I hope. Hugo, we must meet up as soon as humanly possible.'

'Ben, that is a certainty. Goodbye for now.'

Crean handed the smartpad back to Bettony. 'I passed the test then?'

'You passed the test. Now can we go through all this again?'

'Of course... Any chance of a coffee first?'

Crean was privileged, Bettony explained when she returned. Not only did he get coffee, he got biscuits as well.

They sat at adjoining desks in the disused office, eating and drinking. The atmosphere had improved considerably since they first entered, but there was still tension in the air. Partly, this was due to the scale of the challenge they faced, although Hugo in particular was confident that they would win through. Partly, it was down to Bettony's basic distrust of anyone from Erce (Benedict excepted), particularly anyone connected to the Sentinnat.

Partly, without either of them acknowledging it, there was the unspoken realisation that each was physically attracted to the other.

'So my entire report found its way to Erce? To Angland?'

'I'm afraid so. TMB has obviously got himself into a position of trust over here. Either that, or another Sentinnat bod has and they fed it out to Timmbo.'

'We need to come up with a strategy Hugo. And I need to know who Milden-Brewer is. I need to know when I'm dealing with him. Describe him.'

'Smallish, I'd say - medium height or slightly less, light build, light brown eyes, four years older than me. Damn! He gave me his business card but I left it at home.'

'So you know what name he's going under?'

'I ought to didn't I? Everything on the bloody card was in the handwritten script and I have to confess, I struggle with that. I'm ok with the printed stuff we get on screens. But that old-fashioned super-squiggly clutter is a bit beyond me. I thought his title was "Doctor", though.'

'Doctor! That might explain a thing or two.' Bettony explained about the death of Sherian Penck. 'If Timmbo's working at Falmouth General he'd have every opportunity to kill her.'

Crean was quietly pleased to hear Bettony adopting his own nickname for Milden-Brewer. He said, thoughtfully, 'It sounds so odd to me, hearing a doctor described as "her".' He saw the look that passed over Bettony's face and quickly added, 'Don't get me wrong. It's all good. It just doesn't happen back on Erce. Women know their place.'

'Mmm. I'll let you off... you know, thinking about it, one of the other deaths happened at a hospital.'

'One of the other deaths? How many have there been?'

Bettony summarised the violence of the previous few months.

'Good heavens. These people must be doing their collective nut. Strikken... That's the guy I met at the party is it? When I was talking to you? Strikken Flange, aka Will Hartnell.'

'Yep.'

'And you and he are...?'

'Yes. Me and him are.'

Crean nodded. The atmosphere cooled just a little.

'You know, these things have got TMB written all over them. The man's a sadist. And he's a killer. You need to be very careful with him Bettony.'

'I can look after myself.'

'Yes I know. I read your report, remember? But Timmbo has had a lot of combat training. I'm guessing he carries a Tipper somewhere about his person, even here.'

'What's a Tipper?'

In response Hugo reached down, towards his heel. Bettony half-thought he was rubbing his leg, but when he straightened up he held a narrow-bladed knife in his hand. It was small - not much more than six inches in length, Bettony guessed - but it wasn't a friendly-looking kind of implement.

'It sort of tips an argument in your favour,' Crean explained, putting the knife on the desk in front of her. 'It's a throwing knife too. By the way, I understand why you put so much distance between us when we first came in here, but really, it was too much. It made you an easy target for one of these. The safest distance is a couple of yards. Gives you time to react if I try to stab you and it's too close for me to throw something like this. Not that I would. But Timmbo might. Careful!'

Bettony had touched the blade, but then quickly pulled her finger away as though she had been stung. A tiny bubble of blood appeared on her fingertip.

'You're not going to tell me it's poisoned or anything are you?'

Crean smiled. 'You're safe. It's not poisoned. But as you've found out, it's very sharp.'

'Does everyone at the Sentinnat carry one of these?'

'If they're out on a job, yes.'

'And have you -?' The question was only half-formed. She didn't even want to ask it but she wanted the answer to be No.

'I have never used one, no. I have managed to avoid that sort of assignment.'

There was an awkward silence. Then Hugo added, 'And much as I admire your martial arts skills, you should be aware that even without his Tipper, our friend Timmbo is a very dangerous person. The unarmed combat training that we go through is very comprehensive.'

'Thank you for the warning.'

'Yes. You're welcome.' Hugo's blue eyes met Bettony's hazel ones. Despite the seriousness of the situation, she felt that he was almost laughing - but not at her. Bettony felt that he was inviting her to laugh with him - and she wanted to laugh with him. 'Anyway. You mentioned strategy.'

'Yeah... What strategy did you have when you hatched your plot to come over here Hugo?'

'Oh that was simple. Find you. Alert you to the dangers. Enlist your help. Save the world and live happily ever after.'

Bettony couldn't stop herself from smiling. 'It's a great plan but it's a bit lacking in detail. And I'm not too sure about the "enlisting my help" part. That makes me think you want to play the big strong man. On Erce the women might stand behind their man looking pretty and occasionally screaming, but we're not on Erce. It's equal partners here chum.'

But still looking pretty. Just in time, Hugo stopped himself from saying the words. Something passed between them, unspoken. Bettony looked away, her blush returning.

'So who do you think you can trust in this wonderful land?' Hugo asked, breaking the silence. 'Who do you want to be able to trust?'

'Apart from Strik and Benedict and Kagh? Bollie Sneggs.'

'I'm not sure what answer I was expecting but it wouldn't have been Bollie Sneggs.'

'First of all - your society is so racist that even if you could find Bollie's double he would have had a very deprived education. It would take years to either teach him Enceldic or educate him up to the point where he could emulate my friend's scientific knowledge, let alone copy his unique style of conversation. Even assuming you'd be able to get him to co-operate.'

'Not my society Bettony, please.'

'You met Bollie though. At the party.'

'I did. He does indeed have a unique style of talking, albeit one which is not without its charm. And secondly?'

'Secondly, Bollie has a brain the size of a planet. He has the ability to do a deep DNA analysis. Timmbo can fix the records all he wants but Bollie could stand in front of the... machine thing... and tell us who's who. So we can build up a base of people that we can trust.'

'What about Brink Stellish? Mrs Ponch? Your friend Bob? Osian Jelks?'

'All people that I would want to get involved as soon as possible. Bob would be a definite and what with all the Slepwood stuff that's already happened he'd be a nailed-on certainty for being the real deal, but right now he's doing his thing in some alternate world. Mrs Ponch - almost certainly. Same reasons as Bollie, plus she's a woman, and we know what Slepwood said about her. But first we need to be absolutely sure. Cut down our risks as much as possible. That means starting from Bollie. And I want to hunt TMB down... He could be so many people. He could almost be Tweek Golgood, except Tweek's got blue eyes and he's maybe a bit too tall. Oh I wish it was Tweek.'

'The famous Tweek Golgood. I've heard so much about him but I have yet to meet him. Do I gather you're not overly taken with the young man?'

'Ha! That's one way of putting it. Give me a videocall this evening and let me have a look at TMB's business card. If I can't work it out we can ask Kagh.'

'Kagh?'

'That's Dave Potts to you, if you read my report. And probably the best person to have on the interdisciplinary panel would be a guy called Kevin Pantle. I've got his details in my office, we can go up there now.'

'That's great. You've been such a help Bettony, I'm sure you've got better things to do.'

I love this, Crean thought, as an overweight man in an unpleasantly tight-fitting t-shirt walked into the office. *I could just*

*feel what she was doing there, warning me about this gent. She's
as clued up as I am. It's like we're tuned in to the same frequency.
This is exhilarating!*

'Bettony, Brink's been looking for you. She wants to talk to you
in her office please.'

'Oh ok, thanks Garri. Garri this is Hugo Crean.'

'Hullo.' Garri turned without waiting for Hugo to reply, and
headed out of the office.

'We'd better go.' Bettony's voice was barely a whisper. Louder,
she added, 'Come and meet Brink. I'm sure that she'll be pleased
to meet you.'

'I'd love to but I really must get something to eat before the
meeting. Thank you again so much for your help.'

For a moment Hugo felt her fingers touch his, thrilling him.
Then he realised she had pushed a small piece of paper into his
hand. He risked a glance and saw she had scribbled down her video
contact details.

'Danny will be able to point you to the Cafeteria, it's in this
building on the first floor. Good luck with your meeting Pixel.'

'Thank you Bertie.'

'So let's have a look at your house then Hugo.'

'Don't you want to know how I got on today?'

'I'm sure a smart boy like you got on fine. You can tell me what
you thought about Brink, but first I want a nosey around your living
room.'

The picture on Bettony's smartpad wobbled as Hugo carried his
around.

'Here you can see my favourite chair.'

Bettony laughed. 'I expected something bigger.'

'A bigger chair? Large enough for my buttocks, I can tell you.
Oh you mean the house?'

'Ha ha.'

'A cosy cottage, down in the centre of Falmouth and but a short
walk from the seafront.'

'Cool.' *Falmouth. So close... Don't! Don't go there, in any
sense of that phrase!* 'So: Brink...?'

The screen stabilised as Hugo sat down again.

'Very clued up. A hard woman, I thought. Effortlessly authoritative. And very interested in me, for some reason.' Crean pulled a face. 'I've got to say this Bettony, it's still very strange being outranked by a woman. Don't look at me like that! I'm being honest here. It's just not what I've been used to. I've still only been here a matter of weeks.'

'Benedict has never had a problem with that in all the time I've known him.'

'Benedict is unique.' Hugo was suddenly serious. 'Benedict saved my life. Not in some heroic pulling-me-from-an-icy-lake kind of way; he showed me the strength there is in kindness. Anyway: Brink. Very impressive, although very watchful of me. I had the feeling it was more than my good looks that was drawing her attention.'

'Such modesty. Are you worried she suspects you?'

'Not worried no. Maybe, on my guard.'

'Show me the card.'

Crean held the business card up that Milden-Brewer had given him.

'Heavens.'

'I'm glad it's not just me.'

'Hold it still Hugo! It's almost deliberately difficult.'

'That's TMB all over.'

'Ok I'm not sure about that first word. I can see why you thought it might be "Doctor". I think it looks more like "Tree". Or is that the symbol for water, overlaid with something that represents "push"? "Push water"... Fountain maybe?'

'Thank goodness you're around to help, Bettony. I would have been completely stuck if it weren't for you.'

'Shut up. Let's try the next bit... Oh for goodness sake Hugo hold it steady!'

'Hang on I'll send you an image... did you get that?'

Bettony clicked on a small tab that had appeared at the side of her screen.

'You've sent me a picture of a herring gull.'

'Oh. Woops my mistake.' Hugo became animated. 'I took that the other day, just along from here. Magnificent creature isn't it? I'm training it to take food from me. There are quite a few of them.'

'There'll be quite a few more if you start waving food at them. I'd be careful if I were you. If you value your fingers. And your head.'

'It's just so breathtaking to see them! Such a huge wingspan and they can just hover.'

'I've got a feeling the novelty will wear off. Don't you have them in Angland?'

'I suppose we must have had at some time or other... I guess they all got shot. Or poisoned or something.'

'That's dreadful. How about sending me the image of Timmbo's card now?'

They puzzled fruitlessly over the card for several more minutes, then gave up. Crean wanted to contact Kagh immediately, but Bettony insisted they work on a strategy.

They agreed that the first people to check would be Brink Stellish and Zagretia Ponch. Bettony agreed to talk to Bollie Sneggs, to enlist his help and to find out what he would need to be able to do deep DNA analysis. Bettony knew what Sneggs had achieved on the Series Four with DNA that he had extracted from the fingerprints on a gun, but she also knew that he had been making the best of a difficult job; that his DNA analysis had not been in some way as detailed as it could be. What they wanted now was something that was foolproof. Something that would evade anything TMB could do.

Bettony split her screen and logged into the Television House computer.

'According to this, Bollie should be over in Swindon on Thursday. I'll message him and arrange to meet.'

'I suppose if he could get DNA from a fingerprint it should be easy enough to get hold of Brink's coffee mug or something?'

'One step at a time Hugo. Let's hope that's all he'll need but first let's get him on board and find out. Right! Let's talk to Kagh.'

According to her auto-response, Kaghendra was involved in an academic conference in The Magician And His Wand. Bettony had been to that particular pub with Kaghendra a couple of times, and thought that even if they could find a way of contacting her friend, it was doubtful that they would get any sense out of her. There was nothing further that they could do, but Bettony and Hugo were both reluctant to sign off. They talked about life on

Erce, about life on Earth, and about the Abbuthians' occasionally naive understanding of other worlds. Hugo was very easy to talk to. Eventually Bettony realised that it was gone nine and that she had not eaten dinner. They signed off, leaving Bettony feeling a strangely confused mixture of elation and guilt and forgetting completely about TMB's business card.

CHAPTER EIGHT

Stythium shifts and missing mugs

Bollie Sneggs had had a good day. His meeting at Television House had gone surprisingly well. There was no definite decision on the actual funding timetable yet, he had learned, but it looked very much as though his proposed investigation into morhposa in stythium shifts would be going ahead. Bollie was relieved. He had wondered whether his first presentation several weeks before had been too simplistic: There had been quite a few blank looks among his audience. Bollie had spotted this after a while and wrongly interpreted it as boredom. He had tried to counter it by putting more detail into his explanation of each slide, but to his surprise the blank looks had if anything increased. He had apologised at the end of his talk for over-simplifying. He had promised to give more rounded explanations to anyone who wished to speak to him afterwards. To his surprise and disappointment, no-one had.

He had had the nagging fear that he had blown the application.

Still, Sneggs was buoyed by the strength of his case. Quanbitelic morphosa was obviously the way things were going, and where better to isolate them than in stythium shifts? He was amazed that no-one had thought of it before. You set up the eleven-dimensional matrix equations using base pi rather than hexadecimal, and the results simply dropped out. It was so obvious! Today, he had brought with him some printed copies of a more detailed explanation (actually, he thought, "less childish" would be more accurate). He had handed them out before the start of the meeting. But although many had smilingly taken the copies he had offered, no-one had seemed keen to look at them. A few had looked at the first page, blanched, and pushed them into their pockets with a promise to go through them later. Bollie's heart had been sinking right up until the moment when Zagretia Ponch, who as Council Senior with responsibility for science was chairing the meeting, gave him the good news.

'I really thought I'd blown it Bettony. Cheers.'

'Cheers.'

Sneggs thirstily swallowed half of his pint before putting it back on the table.

'Oh that went down well. It just shows how wrong I can be, doesn't it?'

'Congratulations anyway Bollie.'

'Thanks. How's things with you anyway?

Bettony lowered her voice. 'Actually Bollie I've been looking into strange things.'

Sneggs looked interested. 'Are we talking quarks here Bettony? I didn't know you were studying subatomic physics. That's great news.'

'What? No Bollie. Not physics. Just strange in the sense of weird.'

'Oh. Nothing to do with quark-gluon plasma then?' He persisted hopefully. 'Do you want any crisps?'

'No thanks. Bollie, sit down for a minute and concentrate. This is important.'

Bettony explained about Hugo Crean and TMB. Excited as he was by his good news, Bollie Sneggs was brought down to earth by mention of Erce and the Regency.

'You should be telling Brink Stellish and Osian Jelks about all this, not me.'

'I want to do that Bollie. But how do we know they are who they say they are?'

'Who do they say they are?'

'I mean, we can't be sure that they are not imposters.'

'Yeesh. I see what you mean. If this guy you call TMB can hack into the government servers that hold the DNA info... wowzer. You've got a real problem Bettony.' Sneggs frowned. 'Osian Jelks was one of the people who you rescued though, wasn't he?'

'According to Mrs Ponch, the man they've got out at Enysgrume Nowuth continues to insist that he's the real Jelks. That there was some complicated sort of double-bluff going on.'

'That sounds a bit far-fetched. And after all they'll have done the DNA confirmation... ah.'

'Exactly. The chances are that you're right Bollie. But we need to be absolutely sure. That's why we need your help.' Bettony outlined her and Hugo's plan to build up a trusted group of people.

'You're the only person I know who could run a deep DNA analysis.'

'Ah. Right. Gotcha. Yep I could do that all right.' It clearly did not occur to Bollie to wonder why Bettony was so sure that he was not himself an imposter. 'I'd need to get to the Blythe machine at Sputteridge though and that could be tricky. I wanted to use it last month to run a congenital hypothyroidism test on Kat. Honestly Bettony, it was crazy trying to get permission. In the end I gave up.'

'Who's Kat?'

'My dog.'

'You've got a dog called Kat?'

'Well she's a little puppy. Katrine. Such a beautiful little thing.' Sneggs's eyes misted over. 'I suppose I was being a bit over-protective but you can't be too careful can you? They rely on you so much.'

'Yeah... anyway. You don't think you could get at the - what? - the Blythe machine?'

'No. Not without most of Sputteridge knowing what I was up to.'

Sneggs took another deep draught of his rapidly-emptying beer glass and considered the matter.

'Tell you what though. There's going to be a decent enough real-time PCR system at Falmouth General. Strikken will be able to get me access to it. I could adapt its expression profiling facility for what I need. It's not really what it's designed for but with a few adjustments we should be ok.'

Strikken... another pang of guilt. Bettony had not even spoken to Strikken about Hugo Crean's shocking information. She nodded, and said,

'That's what we'll do then. I'll talk to Strik and see what he can fix up, then I'll let you know. It shouldn't be difficult getting hold of DNA samples for Brink, and also for Zagretia Ponch. Once we've got them sorted things should get easier. Thanks Bollie.'

'I'm glad I can help.' Sneggs shook his head. 'You know, I really thought all that Regency stuff had gone away.'

'Good grief.' Strikken's face visibly paled on Bettony's screen. 'And you're sure that this Crean fellow is telling the truth?'

'Yes.'

'I'm not sure if I can be any help though...'

'Strikken! We're relying on you. The whole future of Britannia – no, the whole future of Abbuth itself - could be at stake.'

Strikken's voice was shaking. 'It terrifies me Bettony. You don't understand.'

'It's all right my darling man. I know what a peaceful fellow you are. It's one of the reasons why I feel so strongly about you. But there is no other way.'

There was a long silence. Eventually, Strikken said,

'Well, the answer to your question is yes. I can get Bollie access to our PCR sequencer. I don't know what he's going to do with it exactly but we can usually get results in a few seconds. It would be best if he could get over when I'm on a night emergency shift. Nights are generally quiet.'

** ** **

'Has anybody seen my mug? The one with a picture of Morgan holding his traybake. Stop sniggering Tweek it doesn't become you.'

** ** **

It had been dark for several hours when Bettony got the eight o'clock train to Falmouth. Bollie joined her at Bristol. They got a taxi from Falmouth station to the hospital, where a rather nervous Strikken met them at the entrance and led them down quiet corridors to the room with the PCR machine. Sneggs sat at its control desk for several minutes, tapping and sliding shapes across the screen in front of him. Apart from the sound of Sneggs' movements there was silence. Bettony could feel her pulse racing; the results of this analysis would affect all of their immediate futures.

'Have you got the mug?' Bollie asked, leaning back in his chair. Bettony handed it to him. When she had taken it from the kitchen she had wrapped it in tinfoil, as Bollie had instructed. Now, he carefully knelt on the floor and then smashed the mug on the ground. Bettony gasped in horror. Bollie unpeeled some of the tinfoil, drew tweezers from his pocket and extracted a piece of broken crockery.

'How do you know there's not someone else's DNA on there?' Strikken asked.

94

'I did what Bollie asked,' Bettony replied. 'Waited until it was Brink's turn to wash up and make the coffee. When she left her office I went in, wrapped her mug in foil and stuffed it in my bag.'

'Nobody noticed?'

'Tweek had gone out. Garri doesn't notice much.'

Bollie had taken the fragment of crockery over to a plain metal box that sat on a table behind the desk. He lifted a panel on its front.

'In here?' He asked.

Strikken nodded.

Sneggs carefully placed the fragment in the machine and closed the panel. A small red light winked into life near the top. 'Shouldn't take long.'

They were all quiet, watching the machine. No-one spoke. After what felt like an age, the red light changed colour to green. Sneggs had returned to the control desk; now, he pushed and tapped at the screen and keyboard in front of him.

'Well obviously we don't know whose DNA this is,' he said. 'But whoever it belongs to did not come from Abbuth.'

CHAPTER NINE

There are times when the facts run completely opposite to your instincts. Every one of my instincts told me that the Brink Stellish who I worked for in Swindon was completely and inarguably an Abbuthian. That this part of the process was almost a formality.

As far as I'm concerned, when the facts contradict my instincts then they're wrong.

I realise that this approach has led to some pretty appalling things happening on Earth. It's a dreadful way to make decisions. But I was sure that something somewhere had gone wrong with our plan.

'Try another piece' I said.

'Why?' Strikken asked. 'You said yourself that Brink had washed the mugs and then been the only person to touch her own mug.'

'Please.' I turned to Bollie. 'Try another piece.'

Bollie shrugged his shoulders. 'It's no big deal,' he said. 'We can try as many as you like.'

He repeated the procedure, pulling another piece of broken crockery from the pile on the floor and carefully placing it in the PCR machine. We watched it, until the light turned green. Bollie fiddled at the controls, then said,

'Clear.'

'You mean -'

'Abbuthian.'

'How is that even possible?' Asked Strik.

'Can you try a few more bits please Bollie?'

'Of course.'

'Brink's got a few of these mugs,' I replied to Strik. 'They all look very similar; photos of Morgan, or her and Morgan together. I'm guessing that for her previous drink she had used a different mug, which she then washed, put in the cupboard, and pulled this one out. Maybe she wanted to look at a different picture...'

'This one's clear,' Bollie called. 'Whoever held Brink's mug on this bit was Abbuthian.' He used his tweezers to pick it out and replace it with a different piece. 'Next one's going in.'

'... So Brink pulls a different mug from the cupboard and uses that. But sometime before she did that, somebody else had used it, washed it and put it back.'

'Maybe it was you?' Strik suggested.

'It's possible but unlikely. I'm pretty sure I would have remembered touching that mug. I was being very careful.'

'You realise what you're saying,' Strik said.

'Yes. One of us in that office is not who they are pretending to be.'

'This one's got two DNA signatures,' Bollie said. 'One is Abbuthian, one isn't. The one that isn't has the same signature as before. Let's do an analysis on you Bettony, just to make sure.'

On Bollie's instruction, I pulled a hair from my head and put it in the sequencer. Bollie made a few adjustments on the control panel. We waited until the light turned from red to green.

'Well that's interesting.'

'What's that Bollie?'

'Your DNA signature is different again. So I can see two things here Bettony. One is, we can be sure that it wasn't your DNA on Brink's mug. The other is that at this detailed level of analysis, your DNA becomes sufficiently distinct for me to be able to see clear differences both to Abbuthian DNA and to the unknown DNA on the mug.' Bollie peered at his screen. 'We're looking at three lots of DNA from three different worlds. I'm guessing this reflects historic differences in DNA caused by viral infections. This is fascinating. Have a look Strikken.'

Strik had been watching Bollie's screen from a distance. Now he wandered over and peered closely as Bollie began to point to different bits of the image. He was getting very interested and I felt they were both getting very sidetracked. Words like 'Fascinating' and 'Research' began to bubble out of them. I also began to feel a bit like a specimen.

'Can we get back to why we're here?' I said. I thought I had successfully hidden any irritation from my voice. 'Can we say that Brink is Abbuthian?'

Bollie looked up. 'What we can say is that someone who touched Brink's mug is Abbuthian, and someone else is not.'

Strikken also managed to drag himself away from the screen. 'It's a pity you couldn't have got hold of everyone else's mugs Bettony.'

I reached into my bag.

'Who says I didn't?'

Strikken laughed quietly.

'I just waited until everyone had gone home.'

'I should have guessed,' he said. I walked over to the desk and handed two more tinfoil parcels to Bollie Sneggs. One was tiny. 'Garri always leaves his on his desk so it's a bit grotty. Sorry about that Bollie. And Tweek Golgood doesn't have a mug of his own. Being Tweek he always washes whatever mug he's used straight after he's used it and then puts it away. And also being Tweek, he wears a pair of washing up gloves. So I used a bit of Sellotape to try and lift his prints from his keyboard. Will that work?'

'It should do.' Bollie picked at the tiny piece of tinfoil, and pursed his lips. 'You folded the tape onto itself Bettony?'

'I had to.'

Bollie spent several increasingly frustrated minutes trying to pick the Sellotape apart whilst not touching it any more than he had to. Eventually he put it to one side on the desk.

'Let's do the easy one first,' he said. He knelt down and gently smashed Garri's coffee mug, as he had with Brink's. My stomach turned. I knew Garri fairly well by now. Brink would be puzzled at the loss of her mug. In time, she would think she'd left it somewhere and lost it. She had about half a dozen or more mugs, all basically the same except with different photos of Morgan on them. She would simply use the rest and accept the loss, half-expecting it to turn up again. But this was Garri's favourite mug; one of only two he used. Garri had a different mindset. He would not accept its loss. He would search everywhere. It would affect his mood for a long time. There would be accusing glances.

There would be repercussions.

'Sorry people,' Bollie said once the light had turned to green. 'The same non-Abbuthian who left DNA on Brink's mug has left it on this one. There's also Abbuthian DNA here which is different to that on Brink's mug.'

The DNA checking procedure took around forty seconds. I know this because over the next half an hour, Bollie tested every bit of crockery he could. In every case, whenever a piece contained DNA the results were the same. Brink's mug had either Erce DNA or one of the Abbuthian DNA types. Garri's mug had either the same Erce DNA or the other Abbuthian DNA. A few bits had my DNA too, which just goes to show.

Bollie then returned to picking at the Sellotape, without success. While we watched, I told Strikken about the likely results of smashing Garri's mug. But instead of sympathising he said, accusingly I felt,

'You should have told me. We've got a 3D printer and scanner here. I could've scanned it and printed off a copy. He'd never have known the difference.'

I can't say that I received this news well. I politely pointed out that it would have been convenient if Strikken had given me this useful bloody information before the smashing of the mugs, rather than afterwards. A stony silence fell, broken eventually by Bollie confirming what we already knew. Brink's mug had either Erce DNA or one of the Abbuthian DNA types. Garri's mug had either the same Erce DNA as Brink's, or the other Abbuthian DNA. And he couldn't unravel the Sellotape.

'It's obvious then isn't it?' I said. 'Garri and Brink are Abbuthian. Tweek Golgood is the imposter.'

'... Not really,' Bollie mused, looking up from the Sellotape.

'Surely it's common sense?'

Strikken smiled, rather smugly I thought. 'But what we think is common sense is so often wrong,' he said. 'It could be any one of them Bettony.'

'I can prove that you're both wrong.' I was getting more irritated and it was definitely showing.

'Bettony, I know you want Tweek Golgood to be the imposter, but here on Abbuth we like to follow the facts -'

'It's not a question of what I want! Don't be so self-satisfied Strikken! I was following the facts!'

'Losing your temper won't help either. I know you're under a lot of pressure but - where are you going Bettony?'

I ignored Strikken, and said, 'Bollie I should just be in time to get the last train back. Are you coming?'

Bollie looked uncomfortable.

'I'm going to spend a bit longer seeing if I can get something from this.' He waved the piece of sellotape around with his tweezers. 'I can doss down on Kendra's floor.'

'Bye then.'

I closed the door fairly firmly, and as the echoes died away I headed up to reception. I expected to have to wait a while for a taxi; who knows how things might have turned out if I had. Maybe Strikken would have caught up with me. Maybe we would have talked things out. Maybe... oh well. Maybe did not happen. A couple of worried-looking people were lifting a small child out of a taxi, one of them then carrying it as they hurried up the steps. I opened the door for them, then stepped out and grabbed the taxi before it could leave.

CHAPTER TEN

The Three Mug Problem

The train was very quiet. It was close to midnight; it would be two in the morning or later before I got to bed. The lights in the carriage were dimmed. I switched on the small lamp that was on the table in front of me, and considered The Three Mug problem. I felt instinctively that what Bollie had discovered would give us the proof that Tweek Golgood was from Erce.

Three people (I wrote on my smartpad): *Brink, Garri and Tweek. B, G and T. Three DNA types: A1 DNA, A2 DNA and E DNA. A1 and A2 are Abbuthian, E is Erce.*

What do we know?

B's mug has A1 DNA and E DNA so B must be either A1 or E

G's mug has A2 DNA and E DNA so G must be either A2 or E

T does not have his own mug. He could possibly be A1, A2 or E.

I stared at this. It was obvious: A1 was one of the types of Abbuthian DNA: it had to belong to Brink. Equally, A2 was the other Abbuthian DNA. It was on Garri's mug and therefore it had to belong to Garri. That meant that E - the Erce DNA - must be Tweek's.

Tweek Golgood must be TMB.

Except that he was perhaps too tall and his eyes were the wrong colour...

He could be someone else though. Another Anglish infiltrator. Hugo had told me that there were probably several of them, spies from Erce. Neither Garri nor Brink could possibly be TMB, for goodness sake.

OK, I thought. Run through the alternatives, with the possibility that any one of the three of them could be another agent from Erce.

Unlikely Alternative 1: What if the Erce DNA belonged to Brink? That meant:

Brink had handled her own mug and also Garri's

Tweek had only handled Brink's mug

Garri had only handled his own.

I smiled at the doodle I had used; so similar to the complex Enceldic symbols the Britannians used when writing freehand. That letter to Professor Flange had remained unanswered for a while and had eventually received only a lukewarm, typed response. I regretted not spending more time making the corrections that Kagh had suggested. Or indeed checking it over with her afterwards.

Concentrate Gullivant!

It was a bit like that puzzle about the man taking a fox, a chicken and some corn across a river, I mused. How did it go...? The boat was only big enough for the man plus one other thing. But surely there were all sorts of answers? The man could take the fox over, then come back for the corn; or he could take the chicken over, and come back for the fox... or the corn first... Oh hang on, no...

Concentrate! Empty your mind of aquatically-based riddles!

Unlikely Alternative 2. What if the Erce DNA belonged to Garri? That meant:

Brink had only handled her own mug

Tweek had only handled Garri's mug

Garri had handled his own mug and Brink's.

No. Just... No. There was no way that Garri could be a Sentinnat agent.

And, Most Likely Alternative 3. The Erce DNA belonged to Tweek...

Brink had only handled her own mug

Tweek had handled Garri's mug and also Brink's

Garri had only handled his own.

This was clearly the answer. But how could I prove it to Strikken and Bollie? I stared at what I had written on my smartpad, willing the answer to spring out at me.

It didn't.

I stared some more. My head began to throb.

My eyelids began to feel very heavy. It had been a long and very draining day. The carriage was very peaceful. Despite its speed, the train was rocking in a very gentle sort of way...

I sat up with a start, not realising that I had fallen asleep but realising that I had the answer to the puzzle. It was so obvious!

I checked what I had written.

There was absolutely no doubt.

It rained, the following morning, but not until I was halfway to Television House and it was too late to go back for an umbrella. Also I had missed Maniche, who would have had an umbrella because he was always prepared for stuff like that. Maybe it was something to do with being an accountant, I told myself uncharitably. I managed to stumble in to the office on time, bleary-eyed and foggy-brained from lack of sleep, and also damp. I was not in my most cheerful mood.

This was Welter Hallett's first day at Television House, but the only person in the main office was Garri.

'Hi Garri.'

'Have you seen my mug?'

Here we go... Probably inspired by my frame of mind, I decided to short-cut the weeks of Garri-centred misery.

'I broke it.'

He stared at me. All expression dropped away from his face, except that his lips tightened

'You broke it.'

'I'm sorry Garri. I knocked it off your desk.'

He continued to stare at me.

'I'm sorry all right? Accidents happen. I'll buy you a new one.'

'I doubt very much if you'll get one like that.'

'Why?'

'I got it from Norwich.'

'Huh?'

'I *got* it from *Norwich*.' He spoke very slowly, emphasising the words as if he were talking to a small child. 'When I was on *holiday* there.'

'It was a plain yellow mug Garri. I'll go into town and get you another one at lunchtime.'

Still the idiot-speak. 'Listen carefully Bettony: *I got...it...from...Norwich. I... did... not... get... it... from... Swindon.*'

It had not been the best couple of days. Strikken was being a pain, I was tired and wet, and anyway it had been Bollie who had broken the mug. And if Strikken had only told me about the 3D printer... And now this moron - well, this moron with a brain the size of a planet - was treating me like an imbecile.

My anger, which I have previously admitted does flare up occasionally when I feel threatened or unjustly accused, chose this moment to burst into flame.

'Oh I'm so *so-rry*. I didn't know you had bought it from Norwich. If I'd known that I would have *framed* the *fuck-king bits* and *stuck - them - on - the - fuck-king WALL!*'

Garri was still staring at me, but now his mouth was hanging open and his expression had changed to one of shock.

A voice behind me said,

'Bettony, can I have a word with you in private please?'

Shit.

I followed Brink into her office.

'Close the door.'

I closed the door.

'If I ever hear you talk to someone like that again your employment here will be immediately terminated.'

'Yes. Sorry.'

'Garri is not the easiest of characters but he is an invaluable asset to this organisation. You may find him difficult at times but he deserves respect.'

'And what about me?'

'I beg your pardon?'

'Don't I deserve respect from him?'

'Did he swear at you?'

'No, but -'

'Did he raise his voice?'

'No but -'

'This conversation is finished.' Brink's expressionless eyes bore into me, and I suddenly thought, *this woman is as hard as nails.*

'You must know that he can cause just as much offence -'

'Close the door on your way out.'

I returned to my desk. I was shaking with a mixture of anger and resentment. In front of me, Garri's back was very wide.

At that moment Tweek and Welter walked in. Despite the fact that Welter had clearly not been his choice, Tweek was looking very happy with life, as indeed was Welter. I looked at the two of them and bad-temperedly thought how much alike they were. Welter's going to be a smaller, slightly older clone of Tweek, I thought. All jumping about and enthusiasm and doing things. He'll probably be winding me up as well.

I resented their cheerfulness.

'Ah here we are,' Tweek chirruped. 'You've already met our tame alien.'

I stared daggers at him.

'I'm sorry Bettony,' he mumbled, embarrassed. 'That was meant to be a light-hearted quip but I can see it was in poor taste. Please forgive me.'

Welter was looking at me uncertainly. His *I want to be everyone's friend* look that new starters often adopt was fighting a losing battle against one which said *I want to be somewhere else.*

'You're forgiven Tweek,' I said loudly. 'Unlike some people I know how to *acc-ept an ap-o-lo-gy.*'

They both stared. Garri's back seemed to me to shift uncomfortably. I stood up.

'Hello Welter and welcome. I hope you settle in as well as I did at first. I'm going home now because I have an absolutely stinking headache. Don't forget to let Welter know which mugs he can and can't use, Tweek.'

The two of them stared at me.

'I hope you feel better very soon,' Welter said.

I stamped my way through the rain, back to Perric House. When I got to my apartment I was soaking wet and shaking with cold. I ran a bath, took a couple of painkillers and eased myself into the hot water.

It was true, I did have a bad headache. Probably brought on not only by lack of sleep but also by impotent rage. I half-dozed in the bath, which is probably not the safest thing to do, but when I got out about an hour later I was not only very wrinkly but a lot calmer, and much warmer, and the headache had almost gone. I dressed and made myself a sandwich, ate it, and decided to call Strikken. He should be awake now, I thought, after his night shift.

He wasn't. At least, he wasn't answering my call.

Neither was Bollie.

'Damn them!' I said aloud. 'Damn them all!'

I suddenly felt very tired. I went and flopped onto the bed and fell immediately into a deep sleep.

I woke to the ringing of my doorbell. I must have slept a long time. It was late afternoon, still light, but only just. I opened the door and was surprised to find Mrs Ponch standing in front of me.

'Can I come in?' She asked.

In reply, I pulled the door further open and stood to one side. 'Please.'

I was still grumpy. I was groggy from sleeping at the wrong time of day. I did not really want to see anyone, least of all somebody who I vaguely felt I had let down with my actions today, but I had a huge respect for Mrs Ponch and could never refuse to see her. She sat down in one of my easy chairs and motioned for me to do the same. Such was her authority, I felt neither intimidated nor offended that she had taken control of my own sitting room.

I sat.

'How are you feeling now?' There was genuine concern in her voice.

'I'm ok thanks.'

She looked at me silently for a few moments, then said, 'Not a great day for you.'

I laughed humourlessly. 'You could say that.'

Mrs Ponch said, 'It can't be easy.'

'What can't?'

'Well... You've still not been on Abbuth for long, and here we are throwing you in at the deep end. Pulling you away from the life you were starting to build down in Falmouth and dropping you into the very heart of our government.'

'Have you come to tell me to go back to Falmouth?'

'No!' Mrs Ponch sat up. 'Not at all. I have come to tell you why I wanted you installed into Brink's team.

CHAPTER ELEVEN

Apologies all round...

I made tea for us both, then returned to my chair.

'If it's any help Bettony, I think you are doing an excellent job.'

'Thank you. I take it that you're aware of what happened today.'

Mrs Ponch nodded, but didn't speak. We both drank our tea. Eventually, she said,

'I have a very high regard for you, Bettony. I fear that I have not behaved too well towards you: What you did last year, you did without being asked, and with the utmost bravery. Your actions made a huge contribution to the safety not only of our country but probably of our entire planet. In return I have not been very honest with you and I have put you in danger.'

She shifted uncomfortably, but still met my eyes.

'I have had to make some very difficult decisions. I'm still not sure I've made the right ones. In the process, I have abused your trust.' Mrs Ponch reflected on what she had just said, then repeated, quietly, 'I have put you in danger. Although it seems to me Bettony that you were already in danger. The violence that seems to be tracking you had already begun before you joined us at Television House.

'But I owe you an apology. In particular, it's time for me to explain why I pressured Brink Stellish into appointing you to her staff.' Mrs Ponch took a deep breath. 'When I already suspected her of not being who she claimed.'

'You knew already?'

She raised her eyebrows at that. 'Let's just say, I strongly suspected. Whoever that woman is, she's very clever and she's a marvellous actress. As you would say, a different bucket of fish to Mr Slepwood. But I've known Brink Stellish for many years. People change, I realise that. But.' She shook her head. 'I felt that something wasn't quite right when we first made our entrance in her garden, last year. But I wasn't sure. She did everything that I could have expected Brink Stellish to do but... something wasn't quite right. I needed someone with perception to get close to her. It was I who suggested - actually, more than suggested - that she

employ you.   I couched my proposal in such a way that the
genuine Brink Stellish would have agreed. So the woman playing
the role of Brink had to.

'I didn't tell you of my suspicions because I could easily have
been wrong. The awful thing about what has happened is that it
has made us suspicious of those closest to us. So I thought it was
important that you were free to form your own conclusions. In
any case, you were more likely to play the part of an innocent,
unsuspecting person if that's what you actually were. So I
apologise from the bottom of my heart.'

'Apology accepted Mrs Ponch.'

She smiled. 'Thank you. And now, tell me what makes you
think we're not dealing with the real Brink Stellish.'

I realised that we had still not done a DNA test on Mrs Ponch
but - just as I had felt able to trust her and Bob when I first met
them in Sputteridge - I felt instinctively that this woman sitting
opposite me was the real deal.   I thought too about what
Slepwood had said to me about the impossibility of replacing her.
So I told her about Hugo Crean, and his sad revelation about
Sentinnat agents still being active on Abbuth. I told her about
taking the mugs yesterday, and about Bollie testing them. About
he and Strikken being convinced that there was no solution to the
Three Mug Problem. And what I had worked out, coming back
on the train late the previous night. When I reached the part
about Hugo, Mrs Ponch had shuddered. But when I explained
how I had solved the Three Mug Problem she thought for a
moment, then actually laughed.

'Sometimes, the more intelligent we are, the more we miss the
obvious,' she said. Then she looked startled. 'My goodness, that
sounds terrible.'

I also laughed. The tension was broken now. 'That's ok Mrs
Ponch. After what I've just told you that's pretty obviously the
conclusion.'

'So what are you going to do?'

'Get back to Television House. Continue my hunt for TMB.
Find out what I can.'

'I promise you Bettony, we shall win this battle. It's very
important though that you have confidence in me, so I'm going
to get in touch with Dr Sneggs and have him confirm my DNA.
In fact, let's do that now.'

This time, I managed to get hold of Bollie. He put us on hold while he tried Strikken, who was apparently also available, and Mrs Ponch agreed with them that she would get the eight pm train to Falmouth that evening.

She rose.

'Once I have gained the trust of you all, I would like to meet Mr Crean. I would also be grateful if you would allow me to lead this response to the latest threat from Erce.'

'Mrs Ponch, I would be delighted. I'm sure we all will be.'

When I got to the office the next day Brink was in the main office talking to Garri What I was beginning to think of as the Tigger Twins, Welter and Tweek, were poring over Tweek's smartpad. There was a general moment of embarrassment when I walked in, but I had already decided what to do.

'I was well out of order yesterday,' I said. 'No excuses. Garri, I'm sorry. I've been in touch with a shop in Norwich and a new yellow mug will be delivered tomorrow. Welter, it's good to know you'll be working with us.'

Brink looked up with an expression of understanding on her face. Tweek and Welter both smiled and Garri grunted, which was probably all I was going to get. As I sat down, Brink came over and whispered,

'Well done.'

I looked past the smile on her lips and into her cold eyes. I too smiled, and switched my smartpad on.

Game on, I thought.

★★ ★★ ★★

Timm Milden-Brewer was shaking with rage. His carefully laid-out plan was a brilliant one, but it would have to be amended. True, he had begun to cause mayhem, and suffering, and loss around the freak, but he really could not stand those occasions when he had to be nice to her.

Nice! To the freak!

He really regretted his Oxford mistake now. It hadn't seemed so funny after a while. He should have gone back and killed that spineless nerd and sod the consequences.

Ah well, time to move on to Phase Two. It was a shame, but the greater pain was still to be savoured.

Her pain. And Timm would be the one savouring it to its fullest.

CHAPTER TWELVE

The return of Wether Mapps

Late afternoon a personal message pinged into the corner of Bettony's smartpad. At work, as at home, the pad was docked into a much larger screen; normally, Bettony would wait until her pad was disconnected before reading private messages, but she had stayed on after hours to catch up on work missed the previous day. Everyone else had gone home.

She opened the message and read, '*Am unexpectedly in Swindon. Want to catch up after work? Kagh.*'

'*Sounds good,*' she wrote. '*Want to come over?*'

'*Not actually in Swindon per se. Offsite at Longcot and staying at the Two White Horses. No Transport! Meeting finishes in 15 minutes then we hit the bar. Can you get over here?*'

Bettony chuckled to herself. Then remembered TMB's business card. '*I'll get a bus. By the time your meeting's finished I should be there. I've got something I want you to have a look at.*'

'*What's that?*'

'*It can wait until your meeting's over. Something somebody gave me.*'

Bettony sent her message. She was about to log off when a thought struck her. She quickly sent another message and waited for a response. After two minutes she gave up, and shut her smartpad down.

'He's probably on his way,' she thought.

She had more or less caught up with her work. Everything else could wait until tomorrow. The thought of catching up with Kagh over a beer was a very tempting one. Bettony hurried out of the office and headed for the bus station in the town centre.

The days were slowly beginning to lengthen, but it was pitch black when Bettony got off the bus. The service she had caught ran along the main road between Swindon and Oxford, leaving her a walk of about a mile down a straight, narrow lane to get to Longcot. It was very dark. The wind was getting up and Bettony felt spots of rain driven against her face.

'Fifteen minutes and I'll be in a cosy pub and buying a decent pint of beer,' she thought.

The distance was not in itself a problem. She was wearing a warm coat, and shoes that she had bought in Britannia which were generically and inaccurately called Joggers; these had thick soles and heels and looked vaguely like a smart training shoe. They were comfortable and easy to walk in and were popular among men and women. But the complete darkness meant that she occasionally struggled to stay on the lane. She had stumbled for the third time into long grass that flanked the metalled road and cursed, just as headlights from behind her lit her way. She regained her balance and stood to the side, hoping a kind-hearted driver would stop and offer a lift.

The little electric car did stop. The passenger window rolled down.

'Hi, are you going into - oh hello Welter. Are you all right?'

Tigger Two was sitting in the driver's seat. His face, reflected in the dashboard's pale light, looked ashen. He had one hand on the steering wheel and the other held his stomach. With a weak attempt at a smile, he said,

'Not really. I will be though. Tweek sent me. He said you would be here.'

'What on earth - Welter is that wet on your hand? Is it -'

'It looks worse than it is. You must get in Bettony. Your life is in serious danger.'

'How did you know I was here?'

'Bettony, you must get in the car! I don't understand what this is all about. Tweek will be able to tell you. Aaah...' Welter clutched at his stomach again. 'Please. It's important.'

Bettony climbed in. The car was so small that Welter was able to turn it around on the narrow lane without much difficulty. He still drove with one hand, leaning forward and with the other pressed against his stomach.

'Tweek said I had to get you to safety. He said he would preset a Transition Vehicle for you.'

'What! Listen Welter, I appreciate all this but if you'd only take me down the lane into Longcot one of my closest friends is there. I'm sure I'll be safe.'

But by now Welter was steering them onto the main road, heading away from Swindon.

'Just doing... what Tweek told me.'

'Welter look out! Good heavens you're in no state to drive. Let me. Let me drive Welter.'

'Not far now. Then I'll get to hospital... Goodness Bettony, if I'd known what this job involved I might not have applied...' Hallett tried a weak smile. It was clearly an effort for him to speak. 'Walking to Pellic House with Tweek. We had eaten in a restaurant. Car stopped and people got out. Tweek thinks they thought I was you... never been very tall.' Another weak smile. 'Somebody from your work helped us to fight them off... a big man.'

'Maniche?'

'Don't know. He took Tweek to Hospital. Sent me to look for you. Didn't realise they had...' He looked down at his stomach. 'Oh dear. It'll be ok though. Things always turn out ok, that's what my godfather always said.'

'Welter, how did Tweek know where I was?'

Hallett was concentrating hard, following directions on his car navigation screen. He turned off the main road and onto a narrow, rutted lane, grimacing with pain as the car bounced along. Trees on each side crowded down towards them, scratching from time to time against the car.

'He knows everything it seems to me. He probably knows what the weather's going to be like next Thursday...'

Hallett tried another weak smile. In front, the lane - now no more than a narrow track - came to an end in a small clearing surrounded by more trees. The car's headlights lit up an old wooden shed, sitting in the clearing. Hallett dragged himself out of the car and stumbled over to the shed. He pulled at the big double doors and wincing with pain, started trying to drag them open. Bettony pulled him gently to one side and took over. As the doors swung wide the car's headlamps shone into the shed and she stared at a familiar shape, directly in front of them.

'It's a Two! What on earth is it doing here?'

Hallett shook his head. 'That's one for Tweek I'm afraid. What do you mean, it's a two?'

'It doesn't matter Welter. But you said that Tweek has preset it. How has Tweek preset it if Maniche took him straight to hospital?'

'I don't know Bettony. He was fiddling with his smartpad so I suppose he did it remotely. Please. You get to safety and I'll get to hospital.'

'Welter I don't think you'll be able to. Let me drive you there, then I'll come back.'

'No time! Tweek said tell you Bob will be waiting. Don't ask me what that means either or who Bob is.'

Bob!

'Tweek says you know how to get into one of these. Good luck Bettony.'

'Thanks Welter. You too.'

Bettony pulled the doors shut behind her, plunging the shed into darkness. She felt her way to the Two and started fumbling for the emergency access mechanism. Her hands were shaking and at first she struggled to locate the two retaining nuts which would release the door. Then she found them and turned them. The door sprang open, lights flickered on from within the Two, and she stepped inside. The door slammed shut behind her and she looked at the controls and realised that she had no idea how to use them.

She had no idea what to press, or to switch, even just to activate whatever Tweek had preset...

It might be safest, she thought, if I just sit here for a while and then go back outside. I'll get hold of Hugo. And Strikken of course, and Kagh and everyone.

She sat quietly in the dim glow of the controls.

'Benedict! How wonderful to see you. Would you like a short video tour of my little abode before we arrange our get-together?'

'I would love to do both of those things old friend but first I need your advice, indeed if not your help.'

'Tell me.' Crean was suddenly serious. There was no mistaking the worry on his friend's face.

'I received a message from Bettony about an hour ago. I didn't pick it up straight away, I was in a lecture until six. By the time I got home it had been sitting on my tab for over an hour.'

'That in itself is not a hanging offence old bean.'

'Listen Hugo. She said, she guessed I might be coming over to see Kagh at the Two White Horses. She was checking to see if I wanted her to meet me at the station and we could share a taxi out to Longcot but that she'd probably get the bus and see me there.

'The thing is Hugo, Kagh's working on a project down in Sputteridge.'

'You've tried calling her back I guess? Bettony I mean.'

'No reply. Actually it's worse than that. We're on what they call a Friendslink group. It means I can see where she is. Or more accurately at the moment, where she isn't. She isn't anywhere.'

'Or at least her smartpad isn't.'

'You know what it's like Hugo. You fold them up and clip them to your jacket or whatever. You take them everywhere.'

'Bear with me on this Ben, I'm still learning the ropes here. Couldn't her smartpad have just broken or run out of batteries or something?'

'Each of those things triggers an automessage. I may be getting paranoid Hugo but the way things have been recently...'

Benedict left the sentence unfinished.

'Ok.' Crean checked his watch. 'And you think she's gone off-planet.'

Benedict nodded.

'You're not paranoid Ben. I'm getting the next train. I'll reserve a hire car for Swindon station.' Crean drummed his fingers on his knee, thinking hard. 'Bollie called me last night, Zagretia Ponch passed his whizzy DNA test. Can you get hold of her and also Bollie and Strikken and tell them what you've told me? Let's stay in touch. For what it's worth I'm not letting go of my smartpad so if it disappears you know that I've gone with it. Just go over everything you've told me again and give me some idea of how far Longcot is from Swindon.'

It was the slightest of bumps, but Bettony had transitioned enough by now to guess that she was no longer on Abbuth. She was still struggling to work out what was happening but she was excited to see Bob again. She pushed the door open.

It was very dark outside, and very still. It was also warmer than the world she had left, the air was more humid and carried an acrid smell. On every side, close-packed trees loomed out of the darkness. Somewhere high above a strong wind was playing against the tops of the trees, but it was muffled and distant. Down here all was very quiet. The trees were so thick that at ground level they protected against any wind and deadened all sound.

She called Bob's name a couple of times, her voice dying into the blackness. There was no answer.

She could make out that she was still in a wood, but the trees were thicker than on Abbuth. These were some sort of conifer, packed close and mixing a sickly smell of resin into the warm, bitter air.

Her every instinct told Bettony that this was all wrong.

She pulled the door closed and looked vaguely at the Two's control panel. She had no idea how to operate this machine. She realised that unless it moved itself again in the next few minutes she would have to venture outside. By the dim glow from the controls she searched around for anything that might be of use, pocketing odd items.

Hidden away in a corner, she spotted a familiar linen bag.

How on earth did this get here? She thought, grabbing a couple of metal boxes out of the bag and stuffing them into her coat pockets. *This must be the Two we used to rescue people from Erce.*

She quickly checked through the Two for anything else that could be useful and occasionally putting things into her coat pockets. She was filling a bottle with water (was it drinkable? She hoped so, and guessed that she would find out soon enough) when once again, the door lurched wide open of its own accord.

She looked out into the empty, pitch-black night.

It really was very quiet.

Bettony heard a strange, high-pitched voice that chilled her to the bone.

'Betbet, oh Betbet... I'm here...'

It couldn't be. Only one person had called her Betbet and he was dead, beyond any doubt.

'Dear Betbet, won't you come out and play?'

It was not the idea of Wether Mapps' ghost that chilled her. Bettony had long since stopped believing in ghosts. It was the voice.

The voice was the voice of someone who was quite clearly insane.

Bettony pulled the door closed. It immediately clicked wide open. She closed it. It opened. She frantically looked around for anything that she could use as a weapon.

There was nothing.

She needed space to defend herself, to work the kicks and punches that she had spent so many years perfecting. In here, there was no space. In here it would be a trial of strength and she would probably lose that. Bettony stepped outside again, moving away from what dim light projected out from the Two and stepping into the shadows.

As soon as she did so there was a rush of air.

It was filling the vacuum left by the Two, which had suddenly disappeared.

There was a burst of crazy laughter. It was deadened and deflected by the press of trees and Bettony had no idea where it came from. She heard a deceptively gentle 'pop' and something smacked hard into the tree trunk next to her head. More laughter, it sounded as though someone was struggling to control themselves.

Again the weird, high-pitched sing-song voice. 'I can see in the dark Betbet. We can you know. When you're dead you'll be able to as well. The dark is our natural home.'

She dropped to the ground and crawled as quickly and quietly as she could, grateful for the trees that quickly surrounded her. The ground was soft and spongy. After a couple of minutes of this she thought it safe to stand up. As soon as she did so there was another pop and the sound once again of something smacking into the tree next to her. Bettony dropped to the ground again as more maniacal laughter rang out.

'Oh, this is fun,' the voice sang. 'I must say, it makes up for all the burns you gave me. All that scarring on my face. Did you see my scars? You must take a look, Betbet. Don't you move now my dear, I'll come and find you. I told you, I can see in the dark.'

It was ten thirty by the time Crean arrived at the Two White Horses. The village pub had had a quiet evening and barstaff were clearing tables when he arrived. No, they didn't remember anyone of Bettony's description. Yes, it would have been easy to remember any stranger because the only patrons had been half a dozen locals. A stranger would have been easy to recognise. There had been no strangers.

Crean turned his hire car around and drove slowly back to the main road. There were two lanes which led from Longcot to the Oxford road; he covered both of them twice, crawling along at walking pace, looking for anything that might give him a clue to Bettony having been there.

There was nothing. He drove back along the main road towards Swindon, then turned and retraced his route.

There was something vaguely familiar about this area.

Crean had not returned to his transition point since he had arrived in Britannia, but as he trundled back and forth along the road he became convinced that this was where it had happened, where the filth of a spawling, stinking Swindon on Erce had been replaced by his release into Abbuth.

Instead of looking for anything that might show that Bettony had been there, Hugo began to look for something specific. It took him a while, but he eventually found what he was looking for. A narrow lane, little more than a track leading off the main road.

He turned the little car off the main road and rolled a few yards down the lane. This time, a gate had been closed barring any further progress in the car. Hugo stopped in front of it.

Bettony could just about make out the shapes of trees, closely-packed all around her as she stumbled through the wood. Trying to run was useless. She had already fallen heavily twice, scratching herself as she did so.

She stopped, pressing herself against the trunk of a tree. After a couple of seconds, another shot hit the tree, inches from her head. Bettony ducked, instinctively, and heard the crazy laughter again.

Three misses, she thought. Am I just lucky?

It was a part of Bettony's character that any fear she felt did not last long. It generally gave way to a focussed anger; the intensity of the focus, and the strength of the anger, tended to be directly related to the initial level of fear.

This had, at first, been a very frightening experience.

Bettony was getting very angry.

She began to analyse the situation. She realised that the aim was probably not to kill her - or at least, not immediately - but to terrify her. Bettony did not believe in ghosts, but she did believe in lunatics with guns. Anyone repeatedly hitting tree trunks to within inches of her head would have had to be exceptionally unlucky. Anyone wanting to kill her could have done it silently, as she stood outlined in the doorway of the Two. Nobody would advertise their presence as this nutter had.

Another bullet thudded into the bole, even closer to her. She had a rough idea now, where the shots were coming from.

They had to have night vision, she thought. So let's see how they like this.

She unclipped her smartpad. Reaching behind the tree, and hopefully out of sight of her crazy hunter, she half-unfolded it and put her hand over the end. Then she turned its torch to full. The light was so powerful that it glowed bright red through her hand. Still covering the beam, and trying to conceal it with her body as much as she could, Bettony brought it around.

'Is it you, Wether?' She called out. 'I thought you were dead?'

'I am,' the strange sing-song voice responded. It was still muffled but it was enough to give her a better fix. 'I - aargh'

Bettony had pulled the rolled-up pad out and pointed its powerful beam at where she guessed the voice was coming from. She was gambling that the bright light, magnified many times by the effect of night-vision goggles, would have the effect of a brilliant spotlight. It sounded as though she had gambled and won. Her first instinct was to attack while the person was blinded, but her rage was still too focussed to allow her to attempt the suicidal. Instead, she gave the wood around her a brief sweep with her torch, chose the best route away, and flicked it off. Within seconds she was onto some sort of track, wide enough to take wheeled vehicles. She could still hear shouts of pain and rage behind her and risked another brief flicker from the torch, sprinting lightly down the track and then turning back into the wood to her right. Picking her way carefully again, she headed for the densest thicket she could make out. The ground here was rockier and more uneven. Bettony felt her way down into a stony dip and dropped to the ground. With luck, she planned to stay here until daylight removed at least one of the advantages the other person had over her. Then she would set about reversing their roles. The hunter would become the hunted.

She could hear him blundering around - she thought it was a He, even though the voice had been ridiculously high; and an idea about who this might be was rapidly forming. He was a fair way away though, and not getting any closer. She could still hear his voice. No longer song-song, but still high. Still deranged.

'I'll get you you bitch. You *freak.* I'll make you pay. You think you're getting away but - but -' The final few words were shouted in a scream at the top of his voice. '*You've. Got. No. Chance.*'

I rather think I do, Bettony reflected. Oh Timmbo, you have no idea who you've taken on.

Crean used his smartpad to light the way as he walked on, looking for signs of recent activity. They were pretty obvious. The lane was little used and much of it was overgrown with grass. Fresh tyre tracks were easy to spot. Hugo guessed the car was small. He walked the hundred yards or so until he reached a small clearing at the end of the track, and a familiar dilapidated old shed.

It was too much of a coincidence. TMB must have used the spaceship to take Bettony back to Erce. Crean was filled with rage, mainly at himself. He should have worked this out. Should have prevented it.

Worked what out? A nagging doubt said, somewhere at the back of his mind. *It's been months since Bettony arrived on this world. Why now? Why is TMB targeting her now?*

Crean examined the shed closely. It was difficult to see inside, but he thought he could just about make out the shape of the container that had brought him to Abbuth. Some attempt had been made to black out the small window, and despite its tumbledown appearance there were no splits or gaps in the wood that made up the shed. He found a large stone and hammered it first against the lock and then the window. Neither gave way.

'Toughened glass' he murmured to himself. 'Nice work Timmbo.'

Hugo retreated to the cover of the wood, and leaned casually against a tree at the side of the track. He looked as though he did not have a care in the world but he was cursing himself for a fool. Thinking hard. Watching the shed.

Was Timmbo already back on Abbuth? If the spaceship was back, it would seem so. That would mean a very swift visit to Erce for Milden-Brewer. But this machine would deliver TMB and Bettony directly into Sentinnat hands, so it was possible. Again, Crean cursed himself for a fool.

He tried to fit a pattern to the violence that had stalked Bettony. Hugo had no doubt that this also had been TMB's doing; again, it was all too much of a coincidence. What was Timmbo up to? Why give someone who had shown she was a formidable opponent so much warning? It went completely against Sentinnat training for kidnapping.

On the other hand, Hugo mused, it fitted exactly the recommended techniques for spreading terror.

Milden-Brewer had blundered deeper into the wood. Bettony was pretty sure that was who it was, now that she thought about it. Every so often she could hear him scream in frustration, his voice getting fainter until it died away completely.

She stayed where she was.

Time passed.

She didn't want to lose track of him but neither did she want to move from this dip. She would wait, she decided. If she really lost him she would return to the site of the Two. He would go back there eventually. It might not be so easy for her to find, but -

'Hello Betbet.' The voice was whispered into her ear, he must have been lying on the ground above the dip and leaning into it. In one second Bettony's heart seemed to go from seventy to two hundred. She instinctively jammed an elbow up and back, towards the voice. There was a satisfying crunch and a grunt of pain. Bettony guessed she had made contact with Milden-Brewer's nose. She scrambled out of the ditch and thought of throwing herself at the vague shape writhing around on the ground, then remembered just in time Hugo's warning about the Tipper. If TMB had it in his hand she could be throwing herself onto it. She spun around and ran blindly into the wood, colliding with branches and bushes until fear subsided, replaced once again by anger.

How did he find her? How the hell did he find her?

Breathing heavily, Bettony dropped into a low crouch. If he wanted to, of course, he could kill her now. He had the night vision and he had a gun and he almost had certainly a very sharp knife.

She could hear him, a little way off, cursing and grunting with pain. It was still difficult to recognise the voice.

It had to be Tweek Golgood. Who else could it be? Maybe he had found a way of disguising his DNA. It wouldn't be easy fooling Bollie Sneggs, but what other explanation could there be? Who else could it be? Not Brink Stellish. This was someone who was lithe and cat-like and these were definitely not qualities enjoyed by the Head of Council. Besides, Bettony was convinced it was a man.

The blundering and cursing had died away.

It had to be Golgood. Not that he was particularly lithe and cat-like either...

Something exploded against the side of Bettony's head. Struggling to stay conscious, she had a vague idea that she had been hit with something heavy. Already crouching low, she lurched to the ground, head spinning, dots of light dancing before her eyes.

'Got you now you bitch.' This time the voice was strangled and unnaturally low.

She was reaching into her pocket, conscious enough to know what her only chance of escape was. Her hand closed around the metal box.

Five... Four...

'Not so clever now are you? You're going to die, Betbet.'

Three... Two...

'But you're going to suffer first.'

One...

Crack.

Pain shot through her, reaching into every nerve in every part of her body.

All was silent.

Hugo had been motionless, merged into the darkness and watching the shed for twenty minutes.

He was beginning to crave a cigarette. He had given them up three years ago, despite the health benefits that the manufacturers in Angland claimed they gave. A family friend had given up and had told him about his feeling of improved fitness, and how his sense of taste and smell had returned. Hugo had tried it and had found the same, but there were still times when he really wanted to light up.

He unclipped his smartpad and, still watching the shed, unfolded it enough to allow him to make a call.

Bettony was also motionless, although she was lying flat on a forest floor. She was still in a wood; that much she could make out. It smelt broadly similar to the one she had just left. Perhaps stronger and sourer. Still pine trees, or something similar, but mixed in with a stench of decay.

After a couple of minutes she risked sitting up. Her head hurt, but not too badly. She reached up and felt an egg-sized lump where she had been hit.

There was still the sound of wind, high above. Bettony was mildly surprised at this. Surprised, too, at the humid warmth of the air.

She waved a hand around. The action did not generate any heat.

As far as she knew, the metal boxes had last been used when she and Bob rescued people from Erce, and when Benedict and she had practised their arson skills on the Hablock Mental Correction Unit. The miniature Transition devices had been pre-set to send people to what they had come to know as the Frozen World. Bettony had expected the same thing to happen now.

This was not the Frozen World.

Still moving gingerly, she stood up. Everything seemed to be ok, no dizziness or anything. She switched her smartpad's torch on and swept the area.

She had not really had the opportunity to take in much detail of the world she had just left, but had seen enough to realise that this one was different. Many of the trees around her were either dead or dying. She shone the torch upwards, and saw treetops that were broken and stripped of bark, like huge rotting needles of sickness.

There was no path here, but neither was there any undergrowth, just dead branches and twigs that crackled underfoot. Bettony picked her way cautiously between the trees, climbing over fallen trunks that littered the ground. She thought half-heartedly about climbing a tree; lights of houses or roads would be easy to spot from up there. Better than just wandering around in circles.

But she had not been wandering around in circles because suddenly she was stepping out of the wood and onto hard ground. Somewhere in the distance she could see a cluster of lights. A village? She had been using the torch sparingly and briefly switched it on now. The ground between her and the lights was covered in lines of small shoots, just poking up out of bare soil. She guessed that the lights were about a mile away.

She stepped out of the protection of the dying wood and into the full force of a strong wind. She picked her way as carefully as she could between the little plants and eventually came to a wide path that led towards the lights.

'This is dreadful Hugo. Absolutely dreadful. I feared the worst and it seems with justification.'

'Can you check again please Ben? Just to make sure she's not here somewhere and you've missed her.'

'Bear with me... No. Her smartpad is definitely not anywhere on Abbuth. Have you told Strikken?'

'Not yet.' A twinge of guilt. 'Perhaps you could do that for me? I don't really know the man. What I need to do as quickly as I can is get back to Erce and get after them before our Sentinnat chums have a chance of sealing her up in Hablock. But I haven't got a clue how to work these spaceships. I need Kaghendra's help.'

'Hmm. Not Kagh, I think. Her piloting can be a bit... haphazard. Anyway it'll take too long for her to get to you from Sputteridge. We need Mrs Ponch. I'm pinging you her contact details now. She knows all about you Hugo... unless you don't feel that you can trust her?'

'Ah! What a mess Ben. But Mrs Ponch is ok. We know that from what Slepwood told Bettony last year.'

Hugo's call was answered within a couple of seconds.

'Mr Crean.'

'Mrs Ponch.'

Brief as it was, her greeting seemed to carry a request for an explanation. Specifically, as to why he was calling. Hugo outlined what he knew, and what he wanted to do, and described as well as he could where he was. Mrs Ponch listened without comment. Crean felt that something more was needed.

'Mrs Ponch, I fully understand why I might struggle to earn your trust. I can only ask that you have faith in the judgement of your friends. Particularly of Bettony herself.'

'Indeed.' Mrs Ponch seemed to consider for a moment. A small tab appeared in the corner of Hugo's smartpad. 'I'm sending you a Friendslink request Mr Crean. If you accept it I will be able to pinpoint your position.'

Hugo did as instructed.

'Good. Thank you. I shall be with you in fifteen minutes. Please keep watch until I arrive. In the meantime, you might want to consider...'

'What has prompted this course of action? And, why now?'

'Indeed.'

CHAPTER THIRTEEN

Bettony Gullivant and the Workers' Paradise

Why did the Two disappear? The thought suddenly struck me as I trudged through the darkness. The Two had vanished but Golgood hadn't. How come? Did he have another TV?

It almost felt as though he had been engaging in a duel with me. Not a very fair one, to be sure.

Why?

I was free of him now. But he was a smart man. He must have had a good look around the Two. He must have found Kevin and Dildow's single-use transition boxes.

I had to assume that all of the remaining boxes would behave like the one I had used. He would follow me.

I hurried through the unfamiliar landscape towards the lights.

The houses were small and separated from each other by little more than pathways. Thick wires ran at rooftop height from one to the next. There were no streetlights but few of the downstairs rooms had curtains. Electric light blazed from bare bulbs and television screens in small shabby rooms. Enough light fell on the paths for me to see my way. A dog wandered around a corner, looked briefly at me, then ambled past, uninterested.

Heart in mouth, I walked up to the front door of the largest house. I could hear music blaring loudly. I banged my fist on the door.

Nothing happened.

I banged my fist again.

'Paulette can you see who that is?' A man's voice shouted in English. A few seconds later the door was pulled open and a woman looked at me. She was small and thin and careworn and was definitely surprised to see me.

'Who are you?' She asked.

'I'm lost,' I said. I was about to say, My car broke down, but in a moment's inspiration changed it to, 'My horse went lame.'

Paulette's look of surprise became more pronounced.

'Who is it?' The man's voice called.

'It's a stranger.'

'A stranger?'

'She says she's lost. She says her horse went lame.'

'Where?'

She looked at me. 'Where did your horse go lame?'

I managed to avoid saying, *On its leg*, and instead said 'Somewhere outside the village.'

'She says, somewhere outside the village.'

A man appeared behind the woman. He was slightly taller than her, but still shorter than me. His hair was wet and he was rubbing at it with a towel. Like her, he was thin and wiry.

'You've lost your horse?'

I nodded.

He grinned. 'You've had that then. Somebody's probably eaten it by now.'

'Brian stop it.'

He was still grinning. He glanced at the woman, then back at me. 'You'd better come in. What's your name?'

'Bettony.'

Not much point in using a false name, I thought. If Golgood was tracking me, it wouldn't be difficult identifying me. On the other hand, if anyone from Abbuth managed to get here I would want them to know where I had been.

'Interesting name.'

'Brian!'

The door opened directly into their living room. They ushered me inside. A big old-fashioned cathode-ray tube television took up a good portion of the room. On its screen I glimpsed wildly over-coloured images, all bright reds and greens, people dancing about.

'I'm just saying, it's an interesting name.' He was half-smiling. 'Please, sit down.'

There was a small wooden table in a corner. Three chairs were pushed under it. I pulled one out and sat down and Brian switched the television off.

'Have you registered with the party secretary?'

'Er... Not yet.'

He grinned. 'Thought not.' He pulled another chair out and also sat down.

Paulette tutted at him, then asked me, 'Would you like some tea?' She looked worried.

'Please.'

She went out of a door at the back of the room. Brian continued to look at me, half grinning, half serious.

'There's been some bigwig nosing around the village recently.' He said. 'He's warned us to look out for strangers. Recalcitrant types have been colluding with undesirable elements to betray the people. Apparently they've been extending their devious activities and we are not safe from their counter-revolutionary clutches, not even out here. There's a very dangerous woman seeking to use her feminine wiles to inveigle us into seditious activities.'

'Oh. Right.'

'I'm just wondering how recalcitrant you look. You're definitely a woman.'

'Brian! Stop it.' Paulette had reappeared at the doorway. 'My husband can be a bit of a pillock at times Miss. Ignore him.'

They had a close relationship, these two, that was obvious. Even though Paulette's role in it seemed to be one of trying to rein her husband in. His comments reminded me of some of the more tightly-controlled societies on Earth; and he was a risk-taker, I could already see that. I wondered how much his independent mind (and his willingness to share his thoughts) had gotten him into trouble.

You could almost touch the affection between them.

'Sorry.' Brian was suddenly serious. 'I suppose what I ought to do is take you along to the village's party secretary and let him sort it all out. But I'm not sure he's the right man for this.'

In my pocket, my hand was reaching for the metal box. I didn't know if it would work a second time, but it would be worth a shot.

'The problem is,' he continued, 'I don't trust our beloved party.'

'Brian!' This time the woman's voice was sharp with fear.

'And I didn't trust Senior Party Official Mapps either.'

Mapps?

'In fact, I thought he might be a bit recalcitrant himself. He didn't have a car or –' his mouth twitched slightly '– a horse or anything and yet he claimed he had come from Swindontown and was going to Oxfordtown. And he dressed funny. Our party officials, they love to dress up in their suits don't they? Cheap shoddy badly-fitting suits. Looking like gangsters in some American film and in a way I suppose that's what they are.'

'Brian! You'll get us both put in prison.'

'He'd got his paperwork all right' Brian continued, undeterred. 'Enough to fool Stubbins anyway. But he wasn't dressed like any party official I've ever seen.' He looked me up and down. 'In fact, he was dressed quite a lot like you...' He paused for a few seconds, frowning.

'So anyway, when he left, I followed him out of the village. And although he started out on the track to Oxfordtown, he left it pretty quickly and he wandered into a wood. Which I thought was a bit odd. I followed him into the wood. And what was odder still, I watched him climb into a metal box in the wood and disappear.'

He was watching me closely now.

'I mean, literally, disappear. Pouff! Gone. All of it. Metal box and him inside it. Gone.'

'One day Brian your stories will get us both into trouble.' This was said quietly, as a statement rather than an expression of surprise. I guessed that it was not the first time that Paulette had heard the story. Paulette's steady admonishments seemed to be a part of the dynamic of their relationship.

'I don't believe in magic,' Brian continued. 'Or ghosts. Or vengeful spirits. I used to teach science before the village decided otherwise and if I believe in anything it is in science. But I also believe in what I see and I saw him disappear. And now, just as he predicted, you're here.'

Paulette put a pot of tea and three cups on the table. She poured the tea black, and put a cup in front of me.

'You said you used to be a teacher,' I said.

'Brian's from here,' Paulette replied. 'From Vellia. I'm from London. We met at university. We wanted to come out here and help these people. Help to educate them. But there was a lot of jealousy after we got here. Why should we both be getting teachers' wages when everyone else was earning so much less and working so hard in the fields? So the villagers had a meeting and decided that one of us had to work in the fields. In fact they said it had to be Brian. The party secretary agreed to it.'

'Stubbins is just a dope,' Brian said. 'He'll agree to anything if enough people shout loud enough. You know who one of the loudest voices was?' For a moment there was real anger in his face. 'My brother. *My own brother!*

'It was very easy getting a permit to come here,' he continued, 'but it's a damn sight harder getting one to leave.'

'Anyway,' Paulette said. 'We've told you about us. Tell us about you.'

'And Senior Party Official Mapps,' Brian added.

'You strike me as intelligent, reasonable people,' I said. 'Educated and rational. So I'm going to tell you the truth. But I can guarantee you're not going to believe it.'

'I've stood and watched a big metal box disappear into thin air,' Brian answered. 'You might be surprised at what I can believe.'

★★ ★★ ★★

Hugo watched the woman approach. She walked past him then stood, looking at the wooden shed.

'You'd better reveal yourself Mr Crean. I suspect you're rather better at this sort of subterfuge than I am.'

'I'm here Mrs Ponch.'

Hugo stepped away from the tree and briefly flashed torchlight onto his own face. Mrs Ponch turned and walked towards him. In the gloom, they could just about see well enough to shake hands.

'Our second refugee from Erce,' she said. She was speaking quietly. Hugo could barely make out what she was saying over the noise of the wind. 'And I understand that you are good friends with the first.'

'With Benedict, yes.'

'What a lovely man.'

'Indeed.'

Mrs Ponch fell silent, standing motionless in front of Hugo. He waited for her to continue.

'A very different background to your own, I believe.'

'I'm sorry?'

'My information is that you are a member of the Sentinnat.'

'Was, Mrs Ponch. I was.'

'Although they are not aware of your resignation.'

'I hope to God not!'

'And you believe that a Sentinnat agent has kidnapped Bettony Gullivant.'

'I do.'

Another silence. The wind's dropping, Hugo thought. He also thought, every second is precious. But it was Mrs Ponch who was dictating this exchange, not he.

Eventually, she said, 'And you would like me to pilot you to Erce.'

'That's correct.'

'It would be an easy way to kidnap me, wouldn't it?'

'Believe me Mrs Ponch, if the plan was to kidnap you, we would be back in Erce by now.'

'Yes. Yes I rather think that's correct.'

Another pause. More seconds leeching away.

'Very well. You say that a transition vehicle is hidden in this wooden hut?'

'It's how I arrived here.'

'You have a lot to tell us, Mr Crean. But first things first.' She walked over to the shed's door and tested it. 'Quite an impressive lock. I assume you don't have a key?'

'No.'

'No. Can you break in?'

'I have a toolkit in my car. If you don't mind keeping watch for a couple of minutes while I fetch it?'

'Off you go Mr Crean.'

Hugo returned carrying a small leather wallet. Inside it, thin pieces of metal wire hung from a narrow metal band. They were twisted into differently-shaped hooks and curves. Hugo selected one and pushed it into the lock. There was a spark, and Hugo recoiled with a curse.

'Ouch. Excuse my language there Mrs Ponch. This is a Sentinnat creation. At least I know what I'm dealing with.' He selected another piece of wire and tried again. After a few seconds there was a click. Hugo removed the lock, pulled one of the big doors open and shone his torch inside.

'So there we are,' Mrs Ponch said softly. 'The missing Two. I shall be interested to learn how it found its way here, Mr Crean.'

'Can we get on please?'

Mrs Ponch started to enter the shed. Hugo stepped in front of her.

'If I may. Just in case anyone is waiting for us.' Controlling his impatience, he shone his torch around the shed and checked behind the Two.

'All clear Mrs Ponch.'

'Shine your torch here please Mr Crean. Thank you... there we are.'

Mrs Ponch turned the two disguised retaining nuts and the Two's door opened. Low level lighting flickered into life on control panels and screens inside the machine. Hugo, accustomed to the dark night, suddenly felt that the shed was flooded with light. He pulled the shed door closed, then watched as Mrs Ponch sat at the spaceship's strange controls and brought them to life. It looked as though she was pulling and pushing strange, constantly-changing shapes across the middle of the three screens in front of her. After a few moments she said,

'This Transition Vehicle has been used within the last two hours. But it did not travel to Erce.'

'How can you be so sure?'

'Believe me Mr Crean, Erce's transition coordinates are imprinted in my brain.'

'Can we follow them?'

'Close the door please.'

Hugo did as he was bid and squeezed into the small space behind Mrs Ponch's chair.

'Thank you.'

'When do we go?'

'We've gone. We are already there. Bear with me please...'

The screen on the right flickered into life. Looking over Mrs Ponch's shoulder, Hugo saw an image of a small clearing, smaller than the one they had just left. It was hemmed in by a densely-packed wood.

'It looks quite light out there,' he observed.

'That's the effect of the cameras, I'm afraid.' Mrs Ponch touched the central screen and the image immediately faded. The trees now were almost merging into each other, dark fuzzy shapes on a gloomy background. 'That's how it will appear to us.'

'Shall we go?'

'One moment.' Mrs Ponch moved her hands over the central screen again. She frowned, and repeated the process, still apparently without achieving her goal. She worked at the screen for a while longer, then sighed.

'Is there a problem Mrs Ponch?'

'Before I set off to meet you, I did a location-check on Bettony's smartpad. It was not registering at all on Abbuth. But it is not registering here either.'

'Could it be out of range?'

'Unlikely. On Abbuth of course they are connected to a network of boosters and so are visible anywhere on the planet. But even here, each one will have a range of over twenty miles.'

'So she could be here but more than twenty miles away?'

'It's possible I suppose.'

'Or someone else could have taken her smartpad?'

'Also a possibility.'

'Can you tell whether this spaceship has been anywhere else?'

'Yes, I can. I did that when I traced its journey here. The answer is No, Mr Crean. The Transition Vehicle came here, stayed for a couple of minutes, and then returned directly to Abbuth.'

Hugo searched for possible explanations. He could only think of one.

'Somebody dropped Bettony off.'

'Somebody could have dropped someone off. It seems reasonable to suppose Bettony was the someone. But this is only a supposition.'

'So she must be here somewhere.'

'Just because we can't think of another reason, it doesn't mean that there isn't one, Mr Crean.'

Mrs Ponch moved shapes around again and once more the image on the screen brightened and sharpened. She was able to zoom the camera in and yet retain a remarkable degree of sharpness in the picture. Her calmness contrasted with the urgency Hugo felt.

'See there...' They looked at an imprint in the ground.

'I do.'

'And here.' Mrs Ponch zoomed the camera out a little, following a faint trail of broken branches and twigs. It was almost as though someone had been dragged along the ground.

'If you let me out I'll follow that trail.'

'It will be much more difficult out there, in natural light.'

'Difficult is not impossible.'

Mrs Ponch considered for a moment, then pulled a small metal cylinder from her pocket. She clipped it into a mechanism that sat on the desk next to her left hand, then moved more shapes around on the screens.

'This is an emergency beacon.' She unclipped it and held it out. 'I have just reset it. It will only work once. Twist the end and it will broadcast your coordinates back here, to the control panel in this Two. I suggest that you use it purely to communicate to me that you are in a desperate situation. It will even work if for any reason you transition from this to another universe. However – I must stress this – the device typically has a delay of between thirty minutes to an hour between it being activated, and the signal being received in our own universe.

Hugo took the beacon. He doubted whether Mrs Ponch would be able to help if he were in trouble, but it wouldn't do any harm having the thing.

'Is there anything else here that might be useful?' He asked. Mrs Ponch looked vaguely around.

'I don't think so.'

Hugo pulled a linen bag from where it had been stuffed into a corner. Inside it were a couple of metal boxes.

'What are these?'

'Good heavens. They look like the single-use transition devices that - don't touch that!'

A loud crack rang in Crean's ears. The noise seemed to grip his entire body in a brief agonising moment of excruciating pain; at the same time Mrs Ponch's voice was suddenly fading away. Hugo gave an involuntary gasp and collapsed onto a forest floor, only dimly aware that he should have been landing on the hard metal of the spaceship. Sentinnat training kicked in and he instinctively rolled several times, finishing on his stomach, head down, hands and arms covering his head.

He lay still.

The pain seemed to evaporate away.

He was still in the wood but he was alone. The spaceship had disappeared. Had he destroyed it?

'One way to find out I suppose,' Crean murmured to himself, thinking about the emergency beacon. It was only now that he realised he was still holding the metal box he had pulled from the bag.

He rolled onto his back and stared into the blackness above, clutching the box. He tried to replay in his mind the last few moments.

He had pulled this box from a bag. Fiddled with the end of it. Mrs P had been talking. What had she said? ... Something about transition. That was the term they used for space-hopping. Then she had said, Don't -

Don't what? What had he done?

The silence all around him was oppressive.

What if the reason why Bettony didn't seem to be in the place he had travelled to with Mrs P was because she had done the same thing?

Whatever that was.

He began to notice how unpleasantly the air smelt.

'Something rotten this way comes,' he murmured to himself, smiling as the quote put him in mind of his friend Benedict and his habit of quoting from forbidden works.

Crean sat up, recovered and exultant. He remembered from reading Bettony's Sputteridge report that she had herself used a transition box, when she and Ben had escaped after torching Hablock. The emergency beacon could wait for the moment. He may conceivably have destroyed the spaceship - and Mrs P with it - but much more likely he had space-hopped without a spaceship to protect him and had somehow survived. It must be that! Either way, right at this moment he was ok.

Either way, right now he did not need the emergency beacon.

He could hear voices. Still some way off, but approaching him.

They were talking too quietly for him to follow their conversation but he could pick up enough to recognise Anglish.

Crean's heart sank. Was he in Erce, after all?

He stood up and moved like a shadow to the cover of a large tree.

Two of them. Getting closer and closer...

'Come into my parlour, said the spider to the fly,' Crean whispered to himself as he reached down to his calf.

He barely needed to move. Just half a step out as they passed and his arms encircled the nearest shape, holding his Tipper to its throat. It gurgled. It was small. It was surprisingly strong too, but Hugo held it tight. Like a fly in a web, it could not move.

'Both of you -'

He got no further. There was a strange shuffling sound, and the other shape momentarily appeared to be doing some sort of spinning dance.

Only for the briefest of moments though. Something like a hammer thudded into Hugo's temple. It was as though someone had flicked an off-switch for his body and his brain. He was vaguely aware of the forest floor, rushing up to meet him in an unforgiving, bruising sort of way.

CHAPTER FOURTEEN

'It's a great story, I'll give you that.'
(About half an hour earlier...)

'It's a great story, I'll give you that.'

Brian sat back. Bettony found it hard to read his expression. Paulette had left the room some time ago. Bettony could hear her clattering around in the kitchen. She guessed that the woman had dismissed what she was saying as fantasy.

Brian though...

Eventually he said, 'What you've just told me sounds utterly ridiculous. I'd suggest you spend some time thinking up something that's a bit more believable in case you need to tell it to a party official. It's ok! Don't look at me like that. I'm not going to turn you in and neither is Paulette.

'I'm not saying I don't believe you either. I saw the metal box disappear, remember? But...' He shook his head. 'I mean, different worlds? Really?' He shook his head and laughed.

Paulette returned, carrying bowls of broth.

'Here you go.' Her voice was hard. The comment seemed to have been addressed to the television. Then, to Brian, 'You've skyved out of cooking again mister.'

'You could've stayed in here, beautiful.'

'Hmph. We have to eat.'

Bettony could sense the other woman's hostility, although to be honest Paulette's hostility was so obvious that even Garri with a crash helmet on would have had no trouble sensing it.

'Paulette, if I was going to make a story up wouldn't I have invented something a bit less crazy?'

'Hmph. Crazy. You said it.'

'But what about Brian seeing the Transition Vehicle disappear?'

'Him and his daft stories.'

'Hang on.' Brian put his spoon down. 'When have I ever come up with a story as daft as that?'

'Coming out here. Trying to educate these people.'

'That's not fair! You wanted to do it as well.'

They seemed to be re-opening an old argument. Bettony ate her broth, eyes down, not wanting to intrude on a private quarrel. She reflected that Paulette's hostility was at least having the effect of pushing Brian towards accepting her story.

They ate in silence. After a while Bettony took her courage in both hands and said,

'If you don't mind me asking, what's your explanation of what Brian saw?'

Paulette snorted derisively. But she was an intelligent woman and not as belligerent as her attitude suggested. Eventually she said,

'I don't know.' Her voice became firmer as she moved onto solid ground. 'He can't keep away from trouble, that's his problem.'

The silence returned. After a while Paulette added,

'Maybe he imagined it.'

'You know that's not true, beautiful.' Spoken gently.

'Brian, you know what will happen if people find out that she's here. Things are hard enough as it is.'

'There's not a day goes by that I don't regret bringing you out here.'

That was heart-wrenching. Bettony put her spoon down and stood up.

'I've caused you enough trouble. Thank you for the food. I'll leave now.'

They both stood.

'Don't you be stupid either,' Paulette said. She turned to Brian. 'If I'd known when I was at university how things would turn out...'

'You wouldn't have married me?'

'Of course I would. You bloody idiot.' She wiped a tear from her thin, lined face. Husband and wife hugged.

'I should still go.'

'No!' They both spoke.

Paulette gently released herself from her husband's hug, and sat down again.

'Finish your broth. Both of you. Before it goes cold.'

They returned to eating. It was cold in the room, and getting colder. There was an open hearth with ashes in the grate and a couple of small logs next to it, but no fire. Bettony had not taken her coat off, only unzipped it.

Although a silence returned, it felt a far gentler one. Bettony wondered how to start the conversation up again but it was Brian who spoke.

'So what are your plans?'

'I don't know.' Bettony pulled the transition box from her pocket. 'This is what got me here. Maybe it would work again.'

'Where would it take you?'

'I don't know. Like I told you, it wasn't designed to bring me here. And they're only supposed to work once, I think. Could be worth a try though.'

'Would it help if I showed you where the metal container disappeared?'

'Yes... I suppose it might.'

'Be careful,' Paulette said. 'Don't let anyone see you.'

In reply, Brian leaned over and tenderly kissed his wife on the cheek.

'She worries about you.'

'I know. She worries about a lot of things.'

'Do you think you'll be able to get away from here?' Bettony asked.

They were picking their way into the wood.

'I don't know. I hope so. But it's not easy for the party to get teachers to come to places like this...'

'Where would you go? If you could?'

'I dunno. Bristol or London, maybe. A big city.' Brian laughed. 'Somewhere where they have running water and you don't have to use night toilets out in the fields. And somewhere with heating!'

'Do you get used to the cold?'

'These doublets are quite warm, you know. And the jacket is padded. To answer your question though, no, you don't get used to the cold, but you get used to the idea of *feeling* cold. Not quite the same thing. Not far now, straight ahead.'

'Is Paulette able to see her family?'

'Oh yes. Travel permits are easy enough to get. It's not cheap though and - kugh!'

A large shape seemed to have appeared from nowhere and enveloped Brian. The little man was struggling impotently against its grip. The assailant was starting to speak. Without thinking Bettony spotted, spun and planted her heel on the shape's head.

Bullseye. The shape fell to the ground, poleaxed.

'Are you ok Brian?'

'Yes. Yes I'm fine. I think he was holding a knife to my throat but it felt like the flat side, not the sharp edge.' Brian struck a match and bent down. 'Yes here it is. What a lethal-looking thing. That was a very impressive kick you did there.'

Bettony switched her torch on and played it on the inert shape on the ground. Then cursed.

'Do you know him?'

'His name's Hugo Crean. I thought he was on our side...' This doesn't make sense, Bettony thought. It was Hugo who told us about Regency infiltration and TMB. Surely he can't actually be Timmbo... Has this all been some kind of very complicated scheme of his...?

Without her realising, the figure had regained consciousness. It suddenly sprang up and grabbed her arm and twisted, pulling her to the ground and rolling over her.

'Who have we got here then? I - ooof!'

Bettony had managed to bring her knee up into Hugo's groin as they fell, temporarily paralysing him. He was still holding on to her though, and for several seconds they rolled around until Bettony was able to free herself. They both sprang to their feet. Or at least, Bettony did. It was more of a painful stagger for Hugo, who was still recovering from the blow to his male pride. Bettony tried another kick which Hugo parried with his arm, trying without success to hold on to her leg. They came together briefly then parted again.

'Bettony is that you? It's me, Hugo. I've - ow! Will you stop that!'

They closed again, each warding off the other's attempts at throws, until Hugo was able to make use of his greater strength and put an arm across Bettony's waist, trapping one arm.

'Bettony calm down. I've got you in such a way that - *aargh*'

'Yes and I've got you too Crean. If I squeeze here you'll never know the joys of being a father...'

They struggled for a few more seconds, then Brian said,

'To be honest this is like a more physical form of one of my and Paulette's rows. Letting steam off while taking care not to inflict any actual harm. Perhaps you should stop wasting time and effort and let each other go. You're obviously trying not to hurt each other and the easiest way to do that is to stop this foolishness now.'

This was spoken with the authority of a schoolteacher. Like children caught fighting, gradually, distrustfully, and with a vague sense of having been naughty, Bettony and Hugo disentangled themselves.

'I don't know about not hurting each other...'

'Hugo if that was you who's been shooting at me -'

'Of course it wasn't me! Mrs Ponch and I have been trying to trace you... Who's been shooting at you? And who is this?'

'He's a friend. Is Mrs Ponch here? Have you got the Two?'

'The what?'

With exaggerated patience, Bettony said, 'The Series Two Transition Vehicle. You probably call it a spacecraft Hugo. Or a steam engine or something.'

Misunderstandings slowly fell away, replaced by explanation. Brian handed the knife back to Hugo and listened, absorbed, as these two strange creatures talked fantastical things. He was able to confirm to Bettony that Crean was not Mapps. He gave a rough description of Mapps, which helped to dispel any lingering doubts that Bettony had about Hugo. Crean was sure that Brian was describing TMB; Bettony was equally sure - despite apparently solid DNA evidence that this was impossible - that it was Tweek Golgood. This led to more inconclusive discussion about TMB's identity on Abbuth and what he was up to.

'Do you still want to see where the metal container disappeared from?' Brian asked Bettony.

'I don't think there's much point,' Bettony replied.

'It must have been a few yards over there,' Hugo said, gesturing vaguely.

'It was.'

'That's where the shed is on Abbuth.'

'You'd both better come back with me,' Brian said.

'Sorry old bean. Not a chance.'

'I think what my friend is trying to say here Brian is that we don't want to get you into trouble.'

'Spot on Bets.'

Bettony was about to say, *Don't call me that!* - But realised that she rather liked it. Coming from Hugo, anyway. Instead she responded,

'No problem boy.' And when Hugo smiled, she warmed to him even more.

'Right, look, I can see that you two want to spend some time alone,' Brian said. 'If you need us, you know where we are but please try and make sure you arrive while it's dark.' He paused. Hesitated. 'Look... I don't know if this is possible, but... if your spaceship can manage two more people... Anyway. Good luck.'

'We'll fit you in' Bettony said, on sudden impulse. 'Both of you.'

'Good luck anyway. You know where we are.'

The little man trudged away. There was a moment's uncomfortable silence.

'What did he mean, "I can see that you two want to spend some time alone"?' Hugo asked. Although Brian had gone now, and there was no need to do this, he was still using Anglish/English.

'Don't ask me.'

Another silence. They were sitting next to each other on a fallen log. Possibly slightly closer than was necessary.

'Is your head ok?' Bettony asked.

'Pretty much. A bit sore.'

'Only...' This was difficult for Bettony to say. 'That was how... how I did for Slepwood.'

'I know. I don't think you have anything to worry about Bettony. I've taken much worse knocks at rugger. Thick skull.'

'I've noticed.'

'Good kick though girly. Took me clean out.'

'I can just about tolerate you saying rugger instead of rugby. Calling me girly though, that's well over the line. Unless you want a resumption of hostilities.'

Crean laughed. 'Fair enough. Two cracks on the head in one night might be pushing my luck.'

'So what's the plan rugger-boy? As far as you see it anyway.'

Crean laughed again. 'You should've been born on Erce. You should see the way that women are expected to behave there, doing as they are bid by their menfolk. You'd have shaken them up Bets. Actually no. Just joking. You'd hate it.' He scratched at the ground with his boot. 'What I find interesting is that Timmbo seems to have set this up. He seems to have a special plan for you. Sort of, you versus him. Mano a mano. Or mano a womano.'

'Yes. I thought that. Like a duel, except he's the only one with a gun.'

'He's expecting you here, that's for sure. He must have rewired these magic boxes so that they all bring people to the same place.'

'He'd have to be smart to do that.'

'He is smart. Don't ever underestimate him. He's going to struggle to get here now though, now that Mrs P has taken control of the spaceship.'

'It's a transition vehicle... Except that it must have been he who sent it back to Abbuth.'

'True. Listen Bets, Mrs P gave me one of these.' Hugo produced the emergency beacon. 'She said it works across outer space. Do you think she's right?'

'Realities, boy. It works across realities. Yes, of course she's right.'

Crean looked at the unassuming piece of metal in his hand. 'Astonishing. So I could use it now and she'd come hurtling through - reality - like a taxi? Arrive here and take us home all safe and sound?'

'That's one way of putting it. I wouldn't use those words to her though. And I'd want to talk to her about bringing Brian and Paulette back with us.'

'No, I wouldn't use those exact words. Diplomacy is one of my strong suits my dear. Could be a bit of a squeeze getting your new friends in that spacecraft.'

'I can see that someone as perceptive as you are Hugo will quickly work out that she could make more than one trip. Anyway I'm thinking that we might want to hang around here for a little while longer and see if Timmbo puts in an appearance.'

'That's ma girl. And you can tell me how you were so easily fooled into believing Timmbo was your old pal - Ouch!'

'Sorry did I catch you there boy?'

They were each of them enjoying the other's company. And without realising, they had both relaxed. Neither was as alert as they should have been. Even so, some animal instinct warned Crean of danger. He suddenly pushed Bettony hard to her right, away from him, at the same time raising his left arm to protect his head and dropping backwards off the log to his left. Milden-Brewer appeared like a shadow detaching itself from the darkness around it. He had not been aiming for Bettony, though Hugo's actions had been enough to make him miss his mark: Instead of the Tipper slicing into Crean's left carotid artery it was Milden-Brewer's arm which met Hugo's. Crean was off-balance, unable to stop himself from falling backwards. He grabbed out wildly but Milden-Brewer easily evaded his flailing arm, dancing to one side then launching himself at Bettony. Hugo watched in horror as the two figures became one in the gloom.

And then disappeared.

Hugo's howl of impotent rage filled the wood. But there was no-one there apart from himself to hear it.

He was alone.

CHAPTER FIFTEEN

Adventures on a Hot World

Bettony recovered first. She had previously experienced the paralysis that the pain of the transition device produced, and was half-prepared for it. She forced her body to move, pushing out of Milden-Brewer's embrace and rolling across soft sand. Unable to stand, she carried on rolling, until Milden-Brewer's vague outline was swallowed up by the darkness.

In contrast to the chill of the world they had just left, this one was warm. Bettony felt use begin to return to her body. She staggered to her feet and stumbled away. She could hear Milden-Brewer cursing. She had no doubt that very soon he would be after her again.

It must be two or three in the morning, she thought. She was tired, physically and mentally. This peculiar hunt - that was what it felt like now, a hunt, not a duel - had been going on for hours. Wherever she went, whatever she did, Milden-Brewer seemed to be able to hunt her down. She wanted to check the time, but did not dare light up her smartpad. It seemed to be simple enough for TMB to find her, without her making it even easier.

Despite having been gripped by him, Bettony was not sure if it was Golgood. It was not a large man, she thought. The thickness of the winter coats they were both wearing made it difficult to be tell exactly how heavily-built he was, but not very, Bettony guessed. He could have been as slightly-built as Golgood. He was taller than her, certainly, but their encounter had been too short-lived and too violent for her to guess how much so; and most people were taller than her, both men and women.

Was it even a man, she wondered? But the voice had sounded male, despite the crazy way he had been using it.

She stumbled on, making slow, tiring progress through the soft sand.

Knowing that TMB would soon be following.

Hugo dug the metal cylinder out of his pocket and twisted the end. To his surprise, after a couple of seconds the tube jumped out of his hand, stinging him. Momentarily stunned, he watched it arc through the air, give a loud *crik*, and disappear.

'Whatever next,' he murmured to himself. He sat down again on the fallen log, wringing his hand. His normally irrepressible spirit was feeling crushed. He had failed to protect Bettony

She would say that she doesn't need protecting, Erce boy, a little voice in his head told him.

He half-smiled, but dismissed the thought. We're talking about TMB here, he told the voice. He had failed to protect her and TMB had got her.

Had he?

Shut up. TMB was probably making her suffer right now.

Like Slepwood did? Remember what happened to him?

Crean grinned, despite himself. And then a fragment of a memory from his schooldays flashed before his eyes, so vividly that he could actually see it in the darkness.

And Crean understood what this was all about. Everything suddenly fitted into place.

His spirit, so hard to repress, began to revive. Bettony was in deep trouble, no doubt about that.

But if Crean knew TMB - and he did, he was sure of that - there would still be time.

Hugo settled down to wait. Some time later, his keen ears picked up a muffled sound, rather as though something very large had gently sighed. Then a disembodied voice said,

'Mr Crean, you seem to be alone. Feel free to join me if you wish.'

Hugo waved facetiously in the general direction of the voice, got up and trudged towards the Two.

It was relentless. That was what was so tiring. That, and her complete inability to turn the tables on TMB. To do what she really wanted to do and hunt the hunter.

How was he able to do it?

It could only be through her Smartpad. Bettony wondered briefly if she had ever formed a friendslink with Golgood. Is that how he was tracking her? Would it even work, out on this world, away from Abbuth?

She dismissed the idea. She was certain that she had never linked with Golgood. Still, when it was light she would check.

Was there some other way he was tracking her through her smartpad? She could leave it behind somewhere. But then, if Golgood could track her through the pad so could Hugo or (more likely) Mrs Ponch. She had to hold on to it or face the rest of her life in this other world...

There was the faintest of pressures against the left side of her throat and she knew it was Milden-Brewer's knife. She froze.

A voice whispered, close to her ear,

'If you make even the slightest of movements I will slice into your neck and you'll have around three seconds left to live. So don't do it.'

Stay calm. 'How do you keep finding me Timmbo?' She forced her voice to be light. Without being conscious of it, she was aping Crean's manner.

'Don't call me that!' Boiling hatred strangled the words in Milden-Brewer's throat. The Tipper momentarily twitched away from her, then was back again.

Bettony's right hand tightened on the rock she was holding. Soon it would be time to gamble, but first she wanted to find out why he was doing this. Why she was being targeted. Her heart was thumping. She forced herself to keep her voice steady.

'Are you tracing my smartpad?'

When Milden-Brewer spoke again his voice was back to a whisper. He ignored Bettony's question. 'You think you're so clever don't you? No surprise you hooked up with Crean. One disgusting smartarse attracted to another. I've got plans for Crean but they can wait. You're going to die first but it's going to take a while. In fact it's going to take a week. Do you know why it's going to take a week?'

'Something to do with your religion?'

'Don't push it!' Another twitch of the knife, the gentlest of pressures but this time Bettony could feel it cut into her skin. Milden-Brewer seemed to have a speech prepared and now he returned to it. 'I had the honour of knowing a great man. In fact, more than that. I had the great honour of being his godson.'

Oh... bugger. I think I can guess where this is going...

'And that stalwart, heroic man was taken from us before his time. The world - *our* world, the *decent* world, the world of *moral values* - was denied his presence. I was denied his presence.'

Was he crying?

'It took him a week to die. From when you brutally kicked him in the head, until his poor brain could take no more and -'

A sob, definitely a sob.

'*You killed him you freak!* And I'm going to kill you. And just like my godfather, it will take a week. One week from tonight you will die. But you will know the terror of what is facing you. You will face the next seven days knowing they will be your last. Frightened like only a woman could be. *He* would never have felt terror. He -'

Now or never, Bettony thought. She pushed one hand against the arm that was holding the knife and with the other she swung the rock hard against Milden-Brewer's head...

Except that it wasn't there. He must have ducked or moved. She was trying to grip Milden-Brewer's arm but he twisted easily out of her grip. For a moment or two she flailed around with the rock, then dived to one side. If she couldn't get him, he wasn't getting her.

Maniacal laughter drifted across the darkness. Milden-Brewer had already put distance between them.

'One week from today. One week! Enjoy the last seven days of your life you freak!'

'A clever man, your Mr Milden-Brewer. He must have modified the transition devices quite considerably.'

'Or gotten someone else to do it.'

TMB was always good at techie stuff though, Hugo reflected. There was a big difference between fiddling around with a radio and all this stuff they used on Abbuth but still, once a techie...

The linen bag was still in the Two. While Hugo told her what he knew, Mrs Ponch took one of the remaining metal boxes and looked at it speculatively.

'The way I see it Mrs Ponch,' Hugo went on, 'they must all be modified in the same way because otherwise Timmbo wouldn't know where Bets was going. Can you work out where he programmed them to go?'

'Not with the equipment we have here, no. It's time for us to return to Abbuth and speak to Mr Sneggs, I believe.'

'Time is something that we don't have.'

'I'm aware of that.' For the first time Mrs Ponch's frustration showed. 'Unfortunately we don't have an alternative either.'

'There's always an alternative.' Crean smiled, disarmingly. Hiding the turmoil he was feeling. 'Give me a couple of those beacon things and I'll use my magic box and go zapping my way around outer space looking for Bets. Still plan A. But you can get back to your world while you're waiting for me. Get Ben or someone to pick up one of the spare magic boxes from you. He can whizz down to see old Bollie with it. If Bollie can't crack it no-one can.'

Mrs Ponch smiled thinly. 'I'm not sure which is the more endearing Mr Crean. Your boundless optimism or the head-on collision between our science and your understanding of it.' She stared into space, squeezing the bridge of her nose with her thumb and forefinger. 'We shall do as you suggest. Except that I only have one emergency beacon left so do not use it until you have located Bettony, unless you yourself are in mortal danger.'

'Of course.'

'Are you on a friendslink with Bettony?'

'Sadly no.'

'I suggest that when you arrive in a new reality you send out a link request. Do you have her details?'

'I do.'

'The smartpad will still have a range of twenty miles. If you can link with her you should be able to track each other down. How much battery life does your pad have?'

Hugo unclipped his smartpad and checked.

'Three weeks.'

'Let us hope it doesn't take that long.'

'I'm with you on that one.'

'It's going to take a while for me to get Mr Erwin and Mr Sneggs organised.'

'Absolutely. Bye then Mrs P.'

'You might want to take some -' Mrs Ponch stopped. Crean had managed to open the Two's door and was already pulling it closed behind him - '...water. Although you seem able to charm the birds from the trees,' she went on quietly to herself, 'so finding a drink is not likely to pose you a problem.'

She had walked for an hour and was very tired. Soft dry sand sapped what energy she had left after the night's adventures. If there was firmer ground, Bettony had not found it.

She had hoped to find lights somewhere, some evidence of human habitation, but everywhere was pitch-black. The third time that she stumbled into a rock, she decided to give up any further attempts at investigation until it was light.

She flopped to the ground. The sand was not cold and (once she had snuggled around in it) not uncomfortable. It was probably wildly dangerous, Bettony thought, but in this pitch-black darkness so could anywhere be. Timmbo was not going to kill her tonight (or what was left of it), he had told her that much. So she may as well sleep.

She really was very tired.

She held her hand against the scratch on her neck, and closed her eyes.

She woke when she was too warm. *February*, she thought. *What's this place like in summer?* It was still dark. Bettony took her coat off, feeling the bottle of water in her pocket, and with surprising ease fell asleep again.

The next time she woke she was again too warm, but it was light now. Early, she guessed. A long hill rose in front of her. The sun was hanging in the sky not far above it.

Hanging in the clear blue sky. Not a cloud anywhere. The ones that had so completely blocked out any light from the night sky had long since evaporated away.

Bettony checked her watch. Nine am: Early-ish, anyway. She stood up and looked around.

It was hard to believe that in other worlds this was farmland. Bare rock and sand lay all around, stretching in every direction.

Hard to believe, too, that it was February.

Where had Timmbo gone?

She could smell the sea.

The sea? From Swindon, close to the centre of England?

A humid breeze was blowing from a direction to the left of the sunrise, which she mistakenly congratulated herself on knowing was east. She pulled the water from her pocket, opened the bottle and sniffed it speculatively. It seemed to be ok. She tasted a sip. It was warm, but not particularly unpleasant.

She was intrigued by the smell of the sea. Her first idea on waking had been to pursue TMB, but if he wanted her, she thought, he could come and find her. She wasn't going to do his job for him.

'Talking of which,' she said to herself. She unclipped her smartpad from her jeans, unfolded it and switched it on. Interestingly, the friendslink grid covered quite a distance. There were no unexpected entries in her friendslink contacts. No sign of any contact within the grid either. If there had been, it could only have been Timmbo, whatever the identity.

She picked her jacket up. No need for this here. Could be useful though. Probably. Somewhere. She abstractedly picked at a small bobble, close to the right-hand pocket. It stubbornly refused to budge.

Ah well. She started to trudge south, into the breeze. Uphill.

Crean's use of the transition box landed him, painfully, into what felt like a sandpit. If anything, the night here was even darker than the last place. It was also silent. The pain quickly ebbed away. He waited, motionless, listening for anything that might give him a clue about where he had landed.

There was only complete, blanketing silence.

He tried to remember the layout of the land around the spaceship on Abbuth. Broadly flat, he thought. Perhaps dropping slightly towards Swindon? Whatever else would be different, he thought the actual geography of the place would be the same here.

Why sand? Had the people here dug out a quarry? But he did not think he was in a quarry. His eyes had adjusted by now as much as they could to the gloom around him; he had a reasonable idea that the land here was also flat.

He scooped a hole in the sand, lowered his smartpad into it and switched it on, trying as much as possible to cover the light that its screen gave off. This was a risky thing to do; if Timmbo saw the light, he would be in trouble. But he needed to do this. Hugo pulled up Bettony's contact details and sent her a friendslink request. He turned the screen's brilliance as low as possible, then waited.

There was no response.

Eventually, Crean fell into a light, cat-like sleep.

Mrs Ponch called Benedict immediately she was back on Abbuth. It was well past midnight by now, but her call was answered straightaway. She explained what she wanted from him.

'I'm desperate to help,' he said. 'The only problem is I don't own a car and I don't think the train service runs through the night.'

'I'm booking you a taxi as we speak. It will take you to Swindon station. I'll be waiting for you in the car park with one of the transition devices. I'm also booking you on to the last train to Bristol. If we are quick you should just about make it. I shall make sure that Mr Sneggs meets you at Bristol station. I'm afraid there will be a four hour wait until the first train back –'

'That's not a problem Mrs Ponch.'

Zagretia Ponch signed off and stared for a moment into space, squeezing the bridge of her nose with the thumb and forefinger of her left hand. She sometimes wondered exactly what she and her fellow Britannians had started, with their interquantal transitioning. It was without doubt an astonishing achievement. The discovery that there were other universes and that the people on Abbuth were not alone was profound. It would inform their development forever. But they had opened a Pandora's jam-jar, that was for sure, and the very least it had released was the dangerous inhabitants of Erce.

And yet. One of the nicest people she had ever met was from that dreadful place. Earth, of course, was such a puzzling mixture of good and bad, but again, in Bettony Gullivant it had thrown up a brave and resourceful and very trustworthy individual, albeit one whose ability to jump to wild conclusions was without equal.

Ah well.

There were six message tabs from Dr Flange, but they would have to wait a few moments. She made her next call, and found herself looking at a bleary-eyed winner of the Corngreave Yalta.

'Mr Sneggs. My apologies for waking you...'

It was hard work climbing the hill. There was no path, and Bettony's feet constantly slipped on the loose, barren ground. Half way up she rested on a rock, looking down on the route she had taken. It was quite a view. The barren mixture of rock and sand stretched in every direction, as far as she could see. At least there was no sign of TMB.

'There will be though,' she said to herself.

She checked her pad again. Her heart skipped a beat when she saw a friendslink request from Hugo Crean. He had found her! She lingered over the contact photo, smiling, suddenly happy. Crean was gazing towards the camera, his fair hair cut in a familiar boyish mop, the too-long fringe falling forward over his forehead.

Steady on girl, she thought. You're not a free spirit any more. She tapped to accept the link request, then eagerly opened the friendslink grid to see where he was.

He was three miles northeast of her position.

'You've put some speed on boy,' she murmured. She tried calling him but her pad returned the message Unavailable Service. The thought crossed her mind, I should go and meet him. But curiosity drove her forwards and upwards. It was not that far now and she wanted to discover the source of the sea breeze. She wanted to see what was on the other side of the hill.

Bettony took another sip of the water and set off again. The hill was steeper as she climbed towards its peak. There was little sand here, it was mostly bare white rock which the weather had carved into strange shapes. She had to be more careful, too. The rock was weak, and several times gave way beneath her feet. But finally she pulled herself over the peak of the hill.

And gazed down on a remarkable sight.

The hill fell away gently in front of her, flattening out into mixture of rock and sand, both of which were almost white. Sunlight reflected off both; the effect was dazzling. In the middle distance a broad stretch of blue water widened to her left into a peaceful ocean.

Bettony gasped.

She sat for some time, almost hypnotised by the stark beauty of the landscape below her. Hugo would have to see this, she thought. He would have to climb the hill to meet her, she wasn't going back. She was confident that he would use the grid to find his way to her. She climbed a little way down on the seaward side of the ridge and made herself comfortable against a rock. It was warm and she was surprisingly happy.

Crean woke at dawn. He had the ability to make do for long periods with small amounts of sleep, and now he felt refreshed. He checked his smartpad - there was no response yet to his link request - then surveyed the land around him.

He was not in a quarry. Rock and sand surrounded him in every direction. He moved quickly to the shelter of a large rock. Timmbo was a good shot, no point in giving him a clear target.

After a while he felt safe enough to venture out into the open. There were a lot of tracks around him.

'Tell me your story,' Crean said, studying them...

There was one dip which was probably made by their two bodies when they landed. It looked as though one of them had rolled away from it; Bettony, Crean guessed, from its size. At some point she had stood up, walked a short distance, then dropped to the ground again. Milden-Brewer was not a big man but he was bigger than Bettony, and Hugo could make out his larger footprints, following, then catching her. Hugo was pretty sure about this. Timmbo's footprints were imprinted into the flattening that he thought was caused by Bettony.

Was she injured? Is that why she was rolling, and why she had dropped once more to the ground?

But then they seem to have parted company. Bettony's smaller footprints led one direction, Timmbo's not that much larger ones going in almost exactly the opposite.

This puzzled Hugo. Had they fought? The one escaping from the other?

His first thought was to follow Bettony. There would be time for a reckoning with Timmbo, of that he was certain, either here or on another world. First, he needed to get to Bettony and activate the beacon. Bring Mrs P here and get Bettony home.

He smiled to himself. So Abbuth was home now, was it?

Something nagged at Crean's thoughts. Why was Timmbo heading away from Bettony? He half-smiled. She could be scary, it was true, but he doubted that was the reason.

He would follow Bettony, that was definite. But perhaps he would scout Milden-Brewer for a short distance first.

'Oh fickle soul, inconstant as the moon,' he chided himself as he retraced his steps westwards.

Milden-Brewer's footprints may have started heading away from Bettony's, but Hugo soon discovered that they curved around and ran parallel to hers at a distance of around fifty feet.

How did you do that in the dark, Timmbo? Crean wondered. But then again, from what Bettony had told him, TMB had already successfully tracked her earlier in the night. Hugo recalled his lessons on night-time tracking at the Sentinnat's combat course. The group had been divided into pairs: Each participant had to track his partner and what was euphemistically termed "subdue" them, before the roles were reversed. The oleaginous Toby Osbourne was the unfortunate who had been chosen to track and subdue Hugo. Hugo had remained unsubdued. He had not been gentle with the luckless Osbourne, who to the amusement of the training officer had required a visit to hospital, leaving Crean with no-one to track. There had been a strange shortage of volunteers to take Osbourne's place, and Hugo was forced to sit out the rest of the exercise.

If Timmbo had tracked Bettony in the pitch black of the previous night, from a distance of fifty feet, he was doing very well, Hugo reflected.

After half an hour the two sets of tracks diverged. Bettony's continued in a gentle curve towards a long hill in the distance; Timmbo's swerved away to the left.

'What is your game, little Timmbo?' Hugo mused. He decided to follow Milden-Brewer. He had not gone more than a few paces before his smartpad bleeped. Crean unclipped and unfolded it, and was pleased to see his friendslink request had been accepted by Bettony.

Excellent! He opened the grid and saw that she was located several miles south-east of his current position.

He chuckled grimly to himself.

It was at this moment that one of the nearby rocks heaved itself to its feet. A disproportionately small, wizened head poked out from the main body of the rock, which began lumbering westwards. The giant turtle-like creature was completely uninterested in Hugo, who watched sand channel its way off its back as it slowly departed.

'Well I never,' he muttered. On impulse, he composed and sent a brief message, carefully placed his smartpad on the turtle's large, flat back, then covered it with a sprinkling of sand and pebbles.

The beast slowly turned its head and gave Hugo what he felt was a disgruntled gaze, before it resumed its steady journey.

'Apologies old fellow,' Hugo said. His smile became less grim and his blue eyes seemed to sparkle with amusement. 'And many thanks for your help and assistance.'

The turtle did not reply.

So Crean had made his way here too had he? TMB was not particularly surprised. Even a fool, in time, would have worked out that all the transition boxes were identically pre-programmed.

Timmbo had just opened his smartpad. Now, he looked at the friendslink request and sniggered. What a pity Crean hadn't worked out the rest.

And suddenly, it was one of those times when Milden-Brewer could hardly stop laughing.

He was so much smarter than both Crean and the freak. Well of course, you would not expect much of the freak. A woman's brain is so much smaller than a man's. It gave Timmbo no great satisfaction to outsmart her (apart from the obvious one of course, the satisfaction of leading her terrifyingly to her death). But it felt so good to be getting one over on the famous Hugo Crean.

The hated Hugo Crean.

The stupid Hugo St Monderby Dephwood Crean who would never work out how misleading his smartpad could be.

Timmbo doubled over with glee. The Hugo Crean who would never leave this awful place.

Still, at least he would be here with his bit of skirt. Even if she was dead.

Milden-Brewer collapsed once more with laughter. His smartpad pinged the arrival of a new message and he made an effort to pull himself together. Then just as soon as it had hit him, the frenzied mirth evaporated away, replaced by anger.

Hi Cuddlybits there's something really strange in the distance, to the westish. I'm going to go and have a poke around. Progress is really slow, my leg's no better. Can't put my weight on it. Just need you to kiss it better! Watch out for Timmbo, I've got a feeling he's here somewhere. He's not a problem though, he's so weedy you should be able to blow him over.

Milden-Brewer danced with rage. How could this stupid man be so stupid! Rugby, fighting, that was all he was good for. But actually using what little brain he had...

Crean had got a problem with his leg had he?

That would even the odds up.

Maybe I could have a little fun with him too, thought Timm.

Yes. Crean first. Get him out of the way, then deal with the freak.

Crean rested in the shade of a large rock, twenty yards from TMB's tracks. Hidden in its shadow he was able to watch out for Milden-Brewer with a degree of comfort. A casual observer might have thought Hugo was dozing, and although Crean was completely relaxed, that casual observer would have been badly mistaken. He idly wondered if he had overdone the message. *Cuddlybits*? Hugo chuckled. No, that was fine. And the rest of it would have annoyed Timmbo beyond belief.

An angry opponent is the best sort of opponent, Crean reflected. The best strategies are the ones that are conceived in cold blood. Anger brings mistakes.

Anger is weakness.

An hour later, through half-closed eyes, Hugo saw someone approach. He melted further into the darkness cast by the rock, watching the slight figure of Timm Milden-Brewer walking quickly towards him. His hand reached down for his Tipper.

Predictable as always, Timmbo.

Hugo's plan had been to confront Timmbo. He had every confidence in his physical supremacy over TMB. Just in time, he saw what TMB was carrying.

'Hullo,' Hugo murmured. 'What have we here? A Coppler?'

He peered at the gun in Milden-Brewer's right hand. It was a short, thin-barrelled Coppler and Mann rifle. A large silencer covered the end; an infra-red night-vision sight perched on the top of the barrel.

'It is! A Coppler 50, no less. You naughty boy, Timmbo.'

Milden-Brewer was too far away to hit with the Tipper; and in any case Hugo wanted him alive and able to answer questions. The ground was too open to surprise him. Timmbo would get a clear shot in before Hugo had closed down even a quarter of the distance between them. And Timmbo would only need one shot.

Change of plan then, thought Hugo. He watched TMB pass him and disappear westwards into the distance, then stepped out from the shadow of the rock and hurried eastwards. There was a reason why TMB had gone so far out of his way and Hugo wanted to find out what it was.

Bettony was beginning to get bored. You can only look at a breathtaking view for so long without it becoming a bit samey, and in Bettany's experience that wasn't long at all. Breathtaking was ok, but you had to breathe, after all. She clambered back to the top of the ridge and with the sun now behind her scanned the ground to the north for any sign of life. Crean and Timmbo were both out there somewhere. She pulled her smartpad out and selected the Viewmap option to see the friendslink grid.

What on earth was the man doing? According to the grid he was heading west, away from where she was.

Hey boy, she messaged. *Something new cropped up?*

There was no reply.

Crean left his jacket behind, hidden away in the shade of the rock. His lumpy transition box was stuffed into one of its oversized pockets. Once he picked up Timmbo's tracks again he fell into a steady run. Despite his deceptively lazy movement, he was travelling quickly. Barely twenty minutes later, he found what he was looking for. Milden-Brewer's low camp, sheltering in a narrow dip, still shaded from the morning heat.

Hugo helped himself to a bottle of Timmbo's water and bit thoughtfully into one of TMB's biscuits. It looked as though Timmbo had invested some considerable time and effort into this place. A large piece of thin, sandy-coloured canvas had been pegged out as a low roof, stretched between the ground on one side and against the top of one bank of the dip on the other. Beneath it there was a thin sleeping-bag and a plentiful supply of provisions.

Hugo found a rucksack and filled it with as much food and water as he could carry. He destroyed the rest, emptying the water into the dry ground and scattering biscuits and dried meat and fruit.

Then he pulled the canvas down and shredded both it and the sleeping bag with his Tipper.

He guessed that he had maybe half an hour on Timmbo. It wouldn't take the man long to locate the turtle. Hugo thought TMB could then do one of two things. Either he would close down Bettony, or he would return here. Hugo's tracks were easy enough to see and to follow, even Timmbo would realise what he had been up to.

Ah well, Hugo knew what his own plan was. He summoned a rough map of the area in his mind, visualising the curved path of Bettony's footprints and the straight line that had brought him here. He worked out a rough direction to take that would allow him to pick up Bettony's tracks.

It was getting hot. Milden-Brewer's Sentinnat training meant that he was prepared for this sort of arduous trekking, but it did not mean that he enjoyed it. He was focussed on Crean's position on the friendslink grid and had chosen a direct route to intercept him. Had he followed the tracks he might have wondered about Hugo's strange, four footed and occasionally haphazard progress.

It took him almost two hours to catch up with Crean's smartpad location, which bizarrely was a small island, twenty yards away in the middle of a foul-smelling pool of water. He could make out a few straggly bushes and stunted trees growing among the rocks. Milden-Brewer imagined Crean, in pain and stinking from the fetid water that had soaked into his clothes (and hopefully into the wound on his leg), cowering among the scrub. No doubt Crean had realised at some point that TMB was hunting him down, and had taken refuge where he could. Timm thought briefly about entering the water, but immediately dismissed the idea.

He could wait.

He thought gleefully about Crean, forced eventually from his squalid hiding-place, begging for mercy that would not be forthcoming.

He could wait all right. He had been waiting for something like this for many years. A few more minutes would not hurt.

He had seen the freak's message but ignored it until now. He decided to fill in the time by replying. He would make it look genuine by copying Crean's grotesque phrases.

Finally!

Bettony pulled her smartpad open and read the incoming message. It was not the message that she had been hoping for. Her eyes widened and her mouth fell open in shock.

Hi Cuddlybits I've been poking around to the westish. Thought there was something strange but it's nothing. Progress is really slow, my leg's no better. Can't put my weight on it. Just need you to kiss it better! Stay where you are, I won't be too long now.

'Is he on drugs?' Bettony said to herself. *Cuddlybits?* The phrase *poking around to the westish* was so peculiar that she wondered if it was some sort of obscene euphemism. And what was up with his leg? *Kiss it better?*

She tried, and failed, to compose a suitable response. She would wait, instead. She would get more satisfaction from her reply if it was delivered face-to-face.

Another hour passed before she spotted Hugo. He was some distance away, but moving quickly. Not much problem with his legs now by the looks of it. Bettony reluctantly marvelled at the way he seemed to spring up the steep hill, never losing his footing on the treacherous surface.

'Hi Bets.'

He wasn't out of breath either. Why wasn't he out of breath? She somehow resented that.

'Your leg has obviously made a quick recovery,' she answered coldly.

'What?'

'Cuddlybits?'

'Oh you got that did you?'

'Who else was it meant for?'

'Timmbo.'

'Crean are you drunk or has the sun affected your brain?'

'Whoa steady on girl I recognise that fighting stance! Not the safest pose to assume on the ridge of a steep hill... Wow, what a view.'

'Never mind the view, stop changing the subject. What was the idea of sending me such a dumb message?'

'Can I have a look?' Hugo held out his hand. 'Please?'

Reluctantly, Bettony handed over her pad. Hugo read the message and chuckled.

'First lesson of the day: If it doesn't sound like me, it probably ain't me. It's good to see you again Bets.'

The last sentence was said gently, and perhaps with more warmth than Hugo intended. Bettony looked at him sharply and pulled the smartpad out of his hand.

'I was pretty sure that Timmbo had worked some electrical wizardry and made himself look like you,' Hugo went on. 'In a manner of speaking. No-one could do that in person of course.'

'I should hope not,' Bettony replied. Hugo was gratified to hear that her voice had lost its chill.

'So I sent him a loving message with a bit of bait in it. It looks like he used some of my warm words when he contacted you. When he was pretending to be me. Thinking that was how we converse.'

'Huh. The man's more of an idiot than I thought. How did you realise it was Timmbo linking you, and not me?'

'When I was tracking you both. You came this way and Timmbo forged a path due east. And yet my friendslink request was accepted by the Bettony with bigger feet who had ploughed his furrow eastwards. Anyway I persuaded a native to waddle away with my smartpad, but not before I had very naughtily sent you - by which I mean, sent Timmbo - a rather personal message explaining about my dodgy leg. I wanted him out of the way for the moment and thought he might be keen to take on a wounded Hugo.'

'Hold on boy. Explain slowly, in more detail. And tell me about the native.'

'Let's move out of sight first. The view is so much better on this side too. Can I interest you in a biscuit or a raisin?'

They sat in the sun, eating and drinking while Hugo described his morning.

Bettony opened her friendslink grid. 'It looks like he was playing us both off. I should have realised when you answered my link request. You'd covered too much ground. Even for you.' She pointed. 'Look, that's you now. Couple of miles north-west from here.'

'So Timmbo knows that you're here.'

'Looks like it. Yep.'

'I wouldn't worry. He'd be able to track you easily enough in this terrain. I did. Interesting that he's still following the turtle. Must be the exciting opportunity of taking me on when I'm handicapped by a dodgy pin, it's affected his judgement. Although let's be honest, even a one-legged Hugo Crean would have no problem against Timmbo.'

'Following the turtle. I think you've invented a new phrase there Hugo. Your modesty is one of your most engaging features, by the way.'

'I know. Only one of them though, there are plenty of others. He probably thinks he'll deal with me and then come for you. Talking of which. I've worked out why he's paying you so much attention. I think it's revenge.'

'—Because he's Slepwood's godson. Don't look so downcast boy. He basically told me as much last night when he had a knife at my throat. He wants me to spend a week here in terror, knowing that at the end of the week he's going to kill me.'

'Doesn't know you very well does he?'

'Flattery will get you everywhere.' There was a moment's embarrassed silence, while they both thought about what Bettony had said. Hastily, she added,

'How did you find out?'

'That Slepwood was his godfather? Oh. Er, I remembered.'

'You *remembered*?'

'Yeah... sorry. I remembered Slepwood coming to visit him when we were at school. Sleppy was already a force to be reckoned with. A lot of the boys were very impressed that Timmbo was his godson. Another biscuit?'

'Thanks.' They sat in silence, looking at the view. The sun had moved higher now and although it was still very bright the blinding glare from the rocks was not aimed directly into their eyes.

'We should probably get back to the transition point and activate the emergency beacon.'

'I know.'

Neither of them moved.

'On the other hand,' Hugo said, 'this is a good opportunity to get hold of Timmbo and get him to identify the other Sentinnat spies. I suspect I'll be better at doing that than your well-meaning friends from Abbuth. Putting him in a hotel on an island off the coast of Cornwall and giving him tea and cakes is probably not going to yield a result.'

'He's going to be very cross when he finds out you've trashed his tent.'

Hugo laughed.

'Ain't he just.'

Silence returned. Hugo asked,

'So is he the famous Tweek Golgood then?'

'I think so. It was hard to tell. He was behind me when he had the knife at my throat and he was whispering.' Bettony sighed. 'But that means Bollie somehow missed his DNA. And I trust Bollie, both as a person and as a resident genius. It doesn't make sense.'

Another pause.

'Before we were rudely interrupted last night, you were going tell me how you were so easily tricked into Timmbo's clutches.'

'Pushing your luck again boy?' Bettony scratched at the rock in front of her. 'You're right though, to be honest. It was easy for him. Oh! Poor old Welter! I wonder if he's ok.'

'Welter? Who he? Explain woman.'

Bettony explained.

'Our Timmbo's quite a dab hand at electrical impersonation isn't he?'

'You know Hugo, with your grasp of technological language you should be an engineer.'

'You mock me madam... It sounds as though Timmbo went to an awful lot of trouble. Who were the goons who attacked this Welter character? Why not rock up to Longcot himself?'

'You know how his brain works better than I do.'

'Mmm. I should do shouldn't I? Where is he now?'

Bettony checked the grid. 'Still at the same place.'

TMB was becoming increasingly frustrated.

Time was on his side, of course. There was a whole seven days for the freak to slowly succumb to hunger and thirst. Whatever supplies she was carrying would not last long. He had his base, carefully prepared, and it was not as if he was going to lose track of

her. He could retire to his base, confident that he now had two lazy
ways of locating her plus his own exceptional abilities, learned the
hard way on Sentinnat training courses.

But now that he had Crean at his mercy he was impatient for the
kill.

He began to sing, using the high-pitched voice that he thought
must have terrified the freak, the night before.

'Hugo, oh Hugo...? You can't stay there for ever...'

Something stirred on the island, then was still again. He resumed
his normal voice.

'Hugo let's be sensible about this. You must be facing a terrible
end. I know you and I know you're not the sort of chap to cringe
in a bolthole, waiting for a coward's death to creep up on him.'

He picked up his Coppler and used its sight to scan the island.
He could see nothing of Crean.

'Come back over here. I'll give you a drink and we can finish
this man to man.'

Just one good shot, that was all he needed.

'Finish it honourably, while you've still got the strength.'

He was still sighting the island with his rifle. Even Crean's voice
would help locate him. One shot, not going for the kill, hopefully
leaving Crean alive for a while longer. Then watch him suffer a
prolonged death. Milden-Brewer's mouth actually watered at the
prospect. He flicked a tousled curl away from his forehead, then
continued scanning the island.

'What do you say Hugo. For the honour of Hinton. Do it the
proper way.'

Silence.

Milden-Brewer sighed. *I've got time,* he thought.

'How are we going to nab him?'

'He can come and find us.' Hugo smiled. 'Send him a message.
Tell him to get a move on. No don't do that, ask me how I'm
getting on.'

'Yep...ok. Done that.'

'What did you say?'

'I said, "Hi Huggsy how are you getting on?"'

'Lacking in inspiration but a functional message I suppose. Ow!
Sharp elbows.'

Milden-Brewer was idly lining up shots at random points on the island when Bettony's message pinged in. He cursed himself for not switching to silent mode. It was unlikely that Crean had heard it though. He read the message, swore, then idly opened out the friendslink grid.

Damn! Crean was moving again...

What on Erce was he doing? Without any map to underlie it, there were few reference points on the grid. Away from Abbuth, it really was little more than just a grid. But from what Timmbo could make out, Crean appeared to have slipped silently into the foul water on the other side of the island and was swimming round and round in it.

How stupid was this man? Was this his way of taunting Timm?

Had Crean seen his rifle?

Never mind. It might make good sport, plugging Crean while he struggled in the water. Milden-Brewer jumped to his feet and hurried around the water's edge, all the time scanning the pool for signs of life.

'Still no reply?'

'Nope. As evidenced by the lack of a ping...'

'I wonder what he's up to. Possibly he hasn't worked out that I'm not a turtle and he's watching me lay some eggs or something.'

'What a revolting thought.'

'He's not the smartest boy on the planet.'

'I dunno. On this planet he's only got a competition of one.'

'Ho ho.'

'And he's pretty good with these fancy electrical gizmos.'

'I suspect you're cruelly parodying me again young lady.' Hugo stretched, lazily. 'I can't wait around all day - hullo what's this?'

He had been idly picking at Bettony's coat, which lay on the ground between them. Now, he pulled it up and examined it.

'If you want to look in my coat pocket boy you only have to ask. No secrets between adventurers and all that.'

'It is a jolly good adventure isn't it?' Hugo murmured abstractedly. He was pulling at something. 'Hullo. When did you first notice this?'

'Oh that bobble? Dunno. It won't come off, I've tried. I think it's a bit of gunk that got stuck on sometime.'

'When?'

Bettony was suddenly serious. 'Earlier today probably. Why? What is it?'

'Before today, I'm guessing. It's one of the very latest whizzbang up-to-the-minute Sentinnat trackers. No wonder he's found you so easy to follow. Even before the friendslink thing.'

'Bastard.'

'Cunning bastard, may I suggest. The question is, when did he stick it there?'

'I leave my coat on the coat-hanger at work.'

'Must have been then. It only takes a second or so. Clever really. Ah well, more opportunity for some fun with Timmbo. I wonder if he's planted any more. I can pat you down if you want?'

'I can pat myself down thank you very much.'

'Well if you change your mind.'

'Funny I never noticed it before though. I suppose he could have planted it last night when he had his knife at my throat.'

'My guess is that it was on your coat when you were in that other place with all the trees. I did wonder how he managed to know where you were all the time. That would have tested even my abilities.' Hugo stood up.

'What are you doing boy?'

'I'm getting bored. I'm going to go and see what he's up to.'

'He's moving.'

Milden-Brewer was still walking around the pool's edge when he saw a movement on the water. Yes! A gentle plop was followed by ripples, spreading out over its stillness. But by the time he had raised and sighted his rifle all was still again.

So Crean had seen him coming and decided to dive. Timmbo smiled. Let's see how long you can hold your breath Golden Boy, he thought.

This side of the pool the island was further away from the edge. For a fearful moment Timmbo imagined Crean suddenly surging out of the water at his feet. But common sense reasserted itself. The sludgy green water was shallow here, and from what he could see it only began to deepen several yards further out.

He waited, gun at the ready.

'Can you zoom in any more?'

'Hang on.'

They watched Hugo's identifier shuffling around the grid.

'So he's just walked about a hundred and twenty yards in a semi-circle and stopped again.'

'Metres boy, metres. Get with the Abbuth flow.'

'Metres, yards, what's the difference?'

'About four inches. Sorry, nine centimetres.'

Hugo sighed, theatrically. 'Why would he do that Bets?'

'He's watching something. Circling around it.'

'Probably. Anyway. Time that the hunter became the hunted.' Hugo stood up. Bettony did the same.

'What are you doing?'

'Joining the hunt. Remember, this isn't Erce.'

'It might not be very pretty.'

'Crean, you've read my report. A lot of what I've seen has not been pretty.'

'Ok but please will you also remember what I said about Timmbo.'

'Yes I know, he's a lethal killer. You can catch me when I swoon. Shall we take the smartpad?'

'If we take the smartpad he'll know we're on the move. We'll take the rucksack but let's leave the pad and your coat here. It won't be a problem tracking him Bets. To quote one of your earthly phrases we'll turn the taps on him.'

'The tables. Turn the tables. Are you doing that deliberately Crean?'

'As long as we're super-quiet,' Hugo went on, smiling but ignoring Bettony's question, 'we'll be able to check out what Timmbo's up to. You never know, perhaps he's found a new interest in Turtles.

'Good morning Mr Sneggs.'

Bollie's face, puffy and baggy-eyed with lack of sleep, loomed on the smartpad.

'Hello Mrs Ponch. This was quite an interesting puzzle you set me.'

'Did you meet with success?'

'Yes. Our adversaries from Erce had made some quite clever adjustments to Kevin and Mornder's transition programming. It took me nearly twenty minutes to work it out. Then it was just a question of unpicking it and mapping it.'

'So you can forward me co-ordinates for each successive transition?'

'Yes. That's the good news. But I'm afraid there's some bad news too...'

'What do you think happened here? On this version of our worlds?'

'Beats me.'

'Don't you find it interesting though Hugo? The idea that at some point in the distant past some tiny little thing happened differently, and as a result this version of Earth - of Erce - became an arid desert? So different to the worlds we know?'

'Not really. It happened. We can think about all that when we're sitting by the fireside back in a chilly Abbuth, clutching our mugs of cocoa. For now, we should focus on the job in hand... Speaking of which I think we should leave Timmbo's tracks for a while and scoot up behind that low hill over to the left. I've got a feeling we're getting close. With a bit of luck we might be able to see what he's up to.' Hugo dropped his voice to a dramatic whisper. 'Tippy toes from now on Bets.'

They had been keeping ten metres to the left of Milden-Brewer's tracks. Now, they pulled further away to the left and began almost to double back on themselves, then veered to the right, circling behind the low hill, which was now between them and the tracks. Slowly and quietly they climbed the hill, dropping to all fours as they reached its top.

'Well well, look at that.'

Hugo dropped back behind the shelter of the hill and clutched his sides in helpless mirth. About fifty metres away Bettony could make out a human shape, sitting on a low rock next to a stagnant pool, rifle in hand.

'What's he doing?'

It took a while for Hugo to regain control of himself to the point where he could trust himself to speak.

'I suppose it's possible that he could be fishing. But it's my considered guess that he's followed my friend the turtle and is waiting for me to appear, god-like, from the water.'

'I thought you people were highly trained at tracking? How come Timmbo couldn't spot the difference between your footprints and those of a four-footed amphibian? Hugo? Hugo stop laughing.'

Something in Bettony's tone brought Hugo back to his senses.

'I'm sorry. It's the way he's sitting there, waiting for me. It just looks hilarious...'

'Crean! Be quiet! He'll hear you laughing.'

'There's a lesson for us all there Bets. Follow the physical evidence. Don't rely on technology. It's the whole "follow your SatNav into the river" thing.'

'You've done that have you?'

'Me? Of course not. Not recently anyway.' Hugo pulled himself together. 'Right. I'm afraid this is the closest we can get to Timmbo without him seeing us. If that happened in this terrain the situation would change very rapidly, what with him having a rifle and everything. I wonder how long my old chum will be content to sit and wait for me? If he's here when night falls we could work something out. Cover of darkness and all that. But he might decide to head off to his tent for refreshments before then. If that's the case, I'd rather be there before him. There are opportunities over there for getting up-close and personal before he can use his rifle. Same goes for if he decides to go and pay you a visit.' Hugo stared into space. 'What would you do Bets? If you were Timmbo?'

'If I were a psychotic killer who had finally tracked down my injured turtle-god enemy to a stagnant pool a couple of miles away from my tent?'

'That's pretty much it.'

'Have I remembered to put some food and water in my pockets?'

'Aha. Good question.' Hugo considered. 'I'm pretty sure Timmbo would remember that part of his training, yes.'

'I'd wait then. But since I can track my turtle-god and I'm not too worried about him limping away to safety, I might withdraw in the heat of the day to somewhere not too far away with a bit of shade.'

'Another good point.' Hugo poked his head over the top of the hill and scanned the ground. 'There's not much shade anywhere in this awful place. Must be dreadful in high summer. There's a dip on the other side of this hill that's a bit shady. Down at the bottom where it steepens a bit. Hullo! Target on the move.' He dipped quickly down and sat next to Bettony. 'Looks like you were right. He's heading in our direction.'

'You don't think he saw you?'

'No chance.' Hugo smiled. 'We'll soon find out anyway.'

'You're so reassuring boy.'

Milden-Brewer was mystified. According to his smartpad - which he now had on maximum magnification - Hugo Crean had spent the last ten minutes swimming round and round underwater, just a few yards in front of him. Now, Crean had come to rest, still underwater.

He must have rigged up some sort of breathing tube. Was he waiting, even now, for Timm to give up and walk away, thinking him drowned? Milden-Brewer could think of no other explanation. He took a drink from his flask. The day was getting very warm. Milden-Brewer decided to seek some shade. He could still keep watch on Crean with his smartpad. If the man was somehow monitoring Timm's movements, perhaps this would encourage him to break cover. It was extremely odd behaviour though, even for Crean.

Still puzzling over Hugo's movements, Milden-Brewer got up and looked around for shade. The only real place was the bottom of a low hill, a little way to the south. He wandered across and settled down as best he could on the hard ground.

He wondered what the freak was doing. He had not checked on her for a while. He switched contacts and the grid zoomed out, Crean's identifier being replaced by hers. Good. She was still in the same place. Milden-Brewer double-checked her position with his Sentinnat locator. It agreed.

Hi Cuddlybits, he messaged. *Shouldn't be too much longer. All well here. Plenty to tell you. Please stay put for now!*

That sounded like it was a message from Crean, he thought, mistakenly.

Close by, Hugo and Bettony lay back against the south-facing side of the hill, protected from sight by its brow. Bettony was straining her ears, listening hard for anything that would tell her TMB was approaching. Her heart was thumping. She was sure her breath was loud enough for Timmbo to hear. She looked at Hugo. His eyes were closed and a smile twitched at his mouth. He appeared to be completely unconcerned and enjoying some private joke. For a moment she thought he was asleep. But some sixth sense seemed to tell him that Bettony was watching him: He opened his eyes wide and turned to her, then opened and closed his mouth several times, fish-like, and started shaking with silent laughter. Bettony glared at him.

'Sorry' he whispered, so quietly she could hardly hear him. 'You don't know what it's like being a turtle-god.'

The day dragged on. Bettony felt an almost-irresistible urge to move but did not dare to, for fear of scattering stones and alerting Milden-Brewer. The February sun gave up its struggle to get any higher in the sky and soon began to drop towards the horizon. She thought it would be too weak to burn her, but the air was very warm, and weak as it was the sunshine was uncomfortable. She felt sweaty and dirty and increasingly thirsty. She dared not risk opening her water bottle. Hugo continued to give every impression of a man at rest. His body radiated relaxation. His breathing was light and regular. Bettony wondered if he really had fallen asleep; but she also guessed that the slightest noise would bring him to his senses.

Eventually the daylight faded. Bettony heard stones clunking against each other as TMB moved. The sounds became fainter. Hugo turned onto his stomach and crawled to the brow of the hill.

'He's going back to worship at my shrine,' he whispered. 'And so he should.'

'He's going to need to eat and drink sooner or later. He's not going to wait till it gets dark is he? If he sets off for his tent before we do we might lose the chance of taking him by surprise. Maybe we should get going. Find somewhere around his tent to ambush him.'

Hugo was about to question Bettony's use of the terms We and Ambush, but something in her expression told him not to. Instead he meekly agreed, and they quietly retraced their steps around the hill, picking up Milden-Brewer's tracks and keeping them some ten metres to their left.

Dusk brought with it a layer of cloud that seemed to form from nowhere in the sky. When the last feeble glow of the sun's light disappeared it would once again be very dark.

'I could think of better places to go for my holidays,' Hugo murmured as they trudged along in the deepening gloom.

'Where did you go when you were on Erce?'

'My family have a villa and some land near Barcelona. It can get too hot in high summer though so we usually go to the shooting lodge in July.' He took in Bettony's look of disapproval. 'I used to walk Bets. Over the moors. I'm not a fan of using animals for target practice.'

They found TMB's wrecked camp without any difficulty and settled themselves behind a rock, looking down on the dip which contained it.

'You did a good job boy.'

'I try my best. May I respectfully suggest that you let me have first dibs at Timmbo, and hold yourself back ready to come to my rescue if I struggle.'

'I suppose.'

'Are you comfortable?'

'More or less.'

'Radio silence then Bets. He can be very quiet when he wants to, can our Timmbo. I suspect we might hear his reaction to my handiwork though.'

'Shhh...'

The night was almost as warm as the day. Milden-Brewer had resumed his position on the edge of the pool, checking his smartpad from time to time. He wondered if Crean had thrown his own pad into the pool, but he knew that was wrong - he had of course seen the last of Crean disappearing into the murky depths. And if Golden Boy had thrown the pad into the water, it wouldn't have circled round and round...

Milden-Brewer had not slept much the previous night. For one thing, it had been a hectic time, and on those occasions when the chance for rest presented itself he had been too excited. Finally his carefully-laid plans were coming to fruition! Milden-Brewer did not possess Hugo's ability to cat-nap. Now, sitting in the darkness and the quiet, he felt the relaxation of sleep creeping over him...

He came to with a start, immediately followed by a surge of fear that Crean had used the time to steal up on him. All was silent but Milden-Brewer knew how quiet Hugo could be. Quickly and noiselessly he dropped behind the rock he had been dozing on. After five minutes of complete stillness he carefully reached up and placed his smartpad on the rock, turned it on and quickly crouched down again. The pad's faint blue-green light shone out in the darkness. A further ten minutes passed before Milden-Brewer dared to pull it from the rock and check on Crean's position.

Damn! He had been asleep for four hours and Crean's locator had disappeared. Milden-Brewer had set his grid to maximum magnification to observe Crean's peculiar progress - or lack of it - around the pool; now he reset it to automatic. The scale changed and placed Crean at least a couple of miles away, heading south-east. Milden-Brewer selected the All-Friends option, and noted that Crean had passed well to the east of the freak. So they had not met up then. At least that was something. Crean appeared to be heading for the sea. Well good luck on that one! He was moving slowly, Milden-Brewer guessed his leg was a problem. Maybe he could still have some fun hunting down an increasingly desperate Hugo Crean.

Not tonight though. He had not expected to be away from camp for so long, and had long since exhausted his supplies of food and water. He switched his Sentinnat locator on and noted that it confirmed the freak's position before using it to guide his way back to camp. He had left a tracking bud in the camp and congratulated himself on his foresight.

The freak had not moved all day, Milden-Brewer reflected. Not a surprise really. He consoled himself with the wildly inaccurate idea that a woman needed a man to tell her what to do. Leave them alone and after a while they become completely clueless.

Bettony woke with a start. Something was prodding her in her side. It was dark now, although not quite as completely black as the previous night.

'Only me,' Hugo's voice whispered close to her ear. 'You were snoring. Don't worry, no harm done. He's taking his time though.'

'Do you think he spotted us?'

'Heard you, more likely. No. You'd only just started - hang on. Something noisy this way comes. Heavens, he's even got his torch on.'

Confident in his knowledge that Crean and the freak were both several miles away, TMB was hurrying back to camp. He was looking forward to something to eat and drink and a good night's sleep. What remained of the night, anyway. His camp had been well-chosen and was well-concealed until he was almost upon it; as a result, he only became aware of the mess Hugo had made of it when he began treading on tattered shreds of the canvas.

'What the hell...' He began to play his torch around.

Bettony was aware that Hugo was no longer by her side. Moments later, a second dark shape seemed to materialise out of thin air behind Milden-Brewer, and at the same time that Milden-Brewer started to moan with dismay she heard Hugo's pleasant voice say 'Evening all.'

Hugo's Tipper sliced through the leather strap holding Milden-Brewer's rifle and pulled it away from him. Lesson one in the Sentinnat training manual: Take every opportunity to improve the odds in your favour. But TMB reacted with impressive speed. He knew that his rifle was useless in close combat; he also knew that Crean had got his Tipper in his hand whereas Timm's was out of reach. He was further hampered because he was holding his smartpad in one hand, using it to light his way, and his precious transition box in the other. Crean was inches behind him and Milden-Brewer knew all the combat moves that were open to the man, any one of which was about to be inflicted on him. Without consciously thinking about it - still reeling with terror at the shock - he pushed the transition box backwards into Hugo's stomach, pressing the activator as he did so, and - just - managed to withdraw his hand before the box cracked into life.

Hugo's gasp of pain sounded briefly, then faded away. Silence returned, broken only by Milden-Brewer's laboured breathing.

Hugo had gone.

CHAPTER SIXTEEN

I'll kill you yet

Frozen with horror and disbelief, Bettony hid behind her rock and watched Milden-Brewer. His first reaction was a crowing, shaky laugh; then he played his torch around the wreckage of his camp, taking in the full implications of its destruction. He let out a chilling scream that was a mixture of rage, insanity and fear. Bettony watched as he stormed around. In the gloom, with the only light coming from his torch, it was difficult for her to be sure it was the man she knew as Tweek Golgood.

He had started off by kicking wildly at his tattered possessions. That soon changed to a desperate scrabbling attempt to retrieve whatever he could. He began to make a strange noise, a mixture of a whimper and a sob.

'I'll kill you yet you bastard Crean' he shouted. He found a water bottle somewhere that Hugo had not destroyed, and drank greedily from it. Bettony watched him gather the shredded remains of his sleeping bag and the canvas, and arranged them into a sort of nest, into which he threw himself. She could hear him, still whimpering. After a while this subsided, replaced by heavy and regular breathing, and soon Milden-Brewer's snores filled the night air.

Bettony raked the dry ground with her hands until she found a good-sized rock. Quietly, and very slowly, gripping the rock in one hand, she rose from her hiding place and advanced towards the lip of the hollow in which Milden-Brewer was nestled.

'Well well well. What have we got here?'

A voice that promised violence.

The short-lived pain from the transition box was still coursing through Hugo. He was lying on a grubby wet pavement on a badly-lit street, still momentarily paralysed and holding the transition box. Where had the Coppler gone? He had a vague idea that he was dropping it as he transitioned. He watched two large men approaching and recognised their uniform. Black bomber jackets, black trousers tucked into heavy duty boots that laced halfway up their calves. Good boots for kicking with. Each man held a heavy stick. Oh no. Oh no, no, no.

Hugo forced himself to his feet, still groggy from the transition. He knew that he needed to be very quick. Once these thugs started laying into him it would be too late for explanations.

With an effort of will he summoned all the authority at his disposal.

'I'm Sentinnat. Keep your fucking distance.'

It was not often that anyone spoke to the militia like that. It paused them long enough for Hugo to unroll his sleeve. He felt the effects of the transition box melt away; felt his strength returning as he held out the inside of his forearm, showing them a circular tattoo.

The sight of the tattoo had an interesting effect on the two militiamen. A look of horror replaced the leering grimaces on their faces; their bodies seemed to lose aggression, to sag with fear.

'Shit' the slightly less large of them said.

'I'm sorry sir,' said the one who had previously spoken. 'We didn't recognise you.'

'Take me to your office. I need to contact Mazeley. Now!'

The word Mazeley seemed to inspire fresh horror. The two men formed up respectfully on either side of Hugo, marching – more or less – in time as they led him through the foul, darkened streets. Once or twice Hugo saw shadows shrink away into alleyways. Probably a good job these two goons came across me, he thought. It's safety, of a kind.

The militia office was a squat, ugly structure that stood slightly apart from those around it, as though the other buildings were trying to edge away from it. The militiamen led Hugo through the reinforced doors and up to the desk. The man behind the desk smiled unpleasantly at Crean.

'What have we got here then? Out after curfew sonny? Oh dear oh dear.'

'He's Sentinnat sarge,' the militiaman said urgently. 'We've seen the Authority. He wants to contact Mazeley.'

As with the two men standing beside him, Hugo saw fear hit the sergeant like a gut-punch. He could actually see the colour drain from the man's face as he stood, mouth open, petrified.

'Just point me to a phone,' Hugo said, wearily.

'Sir you can use this one.' The sergeant unbolted the access to his little area and respectfully held it open for Hugo to pass through.

She could not attack Timmbo from here. She wanted to creep close to him and then bring the rock down on his head. Bettony pulled back from the lip of the hollow and tried to work out a route that would bring her around and on to a path that would lead her to him. It was not easy in the darkness.

It was at this moment that she felt a sharp scratching at her hand. She looked down at the rock she was holding and thought she could make out something like four little crabs, one at each corner. Her brain was beginning to come to the conclusion that they were feet when to her horror she watched what appeared to be a long snake push out from the middle of one end of the rock. She let out an involuntary shriek and dropped it. The noise was enough to wake Milden-Brewer who suddenly sat up.

'Who's there? Crean is that you?'

Bettony dropped to the ground. The baby turtle was close to her face. She watched its neck extend grotesquely outwards, its head swaying this way and that, until it was three times the length of the shell. It swung around until it was almost touching her nose. She could hear it making tiny rasps – of disapproval, she guessed. She felt sick but did not dare to move.

Milden-Brewer stood up, trying to peer into the gloom. She could make out his head and shoulders above the lip of the hollow.

'Who's there?' He repeated. He played his torch around but did not move. Eventually he settled down again. The turtle's head retracted into its shell and the feet disappeared. It became once more indistinguishable from the rocks around it.

But how many of them were really rocks? Bettony wondered. Her heart was still thudding hard. This lifeless place suddenly felt very creepy.

Another five minutes and Timmbo's snores once again filled the night air. Timing her movements to coincide with his snores, Bettony stood up and slowly edged away. She knew that this was still a good opportunity to surprise TMB, but could not bring herself to pick up another rock. She needed rest too. She was shaking with nervous and physical exhaustion. She had to get away. She also desperately wanted to get back to her smartpad before Timmbo grabbed it.

It was her only hope of escaping from this hateful world.

Working more from memory than anything else, she tried to retrace her steps. After ten minutes she was completely lost.

'Hugo? What the devil?'

Hugo correctly interpreted this as a request for explanation. He was also pleased to hear that he was still 'Hugo', and not 'Crean'.

'My apologies for calling you so late in the evening sir but it's rather urgent. I have some news for you.'

I'm like a man with a spade, trying to dig his way out of a hole, Hugo thought. But on the spur of the moment he could think of no other way of getting himself out of Regency Swindon. And he certainly wanted to get himself out of Regency Swindon. The place was almost like a private fiefdom for the Brandon Bowles family. Contacting the Regency Earl of Weymouth should allow him to escape the clutches of County Lord Lieutenant Roland Brandon Bowles. Hugo had vivid memories of an altercation with Meredith Brandon Bowles at Hinton. No-one ever came well out of an altercation with Hugo, and Brandon Bowles certainly hadn't. Hugo did not want the inaccurately-named Merry exacting revenge. The Brandon Bowles were well-known for their long and vindictive memories.

There was one thing about Weymouth - what he lacked in intelligence, he more than made up for in low cunning.

'Calling from Swindon, I understand?'

'Yes sir.'

'Put the desk sergeant on.'

Hugo handed the telephone to the man standing next to him. He watched the sergeant's face turn further to jelly as he listened to one of the most feared and powerful men in the country. A leading member of the Regency Cabinet itself.

'...Of course I'll do that Sir. Straight away Sir... Yes Sir. I'll have to let my lord Brandon...' More melting of face. 'Please don't do that Sir. Yes... yes Sir. Right away Sir.'

The sergeant passed the phone back to Hugo. His hand was shaking. Weymouth's voice crackled out of the earpiece.

'Look here Hugo I've told that buffoon to drive you directly here. If he tries to take you anywhere else just kill him.'

'Sir.'

'Quick as you can then.'

The two militiamen who had brought Hugo into the office could not know what words had been spoken by the Earl. But they could see the effect on their sergeant. His paralysing terror leached out of him like the smell of stale sweat and made its way through the air to the two of them. Wide-eyed, they watched him lead Hugo out of the back of the office. No-one spoke.

There was a heavy, large-wheeled car sitting on its own at the back of the building. The sergeant led Hugo over to it without speaking. Hugo wondered if the man was fit to drive. If they were stopped, though, it would be better if the sergeant were driving.

The militiaman started the car up and crashed it into gear. They lurched out of the compound and onto the road outside. Despite the cruel, bullying reputation of the Regency militia – particularly that part of it which occupied Swindon – Hugo felt a pang of pity for the man.

'I'm guessing that you're under orders to report anything like this to the CLL's office' he said. The man looked at him. 'My lord Brandon Bowles...' he began, then he turned back to the road, and negotiated a corner. When he spoke again his voice was low and clear with the certainty of what he was saying. 'My life's not worth shit now,' he said. 'And it's not just me. It's my family.' He focussed on the road, then spoke again. His voice changed, became high-pitched, almost child-like in its fear. 'His Grace the Earl said that if I don't follow his orders to the letter I will die a very slow and painful death.' He sobbed. 'Along with my family. But if I don't tell the CLL's office they'll kill us all anyway.'

'Corner!' Shouted Hugo. The sergeant wrenched at the wheel and managed to keep his car on the road. This is not going to end well, Hugo thought.

'How well can you trust your men?' He asked.

'Those two? The two who brought you in?'

'The very same.'

'They're ok.'

'Do you think they'll telephone the CLL's office?'

The sergeant laughed grimly. 'No chance!' He replied. 'Keep out of it, keep your head down. That's the only way to survive.'

'Right then. This never happened.'

'What do you mean?'

'When we get to the checkpoint can you come up with an excuse for leaving town?'

'I... suppose so.'

There was a little more confidence in the man's voice now. *He's done it before*, thought Hugo. *Wandered out, up to goodness knows what. Getting past the checkpoint won't be a problem.*

'I'll duck down. Put me in the boot if you like. Tell them you're out for a drive or whatever you normally say. When we get to Mazeley, drop me outside the gates. I'll make sure that no-one knows about you. When you get back, tell the two... constables... that this never happened, on the orders of His Grace.'

The man actually sobbed. 'Oh thank you sir. Thank you.'

'What's your name?'

Sluckham sir. Sergeant Sluckham.'

'Well concentrate on the road now Sergeant Sluckham. It would be a shame if you totalled us both before we got to Mazeley.'

'Ha! Yes sir. God bless you. Woops! We're ok. Thank you sir.'

Bettony sat on a rock. At least, she thought it might be a rock. She was lost. And so very weary.

And then her first piece of good luck in quite a long time happened. The clouds parted, and the land was flooded with the light of a three-quarter moon. She looked up, so used to straining her eyes at the gloom that this almost felt to her like daylight. She realised that she had veered off northwards, and that the range of hills was now directly behind her.

She might not be able to find her tracks, but she had a pretty good idea where she needed to be. An hour later and she was scrambling up the hill. Not too long after that and she had reached its top. It took her another half an hour to find her coat and her smartpad. She pulled the bottle of water from her coat and added it to the collection in her rucksack; then she stuffed the coat behind a rock. She opened out her pad and quickly checked on Milden-Brewer's position. Bettony de-linked him and watched his identifier disappear from her screen. Sitting back against the side of the hill, she looked over the bare landscape before her. The white ground almost shone in the moonlight. In the distance, the ocean was a darker area that twinkled with wave-reflected moonlight.

She wanted to sleep but knew she had to put distance between Timmbo and herself. The easiest way to do that was to strike out across the open plain in front of her; but that was also the easiest place for Timmbo to track her. The ground was flat and there was nowhere for her to hide.

On the other hand, there would be a tide.

Bettony stumbled eastwards along the ridge of the hill for half an hour. May as well make it as difficult for him as possible, she thought. She walked down the slope and onto the plain. The sea was further away than it looked, but after an hour's steady walking she reached soft white sand. Soon water was lapping around her joggers. She guessed that the tide was coming in. Good! More of her footprints would be wiped away.

A vague plan was forming in Bettony's mind.

CHAPTER SEVENTEEN

Oh dearie dearie me

'Hugo!' Weymouth's greeting was good-natured but with a hint of impatience. 'This had better be good young man. I'm supposed to be at the opera. The countess will not be a happy bunny.' Hugo guessed it was the thought of the countess's reaction, rather than missing a feast of culture, that was troubling the Earl. If anything he seemed to be relieved. And interested.

'I'm sorry sir. I thought it wisest to come directly to you as soon as I could.' Hugo had had time during Sluckham's erratic drive to think things through, and like with Bettony, vague plans were forming in his mind too. His conclusions from what he had learned were startlingly plausible. Most likely, they had more than a grain of truth in them, but more importantly they sounded believable, at least in his own head. And that was the important thing: that they were believable. That mattered more than if they were true. They would have to be believable enough to get him out of this. It was the best he could do.

But he was still living by the second here, judging his words on the other man's reactions. Despite his warning, Weymouth seemed glad of an excuse to miss his opera. An important clandestine meeting, Hugo thought, was a good reason for missing out on a couple of hours of screeching and wailing by implausibly heavy and aged "young lovers" as they negotiated a Regency opera's convoluted plot and its impenetrable melodies. Hugo had every confidence in his ability to make his story convincing; exactly why it was clandestine would become apparent as he went along.

'Did they give you any problems in Swindon? What the devil were you doing there?'

And then Hugo saw what lay behind the Earl's question. And a wild hope burst into existence in his mind with such force that he almost laughed.

'Your words were enough to persuade the sergeant to bring me here, sir. I suspect he's a loyal man. A Regency man.'

Yes! There it was. A spark of something in Weymouth's eyes.

Hugo had played enough poker to know that sometimes you could win with a losing hand by throwing everything you had into one magnificent bluff. He had to win this one, and quickly. There was no alternative. Losing meant everything could unravel. What would follow would be a painful death, or at the very least being disappeared to Hablock for some "treatment".

They were standing in the reception hall at Mazeley. Weymouth motioned Hugo into the lift, followed him and punched in a code that would take them to the top floor. He waited until the life doors had closed before asking, 'What have you discovered?'

Hugo chose his words carefully. 'Sir, I'm not sure if you're aware that the alien spaceship has been moved to Swindon?'

The twitch of alarm that burst across Weymouth's face was perfect. 'What!'

'I was taken there to make the trip to Abbuth. Something of a surprise, but orders are orders sir. Still, it raised questions.'

'I bet it damn well did. Swindon!'

'Of course I have been following orders on Abbuth, but I have also been... sensitive... to any unusual actions by our people.'

'What's that thing in your hand?'

'It's a device that has been developed by - agent Wellbeck - for space travel. It's how I managed to get back here sir.'

'By Wellbeck! You mean Milden-Brewer, Hugo? Let's not mince our words.'

'Sir. By Milden-Brewer.'

'Do our people know about this... thing?' Weymouth waved his hand at the transition box.

'If I'm right sir, the answer to your question will be "no".'

'Damn it man. Do you know what you're suggesting?'

'Sir.' Hugo decided to throw the last of his chips on the table. It had been common knowledge for a while that the Brandon Bowleses were consolidating an unusual amount of power through their base at Swindon; suspected by some that they would eventually use it to launch a power grab on the Regency itself. Angland under the Regency was always a ferment of alliances and plots, some more real than others. Crean was gambling everything now on the insecurity that this created in the minds of those in power. For all he knew, the rumours – and his own conclusions – could easily be true.

'It's my belief that Milden-Brewer has been inserting colleagues into Abbuth who are sympathetic to County Lord Lieutenant Brandon Bowles. I believe he's running a separate information gathering exercise to that of the Sentinnat.'

Weymouth's face had gone puce with rage. The lift stopped, and he pushed through the doors even as they were opening. He stormed down a well-lit, opulent corridor. He pushed open the heavy oak door that led into his office, walked over to his secretary's desk and punched a button on a console.

'Your grace?' A man's disembodied voice crackled from the console.

'My office. Now.' Weymouth growled. He turned to Hugo. 'So what's your idea Hugo?'

'I can only assume that CLL Brandon Bowles is seeking to gain knowledge from Abbuth for his own purposes.'

Weymouth slammed his large fist onto the desk. 'I damn well knew he was up to something.'

The door was open but the man who was now standing next to it still knocked, deferentially.

'Your Grace?' He nodded to Hugo, who recognised the thuggish features of the Honourable Wilko Bunsen. Honourable! Almost as much of a misnomer as Merry Brandon Bowles, Hugo reflected, as he nodded back.

'Why didn't I know that the spaceship had been moved to Swindon?' Thundered Weymouth. Bunsen looked at him blanky. 'Oh for Jupiter's sake' Weymouth went on. 'Am I surrounded by cretins? Have you ever seen one of these before? Show him, Hugo.'

Hugo held the transition box up with some misgivings. The last thing he wanted to do was to give advanced scientific instruments to the Regency. But there was no choice.

'Be careful Wilko,' he said, handing it over. 'I've got a feeling it might be booby-trapped. I wouldn't put anything past Timm Milden-Brewer.' Bunsen raised his eyebrows at the use of TMB's name. He hesitantly took the transition box and examined it carefully.

'Booby trapped?' questioned Weymouth. 'But you used it to travel back here?'

I thought it was worth the risk sir,' Hugo replied modestly. If Bunsen activated it, he thought, chances were there would be a loud crack and Bunsen would painfully disappear to enlighten some other universe with his unreconstructed philosophies. It would certainly look as though it had been booby-trapped.

'Mmph. Good man. Good man. Well Bunsen? Seen one before?'

'No your Grace.'

'Damn well thought not! Get Peckler here. You think Peckler's sound, Hugo?'

'Yes sir.' *Up to a point.*

Bettony splashed her way along the warm, moonlit shore. All this needs is a bar, she thought. Something a bit ramshackle, made out of wood, with a world-weary barman and a few people sitting around it on stools. And some decent gin.

She had taken her shoes and socks off and had paddled along the water's edge for a fair distance. It was time to head inland, she thought. She dried her feet as best she could and put her socks and joggers back on. The ridge that separated this side of the country from the side with Milden-Brewer was much lower here. She dragged herself over to it, climbed until she found somewhere she could hide herself away, and fell into a deep, exhausted sleep, her head cushioned by the rucksack.

Peckler had been summoned from his evening by the fireside and was standing in the inner office of the Earl of Weymouth, in front of the Earl himself. Weymouth was seated at his large oak desk. Hugo and Wilko Bunsen stood respectfully either side of him.

Peckler was deeply uncomfortable. The spacecraft had originally been centred around an inlet on the Cornish coast; but he knew that it had been moved to Swindon. Peckler was as aware as everyone else of the tensions between the Brandon Bowleses and some members of the Cabinet. He had thought it wouldn't be long before there would be a change in the Cabinet's membership and had decided to turn a blind eye. He did not want to antagonise any of the Brandon Bowleses, but now Crean had shone a new light on their schemes. Peckler guessed that they were planning rather more than simply muscling their way onto the Cabinet.

Peckler's whole career had been built on careful positioning. He had built a reputation for diligent hard work. A go-to man for difficult tasks. He had maintained friendly contacts with important people but had never closely aligned himself with one faction or another. His lack of what they called "breeding" - of links to an important family - had prevented him being considered for the very highest roles, but had helped him to maintain a fairly safe degree of independence. He was very skilful in navigating Regency politics. His betrayals were done in the dark, with a stiletto knife in the back, and never in daylight with a sword to the chest. He thought he would survive any change of control. Any government, however brutal, needed people like Peckler to make it function. But if the Brandon Bowleses mounted a coup - if they took complete control - then the waters would be choppy indeed. It would be dog-eat-dog. And that would just be among the Brandon Bowleses. Peckler doubted that anyone would survive for long.

He was being forced to choose.

So yes, he admitted to a furious Weymouth, he had heard about the spaceship being moved. He had assumed the Cabinet had approved everything. Timm Milden-Brewer, after all, was the nephew of Viscount Milden-Brewer –

'I don't need a history lesson in the family of a traitor!' Thundered Weymouth. 'Get me a list of everyone in his network.'

Peckler glanced meaningfully at Crean and Bunsen. But his grace the Earl of Weymouth - Podger to his friends - was well beyond meaningful glances.

'Fucking now!' He shouted.

Peckler hurried away.

Perfect, Hugo thought. Get me a copy too Pecky. And why not bring some coffee and cake while you're at it? He concentrated on staring at the wall in front of him and keeping his expression completely deadpan.

'Hugo, can you get back to this - this other place?'

'I'll find a way sir.' He could be sure of that, what with the beacon in his pocket and Mrs P poised and waiting for the call. In any case, you never said No to a man like Weymouth.

'Mmph. Damn good work you've done here Hugo. There'll be a promotion coming your way once this is all settled. And I'll damn well see it settled.' Weymouth's tone was lightening as he spoke.

'I'm seeing your father next week. Taking the lady wife over to Dephwood for dinner. He'll be proud to know how you're doing.'

'Thank you sir.'

'In the meantime - think you can run the network in this Abbuth place?'

Oh happy birthday Hugo!

'Yes sir.'

'Good. Good man. Ah here's Peckler.'

Peckler was aware of the Earl's limited grasp of even the most basic technology, and had printed out the list. He placed it on the desk. Bunsen and Crean both peered at it from behind Weymouth's shoulders.

Fifteen pairs of names. The agent's real name on Erce, and their false one on Abbuth.

'Why are there stars next to a couple of the names?' Weymouth asked suspiciously.

'The stars indicate a direct one-for-one replacement,' Peckler explained. 'The originals are brought here for interrogation. Some, such as young Hugo here are given completely fake identities. Most of the stars were uncovered last year. You know, the business with –'

'Yes yes I know' Weymouth interrupted impatiently. He turned to Hugo. 'How many of these are with us?'

Hugo was trying to suppress his astonishment at what he was looking at.

'It's difficult to say sir. None of us on the ground in Britannia have any contact with anyone other than Milden-Brewer.' He decided to stir the pot a little, and assumed a puzzled expression. 'I'm sure there are more of us than this though sir.'

'Mmph. Pull Milden-Brewer in Peckler. Make him talk. On my authority.'

Peckler looked even more uncomfortable. 'Yes sir.'

'Something wrong Peckler?'

The briefest of uncomfortable pauses.

'We're not able to contact him directly sir. We rely on him to get in touch with us. He signs in on a weekly basis unless he has something urgent for us. That's when he picks his messages up.'

Weymouth was becoming irritated at Peckler's evasion.

'Then tell him when he next signs in. When is that?'

There was another brief but very noticeable pause before Peckler replied. 'He should have signed in two days ago sir.'

'Bloody hell Peckler! Hugo do you know anything about this?'

Hugo was still living on his wits but he felt that things were going his way. 'I think something's building to a climax sir. It's why I risked coming back to warn you. If I may make a suggestion?'

'Go ahead.'

'If I can get myself back I could pull some of these people in and deliver them to ACLL Peckler for interrogation.'

'How will you get back Hugo?' Peckler's question was deceptively gentle but the Earl had clearly lost patience with him.

'He got himself here didn't he? He –'

Bunsen's limited attention span had become exhausted. He had begun to fiddle with the transition box. Hugo had spotted this but kept quiet. If Wilko vanished, he thought, accompanied by a loud crack, it would only add to the entertainment value.

What happened was entirely different. Bunsen's agonised scream interrupted the Earl who recoiled in horror, stumbling to his feet and backing away from the man and into Hugo. The three men stared at Bunsen, who was apparently still screaming, although his voice had quickly faded away. It very quickly became apparent that Bunsen's voice was about to be joined by the rest of him. They could still see his face, contorted in a mix of agony and horror, eyes wide and mouth still open. But they could also begin to see the wall behind him - see it through his body. As the moments passed, there was less and less Wilko visible and more and more wall. He was slowly vanishing, frozen in place except for his eyes, which were still moving around as though desperately seeking a way to escape. Eventually – although in reality no more than a few seconds had passed – Wilko disappeared, eyes and all.

There was a shocked silence. Nobody moved. The three of them still stared at the vacant space that had previously been occupied by the Honourable Wilko Bunsen. Then a voice spoke from nowhere.

'Oh dearie dearie me. Who's going to be next?'

It was the voice of Timm Milden-Brewer.

'Fucking hell.' The Earl was almost whispering. Silence returned.

Hugo forced himself to speak.

'Sir? Your Grace? Perhaps we should get you out of here?'

'I'm all right Hugo.' Weymouth moved to put himself where Bunsen had been standing. He waved his hand around in the air.

'Strangest thing I've ever seen,' he said.

Nobody really wanted to move yet. Weymouth sat down again. He reached into one of his desk drawers and pulled out a whisky bottle and three glasses. He poured a generous measure into each, and handed them out with shaking hands.

'To Wilko,' he said. 'A bit of a pratt, if I'm honest. But a loyal one.'

'To Wilko.'

'To Wilko.'

When Bettony woke the morning sun was low and shining directly at her, its light magnified by the reflection from the white ground. She pulled a water bottle from her rucksack and drank, then ate a breakfast of melty chocolate and broken biscuits and reviewed her options.

There were two ways, she felt, that she could escape this world. She could get herself back to somewhere close to the Two's transition point, and wait. Alternatively, she could leave Friendslink open and permanently searching for contacts who she trusted, and hope that one of her friends would have a link open if they arrived in the Two.

Without really knowing why, Bettony fully expected Hugo to find his way back to her, and to bring help with him. He had the emergency beacon, after all. He would activate the beacon, Mrs Ponch would be able to locate him, and she would pilot the Two here, just like she had piloted it to the world where Brian and Paulette eked out their miserable existence.

Easy.

Each approach had its drawbacks. Hanging around the transition point would risk being found by Timmbo. She thought of a nature documentary she had once watched. Lions hid themselves around a watering hole, waiting for tasty lunch to wander up in search of a drink. Timmbo was not a lion, and she thought she would offer him more challenge than a wildebeest would to a lion. But still. On the other hand leaving Friendslink open and actively searching for friends would drain its battery. She also feared that Milden-Brewer could somehow still trace her smartpad's signal.

Of course, Timmbo was seriously short on supplies. Bettony doubted that he would last much more than a day on this inhospitable planet without fresh water. To defeat Timm Milden-Brewer, all she really had to do was wait.

A message popped up on her smartpad. From Kagh! Bettony's spirits lifted, then immediately plummeted. She hesitated, finger over the message tab. Surely Timmbo had been posing as Kagh when he had set all this off, a couple of days ago?

Eventually Bettony opened the message.

Five days to go. Enjoy!

She felt a turbulent mixture of fear and anger. He had to be bluffing.

Wasn't he?

Milden-Brewer sat back in his nest of shredded material. He'd found enough water among the wreckage to last him for a maybe a day. After that there was nothing except the stagnant pool he had tracked Crean to the previous day. Timm did not fancy trying to drink that sickening, poisonous sludge.

He was completely trapped. He had sent his transition box to Erce along with Crean – in that moment there had been nothing else he could do – but the action had sealed his fate. He had trapped himself on a lifeless planet with no hope of escape. Even his supplies would only have delayed the inevitable. Without them, death would simply come more quickly.

The thought of dying terrified him.

Damn Crean! Damn the freak!

Well at least there was still something that he could do. At least he could kill the freak.

Milden-Brewer searched carefully through the wreckage. He found five pieces of broken biscuit and ate them. He sipped at the remains of his water, opened out his smartpad and cursed. The freak had disappeared. Bizarrely, Crean's identifier was still visible and was now showing him to be some miles out to sea. Maybe Crean was not so dumb after all; maybe he had somehow programmed his friendslink to give out false location signals. Whatever. Timm knew that Golden Boy was not on this planet.

First thing then: Use his tracking skills to find the freak. With his supplies low, there was no time to lose. There was always the outside possibility that Ponch or Glank or someone would mount a rescue and if Timm had the freak's smartpad he might yet survive.

He was still able to message the freak, even if he could not locate her.

Five days to go. Enjoy!

If nothing else that cheered Timm up.

CHAPTER EIGHTEEN

Mano a Womano

My trouble is, I don't like to run away. All through the two previous days I had been itching to get at Timmbo Miserable-Brewster, and most of the time I'd had to hide and run. The only time things had changed had been when Hugo was around.

But Timmbo no longer had his gun and he no longer had the advantage of knowing where I was. We were both stuck on this hot dead world with a few strange turtles for company. And the creep had just sent me another of his stupid threats.

Had he really found extra supplies? Hugo had made a pretty good job of trashing his camp. Perhaps he had another store somewhere. If not, all I needed to do was wait. I was pretty confident that he couldn't find me. He would dehydrate and without putting too fine a point on it he would cease to be a threat. But if he really did have food and water...

Despite the risk I was more or less decided on getting back to the transition point, or at least somewhere where I could see it. I thought I could dodge TMB, although I also knew there was a good chance that he would pick up my tracks.

So I took the decision to confront him. The quickest way to do that, I thought, would be to get back to where I had left my coat. Timmbo had stuck a tracking device on it and surely he would at least use that as a starting point. I could pick up a few decent rocks that really were rocks and have a go at ambushing him. If he was still alive when liberation arrived we could take him with us.

I'm not the best at directions. If I had been, I would never have arrived in Sputteridge in the first place and none of this would have happened. I would still be happily working in the marketing department of Happidog. Ok not happily. Anyway, enough to say that several hours later I was still looking for my coat.

★★ ★★ ★★

'What made you suspect Milden-Brewer Hugo?'

Being questioned by Peckler, Hugo thought, was a bit like being stretched on a rack. Each answer provoked a fresh question, picking away at the truth. Tightening the screw. But for once Hugo did not have a problem.

'Swindon.'

Peckler was good at hiding his true feelings but Hugo could see him flinch. He twisted the knife a bit more.

'It must have roused your suspicions sir?'

Peckler shifted uncomfortably in the chair next to Hugo. 'Ah yes. Yes it did. It was too soon to do anything, of course. Better to watch them and collect evidence before going to His Grace.' Peckler's face was completely expressionless. 'We are a disciplined organisation, Hugo. We do not lightly question the actions of our superiors.'

So that's how you're going to try and cover your back is it Pecky? Hugo thought. Good luck with that one. Aloud he said, 'Of course sir.'

'I'm a bit disappointed if I'm honest Hugo that you didn't try to warn me.'

Oh no you don't matey. 'Impossible, sir. And I took the first opportunity that presented itself to me to get back.'

'Indeed.'

A door opened further down the corridor from where the two men were sitting. A junior officer stepped out and walked to where Peckler and Hugo were sitting.

'ACLL Peckler, could you follow me please?'

Peckler visibly paled. He followed the young man into the committee room and Hugo was left alone.

It was not so many months ago, he thought, that he had waited in this very same place. It's probably going to be the very same people too. A bit of a different situation though. Especially for poor old Pecky.

It was eight in the morning now; that in itself was a measure of how serious this was. Senior members of the Regency Cabinet did not as a rule rise early in the morning and they did not like having their sleep disturbed. Or their breakfasts for that matter. Weymouth had had a private chat with Hugo an hour ago. He was still full of praise. His own suspicions had been more than confirmed; not that there was much hard evidence of course.

Except for Bunsen's bizarre death, and except for the fact that the spaceship had been moved to Swindon, everything that Hugo had offered was circumstantial or on his own word. But these were two big "excepts". And in the unstable politics of the Regency world a substantial rumour was more than enough to prompt action. Added to which was Weymouth's intense dislike and suspicion of the Brandon Bowleses. It was quite likely that they really were plotting something. They had certainly made themselves too powerful to be ignored, and although that power was still growing it was not yet big enough to stop them from being taken down. The situation was ripe for Weymouth to act against them and this was just the excuse he needed.

The Regency was a hotbed of this sort of politicking. You could almost say it thrived on it. Hugo had little doubt about the bloodbath that would be the final result, and little interest in it either. He was more concerned about getting back to the desert world before TMB could close in on Bettony. Thank goodness he still had the emergency beacon in his pocket. The problem was manoeuvring things so that he was both in a position to use it and also physically in a position to get into Mrs Ponch's spacecraft before anyone else. Hugo saw the urgency, but he also knew how important it was that he appeared to be the same relaxed man as always.

The door opened again and the same callow youth appeared. He beckoned to Hugo.

'Mr Dephwood Crean.'

I don't get a personal escort then, Hugo thought. Ah well.

And there they all were. Some of them looked a bit dishevelled, as though they had been physically pulled from their beds. Unlike previously, there was noticeable air of tension. Pecky was slumped in his chair, as though he had been pummelled. Probably had been.

'Hugo.' Weymouth alone seemed energised by the situation. 'Please, take a seat.'

'Thank you sir.'

There were muted smiles and nods from the other men, which Hugo modestly acknowledged. There were a few different faces, more senior men replacing some of those from the selection committee.

'Hugo, what is your opinion of ACLL Peckler?'

Oh boy. Here we go, straight in and no mucking about.

'In my opinion your grace the Assistant County Lord Lieutenant has always been a diligent and conscientious member of the Sentinnat. It has been a privilege to work for him. My own abilities have developed as a result.'

There were rumbles of approval. From the far end of the long table behind which they all sat, someone muttered 'Well said that man. Well said.'

It's what they want to hear. Loyalty. Anyway, better the devil I know. There are a lot out there who are a lot worse than Pecky. Maybe not so bright, but not so predictable either. Right now, I want someone predictable in Pecky's job.

Hugo picked up Pecky's expression, which was a mixture of surprise and a pathetic gratefulness.

Anyway, you're going to owe me after this Pecky.

Weymouth was silent. He looked from Hugo to Peckler and then down at the papers in front of him.

'Mmph. The thing is, Hugo. The thing is this. The Assistant County Lord Lieutenant has admitted to making mistakes in his handling of this... situation.'

He had to really. What else could he have said?

'Sir.'

They had already had this conversation in private, Hugo and Weymouth. This was all theatre. And the decision on Peckler - not just on his career but possibly on his life - was Weymouth's alone. Hugo had no doubt that the decision already been made. The rest of them would be happy to go along with it.

'Has there been anything Hugo - anything at all - that could give you even the slightest suspicion of the Assistant County Lord Lieutenant's loyalty to the Regency?'

This was it.

'Nothing whatsoever your grace.'

In truth, Pecky only had one loyalty and that was to himself.

One of the other men stirred. 'He appointed Milden-Brewer though didn't he?'

'That is my understanding sir.'

'So how would you explain that?'

'His grace has mentioned that the Assistant County Lord Lieutenant has admitted to mistakes.'

'That's all you'd put it down to? A mistake?'

'That is my belief sir.'

'Where's this Brewster fellow now?'

Here you go Hugo.

'He's still on Abbuth sir. It's my belief that he is intent on finalising plans for –'

'Thank you Hugo,' Weymouth said, surprisingly gently. 'You told me that he's not yet aware either of you being here, or that you have uncovered him?'

'That's correct sir.'

What's Weymouth up to? Doesn't he trust everyone here?

Weymouth looked up and down the table.

'Any more questions?'

It was more of a statement than an invitation, a statement which said 'There will be no more questions.'

The other men shook their heads.

'Thank you Hugo.'

'Thank you sir.'

Weymouth gave the slightest of nods towards the door. The callow youth opened it. As Hugo passed out into the corridor the young man whispered, 'Please wait in the corridor until his grace dismisses you. There may be further questions.'

Hugo nodded and returned to his chair in the corridor. The door closed. Five minutes later it opened again and Peckler appeared looking completely exhausted. He came and flopped onto the chair next to Hugo. He almost sobbed, 'Hugo, I owe you everything. Thank you for your support.'

'Not at all sir. I'm glad I was able to help.'

Peckler looked at Hugo, still clearly grateful but also showing puzzlement.

'Why did you do it?'

'Respect, sir.' Hugo was a master at keeping a straight face.

Peckler raised his eyebrows, astonished, then stared at the floor.

'And I really couldn't see you wanting the Brandon Bowleses in charge sir.'

Peckler managed a feeble laugh. 'Damn right there.' After a moment, he added, 'They're deciding my fate. Right now.'

Hugo had never seen Peckler like this before. He was a beaten man. His expression was no longer studied, or calculatedly expressionless. Every emotion was playing over his features.

'I'm sure you'll be ok sir.'

'Are you?' Peckler looked at Hugo again, hope in his eyes. 'I'm not.'

The door opened again and Peckler blanched, even before the callow youth said 'This way please Assistant County Lord Lieutenant.'

'Good luck sir.'

Peckler didn't seem to hear him.

Another five minutes passed before Peckler stumbled out of the room. At first he turned to his left, towards the exit; but then he turned and walked back to where Hugo was sitting.

'I'm to remain in post Hugo... I just wanted to thank you for your support.'

'I'm glad I was able to help sir.' For a moment Hugo thought Peckler was going to burst out crying. Then the man gathered himself, forced a smile, turned and headed for the door.

If he wasn't in Weymouth's pocket already, he is now.

Several more minutes passed before Hugo was summoned back to the committee room. He was not invited to sit and stood next to the chair, in front of the table. Weymouth looked up at him.

'We need you to get back to their planet, Hugo. Get Milsen-Brewer back here, alive if possible but dead if you must. Some bit of him we can recognise anyway.'

'Sir.'

'Exemplary work Hugo. Knew we'd got the right man.'

'Exemplary,' someone else repeated. There was a chorus of 'hear hear' and a thudding of fists on the table, a traditional Hinton and Yarrow sign of approval. Weymouth smiled. 'Back to it then young man.'

The tension had noticeably lifted from around the table. It seemed the Regency had made their various decisions and were happy with them.

'Thank you sir.' Hugo turned to the man on Weymouth's right. 'Your grace. Thank you your lordships.'

'He's promoted you Priggins,' someone said, to a round of good-natured laughter. Weymouth joined in the laughter, looked at Hugo, and benignly repeated 'Off you go.'

'Thank you sir.'

★★ ★★ ★★

I was on a wide, flat area a little way down the north side of the slope when Timmbo found me. There was a crack of rock against rock, away to my right. I turned to look but some instinct made me glance back, behind me and to my left. There was a moment of complete disorientation as I found myself looking at Welter Hallett, clutching at his stomach and limping towards me.

'Bettony' he gasped. 'You need to run...'

I stared. Then I watched him straighten up and smile, and I saw the Tipper in his hand.

'Actually,' he said, 'you really do need to run.'

'Timmbo' I breathed. As naturally as I could, I slipped the rucksack off my back. I was surprised that he gave me the time to do it. Instead of putting it down, I held it in front of me. There was at least a chance that it would protect me if Timmbo threw his Tipper.

Instead, he tossed the knife to one side. 'Don't need this,' he said. 'I'm going to kill you nice and slow.' His face contorted with a wild, insane rage. 'This is where it ends you freak.'

We stood for a moment, facing each other. For a few moments I felt incredibly nervous. I was, I knew, in a fight to the end. TMB was a small man but he was still some two or three inches taller than me. I had no doubt of his strength and Hugo had warned me of his abilities. I was confident in my own martial arts skills but he was a trained killer. There would be no rescue. In a few minutes time, one of us would be dead.

In the silence I could hear my own breathing.

I began to shake.

And then the old angry reaction kicked in. This man had killed Sherian Penck. He had put poor, harmless Liz in a coma. He was causing harm and havoc in an innocent world.

I could still feel my body shaking slightly. But now it was the result of a boiling, focussed rage of my own.

I threw my rucksack to one side just as Milden-Brewer launched himself at me. Perhaps he was over-confident, or

197

maybe he had underestimated me. Whatever the reason, he came at me full on, swinging his fists. It was easy to place a front kick between his legs. I knew that I had missed the male of the species' unique on/off button, but I had put some force into it and it was enough to stop him in his tracks. He grabbed at my foot but he was winded and his movement was slow. I had enough time to regain my balance and spring backwards a pace, safely out of his reach. Immediately he came at me again, feinting a side kick with his left foot. I tried to block a kick that never happened, adjusted and spun to my left, raising both arms and moving inside the arc of his right leg just in time to take a crunching contact from his shin on both my forearms. I staggered under the force but still managed to reach out. If I could grab his foot I knew I could break his leg which would be pretty much game over. But he was too fast for me, dropping his leg and stepping forwards, sending a punch which whistled past my ear. He was still moving towards me and I drove my right hand, knife-hand style, into his left kidney, making him gasp and giving me a chance to dance sideways and put a couple of steps between us. He took maybe two seconds to gather himself and then he was at me again, this time leading with his right leg, aiming low, aiming for my kneecap. Again I was quick enough to skip away. As his right foot landed on the ground he stepped inside my guard and punched at my head, connecting just on the edge of my eye socket. Dazed, I tried to stagger back, expecting a furious onslaught. Instead, he stepped back and smiled at me.

'Getting tired yet?' He taunted. 'Don't worry. In a short time from now you won't feel anything.'

He wasn't even out of breath. I was panting hard, trying to suck air into my lungs.

'Here we go BetBets,' he said. 'Round two.'

His attacks were relentless. Most people favour either the left side or the right; Milden-Brewer was equally sharp on both, with his kicks and with his punches. His balance was incredible. He was amazingly fast and all of his attacks carried a lot of power. Some of his kicks were so fast that it was only as they connected that I realised what was happening, only the fact that I was backing away that stopped them from carrying too much impact and felling me. I was still getting through with some attacks of my own but he seemed increasingly able to soak them up and keep coming forward. I knew that I was losing power as my strength ebbed away. I had fought in competition but never against such an opponent. Those fights lasted only a couple of minutes and could be incredibly fatiguing; this one felt as though it had been going on forever and it was non-stop. It took all my willpower just to stand upright, I was so tired.

Milden-Brewer suddenly stepped back and looked around. I watched him while I sucked great lungfulls of air into my body.

We had fought our way across the flat area and into a shallow, rock-strewn dip. His right eye was swollen and closing and his nose was bleeding freely. I consoled myself with the thought that at least some of my attacks had got through.

'Here we are then,' he said. 'Just about to start our final round. How fitting it should be somewhere like this.' He gestured around him. 'It's ironic actually. We have something like this on Erce. We call them fighting pits. They are where grudges of honour are settled.'

I said nothing. I was watching his body. Trying to anticipate his next attack.

He took a step forward. I backed away.

'It doesn't look like Crean will be back does it?' He asked.

I did not reply.

'He's on Erce now. I reprogrammed the transition boxes, but I suppose you already guessed that. Crean will have rather a lot of explaining to do, I think. And if he tries to use his transition box one more time...' He struggled not to laugh. 'It's goodbye Hugo I'm afraid.'

The dip flattened out to my left, before following the natural line of the hill downwards. It was the only way I could escape. Any other direction and I would have to climb. The sides were not steep and not high, but the few seconds spent scaling them would be a few seconds too long and he would be on me in a flash. I took a couple of steps to my left but Timmbo moved to cut me off. It felt like we were playing out a real-life game of chess.

The last two pieces on the board.

'What a strange situation we're in,' he said. 'Neither of us with any chance of escape. The best we can hope for is to be the last one to die. I would suggest you're not the odds-on favourite for that one BetBets.'

He could have walked right up to me. He was cutting off my only way of escape and if he advanced, all I could do would be to back towards the steepish climb behind me. But he stayed where he was.

Maybe if I could keep him talking I could recover enough strength for one last desperate attack.

'All that business in the car,' I said. 'Very clever. I never suspected a thing.'

'You mean my "injuries"?' Timmbo laughed. 'Fooled you there didn't I?' He was obviously pleased with the success of his little charade.

'I thought you were Tweek Golgood - if you see what I mean.' My breathing was beginning to get back to normal. My strength wasn't; it had gone. I could barely stand.

Timmbo laughed again. 'He's so enthusiastic isn't he? And so often he says the wrong thing. Without meaning to, he can be hilariously offensive. I modelled myself on him. Modelled Welter Hallett, I mean. All that puppy-dog energy. But yes, I tried to throw as much suspicion on him as possible. You don't know the half.'

'I never thought Timm Milden-Brewer was Welter Hallett. Apart from anything, you've only just arrived at Swindon.'

'Ah well you don't have to be visible to be pulling all the strings.'

He took another half-step forward. As much to stop him as anything, I said, 'I know Brink Stellish is from Erce.'

That genuinely surprised him. 'How? Who else knows?'

'Everyone,' I bluffed. Out of the corner of my eye I saw one of the bigger rocks shift slightly. I began to look around the dip, at the larger rocks and at the many smaller ones spaced out between them. And I began to wonder...

And the beginnings of a plan began to form.

'No!' Timmbo said. 'Not possible.' He frowned, then kicked out at one of the smaller rocks. I thought I could hear the faintest of hisses. If boulders could tense with anger, these ones were doing it now. 'I knew we shouldn't have swopped a woman,' he finished. 'Weak. Unreliable.'

'What happened to the real Brink?'

'Hmm? Oh she died. Ages ago.'

I tried to hide my revulsion.

'What about Morgan the lifepartner?'

'Who?'

'Her husband' I growled.

'Oh him. That was really funny. He was one of a group of people who were acquaintances of the real Stellish. After I got her inserted she started to cultivate him. He's the real deal. Pretty good cover eh? Being married to somebody who is actually from Abbuth.'

I was still edging round, but instead of trying to move towards the flatter area I was deliberately backing towards the part that ended in a steep climb. In doing so, I had put an area of smaller rocks between us. I looked down at the rocks at my feet, bent down, and very carefully selected two handily-sized ones. Very carefully.

'What are you doing?' Milden-Brewer asked. 'I thought this was a fair fight.'

'Nuts to that.' I threw one of the rocks as hard as I could. I aimed at his body, trying to make sure that I hit him. I'm not the best aim in the world though. My rock caught him a glancing blow on the head.

'What the hell?' He was furious. I held the second rock, making as if to throw again. 'Ok then' he said, 'if that's how you want to play this.' He bent down and picked up two rocks at random.

Please, I silently prayed to Hugo in his role as the god of turtles. This has to work. Otherwise I will almost certainly be facing a valiant and untimely death.

I wanted to keep Timmbo talking as long as possible.

'I suppose that was all Slepwood's plan?'

At first I thought I had overcooked it. TMB began to tremble with anger.

'That's Regency Lord Lieutenant Slepwood to you,' he snarled. 'It was his strategy, yes.' He was probably going to say a lot more on the subject but I can only assume that in his fury he was grasping the rocks very tightly. In any event he suddenly gave a cry of pain, threw one rock to the ground and looked at his hand. 'What the hell -'

The rock had cracked as it hit the hard ground. A loud, high wail came from it. Timmbo looked down, then looked in horror at the rock he was still holding. I watched a long, snake-like head and neck slither out of the shell and bite hard on his hand. He gave another cry of pain and attempted to throw this, too, to the ground. But the turtle had fastened hard onto his hand and was not letting go. He bent down and began to smash the creature against the ground. This one too began to hiss and scream.

Crouching down, hammering away at the baby turtle, he didn't notice the adults. Alerted by the cries, they were coming to life all around us. I very carefully put the rock I was still holding on the ground and stood absolutely still. All around, I watched boulders sprout feet and a head and begin lumbering with surprising speed towards him. At first they looked recognisably like turtles. It was only when they got close to Milden-Brewer that their heads suddenly extended, looking like huge snakes but with mouths opened wide to reveal rows of teeth that were the thickness of needles.

There were now very few rocks between me and the climb out of the dip. Those that remained looked like genuine stone. I scrambled out and watched from the safety of higher ground.

The turtles had formed a ring around Milden-Brewer. Heads lurched forward with amazing speed and fastened on to different parts of him. He realised too late what was happening and began to scream. It was horrific. Revolting as he was, I did not wish that fate on him but there was nothing I could do. The necks of the adults were so long that the creatures were fastening onto his chest and neck, more and more of them. He was staggering, trying to remain upright, unable to step away. When he sank to the ground under their weight I hurried away, trying to block my ears against his screams.

It took a while for him to become silent. I hadn't realised that I was running until I tripped and fell into sand. Then I was sick. After a few minutes I gathered myself. I would have to return to the turtles' nest area - that must surely be what it was - to find the rucksack.

That could wait though, for now. Wait until the shaking had stopped.

** ** **

The callow youth was to be Hugo's liaison. Rodney Cranford-Bright, the nephew of the Regency Earl of Lewis, the man who had sat to the left of Weymouth.

'I used to be your fag sir at Hinton,' the youth said breathlessly. Hugo realised he had attained something of the status of a hero, at least in the eyes of Cranford-Bright. He was obviously being hero-

202

worshipped right now. He vaguely remembered a younger version of the callow youth, who was perhaps not quite as young as he looked.

'Ah,' he said. 'I wondered where I recognised you from.'

The callow youth glowed with pleasure.

'Rodney, I need to get back to Swindon. It's the only place that I can call the spaceship back to. Can you get me a car? You could drive me if you want.'

The callow youth's glow deepened.

'I'll speak to Uncle - I mean, to his grace.' He disappeared back down the corridor. Hugo sat back in his chair, took a deep breath and relaxed into a much-needed cat-nap. It seemed like moments later when he was woken by the youth's gentle coughing. Rodney no longer looked happy.

'His grace says you're to summon the spaceship to another place.' He dropped his voice to an excited whisper. 'The plan is to carpet bomb Swindon out of existence.'

Hugo fought to keep his face clear of the shock and revulsion that he felt. They were doing this because of him. Tens of thousands of lives were going to be lost because of him, and there would be nothing he could do to stop it from happening.

'Where is his grace the earl of Weymouth?'

'He's - er - oh there he is, they're all just leaving.' Rodney cleared his throat deferentially. 'Your grace -'

Hugo had sprung to his feet and in a few easy strides was whispering into Weymouth's ear. Rodney watched the two men move away from the rest of the Cabinet, who were too interested in getting back to their beds to take an interest. After a couple of minutes Weymouth gave Hugo an avuncular pat on his back and headed for the door. Hugo beckoned Rodney over.

'Right then Cranny, get hold of that car pronto. His grace has given me two days to get the spaceship and I really don't know if that's going to be long enough.'

'What are you going to do sir?'

'I'm going to sit quietly somewhere out of sight in Swindon and wait for the spaceship.'

'What if it doesn't turn up sir?'

'If it doesn't turn up,' said Hugo grimly, 'I'm going to die waiting, along with everyone else in that god-forsaken dump.'

I had thrown my bag clear of the turtles' nesting area, but it was close enough to give me the jitters when I went to pick it up. There was no sign of life anywhere around me but there were plenty of rocks. Perhaps that was all they were, just rocks, but I treated each one with a great deal of respect. I examined my bag carefully. It was dusty but I could not see any evidence that the turtles had been interested in it. Everything inside was untouched.

I did not go and have a look to see what remained of Tim Milden-Brewer.

I walked for half an hour before I decided it was safe to stop. I chose a spot that was clear of any rocks, settled down, and treated myself to a meal of water and some tinned sardines. I was bruised from TMB's many punches and kicks, and the swelling that was throbbing on my face had forced my right eye to half-close. And I was so tired. I sat back and rested. And immediately, I fell asleep.

I must have been asleep for a couple of hours but I was still achingly tired when I woke. It was early afternoon by now, enough daylight left for me to try and find my way back to the transition point. Nothing to stop me now. My plan was to use the tracks we had made to help guide me. In this deserted, barren land they were very clear. But my simple-sounding plan was not as easy as it sounds. I have already admitted that I'm not great at directions, nevertheless it came as something of a surprise when I realised I had accidentally followed the tracks back to Timmbo's camp. What was worse, there were now footprints all over the place. I chose a set that seemed to lead in the right direction and began to follow them. I hadn't gone far when I saw something jammed behind a large rock. I approached with care. (I was now approaching all rocks with care, even massive boulders. Especially massive boulders.) I realised I was looking at Hugo's jacket. He must have stuffed it away out of sight when he was trashing Timmbo's camp. I gently pulled it away from the rock.

Something heavy was pulling down in one of the pockets. My heart lifted. It was Hugo's transition box! Of course, he would have had to leave it somewhere. I pulled the box from his pocket and regarded it. It was certainly a way out of here, although only as a last resort. Goodness knew where it would take me. At least here, I was somewhere that Hugo and Mrs Ponch would be able to find me. I did not fancy their chances of guessing which universe I might transition into after this one: There were an infinite number of them, apparently. Possibly even more.

Still, it was a way for me to get out of this place. If the days dragged on and I ran out of food and water I would still have an option left. The box joined everything else in my rucksack. It was too hot to wear Hugo's jacket but I pushed it through one of the straps on the bag. It was far too big for me but I knew it was only February, and I had neither the strength nor the directional ability to go and find my own coat. On other worlds it was cold. Hugo's jacket could be useful.

Well, you never know.

At the very least, it would make a half-decent pillow.

★★ ★★ ★★

Hugo slept in the car. Cranford-Bright kept a respectful silence, and drove quickly and smoothly. As instructed, he pulled to a stop out of sight of the checkpoint. Hugo was awake before the car had stopped.

'What shall I do now sir?'

'Go home Cranny. Get well away from here. Stay safe.'

'I can stay if you like?'

'It's too dangerous. If you were found, the best you could hope for would be getting blown to bits by the bombs.'

'I'd really like to help sir,' Cranford-Bright persisted.

Hugo thought for a moment. Would Weymouth postpone the bombing if he knew that one of his chum's nephews was likely to die as a result of it? Probably not.

'Just go home Cranny.' Perhaps it was a result of the tiredness, but in a moment of affection Hugo added, 'Tell his grace that I would recommend you for advancement if I could. You're a good man.'

'Gosh. Thank you sir. Surely there's something I can do?'

'Just this above all things Cranny.' Hugo climbed wearily out of the car, then leant back in. 'To your own self be true. And get the fuck out of here.'

He left a bewildered Cranford-Bright and wandered away into the grey midday light.

★★ ★★ ★★

My spirits were quite high as I followed the tracks. I still had food and water for a couple of days, Timmbo was no longer a threat, I

205

would shortly be near the transition point and I had a get-out-of-jail card in the form of the transition box. I even managed to spot where the tracks separated and within only a few hundred yards had realised I was on the wrong one.

The transition point itself was easy to find. There were still the marks made by Timmbo and me when we had arrived, and the ones nearby from when Timmbo had grabbed me. Somewhere around here was the point where the Two would turn up. I selected a large rock, made sure it wasn't a turtle and sat in its shade. I allowed myself another small meal, and fell asleep.

** ** **

Somewhere above him, a green neon light advertised the presence of Jed's Self Storage. Or it would have done if all the letters had been lit. As it was, Hugo checked his watch by the light of ed's elf storage, an idea which had made him smile despite everything.

It was three thirty on a cold and gloomy February evening. He had borrowed Cranford-Bright's thick overcoat, for which he was very grateful, and was huddled into it, in a dark corner formed by two brick walls, waiting for help from Abbuth.

It had been easy enough to slip into Swindon on foot, but finding the spaceship's arrival point took a long time. There were militia foot patrols to be avoided, and the occasional hopeful mugger to be discouraged. Eventually Hugo was convinced he had found his first objective – the place where he had arrived in Erce – the site of Timmbo's little camp, on the desert world. He relied on his sense of direction to work out a route in this cold, miserable city that mirrored the one that led from TMB's camp to the point where he had arrived on the desert world. Hugo knew that the spaceship would arrive somewhere close to that point. He had twisted the beacon, felt the stab of pain as it *crikked* into life, and watched it jump out of his hand and disappear.

This was it then, he thought as the silence returned. If Mrs P arrives, and I can get to the Two before any inquisitive local, we're in with a chance. If not... Never mind if not.

Alert to any movement or sound, hidden in the shadows and half-dozing, Hugo let his mind wander around the dreadful problem of how to prevent the forthcoming catastrophe that he had helped to create.

CHAPTER NINETEEN

Happyshack™ - It's like the real thing only better!

Hugo waited in the shadows of a gloomy, neon-lit afternoon.

He had persuaded one of the hopeful muggers into kindly handing over a threadbare old coat, in return for a promise of no broken legs. Hugo put this on now. Cranford-Bright's coat would have attracted attention; this one helped him to fade into the grim background. A couple of times he stretched himself and took a short walk, taking care to keep the transition site in view. There was a greasy cafe across the road, optimistically describing itself as Mr Chuckles' Happyshack™. Another of the hopeful muggers had kindly donated a reasonable amount of money, in return for a similar promise relating to his remaining unbroken arm. Hugo sat in the Happyshack™, eating his Mr Chuckles™ Tastybun© and drinking his Chuckoffee™ ("It's like the real thing only better!"). From his window seat he could watch the transition site. Eventually he wandered out, strolled up and down the road, picked up another Chuckoffee™ and relieved himself of the previous one. Finally he returned to his cold little corner and put Cranford-Bright's coat back on. He used the threadbare coat as a blanket, and watched for the sudden appearance of a tatty-looking metal crate.

One more day and then a lot of people were going to die and Hugo still had no idea how he was going to stop it from happening.

The feeble daylight was beginning to fade when he saw two large men strolling down the road. They had the air of unconcern that told the world they were militiamen. One of them had his torch on, and played the light across the street as they approached. It was just bad luck that the beam picked up Hugo.

'What've we got here then?' The militiamen said. 'Hiding away in the shadows like a naughty boy… Ooh, nice coat. I wonder where you got it from chummy. I'm guessing you stole it.'

It was like a bad dream being replayed. Hugo stood up and began to push the sleeve up to reveal his Authority, but the overcoat was heavy and resisted.

'I'm Sentinnat,' Hugo growled.

'Yeah and I'm the prince regent' one of the men said as he swung his heavy stick at Hugo's head.

The coat made Hugo's movements clumsy. It pulled at his arms and slowed his movements as he tried to protect himself. The cudgel glanced off Hugo's half-raised arm and struck him across the head with less force than a direct blow, but it was still enough to stun him. He felt his legs giving way and tried to cover up but kicks and blows rained down on him. One finally connected hard enough to knock him out.

When he came to, his hands had been tied behind his back and Cranford-Bright's overcoat was gone. He was lying on his side in a small cell. His feet were tied together.

Hugo relaxed as much as he could and waited for the inevitable.

Mrs Ponch squeezed the bridge of her nose with the thumb and forefinger of her left hand.

She was not noted for wavering. Rather the opposite, in fact. Her decisions could often be taken very quickly but were always balanced, always taken after consideration of all available information. She rarely regretted her judgements. She also knew that not taking a decision was a decision in itself; it was a decision not to do anything.

And yet.

Here she was, once again sitting at the controls of the Two. Several hours ago she had received the emergency signal from Hugo Crean. She had readied the Two, prepared to transition... and then had realised where the co-ordinates would take her.

And she had hesitated.

She had no reason not to trust Mr Crean. If he was working on behalf of the people from Erce - if this was all some intricate plot - well, it would have to be all so intricate as to defy belief. She had believed him when he had said that if his plan was to abduct her, she would already be in Erce. And she also knew from Mr Sneggs how the transition boxes had been reprogrammed, which was no doubt how Mr Crean (and probably Bettony Gullivant) had ended up on Erce, and why she was being called to that dreadful place.

And yet.

'Mrs Ponch I implore you to make the transition. It may not yet be too late.'

The appeal was all the more powerful for being so mildly phrased and so gently delivered. Mrs Ponch turned and looked at the slight frame of the man standing next to her.

'If the people from Erce are able to capture the Series Two, Dr Flange - if they capture me and force me to reveal what I know of our science - it could be catastrophic. For our world and for theirs.'

'They have already been in possession of the Two, Mrs Ponch. Please - let me go instead of you. We trained on Series Twos before our expedition last year. I have enough knowledge to be able to pilot it as long as you programme in the coordinates. If they capture me, there's little they could learn except how to heal people.'

A brief silence. Then,

'Agreed. You will come back immediately at any sign of danger.'

'I shall.'

Mrs Ponch moved her hands over the touchscreens.

'I am presetting it with our coordinates and programming it to autoreturn. It will await your instruction for five minutes. If you do not pilot it back within that time it will return automatically.'

'Understood. Thank you Mrs Ponch.'

'I'm not sure that thanks are in order just yet Dr Flange.'

She left the Two and walked away from the wooden shed that contained it. She watched the Two disappear and began to count the minutes.

Hugo was still cursing himself when the door opened again.

'My goodness. It's Hugo Dephwood Crean as I live and breathe.'

Oh shit.

'Hello Merry. What a joy.'

'They said it was someone with the Authority. What a relief that they got the word to me. Fancy a cigarette?'

Merry Brandon Bowles took the cigarette from his mouth and bent down, but held the glowing end towards to Hugo's face.

'I've given up Merry. It's bad for the health.'

Brandon Bowles laughed. He held the cigarette so close that Hugo could feel its heat against his skin.

'Never heard such rubbish. But there are a lot of things that are bad for one's health old fellow.' He flicked ash onto Hugo's cheek and stood up. 'Being here for one. I suppose you're going to do that brave thing where I ask you some pertinent questions and you refuse to answer?'

'I suppose I have little choice.'

'Good, good. I was rather hoping you would say that. Excellent. Let's start with your face then shall we?'

Brandon Bowles bent down again, cigarette at the ready. He was interrupted by a knock on the door.

'Go away.'

'It's a message for you sir.' The voice was muffled by the door. Even so, Hugo was pretty sure he recognised it.

'Go away or I'll have your kneecaps broken.'

'Yes sir. It's from your father the Lord Lieutenant sir. For your urgent attention.'

'Damn.' Merry Brandon Bowles stood up and opened the door. Hugo looked at the bulky frame of Sergeant Sluckham. 'What is it man?'

The sergeant held out a piece of paper. 'It's from your father sir' he repeated.

Sluckham glanced at the prisoner. Brandon Bowles was looking down at the paper and did not notice the sergeant's start of recognition.

'Bloody damn.' He turned and aimed a kick into Hugo's body. 'I bet all this is your doing Crean. Keep him locked in here sergeant. No food or water. Knock him about a bit if you want.'

'Sir.'

Brandon Bowles slammed the door behind him. No more than a minute passed before Sluckham returned.

'He's gone sir,' the sergeant whispered. 'For now anyway.' The sergeant bent down and added, 'I wouldn't be surprised if he doesn't come back neither. Something's going on. My brother brought that note, he's in the Lord Lieutenant's personal guard. He says they're all packing. He thinks they're doing a runner. He thinks they're off to Farnce!'

They know about the bombing. Somebody's warned them. They must have someone in the Cabinet.

'Can you untie me Sergeant?'

'If he does come back sir...'

'He won't. Your brother's right. I need to get out and get word back to the Regency.'

The sergeant hesitated.

'If I don't everyone in Swindon will be in a great deal of danger.'

The sergeant took a deep breath and nodded. He unbuckled the leather straps that were securing Hugo's hands and feet. Hugo stood, gingerly rubbed his wrists and dashed the cigarette ash from his face.

'You're a good man sergeant. This will not go unnoticed.'

'Sir. Thank you sir' the Sergeant replied uncertainly.

'Can we get to your car?'

'It's been commandeered by the palace guard. Wouldn't make any difference anyway. I tried to get out early this morning to - er - collect some post. No chance. They've really tightened up.'

Damn.

'We have to get out Sergeant.'

'I don't see how –'

'I do.' *Possibly. It's worth a shot anyway. Mainly because I can't think of anything else.* 'Can we get out of Swindon on foot?'

'That should be easy enough. What did you mean when you said everyone in Swindon will be in danger sir?'

'You've got to trust me on this one Sergeant. Now get me out of here. We need to find the Mazeley road.'

'Sir. Follow me sir.'

There was an air of tension on the streets. Perhaps word had leaked out that something was happening; or perhaps there was always an air of tension in this dreadful place. The Sergeant had given Hugo a militia jacket and both men carried cudgels. They were able to make their way unchallenged.

The main roads out of Swindon may have been closed but there were plenty of paths that were unpoliced. An hour later Sluckham and Hugo were striding across open country. In fifteen minutes they were on the Mazeley road.

Everything rests on Cranford-Bright. On whether or not he has decided to play the hero. The lives of tens of thousands of people depend on that one single decision.

...And there he was. There was the car, pulled off the road. Hugo increased his pace, hurrying towards it. As he did so he heard the big car's starter motor turning its engine over. Hugo began to run.   Had Cranford-Bright spotted his jacket and assumed militiamen were on to him? The engine had not yet fired. There was still time.

'Hi! Cranny!' He shouted. 'It's me you idiot!'

The engine was struggling to fire. Hugo was still twenty yards away when it coughed into life, spewing black smoke from the exhaust. The car lurched forwards then stalled. It gave him time to reach the driver's door. He pulled it open and looked at a panicking Rodney Cranford-Bright.

'Cranny. Cool it. Friend not foe.'

'It's you sir!'

'Yes I know that.' Hugo gestured towards the approaching form of Sergeant Sluckham. 'And this wheezing gentleman is the officer who helped me to get away, just like he did last night. He is a true and loyal friend of the Regency. The important thing here Cranny is to get a message to his grace the earl of Weymouth. The Brandon Bowleses have fled Swindon' - *a bit of poetic licence there, fully justified if it saves all those lives* - 'and are heading for Farnce.'

'Bastards!' Cranford-Bright almost exploded with anger.

'I know. Does this car have a wireless telephone?'

'It does sir but we're well out of range here.'

'Can you get back and pass the message to his grace? We could call off the raid and - save the Regency a great deal of money and trouble.'

No point in talking about lives. Concentrate on what matters to them.

'I can sir...'

'I can hear a But there Cranny.'

'His grace places a great deal of trust in you sir. I'm not sure I would command the same respect. I'm not sure I could even get to see him.'

Are they so suspicious of each other, these people?

'You really think that Cranny?'

'Yes I do.'

And he's probably right too. Hugo sighed.

He would miss his rendezvous with Mrs P. He would miss his chance of getting away from here. Perhaps that had already happened, perhaps the little spaceship had been and gone while he was out here.

His freedom. Against stopping the destruction of up to a hundred thousand unhappy, miserable lives that stood no chance at all of ever getting any better.

It wasn't really a choice at all, was it?

Hugo walked around the car, pulled the passenger door open and threw himself onto the seat next to Cranford-Bright.

'Come on Sergeant. Get in the back.'

'I'm not sure I should do that sir.'

'Get in the back Sergeant.'

'Yes sir.'

By the time Hugo got the car's wireless telephone to work they were within ten miles of Mazeley, and he had decided he would have more chance of convincing Weymouth in person rather than over a crackly intercom that was liable to break down at any moment.

There was a lot of activity at Mazeley. Security was tight, too. They had only been able to gain access by leaving the terrified Sluckham at the gatepost. It was difficult to get to Weymouth. His private secretary had denied them access at first, but the combined authority of Hugo Crean and the nephew of His Grace the Earl of Lewis was too much for the man.

Weymouth did not look happy. He met the two of them at one end of a cavernous hall that was buzzing with activity.

'Hugo. Back already? Or not gone yet.' Weymouth ignored Cranford-Bright completely.

'I have urgent news for you sir. The Brandon Bowleses have fled.'

'What!' Weymouth looked as though he was about to explode with anger; inside, though, he was thinking, this might work out very well. Not all of the Cabinet had been happy about the bombing. It was going to be costly, and despite the Regency's stranglehold on news media there was always the risk that the news would leak out. Let it, Weymouth had argued. It'll teach the bastards not to do it again. Not much chance of that if they're all bombed to pieces, someone had said. Thank god he could rely on Dephwood Crean.

'I had an unfortunate meeting with Meredith Brandon Bowles and his militiamen' Hugo said, pointing to the cuts and bruises on his face. 'Bowles was called away while he was interrogating me.

The loyal sergeant who gave me assistance last night was able to help me escape. He has contacts in the Brandon Bowleses' inner circle. He told me what they were doing.'

'Sure you can trust him?'

'Yes sir. He's here now at the gatehouse.'

'Think there's anything else we can get out of him?'

'No sir' Hugo replied hastily. The Sergeant may not be a saint but he did not deserve to be "questioned" by the Sentinnat. 'He's one of us. I'd put my life on that. In fact I already have.'

'Mmph. Good. Good man. And that's the sort of fellow we need. Loyal... How're they getting away Hugo?'

'Sergeant Sluckham tells me that they have a private aeroplane sir. He believes they will try to flee to Farnce.'

'Damn them!' Weymouth shouted so loudly that the entire hall went silent. He had gone puce with rage. All eyes turned towards the three of them. 'Follow me. Both of you.'

Weymouth strode across the hall and into a smaller room at one side. A group of men were leaning over a table that contained a map of Angland.

'Hold the exercise' Weymouth thundered. One of the men looked up. The rest of them kept their heads down. *There's always one* thought Hugo.

'Your grace?' The one said.

'Damn well do it! Put all preparations on hold until I tell you otherwise. And get the Regency together. Emergency cabinet now.'

People scurried away, glad to have an excuse to disappear. The One had quickly understood how much better it was to be the One of Many and was leading the scrum for the door.

'You! Potter!'

A small man who was at the back of the urgent free-for-all to leave the room turned, aghast.

'Your grace?'

'What's the latest on this... raider thing. This thing that takes a photo of aeroplanes and shows us where they are.'

'Er...?'

'What are you! Some sort of cretin?'

The small man began to shake.

'His grace wishes to be brought up to date on the latest developments in the radar project Mr Potter.'

The man looked gratefully at Cranford-Bright.

'Damn right I do!' shouted Weymouth. 'Is this what it's coming to here? I need a fucking interpreter?'

Don't answer that anyone, thought Hugo, keeping a deadpan expression.

'We've got it working on an experimental basis sir,' Cranford-Bright replied quietly. 'It covers much of the south of Angland, the coast and the Anglish Channel.'

'Mmph. Good. Think it can spot the Bastard Bowleses?'

'We'll have to ground all other aircraft first. There's a good chance –'

'Damn well do it pronto. Right. Hugo, you're with me.' Weymouth was allowing himself to return to earth. 'Good work Bright. Get all aircraft grounded and get our fighters ready. Intercept and bring 'em back. If they refuse, destroy them. If they've not already gone we should pot 'em. Prize for the chap who does. I want evidence though. And get that Sluckman fellow a beer or something as well on my orders. He's at the gatehouse. Make a note of his details. New house for his family or something,' he ended vaguely.

One thing about Weymouth, Hugo thought, *he rewards loyalty. Likes to keep his power base solid.*

Strikken Flange powered up the cameras. They threw a series of depressing and vaguely familiar images onto the screens in front of him. He knew that it was a late February afternoon here, just as it had been on Abbuth, but the cameras made everything look as bright as a sunny summer's day on Abbuth.

Perhaps bright was the wrong word. He had transitioned to a dull, grey world, nothing but dirt, brick and slate. One of the cameras picked out a brightly lit sign, somewhere high on a building to the left of the Two: ed's elf storage, it said. Strikken had no idea what that meant. Did these Swindon people believe in elves? He knew that exploration was revealing a strange spectrum of religious beliefs, from none at all, right the way through to a rigid belief that anyone enjoying themselves would bring down the wrath of a giant two-headed caterpillar called Theo. An angry caterpillar which would send the stars away and stop the moon from rising. Theo's many followers knew that for a fact: Had he not dictated his sacred thoughts to his representative on earth, many generations ago, over a meal of wild mushrooms? On Theo's sad world, everyone knew it was sinful to have a good time, and often fatal. Especially if you were a woman, for some reason.

Strikken was grateful that the Two was so well disguised. A battered storage crate did not look out of place at all here. He spent three precious minutes panning the cameras around, looking for Hugo or Bettony. On impulse, he opened the Two's door and ventured outside. It was quiet, and there was a strange acrid smell in the air. He edged his way to the corner of a road and, summoning his courage, called out Bettony and Hugo's names.

'Looking for someone?' A voice said just behind him. Strikken jumped, and turned to a thin man who seemed to be dressed in a collection of pieces of dirty black cloths. The man appeared to have materialised from out of nowhere, as indeed did the knife in his hand. He was speaking a familiar tongue.

'I am, yes.' Strikken had a moment of inspiration. 'I've lost my elf.'

'You've what?' The man took half a step backwards. Nutters were unpredictable.

'I've lost my elf. I was hoping to find somewhere round here to store it but it ran away. Do you know anywhere where they store elves?'

The man took another step away which made his waving of his knife slightly less threatening. Only slightly though.

'Coat.'

The man held out his free hand expectantly. Strikken removed his jacket and took a step towards the man who also stepped backwards, keeping the distance between them.

'Throw it.'

Stricken did so.

'Trousers.'

'What?'

'Hand me your trousers.'

'Look! There's my elf!' Strikken pointed desperately behind the man, trying to distract him long enough to allow an escape.

'What the fuck?' The man half-turned, gripping his newly-won treasure tightly in one hand and his knife in the other. Startled by his sudden movement, a cat jumped from a wall and scampered away. The man registered its leap from the corner of his eye.

'Fuck!' He cried. He was thirty-seven years old and he'd reached that great age in Swindon partly by not waiting around to see exactly how dangerous something dangerous might be. He was in possession of a new coat and he was also superstitious and elves had just been added to his collection of paranormal terrors. He ran for his life. Strikken did the same in a different direction, dashing back to the Two, slamming the door closed behind him and staring at another ragged inhabitant of Swindon just as the transition vehicle obeyed its autocommand and returned to Abbuth.

'It's obviously occurred to you sir to wonder how the Brandon Bowleses got the news of the Regency's plans so quickly. We know that they were aware of them this morning.'

'Mmph. What? Oh yes... Damn right Hugo,' Weymouth blustered. They were striding down a thickly carpeted corridor in a part of the building that Hugo had never visited before. The inner sanctum. 'Could be any of about a hundred or more people who know. You saw what it was like down there.'

Hugo prompted Weymouth again. 'There's a fair chance that someone made a phone call. How else would the Brandon Bowleses have known so quickly?'

'God. You're right.'

'And since it's a long-distance call it shouldn't be too hard to trace.'

Bets. Alone with Timmbo. Mrs P must have been and gone by now. Concentrate boy! They'll be ok and so will you. Just keep your nerve.

On the way to the cabinet room Weymouth disappeared for several minutes into an office, leaving Hugo standing in the corridor.

'Soon have the details if there was a bloody phone call' he muttered when he reappeared. 'Bright will interrupt our meeting.' His lips twisted themselves into a smile, although the rest of his face was reluctant to follow. 'This is going to be interesting.'

It was the first time that Hugo had attended a Regency cabinet and he sincerely hoped it would be the last. There were eight men seated around a solid oak table in a fairly small, oak-panelled room somewhere on the first floor of Mazeley Central Block. Two heavily-armed guards stood outside the thick oak door; Hugo stood just inside. All of the eight had been present at the previous meeting that Hugo had attended. Hugo noted that they sat four to each side of the table. At the head of the table was an empty chair, as it was rumoured always to be. A very ornate chair with styled armrests that were each rounded off with gold carvings, one of a lion's head and one a dragon's. The chair that was always left empty for the absent prince regent.

'I've suspended the military action against Swindon' Weymouth said, without preamble. He clearly liked to take the others by surprise and there was no doubt that he had succeeded. There were gasps of astonishment.

'After you argued for it so strongly?' said Lewis.

'They've gone. Fled. The rats have left the sinking ship. Young Hugo here found out.'

He had the full attention of them all.

'What do you mean Weymouth?' Asked another.

'What I say.' Weymouth was raising his voice now. 'The Brandon Bowleses. They're on their way to Farnce. That right Hugo?'

'Indeed your grace.'

There were a few muttered expressions of disgust. Hugo heard the phrase 'and he was a Hinton man too', but succeeded in keeping a straight face.

'How did they know?'

'Ah. Good question Henry. Thing is this old man. We think someone made a telephone call to tip them off.'

Silence.

'A traitor in our midst?.'

'Mmph. Damn right.'

More silence.

'Farnce eh?' Somebody muttered. 'Bastards.'

There was a knock at the door.

Right on cue, Cranny.

'Enter' commanded Weymouth. Cranford-Bright shuffled into the room. 'Well?'

'Er. Could I speak to you outside please sir?'

'Eh? Why? If it's good enough for me to hear it's good enough for the cabinet. No secrets here boy.'

'It's rather embarrassing your grace.'

Someone further down the table said 'Eh? What's he say?'

'Buggered if I know,' Weymouth replied. 'Speak up boy.'

Cranford-Bright summoned all his courage. 'We've traced a call from Mazeley to Swindon. In fact sir there were two calls, one yesterday morning and one late last night.'

'And? Yes?'

Cranford-Bright cleared his throat, then half-croaked, 'They were made from the private office of his lordship the regency lord lieutenant Featherstone.'

More gasps. Seven of the men present at the table turned to look at the eighth, who paled.

'Don't you keep your door locked Arthur?' Asked Weymouth innocently. His voice was deceptively mild.

'What? Yes! Of course I do.'

'Then how could anyone but you have made the call?' Asked the one Weymouth had called Henry.

It was not the cleverest of traps, Hugo thought, but it had worked well enough.

'I - there must be a mistake.'

'I took the liberty of asking for a check to be made for calls from his lordship's home to Swindon,' Cranford-Bright continued. Weymouth looked unsurprised and Hugo wondered if that too had been a part of his instruction. 'Purely to exonerate his lordship.'

'What? Who gave you the right to do that? My private –'

'What did you discover?' Cut in Weymouth.

'There have been twelve calls so far identified over the past six weeks. Some lasted –'

'It's a lie!' Shouted Featherstone. 'It's all lies. I've never –'

'Silence! Make your excuses to your interrogator! Call the guards in Hugo.'

Strikken was discovering that accidentally kidnapping one of Swindon's feral inhabitants was not dissimilar to being locked in a cage with a wildcat. Mrs Ponch watched in surprise through the shed's open door as the transition vehicle's own door sprang open and two struggling men fell out into the gloom. One of them, who seemed to be throttling the other, glanced around him and then shrieked in terror and pulled away from his adversary.

'Dr Flange are you all right?' Mrs Ponch called. Strikken sat up, rubbed his throat and nodded. His assailant was staring around, paralysed by terror while the two creatures conversed in their devilish language.

'Yes I believe so thank you,' Strikken replied. 'Some superficial bruising to the sternocleidomastoid possibly but no real harm.'

The visitor fell to his knees, arms outstretched on the ground in front of him.

'Please do not destroy me oh mighty witch,' he begged. 'I meant no harm to your elf-keeper.'

Mrs Ponch recognised English, or some approximation, and switched languages.

'You must labour under a misconception my friend,' she said. 'We bear to you no malice. Dr Flange does indeed keep health though, as you rather quaintly put it.'

'I knew it! I'll labour under anything for you oh great denizen of terror. I will be your servant now and forever. Please spare me the fiery pits of Nomalice. I did not mean to provoke the elf. Or steal it. I don't know where it is. Honestly.'

'What?'

The man began to sob. 'I have a wife. Children. I can get them if you like. One of them's a bit idle but you'll soon get 'em working hard. Please spare my life.'

Mrs Ponch switched back to Britannic, to the further terror of their uninvited guest.

'Dr Flange what was your purpose in collecting this gentleman?'

'I assure you Mrs Ponch it was completely unintentional. I am deeply sorry.'

'Can you get the gentleman back to wherever you picked him up?'

'Yes, if you reprogram the Series Two back to Erce. I believe he may be a member of a local cult that worships elves, rather than recognising me as a practitioner of health.'

'Ah. I see. Do they really? How interesting.'

The visitor continued to cringe while the mighty creatures debated his fate in their strange, guttural, hellish tongue. The fearsome witch then brushed past him and into the magic crate.

'Come along young man' she commanded in English. 'Shift your arse.'

The way that they turned on Featherstone genuinely put Hugo in mind of rats, all suddenly deciding through some innate instinct to destroy the weakest of their number. How much of what had been said was true, and how much a fabrication by Weymouth to rid himself of someone he disliked, Hugo did not know. If the rumours were true, it would not be the first time that had happened. But something about Featherstone's manner suggested there was truth in what Cranford-Bright had said. And Hugo had some respect for Cranford-Bright. So maybe, Hugo thought, the Brandon Bowleses really were planning a coup. And maybe Milden-Brewer had been involved, somehow. More likely he had been using them for his own ends, as they probably were him. In truth, each side was playing with fire and each side would be getting fatally burned. No doubt about that one.

Milden-Brewer. Had he tracked Bets down? Had she somehow hidden from him or got the better of him?

The room was in turmoil. There were bread rolls and cakes laid out along with jugs of water and coffee, and the other cabinet members had resorted to throwing them at Featherstone, as though they were still at public school and he had committed some minor misdemeanour, instead of aiding a deadly coup. The guards entered the room and began dragging Featherstone away, he was struggling, some of the more active members of the cabinet were pulling and pushing him about and hitting him around the head. Hugo caught Weymouth's eye. The earl beckoned him over.

'Hugo you've uncovered a hornet's nest' he shouted above the noise. 'Absolutely top-rate work. I need someone like you at my right hand.'

Uh oh.

'Sir, I desperately need to get back to Swindon. I had sent the – electrical command to the spaceship before I was caught by the Brandon Bowleses' militia. If it turns up –'

'Mmph. Good point. I really could do with you here Hugo. But you're right. Get yourself off. Well done young man.' Weymouth rapped his knuckles on the table.

'Thank you sir. Goodbye for now and good luck sir.'

'Don't need luck when I've got men like you around me Hugo.'
I think you probably do.

It had taken Cranford-Bright three hours to drive back to Mazeley; it took Hugo barely two to make the return journey. He had picked up Sergeant Sluckham at the gatepost. The sergeant was much more comfortable than when he had first arrived. Word had filtered down that he was a man in favour and the attitude of the hard men at the gatehouse had changed to reflect that fact. Beer had arrived, and had somehow miraculously multiplied into glasses for everyone in the gatehouse. The sergeant was suddenly a popular man. He was almost (but not quite) reluctant to leave when Hugo called for him. Relaxed by the beer, he found Hugo's driving on the journey back exciting rather than terrifying.

Hugo abandoned the car where Cranford-Bright had sat waiting and the sergeant led the way back into Swindon. They parted ways outside Mr Chuckles' Happyshack™.

'Want me to spare some of the boys to look after you while you're waiting sir?' He asked.

'No thanks sergeant.' The last thing that Hugo wanted was militiamen poking around the Two if it turned up. 'Perhaps you could ask them to leave me alone though.'

'I'll certainly make sure that word gets around sir. Er... who do I take my orders from now?'

'My instruction from the earl was that you are to act as though nothing had changed.'

'Right sir.' Sluckham had no idea what that meant or how to do it but he knew how to accept an order.

Hugo found his corner and settled down again. He looked around for the old coat but it had disappeared, which did not surprise him.

CHAPTER TWENTY

A Land of Magic

I woke before dawn. When I had settled down here, there had been almost zero doubt in my mind that Hugo and Mrs Ponch would combine to rescue me, and pretty quickly. I was full of hope. As time dragged on that hope/doubt balance began to shift. Had I got the right place? What if Brian was a bit out when he told us where the Two had been? Had I even allowed enough distance between where Timmbo and I had transitioned and where the Two may have been? Every so often I would reassure myself. They would not forget me. They would work out where I was. But my hope was dwindling away along with my supplies. When the sun rose I had less than half a pint of water left, some crumbs which probably amounted to less than a biscuit and a small packet of raisins. Despite my best efforts, before midday these were all gone but I was still hungry and I was still very thirsty. I was also increasingly worried.

Around midday I pulled the transition box from the rucksack. I waited another ten minutes. Then another five. Then I took a deep breath and pressed its control. As pain coursed through my body the world around me turned from one of empty heat to one of cold brick and concrete. I was still recovering from the transition when I heard an awestruck voice say 'It's one o' them magic elves.'

There was the sound of running feet. As the pain dropped away I sat up and opened my eyes.

I was in an alleyway. Tatty brick buildings loomed up on either side. It was damp-cold and there was an acrid smell that sat at the back of my throat.

And by the sound of it I was in a land of magic.

✷✷ ✷✷ ✷✷

'You still here sir?'

'Hello constable. Yes I am still here.'

'Another long day watching out eh? How much longer are you planning on staying sir, if you don't mind me asking?'

'Until my mission is over.'

'Ah yes... I'm not really very clear what your mission is sir –' the militiaman correctly interpreted the warning look in Hugo's eyes, and hastily added, 'not that it's any of my business sir.'

'Indeed.'

'We were just wondering sir, if it's no trouble to you of course... would it be possible to pursue your mission a couple of blocks across the way? Say... I dunno... down Stremshaw Street? Only we couldn't help noticing how the level of crime went down around here after you arrived. And er, it's gone up a bit on Stremshaw Street.'

'My mission is here constable.'

'Yes sir. Sorry sir. Well, I'll wish you a good day sir. If you need anything in the way of food or anything...'

'I'm fine thank you constable. Some of the local felons have been kindly donating their money to me.'

'They've been - oh I see. Ha ha. Very good sir. Yes. Well, I'll bid you a good morning sir.'

'Good morning constable.'

Funny how their attitude changes when they think you've got the power of life and death over them, Hugo mused. That was one of the two militiamen who had dragged him off to his meeting with Merry Brandon Bowles. His posturing arrogance on that occasion had been replaced by quivering fear.

Another night had gone by. Hugo wondered how many more of Mr Chuckles™ Tastybuns© he would be able to eat before his stomach rebelled and the broken pavement in front of the Happyshack™ became covered in a mixture of half-digested Tastybun© and Chuckoffee™ ("It's like the real thing only better!").

'Mr Crean sir.'

A thin child stood in front of Hugo.

'Hello Ellphick.'

'You said to tell you if anything really weird happened?'

'I did.'

The child looked meaningfully at Hugo's hands, which were where coins were distributed from.

'Ow much did you say again?'

'Five shillings for a useful piece of news.'

''Ave you got five shillins Mr Crean sir?'

'I have indeed Ellphick but you're not going to see it until I get your news.'

'But once you've got my news Mr Crean sir there won't be any need for you to give me the five shillins.'

'I'm a man of my word Ellphick. On a more transactional level, if I don't give you the five shillings I won't get any more news from you in the future, will I?'

Ellphick understood enough of this sentence to realise it was to his advantage to talk.

'There's one o' them magic elves 'as appeared Mr Crean sir. In Deptford Street. About an hour ago.' He held his hand out.

'What magic elves?'

'Oh they've been around for years sir.'

'Have they? What are they exactly?'

'Oh they're elves sir. And they're magic. Been around for years sir.'

'When did you first hear about them, Ellphick?'

'About an hour ago sir. My bruvver told me.'

'And how do you know they're magic?'

'They just appear from out of nowhere sir. Then they *writhe* around on the ground until they assume 'uman form. My bruvver saw it.'

Ellphick had stressed the word 'writhe' with a great deal of relish. Hugo wondered if the boy knew what it meant. Possibly not, he thought.

'And also yesterday sir one of 'em appeared in a magic box and took Sammy Taylor's dad away to a magic wood but 'e managed to escape.' Up to this point Ellphick had given every indication that he was sincere in his descriptions, but now he began to waver. 'E says he fought 'em and they were terrified and brought 'im back and asked 'im to leave 'em alone. S'what 'e says, anyway,' he finished, doubtfully.

'Is he a brave man then, Sammy Taylor's dad?'

'Why are you only telling me now?'

'I just found out from my bruvver. He's just got 'ome. And I need five shillins sir.'

Hugo stood up. 'Take me to Deptford Street Ellphick.'

Ellphick looked meaningfully at his outstretched hand. Hugo reached into his pocket, pulled out two half-crowns and handed the large silver coins over. The child looked at them in awe.

'It's this way sir.' Ellphick led the way down a couple of side-streets. Hugo began to wonder if he was being set up. His senses were at their keenest, waiting for anything that would show an attack was about to be made, but there was nothing and Ellphick was completely relaxed.

'It appeared somewhere round 'ere sir. Then it *writhed* and then it ran off.'

'Did your brother tell you what it looked like?'

'No sir. But 'e told our mam and she told me. She said it was little but it 'ad a big posh coat on, she said. Expensive-lookin', our mam said.'

Could it be....?

'And the magic box? Where was that?'

Ellphick looked meaningfully at his hand and then at Hugo, but this time Hugo looked meaningfully back. 'It's all part of the deal Ellphick. Lead the way.'

'Follow me sir.'

Ellphick led the way back to a point a few yards from where Hugo had been sitting.

'Just 'ere sir. I don't fink the bloke in the magic box was akcherly an *elf* though sir, 'e told Sammy Taylor's dad 'e was an elf *keeper* and 'e was goin' to turn Sammy Taylor's dad into a slave. S'what 'e said anyway.'

'OK listen to me Ellphick. I think the elf was probably a prince who was escaping from the elf-keeper. If he's treated well he will give... er... treasure to those who... er... treat him well. But first he needs to get back to his elf-kingdom and I can help him to do that. So you need to find out where the elf prince is and let me know.'

'And then there'll be treasure for me sir?'

'Oh yes. Treasure.'

'But also will there be another five shillins up front?'

Ellphick will do well in Swindon, Hugo reflected. Or at least, he should survive, which was more or less the same thing for most people in Swindon.

Hugo pulled a ten-shilling note from his pocket. The boy stared at it, hypnotised.

'Ten shillings if you find the elf-prince for me...' He pulled a pound note from another pocket. Ellphick's mouth dropped open. '... and a pound if I capture the elf-keeper and his magic box.'

Ellphick started to run down the street, stopped, and changed course into the Happyshack™. He reappeared a short while later clutching plastic boxes full of Mr Chuckles™ Finest Chikken-Stile Treets© and hurried away.

★★ ★★ ★★

Were there really worlds where magic elves lived? My first impression was not that I was in a particularly magic place. Wherever I was though, I would somehow have to find a way of surviving here. At least they spoke English. I knew also that I must not give up hope.

The acrid, clinging smell was vaguely familiar, reminding me of Hablock, the sinister prison on Erce. But there had not been magic on Erce; far from it.

At least I still had the transition box.

I wandered out of the alleyway and onto a street. Everywhere seemed strangely quiet. It was hard to tell if the buildings on either side housed factories or people. Some distance front of me and heading further away, two men were walking side by side. They wore black bomber jackets and were swinging large sticks. Trousers were tucked into heavy boots that reached halfway up their calves. They looked like the sort of people best avoided; I wondered if they were the cause of the quietness. I watched them wander away.

'Where'd you get that coat from?'

I turned and looked at a thin little woman. She was wearing a long, tatty dress that reached down to her ankles and her shoulders were covered by a grimy shawl. She reminded me of someone out of a photograph of the Victorian poor.

'It's not your'n,' she went on accusingly. 'It's like that one Jerry Steggler gorroff that wizard.'

I looked down at myself. My dirty clothes and scuffed joggers certainly looked mismatched with Hugo's jacket which he had somehow managed to keep beautifully crease-free and clean. It was also about five sizes too big for me. I wondered who else would have something similar.

The woman was inspecting my face closely.

'Ey. There was a photo in one o them pockets. He looked like you...'

Hope flickered, along with a certain amount of resentment at being thought a man. Could someone have a photo of me? And were they friendly or hostile? I tried to deepen my voice.

'Where is he?'

'Who?'

'Jerry Steggler. Or the wizard.'

She backed away, eyeing me suspiciously.

'I dunno do I?'

She looked over my shoulder and started with fear.

'Come ere, tekkin our coats,' she muttered inaccurately, edging away. 'You should clear off back to where you came from.' The edging became something fuller and the woman hurried away, still muttering.

'I'll do a deal with you for your coat young man.'

Did everyone in this place approach from behind? I turned and looked at another thin and undersized extra from a Victorian photograph. This one had a look of rancorous evil.

'So the deal is, you give me the coat and in return I let you live.' He grinned nastily. 'Whaddya fink?'

I was tired, hungry and thirsty and my bruises still ached. Confident in his threat he faced me squarely, with hands on hips and feet spaced widely apart. He was an open target. I stepped forward, executed a fast, simple front kick between his legs and elbowed the side of his head for good measure as he crumpled to the ground.

'No thanks mate,' I replied. 'I think you can buy me a meal though in return for me not crippling you permanently.' I reached into his pockets and pulled out notes and coins.

'Oh no not again' he moaned.

'Where can I buy food?'

'There's a Chuckie round the corner. Can you leave me enough for a pint? It's not been a good day.'

I took Hugo's jacket off and stuffed it as best I could into the rucksack. I was cold without it, but there was no doubt that in my own scruffy clothes, which had now gone several days without being changed, I fitted in much better. I found the greasy cafe, bought some stomach-churning muck and a strange hot drink, and sat in a corner. I was finishing the muck, and wondering what the long-term digestive effects of eating it were going to be, when a small thin child (was everybody thin in this place?) entered the cafe. He spent several seconds staring at me, then ran out of the shop and down the road.

There were a couple of people sitting together in the cafe, and two men on their own. All four of them plus the spotty youth behind the counter (his dirty nylon jacket identified him as "Your ChuckleSheff Kevin" kept glancing at me. It reminded me of when Kagh had accidentally piloted the Two into a dodgy world the previous year, when we had been escaping from Erce. She had immediately sent us off again, to somewhere (possibly) a bit safer. This place definitely had a dangerous feel to it. I remembered some advice our martial arts teacher had once given us: The best form of self-defence is to follow your instincts and avoid dangerous places. You don't need to get yourself out of trouble if you don't get into it in the first place.

I decided to transition.

As innocently as I could, I reached into my rucksack for the transition box. This was more easily said than done. The rucksack was overstuffed with Hugo's jacket; I could get my hand around the metal box, but pulling it out meant pulling the jacket out too and I did not want to do that. I tried a couple of times without success.

I'm obviously not very good at being innocent. All five were now watching me.

'Wot ya got in there then son?' One of the single men called out. 'A ferret?'

The rest of them laughed unpleasantly.

''E's feedin' is ferret,' another said.

More laughter.

'You c'n get arrested for that.'

The first man stood up. He was definitely trouble. Maybe five ten, which was tall for this place, and with a spare frame that still managed to convey both threat and strength.

''Ere let me 'elp you sonny.'

If I could get my hand around the transition box I could maybe trigger it before he reached me. I frantically pushed my hand back into the rucksack. Now I couldn't even find the bloody box.

The rucksack was ripped away from me.

'Well well, look at this...'

He pulled out the coat and held it up.

'Give that back!'

'This is a bit of all right eh?   - Whoa, calm yourself.' I began to get up but he pushed me down into the chair with such force that it toppled over backwards. Still gripping the chair, I hit the floor and, winded, watched him put the jacket to one side and pull the transition box from my bag.

'And this. What you got 'ere sonny, some sort of radio?'

He pressed the box's controls. And then screamed. At first I thought he had triggered a transition, and I watched my hope of escape disappear in dismay. But he carried on screaming. The rest of the people in the cafe stood up and began backing away. No-one was laughing now. Still the man screamed, but his voice was becoming fainter and fainter. I had the impression that he had not stopped screaming, it was just that we could no longer hear him. No-one backed away any further, they were all frozen in fear. His body was rigid, all except for his eyes which looked around wildly in terror. I realised with sickening horror that he was becoming see-through. One of the men watching began to wail in terror.

He became fainter and fainter, all except his dreadful eyes. Soon they were all that was left; then they too disappeared. I could hear people gasping for breath. Suddenly a voice spoke from nowhere.

'Oh dearie dearie me. Who's going to be next?'

It was Timmbo. I realised Kevin the ChuckleSheff had been and was still making a strange, high-pitched wail. Nobody moved, trying to look around while at the same time not moving their heads. Eyes which had widened in terror searched for the source of the ghostly voice. Then the cafe door opened, and a familiar voice said,

'I see you've found my elf. Well done everyone. And well done Ellphick.'

It was as though a spell had been broken. Everyone charged for the door, which Hugo politely held open. They all tried to get out at the same time, which slowed them down somewhat, but they made it in the end. I was still on the floor, sitting in the chair in the wrong dimension, flat on my back with my legs in the air.

'And you've brought me my jacket' Hugo added. 'Thank you Bettony.'

'That's gorra be worf a pound mister.'

The same small child who had stared at me from the doorway of the cafe was staring intently at Hugo and holding his hand out.

'I thought we agreed ten shillings?'

'Come on mister. That's gorra be worf a pound,' the boy repeated.

'Bettony may I introduce Ellphick. I rather suspect Ellphick is going to be a force to be reckoned with in Swindon in years to come. Ellphick, this supine individual is my pet elf Bettony.'

'You owe me a pound.' The boy was still looking at Hugo, unmoved and expressionless.

Hugo pulled a piece of green paper from his pocket and held it out, then withdrew it as the boy went to take it.

'There are conditions.'

The boy continued to stare.

'You don't tell anyone what just happened.'

'I din't see anyfin' mister.'

'Good. And you keep in touch with me. If you want to earn more pound notes. We still haven't found the elf-keeper and his magic box.'

'Orl right.'

Hugo handed the piece of paper over. The boy stared at it for a moment, eyes and mouth every bit as wide as those of the men witnessing their companion's excruciating disappearance. Then he ran out of the door.

'Your elf?'

Hugo leaned down and reached out his hand, helping me up.

'I don't think Ellphick is in the least bothered about elves, real or imaginary, unless they are in some way related to the procurement of cash.'

'You called me your elf. Where are we Hugo?'

'Aren't you pleased to see me?'

My annoyance disappeared. 'Yes. Of course I am.'

I can't remember who suggested it but for some reason a hug seemed to be the right thing to do. It went on for perhaps a moment longer than it should. Relief was flooding through me.

'It would seem that the locals here have come to their own explanation of some strange events. I'm pretty sure that they've seen Mrs P's spacecraft appear and then disappear. I can only assume that Timmbo's visits used to be extremely brief, or that the Brandon Bowleses cordoned off the area when it was being used.'

'So...'

'Bad news Bets. I'm afraid we're on Erce. On the bright side,
it looks as though you've just avoided a rather nasty demise.'

★★ ★★ ★★

Hugo had slipped into a light doze after Ellphick departed on his elf-hunting mission. When the boy had returned, full of excitement, he had startled Hugo into consciousness. Ellphick had news, and a tale to tell...

Tommy Pallance had apparently been peacefully minding his own business, wandering down a nearby street and thinking about what to buy as a surprise present for his poor old mum when he had been mugged by a strange small man. The man had been incredibly powerful. Despite Tommy Pallance's heroic efforts, he had been overwhelmed and had been lucky to escape with his life.

Ellphick had related this tale with a certain amount of doubt in his voice.

'Is he trustworthy, this Pallance?' Hugo had asked. Then he had looked at Ellphick's rather contemptuous expression and thought, *dumb question,* and had said,

'How much of that do you think is true, Ellphick?'

'E also said that a few hours ago 'e 'ad been peacefully mindin' 'is own business when 'e was set on by a bloke oo sounded a lot like you mister.' Ellphick gave Hugo one of his meaningful looks. 'E wears a noilskin coat' he added, by way of explanation.

'Ah. The gentleman in the noilskin coat. I remember him well. He's having an unfortunate day today, isn't he?'

'The point is, mister,' Ellphick went on patiently, ''e says this bloke oo attacked 'im was wearing a really posh coat. 'E finks it was a magic elf.'

Hugo sat up.

'Any idea where the - er - magic elf might be?' Hugo thought about what he knew of Bettony. 'Are there any local pubs, for example?'

'Well... there are... but it asked Tommy Pallance where it could get some food and 'e told it where the Shitshack was.'

Ellphick pointed across the road to the HappyShack™. Hugo turned and looked.

'Also there's some little bloke in there oo's not from round ere.'

Hugo took a moment to translate this last sentence into something that made sense. He peered at Mr Chuckles™ HappyShack™. 'What's going on in there?'

'It looks like a fight to me.' Ellphick sounded interested. 'Shall we go un 'av a look? An' if we find your magic elf-prince you owe me ten shillins.'

Bettony's fellow-diner had been on the point of permanently vacating the world of Erce, and indeed life itself, when Hugo and Ellphick arrived at the HappyShack™'s door. This had prompted a hasty retreat from everyone except the person who was simultaneously lying on the floor and sitting on an upturned chair.

Hugo felt a rush of happiness surging through him as he recognised Bettony, followed by a rush of pain as he took in her bruises. He helped her to her feet. When she said, almost apologetically, 'I think a hug seems to be the right thing to do at this point,' his life suddenly and unintentionally acquired a depth of meaning that had never been there before.

He was hypersensitive to the touch of her body; he felt her body gently moving beneath his hands; felt her shoulder blades and the muscles around them tense as she momentarily gripped him. He felt the wonderful gentle pressure as her arms briefly tightened around him. This single moment burned itself into his memories and would stay with him all his life.

He knew that he could in theory turn his head one way, and she could turn hers, and they could kiss; but he also knew this would not happen. Perhaps the hug had lasted for a moment longer than it should - undoubtably it had - but Hugo knew they were friends, nothing more. He was aware of Bettony's relationship with Strikken Flange and was anxious not to make his embrace in any way romantic. The very last thing in the world - in any world - that he wanted to do was to lose her friendship. He was meticulously careful not to overstep the mark. But he had, nevertheless, for one brief moment in his life, felt part of something wonderfully greater than himself.

He was also, briefly, fully aware of how lonely he was. That too was a memory which would not fade.

CHAPTER TWENTY ONE

Hugs and Affection and Broken Legs

Hugo led me out of the greasy cafe and across the road. He directed me to a sheltered corner between two crumbling brick walls, spread his jacket on the floor, and we settled down. He explained about the transition boxes. It wasn't good news. At least I had avoided a ghastly death. Timmbo had somehow programmed the transition boxes to follow a specific journey across realities. Their last stop on this route was Erce. After that, they seemed to rip their user to pieces, atom by atom.

Hugo had become embroiled in the violent politicking that took place in Angland. We guessed from what he had learned that Mrs P had arrived at Erce but at the wrong time. It sounded as though she had had a narrow escape, too.

'We don't have much of a plan B,' he said. 'All I can think of is that we wait. I can't imagine that Mrs P would move the spaceship.'

'It's a transition vehicle Hugo.'

For some reason I was electrically aware of how close we were to each other.

'I don't know her as well as you do, obviously,' he went on, ignoring my comment. 'But my first impression of her is that she's not the sort of person to give up on her friends.'

'You're spot on there boy.'

'But she may be rather more circumspect on her next visit.'

'Agreed. I suspect she'll keep the doors shut and use the cameras. I found out who Timmbo was masquerading as, by the way.'

'Who?'

'A man called Welter Hallett. He'd only started at Swindon a few days ago.'

'That sounds like Timmbo. Pulling the strings from behind the curtains.'

'An interesting metaphor boy. Anyway that explains why he was able to pick me up on the way to Longcot. All that stuff about Tweek getting attacked was guff. He's a good actor though, I'll give him that. Or was, I should say.'

'Really? Was? Tell me about your holiday on the golden beaches of turtle-country.'

I told him. It was gratifying to see him shudder when I described the turtles, and their attack on Timmbo.

'Good heavens. A turtle-neck jumper's never going to be the same again. Are you sure he's dead?'

'Well he's not going to be much fun to be around. They'd fastened their teeth into him and they pulled him to the ground. His screaming was ghastly and it went on for ages. Honestly Hugo, those teeth were horrific. Rows and rows of needles.'

'Thank goodness they worship me as their god.'

We were huddled against each other, but only slightly and only because it was cold.

'I managed to get a list of Sentinnat people in Britannia from Pecky. There are a few surprises on there Bets.'

'You mean Brink Stellish?'

'Wow. Impressive. How did you work that one out?'

I told him about the Three Mug Problem. He thought about it for a while, and then I told him how I had solved it. When I did, he thought about it for a while longer, then laughed.

'And then Mrs P confirmed you were right?'

'I didn't need her to confirm it boy. But yes, she did. Who else is on the list - uh oh.' I pointed to the two baton-wielding thugs who were walking towards us, side by side.

'Fear not Bets. Those men are our friends.' Hugo raised his voice. 'Good afternoon gentlemen.'

'Hullo sir. And a friend now too. Still on your mission I see.'

'Indeed. May I ask a favour?'

'Anything you want sir. Do you want us to put the stick on whoever bruised your young friend?'

'No, that's a kind offer constable, but I've dealt with that matter myself.'

'Ah yes. I 'spect you 'ave sir.'

'Are you able to put your hands on something warm we could sit on? And perhaps a few blankets as well?'

'I'll see what I can do sir.' The thug fiddled with his stick. 'A bit of news sir that you may not have heard...' The thug looked expectantly at Hugo.

'Go ahead constable.'

'Sergeant Sluckham has been asked to step up as acting district administrator. He's been asked to assume control of Swindon sir.

By the Earl of Weymouth himself. So 'e said.' The thug sounded disbelieving.

'I hope the Sergeant has accepted. It's not healthy to refuse an invitation by the Earl.'

'No sir. Yes the Sergeant has accepted. Although I think he's bricking it sir. Apparently the Earl wanted somebody he could trust... any ideas why he chose Sergeant Sluckham sir?'

'I believe the Sergeant made a strong impression on the Earl on his visits to Swindon.'

'On his...' The thug looked shocked. 'You're not pulling my leg are you sir?'

'Certainly not constable. I was there when the Earl described Sergeant Sluckham as "the sort of fellow we need".'

'Fuck me sideways. 'Scuse my language there gents... I always said that Slucko was the right sort though, di'n't I Denny?' The thug added, recovering himself, and possibly his chances of a long and happy life I guessed.

'You did, yer... So did I though.'

'Yer. We both did.'

'Please pass my best wishes on to the acting district administrator.'

'We'll do that sir. And we'll get the blankets and stuff over.'

'Thank you constable. Remember that when Acting District Administrator Sluckham speaks, from now on he speaks with the authority of his grace the Earl. From now on, he is the voice of the Regency Cabinet itself and he carries their power of life and death.'

'Bloody hell. God 'elp us.' The thug recovered himself. 'Gents.' He put his hand to his beanie hat in some sort of salute and the two of them walked away.

'I'm tempted to ask what all that was about although I'm not sure I want to know the answer.'

'Sluckham's not a bad man. He's devious, corrupt and avaricious but he's not evil.'

'Interesting distinction you're drawing there boy.'

'Everything's relative Bets.'

'They didn't seem to think much of his promotion.'

'They'll get used to it. So will he, for that matter. He'll be a lot better than the last bunch.'

'Who's this Earl you were talking about? Are you going to tell me he's your uncle or something?'

'No thank heavens. Although he was a school chum of pa's and I now know that they still see each other quite often.'

'And he's the top man? More powerful than Slepwood was?'

'Oh much more powerful than Slepwood. Princeps Senatus, primus inter pares. The first among equals.'

'And a friend of your father. I feel honoured to be in such exalted company. You were telling me about a list of Sentinnat agents.'

'Ah yes. A sly cove, our Timmbo. He'd managed to slip quite a lot of people into Britannia. A few of them were like-for-like replacements but I suppose all the planets need to line up for that to work. There are more who have got completely fabricated identities. Like me, I suppose.'

'You told me that Brink was watching you when you were in a meeting with her. Do you think she knew that you were Sentinnat?'

'Dunno. Possibly. Although we were supposed to be kept in total ignorance of each other. According to what Timmbo told me, only he knows who we all were. He might be lying of course.'

'I think it's safe to speak of him in the past tense now, Hugo.'

'Yes.' He shifted awkwardly and looked away. His mockery was gone; his voice was serious and flat. 'I'm sorry I didn't get back. I left you to deal with Milden-Brewer.'

'I've told you before boy, I'm not from Erce.'

'I know, I know. But.'

'And I sorted it, didn't I? Aha! Look Hugo! Your friends are back.'

★★ ★★ ★★

'Mrs Ponch I implore you, please hurry. We have to return.'

'Dr Flange I am very tired. I have been working for almost a day on the Two, with very little sleep. How that strange fellow managed to damage it so quickly and comprehensively is beyond me. Terror can do strange things, can't it? Would you be kind enough to pass me the hybrid stythium isolator… thank you. Almost there…'

'So are we ready?'

'A few more seconds. We have to have a fully functioning transition vehicle. It will be risky enough as it is - they will be waiting for us, Dr Flange. Without any doubt. Word will have spread. That strange fellow was only too keen to flee the Two, but he will have told many people by now of his adventure. Remember what happened last year, on the Series Four? When the man who masqueraded as our Chief Engineer landed us on Erce? Weaponry was ranged against us. Gunfire. We were saved by the Four's emergency failsafes. The Two does not benefit from such devices.'

'If we do not return soon, Bettony may be lost forever.'

'I know, yes. And Mr Crean, too. We have a duty of care to them both.'

'I think you need to do something Mrs Ponch.'

'Indeed.'

'No, I mean now. You need to do something right now. That's Brink Stellish on the screen, if I'm not mistaken. Walking up the track.'

Mrs Ponch had been working on a small junction box close to the Two's door. She slammed the box shut, launched herself into the chair, and quickly moved her hands over the transition vehicle's controls. The Two's door clicked closed, and there was a brief, almost imperceptible judder. Mrs Ponch had not stopped twisting and moving the shapes, and an instant after the first, there was another small judder. All three screens were now showing images of the new world outside.

It was a desert world. There were scuff-marks in the sand, as though someone had been walking and possibly rolling around.

And a great number of rocks, large and small.

'My word it's warm out there. And deserted. No immediate danger… oh that's interesting.'

'What is Mrs Ponch?

'Despite having activated the emergency beacon from Erce, Mr Crean would appear to be on this world, some six miles south-east of our present position.'

'Where are we exactly?'

Mrs Ponch took a deep breath. She felt an explanation was necessary.

'My first reaction just now was to get us away as quickly as possible. I think it opportune at the moment for the person playing the part of Brink Stellish not to be aware that we know about this transition vehicle.'

'Indeed.'

'Before we became aware of Brink – or rather, the person playing her - my intention was to transition for the briefest of moments to

Erce, return to Abbuth and analyse camera footage to ascertain the level of danger that awaited us. I was able to successfully effect the first part of that plan, but obviously could not return to Abbuth, so in my haste I used the next set of coordinates to hand: Those which Mr Sneggs took from the transition boxes which had been reprogrammed by the agent from Erce. Calm down please Dr Flange! The cameras will have captured images of our surroundings on Erce and we can review them shortly. As I say, all rather hasty...' she peered at the screens. 'But we seem to be reasonably safe. The question is, I suppose, was the beacon part of a trap? Is Mr Crean really here? Or has he perhaps left his smartpad behind?'

'There was no trap on Erce Mrs Ponch. Can we review the camera recordings please?'

In reply, Mrs Ponch brought up images onto the three screens. They were basically photographs of a dirty, neglected town. Mrs Ponch zoomed in to each one and moved slowly around it. At first, two large men, carrying sticks and walking away from the camera down an otherwise empty road, were the only people they could see. There was some kind of shop on the other side of the road.

'"Happy shack,"' Mrs Ponch read aloud. '"Where our dreams fill your stomach with fun". What a peculiar idea. Rather at odds with the shop's dirty appearance, too.' She continued to pan across the image.

'There!' Strikken cried, leaning forward over her shoulder in his excitement and touching the left-hand screen. 'Go back and zoom in as far as you can.'

Mrs Ponch scrolled across to the corner of two brick walls. Two shapes could be seen, huddled together. She zoomed in further. They appeared to be homeless people. They were sitting on some sort of mattress and were covered in blankets. She centred the image and zoomed to maximum, momentarily blurring the picture. It came back into focus, a close-up of the wretched couple. A blanket covered their heads and the top of their faces, making identification difficult. The smaller of the two was leaning against the larger, who had its arm around the smaller one's shoulders. The smaller of the two was resting their head against the larger one's chest. What was visible of its face was disfigured by bruises.

Perhaps they had suffered a beating at the hands of the two men with sticks, she mused.

'And yet their affection for each other clearly survives,' she commented aloud. 'It really is dreadful, some of the things we find on other versions of our world. Heart-breaking. This reminds me of some of the things we saw during our time on Earth.' She continued to scroll around the three screens.

After a while, the two of them realised that there were more people in the pictures than they had at first thought.

'They all seem to be taking care to avoid the two men with the sticks,' Mrs Ponch remarked. 'Perhaps the bruised one was unsuccessful, and suffered the consequences... Although one of the other people seems to be waving to the two men behind their backs. See, Dr Flange? The person at the corner of that alleyway.'

'I'm not sure he's waving to them Mrs Ponch.'

'You think he's indicating to his colleagues how many men with sticks there are? That seems rather pointless to me. Surely anyone who can see his two fingers can see the two men.'

'At least we've established that there's no trap awaiting us on Erce. No line of armed soldiers waiting to fire on us.'

'You're right of course. And I understand your impatience to get back there. But before we do, we must investigate why Mr Crean's smartpad is here. For all we know Dr Flange, Bettony may be here too. Fortunately I am Friendslinked to Mr Crean...'

Mrs Ponch tapped a message into her pad and waited several seconds.

'The message has arrived at Mr Crean's smartpad, I see.'

They waited, all the time Strikken becoming more and more impatient.

'Please check the TV's water supply for potability,' Mrs Ponch said, as much to stop Strikken from fretting as anything. 'If we do not get a response from Mr Crean's smartpad I intend to investigate where it is and who has it.'

Three hours' walking, at least, Strikken thought. He tapped at a control panel next to the water outlet on his right. 'It's fine.'

'Come along then. Fill a couple of water bottles please. The sooner we're on our way, the sooner we get back, as my mother used to say.'

There were a lot of tracks around the Two, going in different directions. Mrs Ponch led the way using her smartpad as a guide, and setting a surprisingly fast pace.

'We shall have to climb that hill in front of us,' she said. 'Are you fit Doctor?'

'I thought I was' Strikken panted. The loose, sandy ground made walking very tiring. It did not help that it was so warm, ridiculously warm for late February. Or that Mrs Ponch seemed so comfortable.

'I suspect that in our world, that hill would be the location of the two Ufferton White Horses.'

'Uh.'

'Would you like me to carry your water bottle Doctor?'

'M'ok thks.'

They reached the hill and began the climb. Several times, Mrs Ponch diplomatically suggested they stop for a rest. Eventually Strikken's exhaustion got the better of his pride and he agreed. He slumped to the ground and gulped down half of his water.

'I shall just go and have a look over there,' Mrs Ponch said.

'Uh.'

He closed his eyes and listened to her footsteps as she walked away. Was he really so unfit?

'Doctor, I think you need to see this.'

The urgency in Mrs Ponch's voice brought Strikken to his feet and hurrying towards her. She was standing on the edge of a piece of flattish ground.

'Oh… good heavens.' Strikken looked at the body on the ground and tried to keep himself composed.

It was motionless, in a terminal sort of way. Around it, the ground was stained a dark red. Dried blood. Not very much of it though, Strikken thought, puzzled. Blood had stained its clothes too, but again, there was not a lot of it. It looked, bizarrely, as though the body had been punctured many times with a great number of fine needles. It was surrounded by small rocks, as though it had made a space for itself to lie down.

'I know this man,' Mrs Ponch said quietly. 'He's Welter Hallett, a new colleague of Bettony's. He introduced himself to me last week.'

'I don't understand...' said Strikken. He bent down and placed his fingers against Hallett's neck.

'There's a pulse,' he said, trying to mask any disappointment he felt.

'I saw it Hugo. I definitely saw it.'

'So where is it then?'

'I don't know!' He was beginning to annoy her with his ridiculously sensible questions.

'And how come you saw it and I didn't?'

'I don't know! It was only there for a couple of seconds, maybe less. Maybe you blinked. Or fell asleep.'

'Or perhaps you did. You could have been dreaming Bets.'

'I know what I saw boy.'

'Ok.' Wishful thinking, he guessed. You want to see something badly enough, so eventually you do. He had his arm around Bettony now, purely to make her more comfortable and not for any other reason at all. He gave her a gentle squeeze, and for a moment felt strangely peaceful. 'I hope it turns up again soon, long enough for us to get on board.' For the first time he was unable to hide his concern. His voice was grim. 'Sooner or later word will get back to Weymouth. He'll pull me back to Mazeley. You too, if we're not careful.'

'Can't we just ignore him?

'No-one ignores Weymouth and continues breathing.'

'We need to get this man back to our own world and get him immediate medical care.'

Strikken was examining the wounds, his mind in turmoil. He had lifted the body's clothes and was looking at a huge number of pinpricks that mottled the stomach.

The body stirred, and croaked, 'Please help me.'

And then a small head poked out from one of the rocks. Strikken's first though was that it was some sort of tortoise. But the neck kept extending until it was grotesquely long. The little head, swaying now like a snake's, dropped down towards the body's bare skin, its open mouth revealing rows of tiny needle-like teeth. Before it could reach the body Strikken batted it away, drawing a hiss of anger.

'Good gods. They seem to be feeding off him.' Strikken ran his fingers over some of the pinpricks. 'How strange. At a guess, the creatures bite to draw blood but also inject something to keep the wound clean - to stop it from becoming septic. None of these wounds seem to be infected. Can you stand up Mr Hallett if we support you?'

'Can't move,' the body croaked.

'We need to move this man as quickly as we can,' said Mrs Ponch. 'For all we know these creatures are also paralysing him with their bites. One thinks of spiders and their prey. We may ourselves be in some danger.'

'But –'

'Dr Flange I understand your feelings but we have to help this man.'

With extreme care, the two of them managed to get drag Hallett away from the strange tortoises. As they did so, more of the rocks grew heads and feet and began hissing disapproval that their dinner was being removed.

The injured man was completely unresponsive; it was like moving a deadweight. Somehow, Strikken and Mrs Ponch managed to turn him and each get one of his arms around the tops of their shoulders. Half-dragging, half-lifting, they pulled Hallett's inert body away from the rocks and down the hill, towards the Two. He was not a large man but it was hard work. They had to stop again and again to rest. Eventually they laid him down, a few yards from the Two. Strikken hurried into the machine and returned with its medical kit. He took a device from it, half the length and width of a mobile phone and twice as thick, and held it against Hallet's arm. Then he held a water bottle to the man's lips, squeezing a few drops at a time into his mouth. Hallett coughed a couple of times but was able to swallow the water.

'Mr Hallett, urgency prompts me to ask you several questions,' Mrs Ponch said gently. 'Is that all right with you?'

'Course,' Hallett mumbled. 'Nything cn do to help.'

'Do you know why Mr Crean's smartpad is locating him on this planet?'

'Golgood's here. Turned violent. Don't unnerstand... Took... woman. Took pad. Dunno why.'

Mrs Ponch was silent for a moment, then gasped. 'You mean he took Bettony? Why? Where?'

Hallett's nod was so slight it could easily have been missed. 'Dunno. Tried stop him. Left me for dead. Dngrous man.'

'Do you know what happened to Mr Crean?'

'Disappeared. Pff. Gone.'

'We need to get after Golgood and Bettony' Mrs Ponch said. She stood, quickly; then looked at the wretched figure in front of her. 'This chap needs to get urgent medical help though' she added.

Strikken did not reply.

'Be K,' Hallett managed. 'Feeling better 'lready.'

'That's the painkiller and the stimulant' Strikken said. I haven't done anything to cure whatever it was that those creatures injected into you.'

'Honestly. Feeling better. Think it had a temp'ry 'ffect only. You both go.'

'Can we rig up a shelter for poor Mr Hallett?' She asked.

Strikken looked around distractedly.

'Leave me in the metal box,' Hallett whispered.

'I'm not sure that would be a good idea Mr Hallett. It can get very hot in there.'

Strikken was about to say more but Mrs Ponch held up a hand to silence him. 'Let us move Mr Hallett to the shaded side of the Two, Doctor.' It was a command, not a request. Between them, they arranged Hallett in a degree of comfort against the north-facing side of the Two.

'Doctor, help me in resetting the Series Two's martinet algorithm please.'

'The what?' Strikken followed Mrs Ponch into the Two. 'Mrs Ponch I'm not tremendously technical you know -'

Mrs Ponch put her finger to her lips to silence him.

'Bettony explained to me how she solved the Three Mug Problem,' she whispered.

'The what? Ah. I'm afraid that for various reasons I didn't hear that. I'm not really sure -'

'I was already certain that Brink Stellish had been − replaced. Whatever else it did or did not prove, the Three Mugs showed that only one of the three of them was from Erce. Stellish was. So

Tweek Golgood was not. Tweek Golgood is Abbuthian.' Mrs Ponch sighed. 'I know Tweek pretty well. He has certain... individual mannerisms, but he is fundamentally a good-natured fellow. I cannot believe he would be capable of evil. I do not think that what we have just heard is true.' Strikken felt the force of Mrs Ponch's intelligence and authority as she fixed him with her eyes. 'Think about it. If what Mr Hallett told us was not true, the conclusion must be that he is himself the perpetrator of this mayhem. I want you to give him something to extend the period of paralysis.'

'I can't do that! It's against my –'

'Either you can do that or we shall have to take him back to Abbuth and hope that Osian Jelks and his colleagues are with us, and have not been infiltrated. It will take a great deal of time, of course –'

'No! It would take far too long and it's too risky! We have to find Bettony.'

'And Mr Crean, yes. So what is your decision Doctor?'

Strikken was back in his agony of indecision. He chose his words carefully.

'My first duty has to be towards my patient. I'm sorry Mrs Ponch but I cannot abandon him. I accept that you have assumed control of our effort against infiltration. But I would say the same if we were back on the Series Four and you were formally my Officer in Charge. Immediate medical priorities override all other considerations, even direct orders from a commanding officer.'

'I know that Doctor. And I respect your principles.' Mrs Ponch had been fiddling with something while they were talking. She pushed it against Strikken's leg, and helped him to fold gently to the floor. 'But in this case the immediate threat to life is that being suffered by Bettony and Mr Crean.' She arranged Strikken as comfortably as she could. 'A heavy dose I'm afraid. Peridown Eight. Please forgive me.'

She went outside and without speaking gave a similar dose to TMB. It was true, he was definitely recovering. Although still unable to move much, he was able to use both his hands to grab her arm in a weak but remarkably painful grip. He could not stop her from moving the Peridown dispenser to her free hand though, and moments later was slumped against the side of the Two.

'Thank you for reassuring me that I was correct, Mr Hallett,' she murmured. She collected a water bottle and set off once more, her pace faster now that she did not need to wait for Strikken.

Mrs Ponch had made good progress. Before her responsibilities as an elected Council member put a stop to them, she had led several expeditions to other worlds and she was becoming accustomed to places that were subtly different to her own. Other-Abbuths, she called them. But the differences were mainly to do with human society, or its effects on climate and the environment. This world seemed to have no human representation at all. As she walked she scanned her surroundings keenly for any evidence that humans had previously been here. There was none. There was no sign of life at all, apart from the unpleasant creatures that had overwhelmed Timmbo, as Bettony called the fellow. What a strange mixture of snake and tortoise! And, she mused, well-adapted to feeding from their prey.

But where was the prey?

She pressed on. In the past, whenever she had transitioned she tried to relate her location on an Other-Abbuth to Abbuth itself. She had developed a good sense of direction and was pretty sure of roughly where she would have been on her homeworld.

So it came as a shock when she reached the top of the hill and gazed down on a barren chalky whiteness that led to the edge of a hugely expanded ocean.

Was Mr Crean somewhere out there?

It was possible, of course. Perhaps there really were people. Perhaps Mr Crean had sailed with them, willingly or otherwise.

She knew that time was not on her side. Before too long, the drug that was immobilising Timmbo would wear off. It would wear off for Dr Flange, too, but Mrs Ponch had no doubt about who would succeed in a struggle between the two. Welter Hallett was not a big man but – if he were who she suspected – Mr Crean had warned her against him. He was well-versed in methods of combat, and well-practised. Dr Flange was neither.

They would be at the fellow's mercy. And from Mr Crean's description, mercy was not something which he had much, if anything at all, of.

She sat on a large rock at the very top of the hill, and pulled a metal cylinder from her pocket. She opened the small telescope to its fullest extent and held it to her left eye, closing the right. The device's electronics steadied the image, allowing her to look in detail several miles out to sea. She scanned slowly across the beautiful blue water, zooming in and out, searching for a boat. As she did so, she felt the faintest of nudges against her right leg. Mrs Ponch looked down just as the adult turtle bared its horrific teeth. Its neck had extended sickeningly from the rock she was sitting on, which too late she realised was not a rock at all but its shell.

In the few moments that it took her to react the creature had bitten into her calf.

She jerked away from it, feeling pain as its teeth pulled at her flesh. But she managed to free herself from its grip and roll away. She saw that several other rocks had grown necks, and feet too. At the same time, she felt a warm numbness around the area of the bite. She was already beginning to lose control of her right leg; when she tried to stand it collapsed beneath her. She was at the very top of the hill; as she fell she managed to throw herself onto its northern side. It was at its steepest here. She rolled down the hill as a child would in a game, but much more wildly, hitting rocks as she went, gathering speed. She was out of control now, bouncing off ledges, trying to keep her body extended and stiff so that it would roll as far as possible, as fast as possible, away from her predators. She flew off one ledge and landed heavily on a rocky outcrop, feeling something crack in her ribcage, but this did not stop her descent and still she bounced on, down the hill. She was no longer able to control her right leg in any way and from time to time it folded under her body at strange and impossible angles. She was almost grateful for its numbness, which she guessed was concealing a great deal of pain. Her mind was still sharp though, and she used what was left of the control she had over her body to try and steer herself towards sandy patches of ground and away from rocky ones. When she finally stopped moving she was a good third of the way back down the hill, in a soft, sandy area. Gasping for breath, battered and bruised, she tried to drag herself to her feet. But there was no strength left to do this in any of her limbs. She could not even crawl. She lay there, feeling soft warm numbness spread throughout her body, still awake and half-surprised that she was still breathing.

All around her, everything was still.

Strikken pulled himself to his feet. His head thumped. The Series Two seemed to spin around him and he grabbed at the edge of the desk for support. He felt very sick. He staggered to the door of the Two and pushed against it, but failed to find the manual door release catch and vomited against the handle.

He turned and grabbed at a water bottle and drank deeply. Slowly his wits returned, and with them his control over his body.

His first impulse was to return to the door. His second was to remember who it was that was outside. His third, running hard after the other two and shouting as loudly as it could, was a recognition of the mess that coated the door handle.

Maybe he should see what was going on outside before he opened the door. Strikken thought he knew enough about a Series Two to switch the cameras on; but despite his best efforts, the screens remained blank.

The wisest thing to do, he thought with the confidence of a doctor, would be to wait a couple of minutes. He could already feel his body functions beginning to strengthen. A couple of minutes and then his metabolism would have stabilised; then body and brain would be better equipped to deal with the situation. Have patience for a couple of minutes and then he would be better able to review all possible options. Whatever they might be.

At least he could use the time to look again at the recording that the Two's cameras had made in their few recent moments on Erce.

Strikken had no trouble pulling the recording up. The screens flickered into life. He found the part with the two homeless people on, and zoomed in.

There was no doubt in his mind that the two were Bettony and Crean. It was as much their posture as anything.

He felt a qualified sort of relief, but looked again at the two people on the screen, huddled close against other.

One with his arm around the other.

'*...And yet their affection for each other clearly survives,*' Mrs Ponch had said.

Realisation dawned. Something seemed to die inside him.

He needed to divert himself. He tried hooking up the live feed again. Again, he failed. He could see nothing of the outside.

He could hear it, though. A dreadful screaming started up from somewhere nearby. Presumably the Two's exterior microphones were still working. Strikken thought about those horrific tortoises. He could make out the word *'please'*, repeated again and again. He forced himself to ignore them, aware of the possible consequences of opening the door. Eventually though they became too much for his gentle nature to tolerate. He pressed the electronic release and the door swung open. At the same time the screaming stopped.

'I thought you'd never wake up,' the small man said, stepping lightly into the machine. Strikken was still wondering what to do when the man took him in a remarkably painful grip. *That's the brachioradialis being counter-rotated beyond tolerance* was all he could think as he felt himself being pushed towards the door. *Or is it the flexor carpi radialis? Both possibly?*

He was out of the door before his brain put the pieces together, just in time to watch the Two disappearing.

Light was fading. Acting District Administrator Sluckham approached the sleeping couple as quietly as a wearer of hobnailed boots could do, and cleared his throat.

'Acting District Administrator Sluckham. Do you have news for us?'

The acting District Administrator jumped. 'Oh hullo sir, I wasn't sure if you were asleep. Ah ha. No. No news. Not as yet.' Sluckham edged closer and lowered his voice. 'It's just that... I was wondering if you had any advice sir. On being a District Administrator. I've never had to do anything like this before.'

'Very first rule. Whatever the Earl of Weymouth says, you do. Without question.'

'Oh. Yes sir. I'd sort of gathered that sir.'

'He may well make some request of you in the next few days. It may seem an odd one; ridiculous even. Obey immediately. He will be testing out your loyalty.'

'Bloody hell.'

'It would shorten your life expectancy considerably not to obey immediately.'

The Acting District Administrator made a strange gurgling sound.

'Next. Remember that you hold the power of life and death over everyone in Swindon. Including everyone who works for you.'

'Yes sir.'

'And remember that they are all human beings.'

'Sir?' This was apparently news to the new Acting District Administrator.

'Treat them fairly.'

'Fairly?' The Acting District Administrator tried and failed to keep the astonishment from his voice.

'Fairly. That does not mean being a soft touch. But treating people fairly is the best guarantee you'll have that they won't try to kill you.'

'Are you sure sir?'

'I am, yes. Firm but fair.'

'Firm... so it's still all right to give them a kicking? As long as I do it fairly?'

'I'm not going to try and tell you how to do these things. We each have our own methodology.'

'Methodology. Yes sir.'

There was a pause.

'I don't suppose... you'd like to do the job instead sir?'

'Unfortunately I have my own task. You'll be fine. I have no doubt that you will be one of the best DAs Swindon has ever had.'

'You really think so sir?'

'I do indeed.' *Not a very high bar though.*

The Acting District Administrator's posture changed. His chest seemed a little fuller; his back straighter.

'Thank you sir.'

'You're welcome. And now I see that my taxi has arrived.'

The Sergeant turned. 'Where the bloody hell did that come from?'

Hugo was pulling himself to his feet, and helping the small person next to him to do the same.

'I would ask one small favour of you, Sergeant.'

'Anything sir.'

'There is only one of us standing in front of you.'

'One of you...? Oh I see. Or rather I only see one.'

'Thank you. And congratulations on your appointment. Mrs Sluckham must be very pleased.'

'She certainly is that sir. Thank you sir. Good luck with your... task.'

'Thank you. Goodbye. And please thank your militiamen for the loan of the mattress and blankets.'

'Ah! They did that, did they? I wondered where they went. Of course I shall. I'll do it fairly as well. With plenty of methodology. While I'm reminding them that they should've asked me first. Goodbye sir.'

Acting District Administrator Sluckham watched Hugo and Bettony walk stiffly towards the metal crate which had just appeared from out of nowhere. Its back panel, which was apparently a door, swung open, giving him a glimpse of futuristic machinery. The two of them, of which he had just been assured there were in fact only one, squeezed inside and he watched the door swing shut behind them. His eyes widened as the metal crate silently disappeared.

'Fuck me,' the Acting District Administrator said. 'Strange times.'

Timmbo was beginning to think he was immortal. Those creatures had been sucking at him like vampires for days; his mind, completely detached, had been able to watch them slowly killing him without the least discomfort. But then those two fools had rescued him and it had taken him no time at all to recover. His strength was returning just as quickly as it had left him.

And now he was back on Erce!

There would be questions to answer of course. But that would not be a problem. He would still be able to exact a terrible revenge, both on Crean and on the freak.

He flicked the cameras on, looked at the blank screens and remembered that he had smashed them all. The microphones were picking up voices, somewhere not too far away.

At least he was in Swindon. He was grateful now that he had carefully cultivated the support of Candaver Brandon Bowles.

He would be safe here.

Timmbo flicked a switch to open the door of the Two. At that moment, probably triggered by the stench from the door, a wave of nausea overwhelmed him. There was nothing left to vomit in his stomach and he was bent double, retching violently, when two people entered the Two. He turned to look at Hugo and the freak. Too late, he closed the door and transitioned. Hugo took him in a paralysing armlock and in the same movement reached down and removed his Tipper from its sheath and threw it into a corner of the Two. Timmbo realised that contrary to his earlier thought, he actually had very little strength left in his body.

But enough, unfortunately, to be able to feel acute pain.

Mrs Ponch had drifted into a light sleep. She woke and realised it was dusk. Realised, too, that there were more rocks in the vicinity than there had been.

A throbbing pain pulsed from her ribcage. One leg was completely useless - and fortunately, still completely numb. But the rest of her body was beginning to respond. Not enough yet for her to be able to drag herself away, though. But she could move fingers and the toes of one foot. The rest would surely follow, given time. Hopefully.

She watched one of the little rocks inch itself a little way towards her, then stop. At least a minute passed before another of them did the same thing.

It was, she realised, simply a matter of timing. If she recovered enough to be able to move before the tortoises began feeding from her, then perhaps she stood a chance of survival. If not, she was reliant on her friends to rescue her. Her chances were not completely zero, but not far off, she guessed.

Another small rock inched closer.

'Bets can you fly this thing? And what's that thumping noise?'

'Number one boy - it's not flying. Number two... No. Number three, it sounds like something big outside.'

'But you must have watched people do it!'

There were more thuds against the Two. They were so strong that they made the inside vibrate.

'I could say the same to you boy.'

'All down to you then Timmbo.'

'Go fuck yourself.'

Hugo regarded the man he was holding. 'You've made a surprising recovery old man, I must say. Mrs P give you some get-better juice?'

'Piss off. Aagh...'

'The thing is, as our friend the earl would have it, the thing is this old lad. If you don't help us, I'm going to put you through so much pain that you'll wish my little turtle-friends had carried on biting you to bits. We both know I can do that, don't we? For example...'

'Aaagh!'

Bettony winced. The two of them had crammed into the little transition vehicle and were standing behind the chair. TMB was in the chair, feebly pulling at Hugo's arm which had enveloped his neck and much of his face.

'Well?'

'Take a trip to the seven hells. Aaaaagh!'

More thudding. Whatever it was seemed to be pushing hard against the Two, which was starting to rock from side to side.

'And speaking of Mrs P,' Hugo went on calmly, 'there's the little question of what's happened to her.'

'Wouldn't you like to know? Ha! And not just her either.' As much as he could while Hugo was gripping his throat, TMB turned and looked at Bettony. 'I bet you'd like to know where your boyfriend is? The other one I mean - *Aaaaagh!*'

'Hugo! Please stop.' Bettony turned to TMB. 'What do you mean?'

'Work it out for yourself.'

'You mean Strikken?'

'Or maybe you're not too bothered about him now that you're getting on so well with Golden Boy here - *aaaargh!*'

'So here's the plan old lad. You get us to wherever you left Mrs P. And in return, I don't take you down the path to that little old place where you're in so much pain, you're begging me to kill you. Which we both know I can, and which we both know I will enjoy doing.'

'Piss off.'

The Two was shaking again as more hammer blows thudded against it. Bettony remembered how it had stopped working when Kaghendra had given it some rough treatment, the year before.

'Bettony would you turn away please? I'm going to pull one of Timmbo's eyeballs out and I'm going to leave it on his cheek.'

'God no! Hugo please. There must be some other way.'

'And then I'm going to do the same with his other eyeball. Ready Timmbo?' Hugo was having to shout against the noise of the hammering. 'Pity I don't have a teaspoon, it would make it a bit more clinical. I suppose my little pinkie will have to do. You'd better look away Bets.'

Hugo's eyes glinted venemously. Bettony saw his remorseless expression and turned away, sickened, as his free hand went towards Milden-Brewer's face.

'You see? You see you freak? This is what Mr Golden Boy's really like. This - AAAGH! All right! ALL RIGHT! Let me get at the controls.'

Timmbo leaned forward and moved shapes across the screens. His movements were less certain than Mrs Ponch's had been but the hammering and rocking stopped suddenly, and Bettony guessed they had transitioned again. For the first time, she realised how foul the air smelled in the Two.

'Where are we?' Hugo's voice was calmer now.

'I don't know. Back where her other boyfriend is I guess. Who knows.' Milden-Brewer slumped forwards as Hugo released him. He had no energy left. Not even enough to lift his head from the desk.

'Come on Timmbo. You're going to lead the way.'

There was no reply from TMB.

'Leave him Hugo.' Bettony's voice was flat.

'I'm not leaving Timmbo here while we wander off into the blue yonder,' Hugo replied grimly. 'That would be one way of kissing goodbye to Abbuth forever.'

Hugo gripped TMB by the clothes at the back of his neck and physically lifted his limp body from the seat.

'Can you open the door electrically please Bets? There's some sort of slime all over the handle.'

Bettony leaned forward and flicked a switch. She did not speak. The door clicked open, onto a rapidly-darkening desert world.

'This - can't be right' she said. 'Strikken's here? And Mrs Ponch?'

'Explain Timmbo.'

'How do I know? I suppose they came looking for you.'

Hugo stepped out of the Two, dragging Milden-Brewer's lifeless form with him. 'Explains how you got away I suppose. Where are they now?'

'How the fuck should I know? Aaaagh! The woman went off looking for you. Drugged me and the other boyfriend - aaagh! - I came round first, hoofed him out and left. I don't know where she is, but he can't have gone far.'

Hugo dragged Milden-Brewer a few yards further away from the Two and let go of him. TMB dropped onto the sand, unmoving.

'Dr Flange!' Hugo called out into the gathering dusk. 'Are you here?'

'Strik!' Bettony had also left the Two now. She was standing some distance away from Hugo. 'Strik! It's ok!'

In the gloom, the shape of a man unmerged itself from one of the nearby rocks.

'Bettony? Is that you?'

'Of course it's me you idiot!'

'And Mr Crean.'

'Yes. Hullo.'

Bettony ran over to Strikken and hugged him. He put his arms around her, but without any great tenderness. She looked up at his face but it was difficult to make out his expression in the gloom.

'Why did Mrs P wander off looking for me here?' Hugo asked.

'Is she not back?' When no-one answered, Strikken went on, 'Your smartpad was showing you to be several miles to the south of here Mr Crean.'

'Ah. That would probably be one of my turtle friends.'

'Friends?' Strikken was unable to keep the astonishment out of his voice. 'You can communicate with them?'

'They worship me as a god.'

'They do?'

They could be speaking different languages for all that they understand each other, Bettony thought. She had detached herself from Strikken now, without any resistance from him. *I'd better translate.*

'Hugo had somehow attached his pad to the back of one of the adult turtles,' she said. 'It was a way of misdirecting Timm Milden-Brewer.'

'You mean Tweek Golgood?'

'No Strik,' Bettony replied with exaggerated patience. 'This is Timm Milden-Brewer.'

'But that's Welter Hallett. Are you saying he's not really Welter Hallett? So Mrs Ponch was right?'

'Nice one Strikky,' Timmbo muttered weakly. 'Give the man a bar of chocolate'

'Actually I was right,' Bettony said stonily. 'Cast your mind back, you may recall it was me.'

They're speaking as strangers, Hugo thought, not lovers.

'What do you mean, one of the adult turtles?' Strikken persisted. 'The hideous little tortoise-things that we saw -'

'- Were babies. The little ones were babies.'

'My gods. And Tweek Golgood is not here? Or is he?'

'Shall we leave the finer points till later Strik? Perhaps you can find someone cleverer than me to explain it. Someone you can trust. If Mrs Ponch is out there somewhere we need to find her.' Bettony had an inspiration. 'I've still got my pad.' She unclipped it and flicked it open. Its screen shone brightly, making the surroundings seem darker still. 'I can see her!'

'Where is she?' Hugo asked.

The AI in the smartpads was able to scan and remember areas visited and build itself a working map as a result. Large sections of Bettony's screen were still only gridlines, but there was enough filled in now for her to be able to locate Mrs Ponch. Unfortunately Bettony's map-reading skills were not well-honed and Strikken was in no mood to assist. Grudgingly, she asked for Hugo's help.

'It looks like she's a fair way up that hill,' he said, looking over her shoulder. He carried on watching the screen. 'Not moving.'

They were both acutely aware of how very close they were to each other.

Against his wishes, Strikken's good nature got the better of him.

'We should go and find her,' he said grudgingly.

'We can't all go,' Hugo replied. 'Someone needs to stay here and look after Timmbo.'

'After what you did to him he's hardly likely to cause any trouble,' Bettony said.

'I didn't do anything Bets. He's been poisoned. That's what you get when my turtle-followers don't like you.'

'Hugo I wish you'd stop that stupid game! They're nasty creatures that have a horrible way of killing people.'

'Not the most smoothly-functioning team are you?' TMB sneered. 'That's what comes of one woman and two boyfriends. It could work though I guess. Could be fun if you're all willing.'

'You're a poisonous reptile aren't you Timmbo,' said Hugo quietly. 'But since you've tried to insinuate something that isn't true, I want to make it clear Dr Flange that there is no romantic connection between Bets and myself. Chance has thrown us together in this little adventure. That's all there is to it.'

Strikken grunted but did not reply. Bettony felt a stab of pain on hearing Hugo's words. Aloud, she said,

'Obviously.' And was glad that no-one could see her expression in the gloom.

Strikken thought about the images on the screen, amongst other things, and remained silent.

They decided that Hugo would go alone to find Mrs Ponch, taking Bettony's smartpad. He felt confident that Bettony would be able to keep the situation at the Two under control. The biggest potential issue, he thought, was Timmbo. But a weakened Milden-Brewer was little threat, and Hugo trusted his judgement as to the rest. And Strikken would only have slowed him down.

He was on autopilot, all conscious feelings suppressed. There would be a time, he knew, in the next few days, when it would all hit him. When he would analyse each moment he had spent with her and agonise over whether a different word or action could have brought their feelings for each other out into the open - and he thought, he really thought, that she had found an affection for him that mirrored his own for her. But for now, Hugo had to concentrate on getting Mrs Ponch back from whatever danger she had wandered into. Losing his focus on that would mean endangering them all. He was responsible for these people.

In his mind, Hugo could hear a voice rebuking him on that thought; saying, *'You forget I'm not from Erce, boy.'*

Concentrate.

He reached the long hill and began to climb, checking his progress on the smartpad but mainly using its torch to follow Mrs Ponch's tracks.

'I didn't have you down as the jealous sort Strik.'

Bettony was hoping to get a reaction from Strikken, more than being serious about her accusation.

Any sort of reaction.

'He's got good reason to be, hasn't he?' TMB was still lying where Hugo had left him, although he had rolled onto his back and could now look at them both.

'Shut up Timmbo. You're poison on legs. This is the man who killed Sherian Penck, Strik. The man who tried to run me down and the man who attacked Liz. And murdered that poor man in Oxford.'

Strikken flinched. 'Do you know that for sure?'

'Of course she doesn't you halfwit! She's been caught, making out with Crean, and now she's looking to distract you with irrelevances.'

Another silence. Then Strikken said,

'So what is Tweek Golgood's involvement in all this?'

And maybe it was all the stress, or lack of sleep, or knowing how far this all was from being over, or maybe it was all of them together that burst a bubble somewhere inside Bettony. In a surge of emotion, she shouted,

'For fuck's sake Strikken! Tweek Golgood's not involved in any of this! Maybe just once, consider that this earth-woman knows what she's fucking talking about!'

She stormed away into the darkness. Strikken watched her go.

TMB smiled to himself. 'Nicely played Dr Flange.'

'Mrs Ponch I believe.'

'Mister Crean. How nice to see you.'

Hugo shone his torch onto the small rocks that surrounded the woman, then knelt down next to her.

'Did they attack you?' He asked.

'The tortoises you mean? A very large one bit me some while ago. I was able to escape it by tumbling down the hill... a bit of a mixed blessing I'm afraid, my leg is badly injured and I suspect my ribcage is not quite all it should be. It has been something of a game of cat and mouse since then with these smaller ones. Cats and mouse, perhaps that should be. I have been saving most of my energies for dissuading them from biting me.' She held her left hand up and Hugo saw it was gripping a stone. 'This is a genuine rock and it has so far worked in keeping them away. I am getting very tired though. I think they are waiting for me to fall asleep. Please be careful Mr Crean. We don't want you being bitten as well.'

'Fortunately I have discovered they're not very quick in their movements.' Hugo carefully picked up nearby rocks and threw them some yards away. There was a muted hissing but no other response. He checked Mrs Ponch's leg and tried to conceal a shudder.

'How badly does it hurt?'

'Somewhat. I suspect the worst of the pain is still being masked by the paralysing agent that I was bitten with. The fact that it seems to be wearing off is something of a mixed blessing.'

'Fortunately Mrs P we have a medical man close by. We just need to get you back to him.' Hugo gingerly lifted the woman up. 'Tell me if you would like me to adjust my grip.'

'So far so good Mr Crean.'

Holding Mrs Ponch in his arms, Hugo began the descent. It was almost fully dark now and he could not operate the smartpad's torch nor its map facility, but he was pretty sure of his direction. He went slowly, making sure of his footing. Few people could have carried her any distance at all in this way; even Hugo had to stop twice to rest his aching arms. It was pitch black when he got back to the Two.

'The hero returns. There's been a bit of a lovers' quarrel down here. Something to do with a blond philanderer who's worked his way into the heroine's affections. I think that's what he worked his way into. Is that right Hugo?'

Timmbo's voice was strangely frail and easy for Hugo to ignore.

'Dr Flange?'

'I'm here.' Strikken's voice was dead.

'I hope you're ignoring these outpourings from Timmbo's toxic mind. I have a patient for you.'

Hugo laid Mrs Ponch gently down on the sand. Strikken appeared out of the darkness.

'Can you shine your torch on her please Mr Crean?'

Hugo did so while Strikken expertly checked and questioned her. He was unable to suppress a shudder.

'I'm giving you Peridown Four,' he said. 'We need to operate on your leg as soon as possible although not until the poison has dissipated. I suspect there's a cracked rib there too which will need attention.'

'How are you proposing to do that Doctor Flange?' Hugo spoke quietly.

'Transitioning takes just a few moments Mr Crean.' *Now he's talking to Hugo as if he were an idiot,* Bettony thought miserably. *Poor Hugo.* Another thought replied, *And why not? He deserves it.*

'And then?'

'And then we get her to hospital.'

'How do you propose to do that?'

'Call for an ambulance of course.'

'From the spaceship's take-off site?'

'Er... You mean, how would we explain the existence of the Two and the unauthorised transition site?'

'Not only that. How would you explain Mrs P's injuries, received on another planet from an alien creature?'

'Ah.'

'Ah.'

'We can drive her to Swindon General.'

'I suppose you could. How would you explain her injuries?'

Strikken sighed. He did not enjoy being confrontational. In a gentler voice, he said,

'Do you have any suggestions Mr Crean?'

'I bow to your medical expertise Dr Flange.' In the darkness, Bettony could just about make out Hugo performing a small bow. She could guess the mocking expression on his face. *Poor Strik,* she thought. The other thought repeated, testily, *And why not? He deserves it.*

'The chances are, of course, that your fellow doctor would be as trustworthy as you are.' Strikken winced. 'But could you be sure? And would you be comfortable with the possibility that someone in the hospital might get word out to one of our friends from Erce, that Mrs P has been using their Two and going off-world?'

Strikken winced at this, but did not answer. Hugo went on, 'Could I suggest that you consider keeping Mrs P in a secure place, under your supervision, until the poison has left her system? And then, make sure that you perform the operation yourself. It should be possible to concoct a story to support her injuries.'

'I'm afraid that's more your area of expertise than mine Mr Crean.'

'Strikken! That was uncalled for. I've had enough of your childish sulking. Hugo I apologise for this man's idiocy. It's worse than yours.'

There was the sound of quiet laughter. 'Wonderful,' TMB murmured. 'Priceless.'

'Perhaps we should get back to Abbuth,' Mrs Ponch murmured.

'Ok how about this for an idea,' Bettony went on, fired by a vague feeling of anger at just about everything and everyone. 'We take Mrs Ponch to Earth. Get her operated on there.'

Nobody liked that idea. She remembered another occasion when one of her ideas had united everyone by turning them all against her...

'Where's the Four?' She said, suddenly.

No-one replied.

'Ok look, you can all shoot me down again but just consider this as an idea. The Four has a pretty advanced medical facility -'

'- More basic than advanced, I would say.'

'Shut up Strik. Compared to our health service in the UK, it's pretty advanced. Could you operate on Mrs P if we got her to the Four? ... You don't need to stay shut up Strikken you can answer that.'

'Yes... I could. I could operate on Mrs Ponch on the Four. There are enough resources on the Series Four for straightforward surgery. But there's already a medic on the Series Four, by the name of Blazer. Kelham Blazer. She's a good doctor. Probably a better one than me.'

Bettony sighed. *Come on Strik, think! How do we know she's who she says she is?* She said, 'Mrs P how can we get hold of the Four's transition co-ordinates?'

'They're stored on the Sputteridge database. If we were on Abbuth I could access them from the Series Two via my Television House connection.'

'Are you feel up to doing that Mrs P? As well as piloting the Two back to Abbuth?'

'Yes. I'm a bit fuzzy from the Peridown but that's ok.'

'Thank you Mrs P.'

'The Four will have transitioned from Sputteridge Bettony,' Strikken objected. 'That's two hundred miles from Swindon. That's the distance we would have to move Mrs Ponch.'

'I know. Can you think of a better plan Strik?'

'Not right now...'

'Good. So we go with mine. Anyone else got anything to say? Mrs P? Hugo?'

Hugo shook his head. He thought, *It's just wonderful, watching her in action.*

Mrs Ponch managed a weak smile. 'Now can you see why I wanted you in Swindon?' She murmured.

I know she'd accuse me of being patronising if I told her that though.

Bettony was grateful to hear Mrs Ponch's comment but she was completely focussed, driven by a low-burning anger, and did not acknowledge it. 'Hugo, help Mrs P into the Two' she continued.

'Right you are.' *And she'd be right, too. I need to learn a whole new set of rules.*

'You're the best person to go with her. If there are problems in Abbuth you're the best equipped to handle them.'

'Do as you're told Golden Boy.' TMB's voice was weak, and barely carried to Hugo. No-one reacted to him; no-one was interested any longer. Hugo gently lifted Mrs Ponch into the Series Two and helped her onto the chair, trying as best he could to settle her useless right leg. He found the bag containing the transition boxes, emptied it and used it to wipe down the door handle and the floor below it, then threw it out of the vehicle.

'Back in a mo,' he said brightly. 'Toodle-oo. Stay on your toes Bets, danger lurks at every turn. Where you least expect it, that's where you'll find it. Blah blah cliché cliché.'

The Two disappeared. Silence returned. Even Timmbo did not break it. Eventually, Strikken could bear it no longer.

'I saw you and him,' he said, flatly. 'The Series Two dropped into Erce for a couple of seconds before we lost control of it to this man here. Its cameras recorded the two of you. Huddled together.'

More silence.

'*Cuddled* together.'

'We were tired and we were trying to keep warm.'

More silence. All light had gone now, neither could see the other. They were just voices in the darkness.

'He obviously has... feelings... for you, Bettony. And you obviously have feelings for him.'

'Don't be silly. Of course I don't.'

'I'm sorry that I have behaved so childishly. I didn't want to lose you, that was all it was. I behaved very badly.'

'You haven't lost me Strik.'

'I rather think I have. Perhaps you don't know it yet Bettony but believe me. It really is obvious.'

Bettony blinked back tears. *Not now.*

Silence returned.

'Nothing to say Timmbo?' Bettony called out. 'No nasty comment?'

The thought chased through her mind, *He's escaped!* But he was still there when she shone her torch. Not moving, though. Not responding in any way.

Carefully, in case this was another of his tricks, Bettony checked Milden-Brewer for a pulse. She found none. His hand was cool and strangely unreal to her touch.

'Strikken! I think he's dead.'

Strikken hurried over and checked for a pulse. He tensed his hands against Milden-Brewer's chest and pressed them down against it in a series of short jolts. After half a minute of this he checked for a pulse again. He was fighting to keep his emotions and his professional responsibilities separate.

He repeated the procedure.

When the Two reappeared Strikken was still trying to resuscitate the lifeless body. Its door opened, throwing light on the scene.

'Got them!' Hugo called. He saw Strikken and Bettony, bent over Milden-Brewer. 'Ah.'

Strikken beckoned him over. 'Bad news I'm afraid,' he whispered. He watched as Hugo bent down and checked Milden-Brewer with surprising gentleness. Hugo looked up, asking a silent question. Strikken quietly shook his head.

'This may be a long-term effect of the bites from those animals,' Strikken continued softly. 'I'm worried about Mrs Ponch.'

'From what I understand Timmbo had been bitten a lot,' Hugo murmured. 'Mrs P only had the one bite. Although admittedly that was from an adult.' He checked again for a pulse. 'Has Timmbo really coughed it? He's not in some sort of trance?'

'He's dead, Mr Crean.'

'Better not waste any time then.'

Without cameras, there was no way of knowing what they would find when they transitioned to the new coordinates. Hugo once again accompanied Mrs Ponch, this time to have a quick scout around. They returned after a minute or so.

'Well it's a lot colder there, that's for sure,' he said. 'You're going to be a bit chilly Bets.'

'What did you see?'

'Nothing much. Grass, and trees, and a clear sparkly sky. Lots of stars. Sweet-smelling air.'

'No road lights or town lights or anything like that?'

'Nope. No sign of people.'

'There must be something of interest,' Mrs Ponch managed. 'It should be fairly safe as well. Otherwise the expedition would have returned.'

Mrs Ponch piloted the Two again. She followed Hugo's suggestion, taking Hugo and Strikken and then returning with Hugo to collect Bettony. The old chicken-fox-grain puzzle again, she thought. Except we're not going to eat each other.

At least the new world had trees. Strikken was able to use a branch to fashion a home-made splint for Mrs Ponch's leg, although it was obvious that this was going to make it even more difficult for Hugo to carry her. Bettony suspected the woman was in a lot more pain than she was letting on. Progress was going to be so slow that Bettony doubted they would ever get to Cornwall.

Impossible, in fact, they reluctantly agreed, in a world that seemed to be lacking any form of transport.

'Plan B then,' Bettony said. 'Transition to Abbuth, make the journey down to Sputteridge, steal a Two and get to the Four from there.'

'It wouldn't work,' Mrs Ponch said.

'Oh I don't know,' Hugo replied. 'We can get into Swindon, pop Mrs P on a train and rely on our wits.' His voice suddenly serious, he said, 'You had a good plan Bets. It's not your fault we can't make it work.'

'We would be discovered immediately, Mr Crean. Immediately we boarded the train.'

'What is there to discover?' Strikken asked. 'In any case, it doesn't look as though we have any choice. The worst that might happen is that I have to operate on you in Swindon General.'

'That's not the worst Strik, that's the best. The worst is that we never get to Swindon General.'

They were standing outside the Two while Strikken put the finishing touches to Mrs Ponch's splint. Reluctantly, they agreed to return to Abbuth and take their chances.

With her leg in the splint, Mrs Ponch would not be able to sit at the control desk. Hugo lifted the chair out of the vehicle, then helped Mrs Ponch towards the door. As they entered the Two, red lights began flashing on all the control panels. A disembodied voice began quietly repeating,

'Alien infection detected. Do not attempt transition. Seek immediate medical assistance. Transition request will be refused.'

'Well there we are,' Strikken sighed. 'We must follow Bettony's plan. We have no choice.'

'What's happening?' Bettony asked.

'I can only guess that the animal which bit Mrs Ponch has infected her with something,' Strikken replied. 'Maybe the same thing that infected Mr Milden-Brewer. All transition vehicles have detection systems to prevent infections being transferred from one reality to another. Accidentally introducing an alien infection into a reality could be catastrophic for it.'

'But how come she was ok just now?'

'I don't know Bettony! Perhaps the infection has been incubating. Or perhaps it's multiplying. It could have been at such a low level as to avoid detection. The Two's systems are not perfect.'

'Can we try calling the Four?' Bettony asked.

'Much too far away' Strikken replied.

'Can we at least try?'

They tried. Or at least, Mrs Ponch tried.

There was no reply.

CHAPTER TWENTY TWO

Jimmy Grinns

After the warmth of the desert world it was a shock to be back in a normal February. We were all tired and the other three were a bit irritable, probably from lack of sleep, but it was too cold to rest and the Two was no use to us. We started walking towards where Swindon ought to have been, in the hope that there was some sort of village or town that we couldn't yet see.

In a few minutes we had found a track; a few minutes more and there were fields around us. Soon after that we reached a house, lights blazing from the downstairs windows. It was surrounded on three sides by trees, which would have obscured it from us until now.

The other three stopped on the track and began to debate what to do. While they were woffling away at each other I walked up the path and knocked on the front door. Sometimes it's better just to do stuff. Especially if the alternative is to spend half an hour in the biting cold arguing about it.

The door was opened by a small, elderly man, barely any taller than me. A blast of warm air from inside the house hit me.

'Oh hello,' he said hopefully. 'I'm not back in am I?' He looked at my bruised face. 'Bloody hell. Are you all right?' He was speaking in English.

'I had an accident on the way here. We're tired and lost,' I said. 'And cold. I know this is a bit cheeky but can we come in please? Just for a few minutes? To get warm?'

He looked over my shoulder. 'How many of you are there?' There was still a strange hopefulness to his voice.

'Four including me.'

'Of course you can.' He stood to one side. 'Come on! They didn't forecast rain in the dining room!' He twisted his face into a strange sort of smile, which was achieved by tensing the muscles in his cheeks and slightly dropping his chin to reveal his teeth. His eyes refused to go along with the exercise, and managed to simultaneously convey both a tattered hope and a pathetic hopelessness.

'I said, "They didn't forecast rain in the dining room!" ' He repeated, looking at me expectantly. 'Hur hur,' he added, still watching me for any sort of reaction.

'Ah. Yes. Hur hur.' I said. I began to feel grateful that Crean was still with us. His brutality towards TMB still sickened me but his was a muscular presence and however weird this little man was, I was pretty sure that between us we would be able to cope with him.

'You'd better give them a shout,' the little man said. He looked deflated.

I called to the others. The two of us watched them slowly approaching down the path.

'You don't know who I am do you?' He asked me. His voice was flat.

'You're a very kind person,' I said guardedly.

'And you're nothing to do with the production company?'

'I'm afraid not.'

'No. Silly really. You live in hope. But it's better than living in Birmingham. Hur.' He looked at me, waiting for a reaction, then sighed. 'I'm Jimmy Grinns.'

I looked at him blankly.

'You know, Jimmy Grinns and Leopold Laffs? No? Come on darling you're not that old. The kiddies' favourite and the Mammies' menace?'

Humour him. 'Oh yes. Of course. Ha ha.' I managed what I hoped was a smile of recognition. The others were joining us now and I felt a lot safer.

'It's Jimmy Grinns!' I exclaimed to them, hoping desperately they would pick up on my cue. Strikken and Mrs Ponch looked vaguely worried, but Hugo Crean beamed.

'Jimmy! What a delight! Jimmy Grinns and Leopold Laffs!'

He's good, I thought bitterly. *He must have heard us talking as he was helping Mrs Ponch down the path. And he looks so pleased, like a man who's meeting his hero. The two-faced bastard.*

'Well at least here's someone who recognises me!' Jimmy Grinns suddenly looked a lot happier. 'Come on in, come on all. They didn't forecast rain in the dining room!'

'Didn't they?' Asked Strikken, puzzled. 'Why would they though?' Crean and I bundled the other two into the house. We followed Jimmy into a warmly-lit room. A coal fire was blazing in a hearth.

I introduced everyone by their first names.

'Come on in, come on all,' Jimmy Grinns repeated awkwardly. There was an embarrassed silence. 'Tea all round?' He asked.

'That would be great thank you,' I answered.

'Can I help you Jimmy?' Crean asked. *The creep.*

'No no, you people sit back and relax. Jimmy's on the job.'

'Ha ha.'

The little man left the room. We heard him opening another door, presumably into the kitchen.

'Just going to check,' Crean whispered. 'Can't be too careful.' He moved silently out of the room, returning a few seconds later. 'All good.'

'What a peculiar person,' Strikken whispered.

'I'm guessing he was some sort of children's entertainer,' I said.

'My gods!' Strikken exclaimed. He was looking wide-eyed at the door. The head of a strange creature was poking around it, half-way up. It had very large sightless eyes and spiky blue hair, some of which was missing, revealing coarse matting. It waggled its head manically.

'Hello doys and girls!' The voice came from behind the door, rather than the creature itself. Mrs Ponch gasped.

'Hello Leopold!' Crean said excitedly. He looked around at us and gave a small gesture.

'Leopold!' I said. 'Is that you?'

Jimmy Grinns came back into the room. His free arm was wrapped around the hand that held the glove puppet. He looked at me.

'Remember now?' He asked.

'Of course!' I forced a smile of recognition onto my face.

'Is it Tuesday at two or Friday at four,' chanted Jimmy, 'there's Jimmy and Leo a-knocking at your door!' The strange open-mouthed rictus had returned to the lower half of his face. His eyes still hadn't made it yet but they were trying their best.

'Wow!' Crean gasped. 'I never thought I'd hear that again.'

'They wouldn't let me bring him on Only One Can Win,' Jimmy Grinns said. 'Apparently he wasn't the right image.'

'Shame on them.' Crean looked outraged. 'Shame on them!' He repeated.

'I'll get the tea.' Jimmy Grinns looked much happier now. He took the tattered glove-puppet off and laid it carefully on a side-table. Once again Crean gave him a few seconds, then followed him out and returned, nodding.

'Are you familiar with this character Mr Crean? Do they have a similar entertainment on Erce?' Strikken asked.

'I suspect Mr Crean is doing what we all should be doing, and playing up to this gentleman's expectations of us,' Mrs Ponch murmured wearily.

'How are you Mrs Ponch?' I asked.

'Tolerably well thank you. Very grateful for this rest.'

We had travelled less than a mile, we were around two hundred from the Four, and already Mrs Ponch was grateful for a rest.

There was a rattle of teacups and Jimmy Grinns came back in, carrying a tray. He set it down on another side table and handed the cups out.

'I think,' he said conspiratorially, 'that you're my next test. They're giving me another chance aren't they?'

'Honestly, we're not.' Even as I answered, I could see his pathetic hope clinging on. He still wasn't sure.

'Did you at least watch Only One Can Win?' He asked, sitting down.

'We haven't had the chance,' Crean said.

'No. Well. Episode one aired on Monday. I was the first to be voted out. All those young kids doing those dumb things. What did they expect? How could I hop through wet cement with these knees? They said it was meant to raise a laugh. Well it did that all right but they were laughing at me, not with me. All the other contestants were anyway. Bastards. It was humiliating. I'm glad to be out of it. Career relaunch my arse. I think they only wanted someone to take the piss out of.'

A thought seemed to occur to him.

'You're not recording this are you? It's not for Only - The Second Take is it?' As an afterthought, he tensed his cheeks again and added, 'Hur hur.'

Crean shook his head. 'Honestly Jimmy, it's not.'

'What are you doing here then? Are you on another show?'

'Yes!' I said in a burst of inspiration. 'We're on The Long Haul.'

Everybody stared at me, for their different reasons.

'The what?' Jimmy asked. He looked around the room nervously. 'Are there cameras in here? They said there wouldn't be. It's in the agreement. No cameras in the accommodation. I didn't mean what I said about them being bastards. Just a cheeky jape. Hur hur.'

'It's not live to air,' I said, trying to sound reassuring. 'It's not that sort of a show. The crew visits us once or twice a day to check how we're getting on.' I thought about what I'd just said. 'Sometimes even less. Sometimes once every few days. Or longer.'

'Nobody said anything to me about it. Is there an extra fee?'

'We didn't know you were living here,' Hugo Crean said. He lowered his voice. 'Things haven't been going too well. We think we've been set up.'

I had to admit, Hugo and me, we definitely worked on the same wavelength.

'Why?' Jimmy leaned forward, sympathy showing on his face. 'How have you been set up? What's The Long Haul anyway?'

'It's going to be on this autumn,' I lied. 'It tracks teams of people as they make their way across the country. Secretly. And one of them is supposed to be injured.' I pointed at Mrs Ponch.

She gave a little wave. 'That's me,' she said. *Thank you Mrs P!*

Jimmy Grinns looked at her. 'They've done a pretty good job on you,' he observed. He was getting interested now. 'And they've started you from this Vintage location?'

'That's right.' *What the hell is a Vintage location?*

'Saves money I suppose, hiring the place out to do two shows at once. Where do you have to get to?'

'Falmouth. Just outside it. Sputteridge.'

'Sputteridge?' A genuine smile spread across his face. 'Do you know, that was one of the last places I played? Ten years ago. Third on the bill. I thought it was a new beginning, playing Vintage locations, Mams and Dads willing to go along with a bit of good old-fashioned humour.' He shook his head. 'Fat bloody chance of that.'

A polite silence fell, while we waited for him to continue. Eventually he pulled himself out of his reverie and looked around at us.

'So you're starting from a Vintage and you're ending in a Vintage. That explains the way you're dressed I suppose. And do you have to get from one to the other using Vintage connections?'

'That's right.' I was grateful for the prompt but now totally lost.

Luckily, Hugo wasn't. 'They haven't given us any maps or anything,' he said. 'There's a second group after us. If they find us before we get to Sputteridge, they win.' His face fell. 'We don't stand a chance Jimmy. We're going to be laughing stock.'

Jimmy Grinns shook his head angrily. 'Bastards!' He exclaimed. 'These days that's all they do isn't it? Just make fun of people. What's happened to this world? People calling themselves comedians when all they can do is mock other people? I know we had a few issues in my day, but Arthur Tasty and his cripple jokes were nothing compared to what they say now. Why ban a man from television just because of his wheelchair gags? Although after that business with the sheep he really didn't have a leg to stand on.' He smiled ruefully. 'Apart from the four that belonged to the sheep of course.'

There was a stunned silence. Strikken's eyes had widened in shock, and I could see he was about to speak. Luckily Hugo beat him to it. 'Have you got any maps here Mr Grinns?' He asked hastily.

'Jimmy. Please call me Jimmy.' He looked around vaguely. 'I don't know. I haven't had much of a chance to explore.'

'They wouldn't be maps on the top shelf of that bookcase would they?' Hugo prompted.

Jimmy Grinns twisted around. 'My goodness young man you're observant.'

He took a handful of maps down, and whispered, 'Let's look at them in the dining room.' He looked towards Mrs Ponch. 'Your friend's nodded off.'

The three of us followed the little man into another warm, brightly-lit room. He selected a map and spread it out on a large polished walnut table.

'There's a vintage rail line that runs from just outside Bristol, down to Falmouth.' He pursed his lips. 'I don't see how you're going to get from here to Bristol though. There's a vintage coach runs from Falmouth to Sputt of course.'

'They're expecting us to use vintage cars,' I said.

'It's a fair old way from here to Bristol in a Morris Minor! Still, you could do it I suppose. Might be tricky with that lady's leg in a splint.'

It was still a strange experience, looking at a map of a Britain which was so different to the one I knew. I had seen maps on Abbuth of course, and also the one on the frozen world. This was another, completely different layout. London was huge, at least three times its size on earth, and seemed to reach out in a star shape into the surrounding counties. Its southern tentacle spread south in a corridor of development that reached as far as Brighton, then for some miles in each direction along the coast. Other cities were smaller than on earth. Straight lines ran between many towns and cities, criss-crossing each other to form something like a webbing. I had no idea whether these represented roads or rail lines or something else, and I didn't want to show my ignorance by asking.

We pored over the map for a while. My eyelids were getting heavier and heavier. My body was crying out for rest. Strikken had fallen asleep in his chair. Only Hugo seemed as wide awake as ever.

'We could go through this again tomorrow if you like,' Jimmy Grinns said. 'It's very late and you're all tired. There are plenty of spare bedrooms. You can stay if you want.'

'Thank you Jimmy,' Hugo said. 'That would be wonderful.'

I found a room with a lovely big bed. It was covered in crisp white sheets, which I spoilt by lying on in my grotty clothes. I think I was asleep before my head reached the pillow.

★★ ★★ ★★

It wasn't that Hugo Crean did not specifically trust Jimmy Grinns. He trusted very few people, and Jimmy simply fell into that very large group. Hugo made sure that everyone had a bedroom, found one for himself, and waited a few moments. Then he crept out onto the landing and took up a position at the top of the stairs, from where he could see down into the living room. He watched Jimmy collect the glove puppet from the side table. Jimmy also took a small glass from a cabinet, along with a bottle. The little man poured himself a small measure of something and sat quietly with the glove puppet in his lap, stroking it as though it were a cat or a small dog. After a few minutes he pulled a handkerchief from his pocket, wiped his eyes and blew his nose.

Hugo watched for several minutes. He returned to his room, then less silently re-opened the door and went downstairs.

It was basic Sentinnat training. Learn as much as you can about persons of key importance. Right now, Jimmy Grinns was a Person of Key Importance.

Hugo tapped softly on the open door.

'Mr Grinns? May I come in? I'm not that sleepy yet.'

'I've told you son, call me Jimmy.' He pointed to a nearby armchair. 'Take a pew. Fancy a snifter?'

'Thanks.' Hugo had a rough idea of what the last sentence meant. He sat down and accepted the glass of spirit that Jimmy Grinns offered. They sat for a while in a comfortable silence.

'How did you come up with the idea of Leopold, Jimmy?' Hugo asked, eventually.

The little man smiled and reached down to the puppet again. 'He was my Danny's. When he was a tot. I used to put him on and make funny noises. Just to make Danny laugh. Just to hear him gurgle. You got any children son?'

Hugo shook his head.

'You should. It's the best.' Jimmy smiled a brief, genuine smile and took a sip of his drink. 'Anyway. When Danny was old enough to have his little friends round he wanted me to show them so I put Leopold on and started to make up funny stories. That was the best, son. My little lad's friends all laughing away and him looking at me as though I was some sort of hero. That was the best time of my life. Ever.' He laughed, looking into the warmth of his past. 'Proper little happy family we were. Till the wife left. And she took Danny with her. I tried of course, but... the courts, you know... they always go with the mammy. Or they did in them days anyway.'

'I'm so sorry Jimmy.'

'Yeah well he was growing out of it by then. I could see he was starting to get embarrassed even when I just did the voice. And we managed to stay in touch, sort of. So that was ok.'

'What happened?'

'What happened? What always happens? He grew up. But after they left - after the wife took Danny away - I realised that other little kiddies might like to see Leopold. So I started to do kiddies' parties and it just grew from there. For a while anyway. A good while, if

I'm honest. And then television and everything.' Jimmy took another small sip from his glass. 'Tastes change though, don't they son? In the end the bookings began to drop away. Then I did that one series of "What's In the Window?" That was a mistake! Saturday early evenings, a show for all the family. Not really my thing, I was a children's entertainer and trying to follow Lenny Sarga, he was the best... I was a disaster, really.'

Jimmy Grinns sighed. 'That was it. Done. Still I'd had a good run.' He smiled again. 'We're like old dogs aren't we, entertainers? Don't know when we're passed it. Don't know when to stop. But do you know what - Hughie, isn't it?'

'Hugo.'

'You know what Hugo? All the time I was making those kiddies laugh, it was a pure joy for me. And when I was looking out at them, I wasn't really seeing them. I was looking at Danny. Looking at his lovely little happy face. And hoping that maybe he was watching me on the tv and feeling proud of his Dad.'

'Do you see much of Danny these days?'

'Oh. Yeah... sort of. He lives in Scotland. He's doing well. His house looks lovely. He screenshotted me last Christmas, ten minutes. He's got two boys, eight and ten, right strapping lads they look.'

Jimmy blew his nose again and took another sip of whisky.

'I'd hoped that they'd enjoy meeting Leopold when they were little but... I never got the chance to introduce him. It's a long way, isn't it, Scotland? Time passes so quickly doesn't it?   We keep saying I must get up there but it never seems to happen. There's always something gets in the way.' He raised the glass to his lips again and took another tiny sip.

'We keep in touch though. You've never heard of me have you son?'

'No.'

'No. I thought not. You the one they put on the team to make it work?'

'Sort of.'

'You're a plant? No offence.'

'Well, you know...'

Jimmy tipped his nose. 'Your secret's safe with me son. Good luck to you, that's what I say. You've got the looks. You'll be putting a hit single out soon I suppose. And why not? Milk it while you can. And know when to walk away. That's the only advice you'll get from Jimmy Grinns. Know when to stop before you humiliate yourself.'

He stood up and finished his drink.

'I'm off to bed. Stay up as long as you like. It's nice to have company, even though you're all a bit odd.'

'Goodnight Jimmy.'

★★ ★★ ★★

I was the last to wake up. Outside, a wind lashed rain against the bedroom window, but the room was warm and the unmistakeable smell of bacon was creeping under the door. I had a quick shower, put my rather smelly clothes back on and went downstairs.

Jimmy Grinns and Hugo were working in the large kitchen, and had got to that magical point in breakfast preparation when sausages and eggs and other interesting stuff are being put onto plates.

'Good morning Miss Sleepy Stop-in,' Jimmy said. 'Make yourself useful and start taking these into the dining room.' He had an air of innocent happiness that completely disarmed me.

Strikken and Mrs Ponch joined us from the living room. It looked like a dreadful day outside. Mrs P didn't look too bad. Bizarrely, although the breakfast was delicious I had a strange longing for the muck I had swallowed in the Happyshack.

'So look,' Jimmy said as we were finishing. 'I've had a think about this. I know you've got to get to Sputt using Vintage routes but I've got the Landunit outside. Hired for the week courtesy of Only. Tinted windows all round. One of you in the front with me, rest of you in the back. The lady doesn't even need to take the splint off. I can get you all down to Sputt today and no-one would know. I've got a friend down there, he'd put you up if I asked him, till you need to make an appearance. We can get one over on these TV idiots. What do you say?'

'I don't think the people in the TV are idiots Mr Grinns,' Strikken said. 'How do you know about them anyway?'

'I've met enough of them to know, young man.'

'Have you?' Strikken and Mrs Ponch were both regarding Jimmy with some interest now. 'Where did that happen, if you don't mind my asking?'

Jimmy looked puzzled. 'Er - loads of places. Here. Obviously.'

'*Here?*'

'Good greeks.'

'Pardon?'

'My teammates are new to the world of *Television*,' Hugo interrupted smoothly. 'Strik here is a doctor. When someone says "TV" he still thinks they mean - er - the "Terminal Virus" department of a hospital. Not "Television."'

'Terminal Virus Department?' Strikken looked as puzzled as Jimmy. 'I think you labour under a misapprehension Mr Crean. I understand -'

'Ah' Mrs Ponch exclaimed. 'Yes. TV stands for Television! Of course.' She smiled knowingly. 'Of course it does. I realise that now. Ah ha. Hahahah. I knew that already dude. Of course.'

Jimmy looked from one to the other as though they were mad, then turned to Hugo. Somehow, Hugo seemed to have gained his confidence.

'Help me out here mate,' he said.

'It's a great idea Jimmy. We'd love to take you up on it.'

'And you never know, it might work out well for me. "Jimmy Grinns helps The Long Haul team get one over on TV moguls" ...Who am I kidding? But anyway. Why not? It could be fun. And when it gets aired my son Danny might be impressed with his old dad.'

That made me feel guilty.

We decided to get going after breakfast. Jimmy invited us to stay on for a couple of days but we were keen to set off.

I got the impression he was quite a lonely old man.

The Landunit was a people carrier the size of a large van. We were able to turn some of the seats in the back of it into a sort of bed that Mrs Ponch could lie on. Strikken and I sat with her, with Hugo alongside Jimmy in the front. The little man seemed to have no trouble manoeuvring the huge vehicle. Soon we were making good speed on a smooth, straight road. The Landunit was very comfortable; there was no engine noise at all, just an occasional thud from the windscreen wipers as they cleared the last of the rain.

As we drove, my longing for the strange food I had eaten in the greasy cafe intensified, which was bizarre, because at the time it had made me feel sick. Mrs Ponch soon fell asleep again, but Strikken and I had little to say to each other. Every so often he would check on Mrs P, and frown, but he did not explain his worries.

We stopped for lunch at a small service area. Jimmy and Hugo swung their chairs around so that they faced us.

'Got any non-Vintage money?' Jimmy asked. He looked at us. 'Thought not. Don't worry.' He pulled a metal stick from his pocket, about the thickness of a pencil and half as long. 'Courtesy of Only. More or less unlimited credits from what I can see. What do you fancy?'

We let Jimmy choose lunch for us. After he had gone, I said to Hugo,

'The funny thing is I want to go and look for a cafe like that one on Erce. I'm really missing that rubbish.'

'You'll get over it Bets. You've got a bit of withdrawal.'

'Withdrawal? You mean they put something addictive in it?'

He nodded. 'It's called frost.'

'Frost? What's frost?'

Hugo shrugged. 'I don't know. I think they extract it from poppies.'

'Poppies!'

'Steady on Bets you'll wake Mrs P.'

'They put *heroin* in the food they sell?'

'I don't know what you mean by heroin. It's only very small amounts. It's supposed to be nutritious.'

'Nutritious? My god! Children eat that stuff?!'

'Bets calm down. Nobody has to eat it. And surely it's better for a kid to eat a Happyshack meal than to go hungry? It's a very cheap way for some people to get food.'

'Hugo there are so many things wrong with what you've just said that I don't know where to start!'

The back door of the Landunit opened and Jimmy climbed in. He handed paper bags around.

'Cheese and tomato sandwiches and bottled water. You can't go wrong with cheese and tom!'

He looked exhausted. I realised how tiring it must have been for him to drive us. Hugo must have had the same thought because he offered to drive.

'Ever driven one of these before son?'

'A while ago. I'll need you to remind me Jimmy.'

Jimmy looked at Hugo doubtfully but was too tired to argue. 'It's easy enough,' he said. 'I'll show you after lunch.'

I'm aiming for an exciting narrative here, even though it's only me who's ever going to read this particular journal. And I know that an exciting narrative needs to be full of excitement but I have to be honest, the journey down to Sputteridge was pretty uneventful. I think that's fair enough. There had been a lot of exciting events over the past few days and many more would have driven me nuts. At one point we were stuck in a traffic jam, and at another Hugo overtook a group of cyclists. And it's true, we hadn't been going long when Hugo called quietly from the front,

'Bets? Can you navigate please? Jimmy's fallen asleep and I don't want to wake him.'

There were three seats at the front and more than enough room for me to climb through and sit between Jimmy, gently snoring on my left, and Hugo, intent on the road to my right. I took in the controls for the first time. The vehicle did not have a steering wheel. Instead there was something more like the sort of thing a pilot uses to guide an airplane.

'I can't believe this thing hasn't got a navigation system,' I said. In reply, Hugo waved a hand at the array of switches buttons and screens in front of him.

'Want to have a guess?' He grinned.

'No thanks.' I gently pulled the opened map from Jimmy's lap onto mine. 'I'm probably not the best person for this sort of thing,' I said.

We were almost whispering, trying not to wake our slumbering guide.

'It's ok. It's pretty much a straight drive, as far as I can see.' Unusually for Hugo Crean, he looked uncomfortable.

'Actually,' he whispered, 'I wanted to talk to you.'

He paused, waiting for me to say something. When I did not, he went on,

'I think - er - what I said to Timmbo... well, I had to be pretty forceful...'

'Forceful!'

'Shh!'

'*Forceful!* You were brutal.'

'No I wasn't Bets. I may have said some... brutal things. But I didn't do anything.'

'I got the very strong impression you were going to.'

'It was important that Timmbo got the same message. Our lives depended on it.' He cleared his throat then mumbled, 'I suppose I would do anything to keep you safe.'

An uncomfortable silence followed. Hugo seemed to be concentrating even more on the straight, smooth, empty road ahead and I was concentrating on the map.

'I don't need anyone to keep me safe. I'm not –'

''You're not from Erce. Yes I know. I keep reminding myself of that. It's one of the things that I find... very... appealing about you.'

For a moment neither of us spoke. Then I said,

'The road splits about a mile in front of us. Take the left-hand fork, signposted Truro. Or it could be Pucklehampton. Is it a mile? Maybe a bit more. Five miles, possibly. Oh here it is...'

CHAPTER TWENTY THREE

We've got friends here too tubby lad

Much of the journey to Sputteridge had been through open countryside. As the road approached Truro, low, functional buildings began to appear on each side. Bettony did not know whether they were homes or work buildings. Mixed in among them were recognisably Cornish cottages and occasional rows of old terraced houses. As they skirted around Truro the mixture changed, becoming more and more what Bettony thought of as traditionally Cornish. Soon they were back in the countryside, on a lane that was vaguely familiar.

Sputteridge itself was exclusively "Cornish". Stone houses and pubs nestled together, connected by meandering lanes. There was a small post office and they passed several general stores, as well as an unusually large number of cafes and restaurants. Although it all looked very old, this Sputteridge was much larger than any version she had encountered so far. It was strangely clean and tidy, all the houses brightly and freshly painted. She wondered if they were now in one of the Vintage areas. The narrow lanes became even narrower as they headed down the hill towards where the village square had been in other worlds. She found it difficult to relate it to the Sputteridge that she knew.

A clanging of bells woke Jimmy with a start. Eyes suddenly wide open, he said urgently,

'Stop! Hughie, stop right now!'

Hugo pulled to a halt. A very old-fashioned black car was pulling in behind them. A sign across the top of it read "Police".

'Oh, no, Hughie what have you done?' Jimmy wailed. 'You should have woken me before now. We don't have a permit for the Landunit in this Vintage!'

A policeman got out of the passenger side of the car and in the style of police officers everywhere walked steadily and with measured tread towards the Landunit. *Not a young man,* Hugo thought to himself. *Out of condition. No visible weapons. An easy takedown, if needs must.*

Jimmy had already dropped his window, and the policeman glanced up at him as he inspected the vehicle.

'I hope you've got a permit for this, sir,' he began, in a tone which managed to convey his sad doubt that his hope would be realised. Then he stared.

'Wha- Jimmy Grinns! It is isn't it?'

Jimmy smiled down from his seat and nodded.

'It's Tuesday at Two, or Friday at Four...' the policeman said breathlessly,

'...There's Jimmy and Leo a-knocking at your door!' Finished Jimmy. He switched on his cheeky grin. The policeman stared, awestruck. Eventually he turned back towards the car. 'Kevin!' He called. 'Kev! It's Jimmy Grinns! The *real guy!*'

The driver of the police car got out and ambled over with some urgency to join his colleague. *Similar build and age. Still not a problem if the worst comes to the worst.*

'Jimmy Grinns?' He asked incredulously. 'Really?'

'Really.' The first policeman riffled excitedly through his pockets and finally found his notebook and pencil. 'Sir, could I have your autograph please?' He passed it up to the open window. 'Could you put something like, "To Martin, with best wishes from Jimmy"?'

'Course I can son.' Jimmy took the notebook, wrote in it and passed it back down to the policeman's eager hand. By now the second policeman had joined him. They peered at the notebook like excited schoolboys.

' "To Martin",' gasped the officer. ' "Here's hoping it never rains in your living room! All the best from Jimmy Grinns" ...would you believe it?'

He's going to cry, thought Bettony.

The second policeman hastily passed up his own notebook and received a similar message of goodwill which he was now staring at rapturously.

'Look I'm sorry we stopped you sir,' the first policeman said. 'If we'd known it was you we'd've nodded you through. We have to be a bit strict about these things, you wouldn't believe how many people try to drive into Vintage areas.'

'Not a problem officer,' said Jimmy. 'I can see you were only doing your job.'

'Can we give you an escort anywhere sir? It would be an honour.' Before Jimmy could reply, the policeman went on, 'It's a funny thing but we were only talking about you this morning.' He turned to his companion. 'Weren't we Kev?'

His companion nodded. 'Why did you only do that one series of "What's in the Window" sir? You were a breath of fresh air after Lenny Sarga.'

'Well, I had other commitments and the contract was only for one season...'

'You should've done more sir.' The policeman shook his head. 'Look, don't worry about the permit. I can see it shining on your windscreen. Where can we help you to get to?'

'We were going to visit Brian McShane.' The policemen looked blank. 'Charlie Jerome,' translated Jimmy.

'Charlie Jerome! Do you know sir, he was guest of honour at last year's Christmas party? What a funny man. He's still got it sir.'

'Yes but it's not catching officer.'

'It's not catching!' Both policemen convulsed in laughter. 'Look sir I can see what's happened,' the first one said when he had regained his breath. 'You've come a bit too far. You should've turned right about a mile ago. Would you like us to show you?'

'Well if it's no trouble...'

'It would be an honour sir. A genuine honour.'

'Just follow them Hughie,' whispered Jimmy. His cheeky smile was still fixed in place. 'Bloody hell we were lucky there. You should've woken me.'

Hugo managed to turn the Landunit around and trundled after the black police car. It led them out of the village and back along the lane that in another world had so transformed Bettony's life. It turned into a gated drive and stopped. The policeman spoke into an intercom next to the gate, there was a clicking noise and the gate swung open. They followed the car down a long drive and pulled to a stop in front of an impressively large house. A very overweight man was waiting by the front door, a cheery smile on his face.

The policemen reluctantly refused an offer to call in for a quick snifter and took their leave. The overweight man waved cheerily to them as they left and then switched his smile off.

'You all right Jim? The fuck you doing?' He nodded towards Hugo. 'Who's this?'

'I'm all right Bri. This is Hughie. Can we come in? We've got a couple more in the back.'

The overweight man glanced nervously in the direction of the departed police car.

'Course you can mate.'

'Thanks' Jimmy said wearily. 'I'll get the others.'

Brian McShane stared as Bettony and Strikken helped Mrs Ponch out of the Landunit's side door.

'The fuck is this Jim? You in trouble mate?'

'I'm all right Bri. They're on a reality show.'

'They must be. Looks fuckin' real to me.'

'Let's get inside. I'll explain.'

McShane led them into a large and garishly-decorated living room. He poured shots of whisky for anyone who wanted one, which was everyone except Strikken and Mrs Ponch, and looked at the people gathered around him.

'So it's Only is it Jim? Some sort of twist? I thought you'd been voted off. And well out of it mate. All them kids with more muscles than brain cells. What's the world come to?'

'This lot's on something called The Long Haul. It's new. I wondered if you could put 'em up for a couple of days Bri? As a favour to me?'

McShane looked uneasily at the people seated around him.

'If they're friends of yours,' he said doubtfully.

'It's a big no problemo if you can't, Mr McShane,' Mrs Ponch said. 'We've got friends here too tubby lad.'

She had regained some of her old vitality, thought Bettony as she cringed. But then again Timmbo did that too. For a while.

McShane was staring at Mrs Ponch. Before he could speak, Jimmy Grinns said 'Bri? A word please?'

McShane levered himself out of his chair and followed the little man into the hallway. A whispered conversation could be heard, with the words "tubby lad" angrily prominent among them.

McShane re-entered the room and glared at Mrs Ponch.

'I'll show you to one of the bedrooms,' he said coldly. 'Jim thinks you're not well.'

With Strikken helping her, Mrs Ponch followed McShane and Jimmy out of the room.

'I should be able to use my Smartpad to confirm the location of the Four,' Bettony said. 'Then we're home and dry.' She hurriedly unclipped the device and opened it out.

'That's odd. Nothing.'

Hugo peered over her shoulder. Once again, each of them was very conscious of the physical proximity of the other.

'Could it be blanketed?' Hugo asked. 'Would that stop it showing up?' He thought he had succeeded in keeping his voice steady.

'Dunno. It's possible I suppose. That's one for Mrs P.' Bettony noticed Hugo's strangled tone and congratulated herself on not letting her own voice betray any emotion.

'Try a wider search area.'

There was the sound of footsteps. Bettony hurriedly folded up her smartpad. The door opened and Brian McShane and Jimmy Grinns returned to their seats and their whiskies. Neither looked very happy.

'What's going on, Hughie?' Jimmy Grinns asked, glancing at the smartpad. 'Is that lady genuinely ill?'

Hugo nodded, sadly.

'I dunno Jim.' McShane shook his head. 'The things they do these days. It's sick. What sort of a show would take a sick old lady and put her in a reality show?'

'You didn't tell me that Hughie,' Jimmy said accusingly. 'And you didn't say anything about knowing people here.'

'I don't,' Hughie replied.

'They said we were supposed to find out more about each other as the show progressed,' Bettony said.

McShane ignored her.

'You've got a funny accent as well,' he said to Hugo. 'Are you English, sunshine?'

'He's Austrian' Bettony said, in a moment's inspiration. Jimmy sat back, a wildly mistaken enlightenment dawning across his face. McShane continued to look at Hugo but his hostility had gone.

'You're Austrian are you?' He asked.

Am I invisible? Bettony thought to herself.

'I can see it now,' McShane went on. 'Blond hair and everything.'

'It's a co-production Bri. Got to be. You know what them continentals are like.'

'Bloody hell. Big budget eh?' McShane suddenly became a lot friendlier. His cheery smile returned. 'You all Austrian?'

'Only me and - er - Strikken.'

'I should've guessed from the name,' Jimmy said. 'Strikk. Strikken. It's not English at all is it?'

'I'm sorry Jimmy,' Hugo lied. 'I wasn't supposed to say anything. But I didn't know about the people in Sputteridge. What we have to do now is find them before Team B find us.'

'In *Sputt*?'

Hugo nodded.

'Must be big budget,' McShane said.

'Bets here needs to get - er - some codes off the old lady. Then she can head into Sputteridge and find the contacts.'

'She got a pass?'

Hello? I am still here aren't I? You can ask me directly if you want...

'No.'

'Hang on.' Moving surprisingly quickly for a big man, McShane got up and left the room again.

Jimmy turned to Bettony and smiled ruefully. 'Sorry luv, he doesn't mean to be rude. We're just from a different age, that's all it is. Your friends are up the stairs, second door on the right.'

Bettony hurried up the stairs. Mrs Ponch was lying on a huge bed, still awake. She took the smartpad and make a few adjustments.

'I've authorised it to show blanketed TVs,' she said. 'Can't see the Series Four, although the range is very small for blanketed craft. So it could be here somewhere. You might just need to get closer to it.'

'That's ok Mrs Ponch. We'll sort it.'

Back in the living room, Hugo handed Bettony some copper coins and a small disk.

'Courtesy of Mr McShane,' he said. 'A very kind gesture. This is the money you need for the village. There's a regular bus service that stops just across from this house.'

'Have you used one of these before?' Jimmy asked her, pointing at the disk. Bettony shook her head.

'You don't need to do anything with it,' McShane explained to Hugo. 'It does it all itself. Just keep it in your pocket. Even gets you into the Parry!' He turned to Jimmy. 'Know who's on tonight Jim?'

Jimmy Grinns shook his head.

'Max Morris.'

'No!' Jimmy was incredulous. 'Max Morris?'

'Well it's February mate. Low season. Scraping the barrel time. Mind you he's got a good show. Clever tricks. I still haven't worked out how he does it. Selling out, he is. *Selling out*, Jim.'

'It's ten years since I was on, you know, Bri. Went down like a stone in a duckpond.'

'I'm off then,' Bettony said, to no-one in particular.

'Ten years! Well it's five since I did Sputt. I'd had enough mate. We're well out of it.'

'You're telling me Bri.'

Hugo looked up at Bettony, grinned and gave a little wave.

CHAPTER TWENTY THREE

Greasepaint, The Paramba and a Humber Hawk

It was late afternoon by the time I got into Sputteridge. Brian McShane's house was a fair way away even from this much bigger version of the village, but there was a bus stop opposite his driveway and a bus turned up after a few minutes.

A very old-fashioned bus, small and slow and noisy and spotlessly clean.

The driver took one of the large copper coins from my hand and gave me a ticket. He was immaculately dressed in white shirt, green tie, green jacket and trousers and a green cap. He was also extremely cheerful. I took a seat near the front. He ground the gears noisily before engaging them and sending the bus lurching forward.

'Sorry' he called. 'These four-twenties had a semi-synchronised gearbox. Built like tanks they were but an absolute bugger to get going. Woops.'

He concentrated on turning the huge polished-wood steering wheel and slowly succeeded in avoiding a ditch, then continued a detailed account of the way the bus worked, comparing it favourably to what he called "the rubbish we get these days". He did not seem either to notice or care that I wasn't listening to him: His joy seemed to lie in speaking, rather than conversing.

He was certainly having a joyous time.

It was still light outside. I tried to work out where I was compared to the Sputteridge that I knew, and got off the bus close to where I thought Bob's police house might have been in another world. The village here was just as old if not older than the one I had stumbled upon less than a year ago, but was confusingly different. As well as being much bigger it had many closely-packed lanes, some of which were too narrow to get even a small car down. All of the houses and little shops were spotlessly bright and perfectly painted. The lanes and pavements were cleaner than my kitchen floor back in Croydon.

I unclipped the smartpad, switched it on and immediately a blank grid lit up the screen. Then it updated and gave me the best news I had had for ages, triggering a surge of relief. It was showing the Four! About a mile away, I guessed. (Or possibly slightly more. Or less.) But there was no image of the labyrinthine streets and lanes that separated me from it.

Surely it wouldn't be that hard? I wandered around for a while, and inexplicably ended up further away from the Four than when I had started. Luckily I came across a post office. I thought I might be able to get either a map of the village, or directions. Or maybe both.

A bell over the door clanked as I went in. Behind a wooden counter to my right, shelves contained large jars of sweets. In front of me, an old-fashioned weighing scales sat on a smaller counter.

I waited.

Overhead, a dim lightbulb glowed. It seemed to suck more light from the room than it gave out.

'Hello?' I called.

Even the smell was old-fashioned. A mixture of sweets, and wood, and paper and cardboard. Somewhere a clock was ticking.

'Hello?' I called again, more loudly. I noticed a brass bell on the counter and hammered it, perhaps more vigorously than I had intended. Its sound echoed around the little shop. Stumbling, bumping noises came from beyond a doorway behind the counter, accompanied by mumbled curses. A middle-aged man staggered in. He wore a waistcoat that failed to meet across his large belly; underneath it, his shirt was open at the neck. He looked panicky and also very tired.

'I'm sorry' he said. 'I fell asleep. Have you been waiting long?'

'Only for a minute or so.'

'You won't report me will you?'

'No of course not.'

'Only I'm already on a warning for not opening on time.' He looked at me indignantly. 'They didn't tell me it was a five thirty start! Five bloody thirty! It's not even light then!'

'I'm not going to report you. I wanted a map of the village.'

He didn't seem to hear me.

'One more warning and I lose my deposit. Five hundred pounds! I'm going to complain about this. Put something up on HolidayNow.' His bleary eyes focussed on me for the first time. 'What do you want?'

'A map. Of the village.'

'Ha! Somebody else who didn't get everything when they arrived. You should complain. Post a bad review. That's what I'm going to do.' He rummaged in a drawer under the counter and pulled out a folded, dog-eared map. 'Here.' He pushed it across the counter.

'Thank you. Er. How much?'

'Oh no, just take it. Somebody else must've left it behind.' He sighed. 'I've been saving up for this experience for years. I honestly wish I'd never bothered. Slave labour that's what it is.'

'I'm sorry.'

'Mm. What're you doing here? In Sputt I mean?'

'Oh, er, nothing really.'

'Nothing? I thought everybody had to do something.' He looked at me suspiciously. 'You're not checking up on me are you?'

'Honestly, no. I'm - er - helping out at the Parry.'

His eyes opened wide in envy. 'You mean the Paramba? Wow. You struck lucky there. What're you doing?'

'I'm - er - rehearsing. Charlie Jerome.' I edged to the door. 'Got to go. Sorry.'

'Hey! Wait! Can you get me his autograph? I'll let you have a go behind the counter here if you do...'

'Sorry.' I hurried away, turned a couple of corners, then stopped and looked at the map. I opened out my smartpad as well. On impulse, I used it to scan the paper map. Hah! This would show them. Gullivant the IT whizz! I selected an option instructing the technologically-advanced pad to assimilate the scanned image into its Viewmap function. Once it had done this, finding the Four on the Friendslink grid would be a cinch.

'*Assimilating information,*' a warm and well-educated voice assured me. '*Please wait.*'

Brilliant. I imagined myself in a few days' time, smugly explaining to Kagh and Benedict what I had done. For some reason, Hugo was there as well.

After five minutes the screen went blank. I tapped it.

'*Assimilating information. Testing...SEVEN...of ninety-one possible physical matches. Please wait.*'

I was getting cold. I gave it a couple more minutes and tapped the blank screen again.

'*Assimilating information. Testing...TWELVE...of ninety-one possible physical matches. Please wait.*'

For goodness sake. My faith in Abbuthian technology began to wobble. I tried to do a quick bit of mental arithmetic. Twelve in about seven or eight minutes, so ninety-one would take...

I gave up and tapped the screen again.

'Assimilating information.   Testing...EIGHTY-SIX ...of ninety-one possible physical matches. Please wait.'

Phew!

After five more long, cold minutes I tapped the screen again.

'Assimilating information. Retesting...THREE...of ninety-one possible physical matches. Please wait.'

I folded the notsoverybloodysmartafterallpad up rather more forcefully than was absolutely necessary and set off. I would follow my own well-tuned instincts. It couldn't be that hard. Just keep going downhill and I would reach the bay and the spot where the Four should have transitioned to.

I don't know how I ended up at the top of the cliff looking down on the village, but it gave me a good view of the whole place. I congratulated myself on my unexpected ploy.

From up here, the village looked beautiful. Stone houses and cottages nestled up against each other along erratically meandering lanes. Some of them glowed gold in the last rays of a weak sun. Thin wisps of smoke floated out of many of the chimneys.

I used the coastline and the shape of the bay to help me work out where the Four would have been in other Sputteridges. There was a very large building covering the whole of that area. A large sign arced across the front of it, but from here I was looking at it almost side-on and couldn't read it. I wondered if it was the Paramba. As good a place to look as any, I thought. I made my way back down the path and headed towards the big building. The dumbpad was still updating, making it impossible to see where the Four was.

The Paramba was more difficult to see from down in the village, but I found it before too long. It wasn't even dark when I headed up to the big slab of Victorian brickwork. Steps led up to big double-doors; at the bottom of them, a small metal sign read, "The Jethro Parry Memorial Building, established in 1867 to assist in the educational, religious and welfare needs of local fisherfolk." Arcing over the double doors was the sign that I had seen from up on the cliff path, which simply said "THE PARAMBA"

On one of the doors was a poster, advertising

Max Morris in Double Trouble

I wandered up the steps and looked at the poster. "Sold Out Tonight" was plastered across the top. Below it, I read,

"Max Morris is Teddy Fey in a hilarious adventure of mistaken identity". I looked at the cartoonish drawing alongside the text.

I stared.

That face, grinning out from the poster.

Of all the....

It couldn't be.

It bloody could.

I checked down the cast list. The names got smaller, the further down, but sure enough there it was.

Bob Jenkins.

So all the time I had been risking my life, fighting trained assassins to the death, getting hurt and bruised, facing monster turtles and being forced to eat strangely addictive muck – Bob had been here! Indulging his passion for local dramatics! No wonder the Four had been away for so long. Its captain's lengthy research into the customs of alternate versions of reality involved nothing more than slapping greasepaint on and having a good time!

The big front doors were locked. I marched around the building and found a small door at the side. A large man was blocking it. More accurately, he was a tall man with a large stomach.

'You can't come in 'ere luv,' he said, planting his feet wide apart.

Perfect. His balance is completely wrong. Amateur. 'I rather think I can.' *Open palm, upwards, high into his chest, straight arm. Drive through from the legs.* Basically I pushed him over. The man and his stomach crashed backwards. I stormed past both of them.

I was in a narrow corridor with a row of closed doors. I pushed the first one open and looked into a large, empty dressing room. The second room was even larger and contained a very familiar face. I marched over.

'Do you mind?' Bob said. 'I'll do autographs after the show.'

'I don't want your autograph! This is no time for jokes. While you've been flouncing around here some of us have been risking our lives!'

His eyes widened. He took a step backwards.

'Listen darlin' I've got money here.' He nodded nervously towards a cupboard. 'In there. Take it. Take as much as you like.'

'Darling?! – What do I want with money? I'm in trouble and I need you to get me out of it. What's happened to you?'

He was about to reply but then stopped himself. He straightened up, suddenly looking more confident, just as an arm reached from behind me and wrapped itself around my neck.

Right leg back, grab the arm with both hands to lock it in place, very quickly bend forward which will lever even a heavy assailant off the ground and rotate the hips anticlockwise. Put as much power in as you can but let gravity and the opponent's momentum do the work for you. The bigger they are, the harder they fall.

The tall man and his unfortunate stomach took a dive over my right leg and once more crashed to the ground. Out in the corridor a woman screamed.

'Stay there' I ordered the stomach.

The stomach - or possibly its owner - groaned.

'What's going on Max?' It managed.

'She says I got her into trouble. Honestly I've never touched her. I've never seen her before.'

'Stop playing games Bob! This is for real.'

'He's not Bob.'

I turned. Paralysed with confusion, I stared at a second Bob, dressed identically to the first one and standing in the doorway.

'Hello Bettony. You certainly know how to make an entrance. Goodness what's happened to your face?'

It took a while for things to settle down, and even longer for Max Morris to stop shaking. We explained that I was Bob's stepdaughter, over-tired and worried about faulty electrics back at home. It was embarrassingly feeble and I felt reflected badly on the status of women in this world, but it was the best we could come up with. Max Morris just seemed to be grateful that no-one was going to hurt him. We managed to persuade the stomach and its owner that there was no need to call the police; that it was all a misunderstanding. A smooth resolution to the incident was aided by the fact that Bob was essential to the success of a very successful play and Morris was clearly reluctant to upset him. Or get him arrested.

Once Max Morris had been settled, Bob led me back to his own dressing room. It wasn't quite the same as Morris's but we both managed to squeeze in.

'What on Abbuth are you doing here Bettony?' My friend's face showed his worry.

'There's a lot to tell you Bob, but the most important thing is that we've got Mrs Ponch here and she needs urgent medical care.' I explained as quickly as I could about her injuries. Bob's eyes were nearly popping out of his head.

'I've got a lot of questions,' he said, 'but they can wait.'

'Where's the Four?' I whispered.

'At the back of the Parry. We're keeping it blanketed. We've managed to run a cable from their power supply. Bit naughty I know but this place is more tightly controlled than a Tactile's toilet. Where's Zagretia now?'

'A couple of miles out of the village. I got the bus in.'

Interest flickered in Bob's eyes. 'Oh yes? One of the four-twenties?'

I must have conveyed something with my body language because although I didn't speak Bob quickly became serious again.

'I'm on in about five minutes,' he said. 'Will Zagretia be ok for a bit longer? I think if I missed the show it would cause more problems for us than it would solve. Ninety minutes, then that's it for tonight. Early finish on a Wednesday. Curfew's at eleven –'

'Curfew?'

'Don't ask, Bettony. This place even has its own security force. Drive around in old police cars, they do. Most of them are retired bobbies though so they're ok. Anyway after we finish I'll borrow Max's car and we can collect Zagretia and get her to safety.'

'And everyone else.'

'What –'

At that moment the door opened and a boy's head peered around it.

'Two minutes Mr Jenkins.'

'Thanks Neville.' Bob tensed up. 'One last look at my lines Bettony. Damn! I need a bit more greasepaint on.'

I watched from the wings. The play was set in a hotel and was a farce of modest ambitions, a lot of which it achieved. The audience generally accepted it quite stoically, chuckling dutifully at the weak jokes, until the third act. At that point I could feel the change. Electrically charged expectation took over from placid acceptance.

The thing was done well, building to a strange climax. Early in the act, Max Morris walked off into one wing. A few seconds later Bob appeared, dressed identically, from the other. The audience must have been puzzling how Morris could run round the back of the stage so quickly. The trick was repeated several times, to the apparently humorous confusion of the other characters on stage, with the time interval getting shorter and shorter. Finally, the other characters made their puzzled excuses and departed. Left to himself, Max Morris fumbled his way to a bathroom at the side of the stage, debating with himself what to do. He turned his back to the audience but stayed in view. Bob suddenly appeared from the other side and carried on the debate, now arguing the opposite. The spotlight was on Bob but a dimmer light still picked out Morris. There was an audible gasp. Bob delivered a few more lines then turned away, as Morris had done. At the same moment the lights reversed. Now fully spotlit, Max Morris turned back to face the audience, who gave another gasp. They repeated this several times. Apparently one was in favour of running off with the vicar's wife, and one not. Eventually Bob left the stage, the plot resolved itself and the play closed to a standing ovation. I noticed that Bob did not reappear to take a bow at the end.

There was a nudge at my elbow.

'Bettony!' Bob whispered urgently. 'Let's get going. I've got his car keys.' He still had his stage makeup on.

'Won't he miss them?'

'He won't miss them. He always has a few drinks after a performance. More than a few to be honest.'

I followed Bob out of the back of the theatre and into a car park. All the cars were Earth 1950s-era or earlier. We climbed into something that was identical to a Humber Hawk – including the name – and Bob brought the car to life. I described to him where Brian McShane lived and he negotiated the big car erratically around the narrow streets, then onto the lane out of the village. It was dark now and the car's powerful headlights cut into the night. I started to explain about Timmbo, and about Hugo and Strikken, but Bob cut me short, saying with an apology that he had to concentrate. Very soon we were outside the locked gate of McShane's house; moments later we were pulling up outside the front door. McShane was already standing outside it.

'Max! We were just talking about you. I was saying how well Double Trouble was doing,' McShane lied.

'We're here for the woman,' Bob said without preamble.

'Wha - *you* are? Are you part of it too?' Even I could hear the jealousy in McShane's voice.

'Sorry mate I don't have the time.' Bob pushed past McShane and into the house, coming face to face with Hugo.

'Where is she?' Bob demanded. Hugo regarded him and smiled affably, looking dangerously relaxed I thought.

'Hugo! I called quickly. 'This is Bob. He's a very good friend. He's here to get Mrs P to safety.'

Hugo nodded and led the way up the stairs.

We managed to get Mrs Ponch lodged across the Humber's back seat with Strikken squeezed in beside her. Hugo and I sat next to Bob on the front bench seat. Before he got in, Hugo spoke quietly to Jimmy Grinns, at one point putting his arm around the little man's shoulders. They hugged each other before Hugo climbed in next to me. Bob set off, once again concentrating hard on the road in front of him and not joining in conversation.

'Have you upset Jimmy?' I asked Hugo. 'I'm sure he was wiping his eyes afterwards. What did you say to him?'

'Oh - er, nothing much. I told him to think about what was important. I told him to go visit his family. Just tell them he was coming, and not wait for an invite.'

I looked at Hugo quizzically but he did not say any more.

It was a quiet trip back into Sputteridge, except for the continual grinding of gears, the curses from the driver and screams from his passengers, and of course the occasional screeching of tyres.

Bob steered the Humber back into the car park behind the Paramba. I had a final moment of terror as he drove across the car park and directly at a solid brick wall, but when we were two feet away from it the wall dissolved away and I was looking at the very welcome sight of an old brick-built public toilet block. Bob managed to stop the car before it collided with the Four and hurried inside, then reappeared followed by a stout middle-aged woman and a younger, slimmer man who between them were carrying a stretcher. It seemed that Strikken knew the stout woman, who was Dr Blazer. Between them and Hugo they got Mrs Ponch out of the car. Mrs Ponch declined the stretcher and insisted on walking inside, helped by Hugo and Strikken. Alarms went off as they entered the transition vehicle. They paused for a moment, Strikken spoke to Kelham Blazer and they continued their slow progress.

'It's Mrs P,' I explained to Bob. 'She's got an infection.'

'We need to have a conversation,' Bob said as we watched the little group slowly enter the Four. 'And if you don't mind me saying this old friend, you need to get a change of clothes.'

'Cheeky bugger.'

'Who's the blond lad? I don't think I've met him. Is he from Sputt?'

'From Sputteridge, yes. Listen Bob, I know there's a lot to explain but this is really important. Strikken has to do the medical stuff on Mrs P.'

He looked at me curiously. 'Kelham's every bit as good, Bettony.'

'Maybe she is. Please Bob. I can explain everything but this is really important. We can say - er - I dunno...'

'We don't need to make anything up Bettony. I'll just tell her Strikken's doing the work and he can explain later.'

A few minutes later Bob and I were sitting in the Officer in Charge's private room. I was mildly annoyed that my friend was sitting as far away from me as possible and had switched the air conditioning on. It was also a bit odd carrying on such an important conversation with a man who was clearly, from his greasepaint and style of dress, about to go on stage and tell a few gags. However. I described as quickly as I could how we had come to be in this world, with an injured and probably infected Mrs Ponch.

Bob raised his eyebrows when I explained about Hugo. He was gratifyingly worried for me when I described my fight with Timmbo, and satisfyingly horrified at my description of the turtles. He shook his head in disgust at the murders TMB had perpetrated on Abbuth.

'I honestly thought we'd put all that dreadful Erce business behind us. Are you sure that this Hugo Cream is on the level crossing?'

'Crean. Yes... Yes I am.'

'You don't sound too certain.'

'He can be brutal.' The words were out before I could stop them. 'No that's not true... He can threaten brutality. But he doesn't want to be...' My voice tailed away. Why was I defending Hugo Crean? And why did I feel that I was arguing against myself?

'That's hardly a ringing endorsement.'

'If it wasn't for Hugo we'd never have found out that there was still a problem with Erce. And I wouldn't have known about Timm Milden-Brewer. I'm here now instead of being stuck on some other reality because of Hugo.'

Bob sighed. 'All this suspicion. Not being able to trust people. It's terrible.'

'I know.'

'Go and get a shower and something to eat. I'll get Fluzz to keep an eye on Mr Cream. We'll gather in meeting room two in forty minutes. You remember where that is?'

'Yes. Crean Bob, not Cream. Who or what is Fluzz?'

'My Chief Operations Officer. Nice lad, you'll like him. Use room three in the guest quarters. I'll get someone to bring you something to eat and some clean clothes.' He wrinkled his nose at me. 'We can have a go at getting the ones you're wearing cleaned up, or failing that we can incinerate them.'

'Ha ha.'

'It's nice to see you old friend. Even in that state.'

'You too Bob. Even if you do look like you're about to do a song and dance act.'

CHAPTER TWENTY FOUR

Spaceships and body parts

Somebody showed Hugo to one of the guest quarters. He chose to take a long bath, rather than shower. By the time he had finished, his freshly-laundered clothes were laid out on his bed.

He dressed and wandered out into the corridor in search of something to eat. He had read about this spaceship of course, but still it was very impressive. Completely different to the little tin box that they called the Two. It was so big! The smoothness of the walls and floor spoke of efficient high tech, albeit combined with poor taste in interior design. Hugo found the kitchen, where he was welcomed by a group of crew members, and gratefully accepted their offer to share their evening meal with him.

He was operating almost on autopilot. His unexpected arrival, combined with his charm and good looks, meant that several of the crew were paying him a great deal of attention; Hugo replied non-committally to their questions, but his mind was racing.

There was a lot to consider.

Hugo was still eating when a disembodied voice called out *'Hugo Crean would you please join us in meeting room two.'*

'I'll show you where that is if you like,' one of the crew said. A pleasant young man, Hugo had a vague idea his name was Fluzz Wilson. He was slimmer than Hugo but about the same height. Probably a similar age, too, although already losing his hair. Like flax on a thinstaff. Hugo could hear Benedict's voice in his head, and smiled at the quotation.

'You seem to have had a rather adventurous time,' Fluzz said as they walked.

'That is certainly true' Hugo answered. Deflecting, he added, 'I'm sure you've had a few adventures of your own though.'

'It's just incredible. This is my first transition. Honestly, the differences in this society! And yet also the similarities! Such a rich source of material to study. We've just about finished here now.' Wilson looked slightly shifty. 'At least, most of us have. The Officer in Charge is pursuing an in-depth study of his own. Er. Oh here we are!'

They entered a room where Bob and Bettony were already seated at a table. Hugo registered Wilson's expectation that he would also be joining the meeting and his surprise when it became clear he was not.

Bob had changed into less garish clothes, and also cleaned the stage makeup from his face. Like Hugo's, Bettony's clothes had been cleaned.

What a freshly-laundered trio we are, Hugo thought.

The Officer in Charge waited until Wilson had closed the door.

'I feel bad about that,' he said. 'Fluzz is a good COO.' He looked at Bettony. 'We're not big on keeping secrets from each other, you know that.'

Bettony nodded. 'I've given Bob quite a bit of detail already Hugo,' she said. 'I'm not sure where the best place to start is.'

'So you're aware of the activities of my old schoolmate Timm Milden-Brewer, or Welter Hallett to those who know him on Abbuth?'

Bob nodded. He's watching Hugo very carefully, Bettony thought to herself.

Hugo pulled a piece of paper out of his pocket and unfolded it.

'Perhaps we should start here then. This is a list of all of Timmbo's agents in Britannia.'

Hugo had told her about the list, but it was the first time that Bettony had seen it. She and Bob both stared at pairs of names, handwritten on the paper. Hugo's included.

'My gods,' Bob whispered. He shook his head. 'I mean - Bettony has already told me about Brink Stellish. That's the most shocking name here. But you've got - what - fourteen names? Are you sure about this?'

'Positive.'

Bob was looking through the list.

'I mean - I know some of these. Trevor Kittern - the bloke's a bit of a tulip, but - Reanne Fyerson. Really? *Reanne*?'

Hugo nodded. Bob continued working his way down the list, every so often expressing more shock at a name he recognised.

'Do you know what happened to the originals?' Bob asked. 'I mean, the Abbuthian people? I thought we'd rescued everyone last year.'

'Most of these agents are using false IDs sir. Like me. There was no Nixel Flines. It was an identity created by Timmbo.'

'Call me Bob. I don't do that Sir stuff' Bob said tersely. He looked suddenly at Hugo. 'You said "most". Who does that leave?'

'I don't know. I'm just going on a throwaway remark that Timmbo made. But I know Timmbo of old. There wouldn't have been any survivors. He would have enjoyed making sure of that.'

'After everything we did last year. I thought we'd finished all this.' Bob's sigh was almost a sob.

'Is this the original list?' Bettony asked.

My goodness she's a smart girl.

'I copied it from the original Bets. Word for word.'

'So where's the original?'

'A man called Assistant County Lord Lieutenant Peckler has the original. He was Timmbo's contact at Mazeley - at the Sentinnat.'

'And you're sure about this Hugo?'

'Absolutely certain.'

Bob was staring at the piece of paper, shaking his head.

'It's like last year, all over again.' He looked at Bettony. 'Isn't it? What have we done Bet? We've opened a Pandora's jamjar and we'll never get the lid back on it.'

'It's not so bad Bob. We've got a full list here. It's not really like last year because we know everybody who we have to deal with. As a backup, we've got Bollie's unbreakable DNA test. And there's no Timm Milden-Brewer to interfere.'

'Mmm. I hope you're right old friend.'

Bob stared at the list, every so often repeating one of the names disbelievingly.

'No Osian Jelks,' he said eventually. 'So the punter out at Enysgrume Nowuth really is from Erce. He was trying to insist he'd been set up and they'd got it all wrong.'

'I know. Mrs P told me. Come on then Bob, we need to work out a plan.'

** ** **

'If I may?' Hugo murmured.

'Hello.'

'Hello sir. In answer to the questions that you are about to ask - I got in because your security is not as tight as it should be; No, I haven't hurt your guards, I have very carefully but quite gently tied

them up; Yes, I am from Erce. No, I do not wish you any harm -
rather the reverse; And finally - because I would never have been
able to make an appointment to see you without all the wrong
people knowing about it.

'So. Please accept my deepest apologies Mr Jelks, but would you
be kind enough to accompany me outside to a waiting car? My
friends are expecting you there. They are well-known to you and
should be able to give you some reassurance about my good
intentions.'

Hilda-Bellane Hart - the woman impersonating Brink Stellish - was
the most difficult to arrest. She insisted that it was a setup. That
she was the victim of an attempted coup, led by recidivist elements
working in collaboration with agents from Erce to undermine the
security of the state and the people. It was her language as much
as anything that gave her away. There were a few though who
believed her, and more who were not sure. But as predicted by
Bettony's bizarre solution to The Three Mug Problem, she failed
Bollie Sneggs' DNA test, which she insisted was a fake. Her private
documentation of her proposed third security force, Section Three,
was discovered, and provided damning proof of her intention to set
up a fifth column of infiltrators from Erce; people who would
eventually be used to mount an armed takeover. She never
admitted any wrongdoing and swore that the whole thing was a
deepfake. Interestingly, the more wildly that she protested, the
easier it became to recognise her guilt.

The facility at Enysgrume Nowuth was expanded to
accommodate an additional fourteen people. Bettony
accompanied Mrs Ponch there when she interviewed Hart. She
was impressed by the place, if not by the trip across to it on a small,
wildly-pitching boat. Enysgrume Nowuth comprised a series of
small islands twenty miles off the coast of Cornwall; the Erceans
were housed in an impressive building on one of the smaller islands.
Accommodation was better than many hotels that Bettony had
stayed in. Residents were given the opportunity to take part in
many activities, educational and sporting. The grounds were well-
kept and open to all.

'Why are there so many armed guards?' Bettony asked. 'It's not
as if they can escape.'

'The guards are here to protect them from each other' Mrs Ponch replied. 'They are constantly plotting serious harm against each other. Groups form, dissolve, then reform with different members.'

'But it's so beautiful here.'

'I don't think they even notice.'

Bettony persuaded Mrs Ponch to authorise her and Kaghendra to make a trip to Brian and Paulette's world. As Bettony had before, they arrived late evening. This time it was Brian who answered the door.

'Oh hello,' he said, surprised. 'I was beginning to think we'd never see you again. How are things going, out there among the stars? You and that man an item yet?'

'Things have gone very well thank you.' Bettony ignored the second question.

'Actually I thought you were Paulette. She's at a meeting tonight. Come in, come in. Who's your friend?'

'Kaghendra. She's the - er -pilot. Of the starship.'

'Hello Brian I've heard all about you.'

'It's all lies.'

They sat at the small table and Brian supplied tea. There was a fire in the grate and the room was warm.

'Listen. You asked me if I could come back for you. So I have.'

'Oh! Thank you.' Brian looked sheepish.

'So... if you still want to come with us...?'

'Well... it's a lovely offer. Thank you. And believe me, I really appreciate you remembering us. But things have changed a bit in the past month. Stubbins has been moved up to Bristol. And... er... actually, Paulette's been made district party secretary. More money, more allowances and everything. And we can look forward to moving up to Bristol as well in a couple of years. Ah! Here she is. Hello Trouble. Have you solved all the world's problems?'

Strikken had finished his afternoon shift at Falmouth General. The hospital's car park was less than half full but another small car was parked next to his own. As Strikken approached the two vehicles, Hugo Crean climbed out of the second.

'Ah. Mr Crean. I was wondering when we would meet again.'

'Would you be kind enough to accompany me Dr Flange?'

Hugo held the passenger door open and Strikken climbed in.

Hugo drove for several hours, turning off the main road and choosing a narrow lane that led up onto wild, deserted moorland. Strikken did not question what was happening. For the whole of the journey, neither man spoke. Eventually Hugo stopped at a deserted stone hut. He pushed the broken door open and led the way inside. The hut was one single room. At the far end was a table and two chairs, one each side of it. Hugo gestured towards the chair on the far side.

'Please, Doctor. Take a pew.'

Strikken sat down, facing into the room, the outside wall at his back.

'I've been waiting for this moment,' he said.

Hugo sat facing him.

'Yes. Sorry about that. It must have been a bit of a sword of Damoclesius. In my defence, I have had to attend to many things. And I thought I could rely on you. I've given you plenty of chances and you've never tried anything on. And between me and you Doctor, I reckon I'm a good judge of a person's character no matter where they are from. But still.'

Silence fell. Hugo was clearly prepared to wait a long time for Strikken to speak.

Eventually, Strikken said, 'When did you find out?'

'I had a vague idea that I'd seen you before, the very first time we met. At that party. But that happens, doesn't it? Especially now. With all this space travel stuff.' Hugo frowned. 'When did I know for certain? When I saw Timmbo's list. Old man Peckler kindly gave me a copy. Two sets of names. The Abbuthian, and here and there its Ercean opposite. And there you were. Strikken Flange. Aka Nils Glubson.'

Hugo pulled a small pistol from his pocket. Strikken watched him toy with it for a moment then place it on the table.

'Why did you remove my name from the list, Mr Crean? Did you do that for many people?'

'Only you old bean... Why did I do it?' Hugo looked pensive. 'No one specific reason. It wouldn't have gone down very well with Bets, would it? I mean - you may not believe this, but it's true - I've never put out to her, you know? Any worthwhile relationship between me and Bets could only happen ceteris paribus, after she had decided that things weren't working out with you. So I suppose there was that. But also... I dunno. You remind me a bit of an old schoolfriend. Did you kill Sherian Penck?'

'Good god no! Although I regret to say, she probably died because of me. I can only think it was some sort of warning. From ... him.'

'I wouldn't worry about it. Timmbo was a psychopath. He was killing people around Bets and I'm pretty sure it was purely for the joy of knowing how much she would suffer. He enjoyed killing people. Some people collect stamps, Timmbo's hobby was killing people. I'd put money on him being behind the murders in Swindon and Oxford. Slepwood was his godfather, you know.'

'Was he? Oh lord.'

'Bets told me about a meal that made Hule Flange ill. Was that your doing?'

'It was.' Tears welled up in Strikken's eyes. 'I wouldn't have let any harm come to them' he protested. 'Any real harm. I had to do it. I have family, Mr Crean. In Angland. Without any powerful connections to protect them. He...' Strikken shook his head. Took a few moments. Composed himself. 'He told me what he would do to them. If I didn't do everything he wanted. That was why I had to come here in the first place. To protect my family.'

'When was that?'

'Oh, nearly four years ago. I was one of - his - first.'

'You were a doctor on Erce?'

'Of course.' Strikken brightened for a moment. 'It was a revelation, coming here. The advances they have made! And how much resource they put into healthcare!'

'What happened to the real Strikken Flange?'

'Ah.' A thin smile forced itself onto Strikken's lips. 'I did manage to get one over on - him - with respect to Strikken Flange. It was a bit risky. But... The real Strikken Flange, as you describe him, had... issues. He was a junior doctor but unfortunately he had experimented with some of the drugs that we use. They had affected him. Damaged him. He was delusional when I met him, he must have been a danger to his patients. I have no doubt that he would soon have lost his job. But I managed to persuade him to leave. Or to escape, as he saw it.'

'If he was delusional it must have freaked him out seeing you.'

'In a way it may have helped. He thought I was him. His other self. Perhaps I am, in some way. Anyway, I got him away. I spent hours... days, scouting the country. Eventually I found a caravan towards the east coast. I've been to see him a couple of times. I take him money. He's been pretty much forced to give up on his drug habit. You can't get them here like you can back on Erce.'

'Timmbo wouldn't've liked that. He likes 'em dead, not being rehabilitated into society.'

'He never found out.' The thin smile returned. 'I managed to get hold of a cadaver that was pretty similar to the original Strikken.' He shuddered. 'It was terrifying. Not the handling of the body, I've done that many times as a doctor. It was the fear that - he - would find out.' Strikken took a deep breath then exhaled. 'But he didn't.

'He got me onto the crew of the Series Four. I don't know why, you didn't ask him why he did things. I guessed there were others, but none of us knew about each other. And I think I was one of his "special ones". That was what he said, anyway. Whatever that meant.'

'It meant that you were one of little Timmbo's private army, old bean.'

'What a revolting thought.' Strikken shook his head in horror and stared into space for a few seconds. Hugo watched him. Waited for him to continue.

'Then I met Bettony. And... there was something there. I tried not to let it happen. I thought it would put her in danger. But she can be very... persuasive. So it did.' Strikken swallowed. 'It did happen.'

Silence returned. Hugo stood and walked to the doorway, staring outside. When he turned back, Strikken had picked up the gun from the table.

'Is it loaded?' He asked.

Hugo nodded. 'Yes. Try it if you don't believe me.'

'I wouldn't even know how to. They have safety catches and things don't they? That you have to release before you can pull the trigger?'

'Not this one. Too basic for all that. Point, squeeze and shoot.'

Strikken shook his head. He looked at the gun as it rested, flat on his hand. Disgust was written across his face.

'These things revolt me. Pieces of metal that produce pain and injury and death.'

He regarded it for a moment longer, then threw it across the table. It clattered onto the floor.

'I pass the test,' he murmured, then repeated to himself, almost silently, 'I pass the test.' He watched Hugo walk over and pick the gun up.

'Are you going to kill me?' Strikken asked.

Hugo shook his head. 'Not the sort of thing I do,' he replied. 'Never have, despite all the rumours. Which I blushingly accept, I did nothing to discourage. "Old Dephwood Crean, his legend, it was greater than the fact". Could be a poem somewhere there. Lesser than the fact, that's more accurate perhaps. It's greater not to kill isn't it?' Hugo put the gun back in his pocket and sat down again. 'How come old man Flange didn't suss you out?'

'Strikken and his father weren't that close. Whether that was because of Strikken's drug problems, or whether it caused them - I don't know. It's a terrible indictment of a father-son relationship isn't it? That he doesn't even know when someone else is masquerading as his son? I felt something of the difficulty in the relationship when Professor Flange came over for dinner. Up until then, it had never been difficult to avoid him. In fact, it felt as though he were avoiding me.'

'It rings a few bells though,' Hugo said softly. 'Where I come from - I mean, the class that I come from, back on dear old Erce - a lot of fathers wouldn't know if their son was replaced by a plastic doll. Mothers too. Sent away to boarding school at five years old and sometimes allowed back briefly when term ends. Then Oxbridge and away we go, marry some witless wonder and the whole thing is repeated. I count my own family in that dreadful carnage of emotion.'

'So what are you going to do?'

'With you? I don't honestly know.'

'You could leave me to carry on my work at Falmouth General.'

Hugo laughed, briefly.

'Too risky. What if for the first time in my life I'm wrong, and you're not the fine upstanding fellow you propose yourself to be?

These lovely people have finally broken the link between here and Erce. But that all rests on you not being naughty.'

'Turn me in then.'

'And consign you to the little hell that Bets tells me our countryfolk are creating for themselves? In that small strip of heaven they call Enysgrume Nowuth? You deserve better than that.'

'What then?'

Hugo could feel the void opening inside him as he spoke. 'I have an idea, NewStrikken. It involves you doing what you do best, which is caring for people. Return to Erce with me. Go back with what you've learned. I'm giving you the opportunity to make a difference to the lives of thousands. And you get to see your family again. Don't worry! You'll be fine. Timmbo's dead, you'll be perfectly safe. You'll be under my wing, as t'were.'

What choice do I have? Hugo Crean had thought to himself, when the idea first occurred. *I will genuinely have the chance to make life better for a whole city of people and at the same time guarantee safety for this lovely world.* It had taken some planning. But he was pretty sure that Weymouth would jump at the suggestion he was going to make to him; and Bollie had come up trumps with the transition box. Sneggs had succeeded in adapting and reprogramming it to do an instantaneous transition, deliver a false message purportedly from Brink Stellish, then transition out again. So no problems there. And Hugo would be in a perfect position to monitor any other communications, just in case Timmbo had left anyone off-grid in Abbuth, and they managed to get through to Erce.

★★ ★★ ★★

The metal crate appeared silently, as it always did. A few turtles lumbered heavily away, startled by its sudden appearance. The back end of the crate swung open and two men appeared, one tall and muscular and blond-haired, the other smaller and slighter in build. They examined some tattered remains that were lying on the ground and carefully selected certain bits of them. They put their choices in a large bag, and disappeared back into the crate. Which itself then also disappeared, leaving a mild gust of air. The turtles regarded the non-existence of the metal box mournfully, then returned to feeding on what remained of the remains of the remnants of their meal.

'Hilda-Bellane Hart?' The Earl of Weymouth frowned, just for a moment. 'Married the late lamented Slasher Hart. She's one of the Forbes-Mabberleys? She's a woman, isn't she?'

'I believe she is sir. But one with the backbone of the Forbes-Mabberleys. They know her as Brink Stellish, sir. She's the - er - head of their council. Their leader, basically.'

'Hah! Bloody fools, letting a woman rule them. Still - Forbes-Mabberley... Toffy! I say, Toffy!'

'Podger?'

'Got news for you. Young Crean here's got one of your mares in charge of the –' Weymouth dropped his voice to a whisper – 'the aliens.'

'What? You mean the crazies with the spaceships?'

'Shh. Yes. That's the fellas. Bellane.'

'...'

'That's one of Connolly's brood isn't it?' Weymouth prompted, seeing his friend's blank look.

'Oh you mean Bunty. *Bunty!?*' Forbes-Mabberley pulled a face. 'God 'elp em.' He looked at Hugo.

'Hope you know what you're doing young man. She'll have 'em invading us if we're not careful.'

A moment of uneasiness passed between the two senior men.

'Just a joke Podger. Just a joke. Ahem. Er. She been in touch yet Hugo?'

'I believe so sir although that's ACLL Peckler's area, not mine.'

Weymouth leaned forward. 'Just call him Peckler now, Hugo. Now you're a County Lord Lieutenant.'

'Call him Greasy, that's what I do' Forbes-Mabberley said. The two men laughed. Hugo smiled politely.

'I saw what you brought back,' Weymouth said to Hugo. 'Of Milden-Brewer.'

'Sir. I thought the part of his arm with the Authority on would be appropriate, as well as his head. Most of it anyway.'

'Indeed. It was good work Hugo. Good work.' Both Weymouth and Forbes-Mabberley had paled. 'Slightly - er - above and beyond, that was. Not sure what you did to get him into that state.'

'Not too sure I want to know,' Forbes-Mabberley muttered.

'No. Indeed. Ahem. Bastard deserved it though,' Weymouth added, rallying. 'I should've put you in charge of interrogating the Bastard Bowles, Hugo.'

'Thank you sir.'

'Mmph. Good work. Shows people what happens when they mess with the Regency.'

Weymouth had raised his voice again. A few men raised their glasses and chorused, 'The Regency.'

'He didn't talk though?' Forbes-Mabberley said.

'No sir.'

'The man had balls,' Weymouth said. 'I'll give him that. Ahem. At least, he did before you started working on him. Ahem.'

Forbes-Mabberley went a more sickly shade of green. 'You're taking on Swindon aren't you Hugo?' He croaked. They paused as a waiter refilled their glasses with whisky.

'That's right sir.'

'We've got a good man down there Toffy, name of - er - what's his name Hugo?'

'Sluckham sir.'

'That's the fella. A good man Toffy. *Loyal.* But I think he needs someone with breeding in charge of him. Wha'd'ya say Hugo?'

'Indeed sir.'

'It's so good to see you sir!' Sluckham was almost crying with relief.

'Good to see you too DA Sluckham. Been keeping things in order?'

'Been doing my best sir...' Sluckham blanched. 'Did you say *DA* Sluckham?'

'That's right. Calm down DA Sluckham! You're being confirmed as District Administrator. That's a good thing.'

'But I thought you were taking charge sir.'

'I am. But every Lord Lieutenant needs a DA to support him. I hope you'll be happy to do that?'

'Oh yes sir! Thank you sir.' Confirmed as DA, not having to be in charge, and working for the terrifyingly fearsome yet somehow very nice Mr Crean - no, for *Lord Lieutenant* Crean. The wife would be happy with the DA thing and this man would know what to tell him to do. And discipline would not be a problem. News of the interrogation methods Hugo had employed when dealing with TMB had leaked, far and wide. Everyone knew what happened to people who didn't do what Hugo Crean wanted. The new DA couldn't see anyone volunteering to have their body dismembered – very slowly, and while they were still alive, if the rumours were to be believed. Very suddenly, Cornelius Sluckham was indeed a very happy man...

He realised that the Lord Lieutenant as still speaking.

'...I have plans, Mr Sluckham. I am appointing an administrator of medicine, a Dr Glubson. And we shall put money into educating the people of Swindon. They will become healthier and more knowledgeable.'

'Yes sir! Er... Why, sir?'

It was a question that Weymouth had asked. Hugo had given a similar answer:

'Because then they will earn more money. And become richer. And pay more in taxes to the Regency. Swindon will cease to be a cesspit of rebellion. In time, it will become the loyal jewel in the Regency's crown!'

'Ha! Yes sir.'

And who knows, maybe it will give birth to something better. A better way of going on. The Regency will not be easy to dislodge. But somebody has to start somewhere.

★★ ★★ ★★

Bettony unfolded the piece of paper again and read it for the fortieth time.

'Come on girl,' Kaghendra said. 'Put it away and get outside of that beer.'

Bettony stared at the paper, re-reading Hugo's farewell. She was not crying, she was absolutely firm about that, even though water was collecting in her eyes and then making its way in droplets down her face.

'Both of them,' she said. 'Both of them Kagh! Didn't even give me the chance to choose.'

'Maybe it wasn't your choice to make.'

'But *why?* Hugo was so happy to escape from that place. Now he's gone back and taken Strikken with him.'

'I thought he told you why. In the letter. A chance to make things better for so many people.'

In reply, Bettony shook her head.

'At least Strikken had the good grace to say goodbye to me face-to-face.'

'Good old Strikken,' Kaghendra said. 'I can understand him wanting to do that, anyway.'

'Well I can't!'

'Drink up girl. Time for one more before the bar closes.'

MRS PONCH EXPLAINS THE SOLUTION TO THE THREE MUG PROBLEM

'Just go through it once more Zagretia. I thought I'd got it that time.'

Mrs Ponch smiled. 'Perhaps we shouldn't have had that second glass of red with dinner. Don't worry Pildew! And stop frowning! Bettony's brain has its own unique way of processing information. It's part of her charm and it certainly throws "New light onto old curtains", as I believe they say on Earth. The important thing to remember is that she did not just use logic, but she also used her human intuition to adjust for the known behaviours of three people, any two of whom, being Abbuthian, would be respectful of the character quirks of others. That's the key to the whole thing. Right. Here we go…

'Apart from Bettony herself, there were three people in the office. Let's call them B, G and T.'

'I did manage to understand that bit Zagretia. Brink, Garri and Tweek.'

'…And three DNA types: A1, A2 and E. A1 and A2 are Abbuthian, E is Ercean.'

'Yep. Got that.'

'B's mug has A1 DNA and E DNA. G's mug has A2 DNA and E DNA. T does not have a mug of his own. Bettony's solution was not to try and work out who had Ercean DNA, but to assume each possibility in turn and look for inconsistencies, or illogical results. But at the same time, allowing for the individuals' personalities. What we might describe as making a null hypothesis and looking for a contradiction.'

'Sounds like the maths I did at Uni.'

'I'm surprised you remember your uni days from what I've heard… anyway. Her first assumption was that Brink had E DNA. This threw up the result that Garri had not handled her mug, which would be consistent with his somewhat unique personality if he were indeed Abbuthian.'

'Remind me why…'

'Because Garri's own mug showed him to possess either A2 or E DNA. If Brink has E, Garri must have A2. A2 is not present on B's mug. Under this scenario Garri handles only his own mug. And we can then also infer that T has A1 DNA. This means that he did not handle G's mug – also consistent with an Abbuthian respect for character quirks. As Bettony discovered, Garri is somewhat protective of his mug.

'Now take case number two – that Garri has E DNA. As Bettony pointed out, the conclusion is that Brink handled only her own mug – fine – but that Tweek only handled Garri's. Doesn't make sense, if Tweek were Abbuthian, for reasons already explained. Put the glass down Pildew and concentrate. The final scenario is that the E DNA belongs to Tweek.'

'I am concentrating. If T was E, then B only handled her own mug and so did G – Garri, I mean.'

'Um… yes. Ok… I've gone wrong somewhere. Hang on. It made sense when Bettony explained it…. Um…

…

…

Pass the wine, Pildew.'

Bettony Gullivant wanders down the high street. Only the veg to buy and she will have all the ingredients for a delicious dinner. And this time it will come out right. She's fairly sure. Good old Kagh and Ben. They deserve a decent meal. They've put so much effort into supporting her. Getting her back on her feet.

The wonderful smell of freshly-ground coffee pulls her towards the café. She knows the coffee is good in here. She's been here before.

Plenty of time...

And they're still open. Not too late. She catches a glimpse of her reflection in the café window. She stops for a moment to admire herself. Not quite the same as seeing herself in the flesh, but -

She watches her reflection wave at her.

For one chilling moment Bettony is frozen to the spot. But she's been through a lot these past few months and no waving reflection is going to -

She's closer to the window now, can barely make out her reflection which has become a vague shadow of herself on the glass. She's looking through it and into the café, which is empty except for an indefinite shape heading towards the back where the toilets are.

Bettony goes in and buys a coffee and sits and watches the door to the toilets. No-one comes out. After a couple of minutes she walks over and pushes it open.

There are two unisex toilets. Neither have windows and the doors to both are open.

There's no-one there.

THE END?

DANGEROUS PHYSICS:
ADVENTURES IN SPUTTERIDGE
Rose Mandelson

The first Sputteridge Chronicle

"Only by the act of looking at it do we make an object's position definite. The paradox of Humdinger's Cat, we call it, after the physicist Gerhardt Humdinger who lost his cat and then claimed he never had one in the first place."

Bettony Gullivant has taken a break from her boring office job and her broken relationship and gone on holiday to Cornwall. There, she stumbles across a strange, deserted village and a marooned alien spaceship disguised as a toilet block.

The bestselling Book One of the Sputteridge Chronicles.

ISBN 9781739781439

CONCORD: SABOTAGE

Allen M. Trager

When Humans nearly destroyed themselves with catastrophic climate change and the resulting wars, they were contacted by the seven-billion-year-old galactic federation known as Concord. The aliens granted Humans probationary membership in Concord and helped us begin to reverse the damage done by centuries of neglect. Select individuals were allowed to serve as crew on Concord spaceships. Five hundred years later, Emma Fuji is the sole Human among a million aliens aboard a spaceship the size of Pluto called Violet Enforcer.

An unknown group begins sabotaging surveillance drones in several systems, and Violet itself is nearly destroyed. Initial suspicion that Humans are responsible is dismissed out of hand. But a Human-crewed ship is vaporized by the same tech, and a group of fanatics on Earth who have renounced any dealings with Concord claims responsibility. Humans are once again under suspicion.

The goal of the Renouncers is to convince humanity to withdraw from Concord, and if they are truly responsible they'll get their wish. Unfortunately, history shows that Tribes that resign or are banished from Concord don't last long. If Humans are responsible for the tens of thousands dead so far, it will mean the end of the Human race.

As the number of sabotaged systems continues to climb, Emma and her closest alien friends race to prove that Humans are blameless. Ranging across an entire quadrant of the Milky Way, Emma and her team search for clues to the true identity of the saboteurs.

In the end Emma's strength, intelligence, and compassion are nearly enough to solve the problem. But the final evidence is revealed by the charm and instincts of the galaxy's most famous canine, Moondog.

ISBN 9781739781422

9 781739 781460